THE
SQUAD
ROOM

ROBERT NIVAKOFF
AND JOHN CUTTER

THE SQUAD ROOM

A NOVEL

BEAUFORT
BOOKS

SQUAD ROOM

Copyright © 2016 by Robert Nivakoff and John Cutter

FIRST EDITION

Hardcover ISBN: 9780825307911
Ebook ISBN: 9780825307201

Library of Congress Cataloging-in-Publication Data on file

For inquiries about volume orders, please contact:

Beaufort Books
27 West 20th Street, Suite 1102
New York, NY 10011
sales@beaufortbooks.com

Published in the United States by Beaufort Books
www.beaufortbooks.com

Distributed by Midpoint Trade Books
www.midpointtrade.com

Printed in the United States of America

Interior design by Mark Karis
Cover Design by Michael Short

1

William Morrison pulled his black Crown Victoria out of his Levittown, Long Island driveway, and headed for the Long Island Expressway.

For the NYPD, Levittown is Copland; and for a cop, Bill Morrison had sort of made it. He wasn't wealthy, but his home was comfortable: stone fireplace, central air, hardwood floors over the old-fashioned heating system built after World War II. It also came with a wife who drank Chardonnay by the box—a far less comfortable detail, but Morrison had learned to cope with it. He was an accomplished, awarded, decorated, and wounded member of the department, and an appreciated leader by the men and women who worked for him. His name at work was "Cap," or "Boss"—"Captain" when things got formal. Specifically, he was the Major Crimes Captain, specializing in homicide, of the New York City Police Department's Detective Bureau: a position he often called "a front-row seat to the greatest show on earth."

This was a trip Morrison had made countless times since he'd graduated from the Academy at twenty-one. As he left his street behind him, he couldn't remember a time when the trek wasn't part of his daily ritual. There had been no life before this, really. Back then he'd lived in Queens, home of Archie Bunker and *All in the Family*, two-story row houses, the

New York Metropolitans—better known as the Mets—and two million other people struggling to make their way in "the city." Back then the trip had been a different one: he'd take the Q42 bus to the E train at 179th Street; then take the E to Manhattan, where he'd switch to the 6 train at 51st Street; then take the 6 down to 23rd and Park Avenue; then walk the rest of the way to the New York City Police Academy.

At six-foot-one and two hundred and fifty pounds, Morrison was an imposing man, but he still remembered the challenge of the Academy. In those days they'd had rigorous standards for everything: you had to be a certain height, had to have perfect eyesight, had to submit to background checks and four-year waiting lists. He also remembered how cruel the job had been, as he'd come on just after the layoffs. No one remembered the layoffs anymore, when the city had been completely in the dumps; when Times Square, 42nd Street was called the Deuce, and prostitutes and pimps strolled up and down like they were on a catwalk. In those days a gun run—a police radio call—from Central, calling in a man with a gun at Rockaway and Livonia, would have led to a snappy retort from 73 Eddie that *everyone* on that corner had a gun.

As Morrison approached the Queens border, he sighed bleakly. Winter was well underway in New York, and the mixture of snow, sand, and typical highway litter piled alongside the roadway created an ominous grey backdrop to an already depressing day—a tone that certainly didn't help with how he was already feeling. Like the bitter winter weather, the Captain's battle with depression, alcohol, sleeplessness, and his failing marriage already felt as though it had gone on forever. He counted the days until March first—the day most cops fighting the Northeast weather, along with its crime, say they've made it through for the year. Even if it wasn't exactly spring weather, it was close to St. Paddy's Day, and that was enough to give most of them the necessary boost in morale. Yet that was a long way off.

It was Christmas day; and as usual, holiday plans for the men and women working under Bill Morrison would be brought to a halt. The holidays always seemed to bring out the bad in some people, which meant that good people like the sergeants and detectives of the NYPD had to work harder. Yet despite the fact that they were responding to violence and crime, some of them were downright happy for the chance to get out of the house and away from their families for the day. The holidays always underscored divisions within families; and for cops, those divisions sometimes ran as deep as they did everywhere else. Morrision remembered the shirt he'd been given once, by a similarly estranged LAPD detective: above a picture of a dead body on the ground with several detectives standing around it was the motto, "Our Day Starts When Yours Ends." It had somehow seemed to him the perfect summary of the everyday separation between the police and everyone else—the stark contrast in experience that made it so much easier for cops of any background to understand one another, than for even their closest kin to understand any of them. Most cops, as they say, aren't white, black or any other race; they're blue—and blue, as Morrison knew well, was a hard color for most others to relate to.

Now, as always on his morning ride, it was difficult for Bill Morrison to keep his mind on the job and off of his own familiar demons. His present marriage wasn't the only one that rankled; these days he actually found it harder to keep from thinking about his first wife. Despite providing him with two children he loved, she'd been a vile, manipulating woman, and had taken him for every cent she could get. And to make matters worse, she'd left him for another guy on the job—the money was bad enough, but *that* had been degrading, and almost took him over the edge.

It had been years since, and the kids were grown and doing well, with families of their own whom Bill spoke to all the time. But if time had somewhat healed those wounds, it had only replaced them with others deeper still. His family was a big one—like most cops' families, despite their difficulties with them—but Morrison's was now smaller by one: a fact that no degree of therapy, psych services, employee assistance, alcohol, or drugs could erase from his mind.

It was my fault, it will always be my fault—

Morrison switched on the radio to clear his head. On a good day, when the stars aligned and the weather was clear, he was outside the Midtown Tunnel, fifty minutes from home, when the police radio was first able to come through. The radio was the life blood for the men and women on patrol, and for investigators it was a barometer for what lay ahead; listening to it, Morrison could instinctually tell, by the energy level of the transmissions to Central, how each job should be responded to. Today it was just a lot of radio chatter with the usual calls, and he lowered it. It had been a long time since radio calls—or anything else, for that matter—excited him.

Most days he listened to the traffic report to find the quickest way to the Midtown South Precinct, where invariably he'd struggle to find a parking spot. Yet today was not one of those days. Today he wasn't on his way to the precinct, but to Sutton Place, an exclusive neighborhood on the Upper East Side of Manhattan. It was an area many considered to be the city's Boardwalk and Park Place—the best of the best. Yet Captain Bill Morrison wasn't visiting Sutton Place on a whim. Violence had shattered the elite utopia, and violence of a particularly shocking kind: a home invasion, involving the brutal rape and murder of a lone woman, whose body had been left disfigured at the scene.

In Morrison's experience, most home invasions were drug robberies, with the victim tied to a chair and the whole family watching as hiding places were revealed. Home invasion homicides, accordingly, were typically drug robberies gone badly, with said victim refusing to give up the drugs or cash. From the moment the call came through on his cell phone at 0530, however, Morrison had known this one was different. It was possible that the victim here had known her assailants or could identify them, so they'd had to kill her, but Morrison suspected otherwise. Drug robberies, along with most other kinds of crime, were nonexistent in Sutton Place.

What had happened there?

2

When Captain Morrison had cleared the Midtown Tunnel, he got a call on his cell phone from Sergeant Andre Simmons.

"This is no grounder, Cap," Simmons told him, echoing Morrison's own fondness for baseball euphemisms as a way of taking the edge off their work. "It's way up there on the brutality meter. We have everyone going; Sergeants Rivera and McNamara are coming in with their squads. Crime Scene will be here for quite a while—there's a lot of work to do."

"Who from Crime Scene do we have there?" Morrison asked.

"Williams and Kelly."

Morrison had known both of these investigators for a while. Otis Williams, a 6'2" African-American guy, had been on the job almost as long as he had; the two of them used to chase sneakers together for the 34th Precinct back in Fort Tryon Park. Morrison couldn't imagine doing that himself these days, but the last time he'd seen Williams the guy looked like he could still run down a dealer in new Jordans. Kelly, a white Irish cop from Gerritsen Beach in Brooklyn, was a little younger, but no less capable than Williams when it came to processing a crime scene. The two had been partners since Kelly joined Crime Scene.

Given the diversity of the Crime Scene unit, Morrison was happy to hear it was going to be these two on the job. You had the guys who were running away from dirty police work, for whom the unit's two-days-on-four-days-off schedule was a bunt. Then you had the Williamses and Kellys of the department—guys who loved putting bad guys in jail, and had a passion for evidence collection. Morrison knew he wouldn't have to direct them beyond pointing them to the scene; they considered it a badge of honor to collect evidence that would put a dirtbag behind bars, and would pull out all the stops vacuuming for fibers, bagging the deceased's hands for potential DNA evidence, and documenting every inch of the scene before it was disturbed by others.

"All right, great. Thanks, Andre," Morrison said. "I'm on my way—I just cleared the Midtown Tunnel, so I'm about ten minutes out." He paused, an intuition crossing his mind. "Are you okay?"

"Well," Simmons started, and took a deep breath. "Cap, I've worked a lot of cases with you, and everything's moving here—we've started a canvas, searching for video, you know, we're good. But this is really brutal. There's serious bite marks, and it just gets worse from there." He took another breath, then added quickly, "I'll speak to you when you get here, okay? There's so many bosses here it looks like a CompStat meeting."

"All right, Andre. See you soon."

Morrison hung up, vaguely perturbed. He hadn't heard Simmons talk that way about a crime scene in five years, and it affected him to hear someone on his team so rattled. As the Major Crimes Captain, he had all the specialty squads at his disposal—Homicide, Special Victims (formerly known by the blunt moniker of Sex Crimes), and the robbery and gang squads—and every one of the men and women who worked for his team were near and dear to him. He probably—no; if he was going to admit it, he *positively*—spent more time with these people than anyone else. They were an eclectic bunch of misfits by some standards, but to Morrison they comprised one of the best investigative teams ever put together. It was an odd thing to admit sometimes: he lived with Kathleen and their daughter, but *this* was his real family.

Kathleen. He was emotionless these days when it came to her. He couldn't remember the last time he'd cared much about anything in his life outside of his work, and his wife was no exception to the rule. She was frumpy, drank to passing out, and went through more Ambien than a patient locked down in the psych unit at Bellevue. Most of all, she hated him—she really hated him. But then, he couldn't entirely blame her for that.

He should never have talked her into letting their son take the police test. He remembered telling her that it was a legacy job—a job to be proud of keeping within the family. There were generations of Fitzgeralds on the force dating back to the 1800s, and they held their red heads high. Why shouldn't the Morrisons enjoy a similar legacy? Besides, Bill Junior wasn't going anywhere else in a hurry. He wasn't much of a student, and didn't have a trade he wanted to follow; if anything, he admired his father and what he did for a living. If he hadn't wanted it, Morrison would never have forced him. Still, why hadn't he pushed him to finish college and become a schoolteacher, a principal—anything but a cop?

God, did he miss that kid. Five years in, and it was still like yesterday. Bill Morrison could still hear the bagpipes from Our Lady of the Snows, where they'd held Billy's funeral. Ten thousand cops at the service, from all over the country. Amazing Grace. Shield 21336, killed in the line of duty.

It will always be my fault.

When he'd graduated the academy, Bill Junior had needed to work in a place where there was still enough crime to keep him busy, and teach him the ropes, and his dad had made sure of it. Ninth Precinct, Lower East Side—Alphabet City, as it was known, for its lettered avenues. It was a dangerous area, the same area where officers Gregory Foster and Rocco Laurie, two former Marines put on a foot post there, had been gunned down by the Black Liberation Army in the '70s. But that had been in the really dark times, when the city was filthy with crime and none of the cops wore bulletproof vests; when the population was under siege, and cops were being dropped by the dozens from the payroll to make ends meet.

Surely things would be different for Bill Morrison Junior.

They weren't.

On a steamy July midnight tour, he and his partner stopped a car that had just blown a red light. What they didn't know was that the two occupants of the car had just pulled an armed robbery. As they rolled up on them, the suspects jumped out of the car and opened fire on the officers, who rolled out of their car to return fire. One of the suspects was wounded, but William James Morrison Junior received multiple gunshot wounds to the face and was struck twice in his state-of-the-art bulletproof vest. He made it to Bellevue alive, but never made it out. The 45-caliber grease gun they'd shot him with was a fully automatic weapon, and he didn't have a chance.

Morrison still felt the pain every day. If there really were five stages of grief, as they said, he didn't know anything about the fifth. Kathleen didn't make it any easier on him—they never spoke of their son's death, but the hatred in her eyes spoke loud and clear. He couldn't give up any more of his pension to divorce her, but they slept in separate rooms, and practically lived separate lives. Their daughter Nadia, sixteen now, and Morrison's two other grown children were bright spots in their lives; but the rest of it was all just going through the motions. If they'd spoken, she might realize that he hated and blamed himself enough for both of them; that Billy's death had been the end of his life too; that he still often wished, desperately wished, that it had been him who'd died that day.

But the words never came.

3

At the scene at Sutton Place, Morrison groaned inwardly as he stopped to acknowledge a number of high-ranking officers and commanders who had already arrived. High rents bring high ranks; and this being Sutton Place and not East New York, the armchair detectives were coming out of the woodwork. Thankfully, it was Christmas, so Morrison knew the worst of them wouldn't arrive until the following day, when he knew he'd be able to deal with them. The job was not only a science, but an art: it required the ability to speak not only with suspects, but with the bosses who thought they were capable of running things—with whom you could only disagree when you knew you were right. Bill Morrison was one of its few artists, and always knew when he was right.

Getting past the brass, Morrison found Sergeants McNamara and Simmons waiting for him. The two men were typical of the new age of policing: smart, driven, and—above all else—loyal to the mission. They were as close as brothers; a striking fact, considering their respective backgrounds. Patrick McNamara had grown up in Woodside, a longtime Queens stronghold for Irish immigrants and their families. He was one of a long line of policemen, and though he was the first in his family to make it past patrolman, he'd known he would be a cop from day one. Andre Simmons, on the other hand, a second-generation Haitian-American, had grown up poor in the Tilden projects in Brownsville, Brooklyn—a place where it was remarkable for a young black man to come out alive, to say nothing of coming out a cop. His parents, appreciating the new freedom and opportunities they enjoyed in America, had made sure to keep him on the straight and narrow, even to the extent of walking him to school every day as a teenager; and despite growing up tough—as he did by necessity—he'd also picked up a big smile and a perennially sunny disposition, along with a deep sense of compassion. When his father had suffered a heart attack in their apartment, he'd seen caring and reassurance intermingled with the commanding presence of the Housing Police officers who'd escorted his family to the hospital, and young Andre had decided that day to become a police officer himself.

Despite the difference in their lives before they joined the force, both Simmons and McNamara had worked extremely hard since then to get where they were now. Short of Detective Sergeant, Sergeant was the best policing job there was; and they had both put in countless hours of study and hard work to gain the necessary promotions. They'd each read the book of Penal Law and Criminal Procedure Law so many times, they probably dreamt about it, and had each been decorated numerous times for valor in the line of duty.

Simmons spoke up.

"Hey, Cap," he said, and got right down to business. "Patrol picked up one guy a few blocks away, but I don't think he's even close to being a suspect."

"What'd they pick him up for?"

"Possession of drugs—he'll be going through the system anyway. I told the detectives to go slow with him, but I'm just not getting the feeling he's our guy." He leaned in confidentially. "Can you please just make sure to keep the Coke Brothers away from him during his interview?"

Morrison smiled. The request was typical Simmons—diplomatic

and polite. Others, he knew, might have used far more direct language. The "Coke Brothers" were detectives Mike Marchioni and Leo Kasak, who were still back at the house—almost certainly cooped up in their private office. Most detectives shared one common office area, commonly known as the squad room, but Marchioni and Kasak had their own office within the squad room, complete with a perennially closed door and two desks facing one another, so they could each speak to the only person—besides Morrison himself—who mattered. Their spectacular aloofness had been cause for quite a bit of speculation among the squad, and not all of it friendly. Everyone was loyal to the Captain, but these two were more than loyal; there was something almost fanatical about it, and to many of the others it was just plain insulting. Even in situations where talk was necessary, they'd withhold most of it for Morrison and each other, chain of command be damned. To say they were detectives of the old school would be putting it mildly. They were about as unorthodox as they came, and not always acceptably so. A lot of the young cops didn't know it, but their nickname came from an interview they'd held with a particularly tight-lipped suspect back in the day, in which Marchioni had finally elicited a confession from the guy by pulling his head back by the hair and waterboarding him a few times with a shaken-up bottle of Coca-Cola.

"All right, all right, I'll keep 'em busy," Morrison laughed. "We wouldn't want any complaints."

"Thanks, Cap. I know you have a soft spot for the old-schoolers."

Morrison watched thoughtfully as Simmons got back to work. Simmons was right; he did have a soft spot for cops of the Coke boys' pattern. But unlike many of the young cops who looked up to them, he didn't appreciate them for their toughness, but for their integrity. Below their grandstanding, macho exteriors, Kasak and Marchioni had the hearts of true defenders of the public good. All too many cops nowadays, of the "collars for dollars" mindset, were happy to spend days processing their arrests, raking in the overtime hours while their shoplifters squirmed in a holding cell with rapists and murderers. The

Coke boys, by contrast, got that part of their job over with as soon as they could; and when it couldn't be done quickly, they more often than not gave the credit for their arrest to somebody else in order to get back out on the streets. Theirs was the thrill of the chase; and they pursued it tirelessly.

Still, Morrison thought with a smile, it was a damn good thing he had cooler-headed cops like Simmons on his force to balance them out.

Once the Crime Scene Unit had finished collecting their evidence, it was Captain Morrison and his team's turn to go through the scene in greater detail. The processing of this scene was going to take more time than usual; but Morrison sensed that removing the carpet for forensic analysis would be worth it. He knew a crime like this, with a socialite victim in a neighborhood like Sutton Place, would bring tremendous scrutiny from every angle, and it wouldn't do to be caught having left any stone unturned.

All of the major media outlets had reporters assigned to police headquarters at One Police Plaza—otherwise known as the Puzzle Palace—so Morrison was quick to instruct all of his people to keep the lid tight on this case. Anyone outside their group was not to be spoken to—and that included other police offices. News traveled fast, but none faster than whispers in the hallways at 1PP; and an unfortunate reality of policing in the modern era was that even a notification to the Chief of Detectives' office could quickly lead to an out-of-control press leak.

"So what do we tell Arndt when he gets here?" Sergeant McNamara asked.

Morrison laughed out loud.

"Sergeant," he said, "I doubt you have anything to worry about. There's no way our illustrious Chief of Detectives is coming out on Christmas Day—not unless the Commissioner himself lights a fire under his ass. But to take your question seriously," he added, "if by chance Arndt *does* show up, I don't want you or anyone on our team telling him *anything*. Just call me. Got it?"

McNamara nodded. Morrison dismissed him back to work, chuckling again. There was no way *that* phone call would be coming through today.

Just then he saw Sergeant Rivera walking in the door, and grabbed him. Frankie Rivera was a distinguished Vietnam vet and longtime commanding officer of the Homicide squad, and was Morrison's go-to guy to put in charge of touchy situations like this. He was a very funny man, despite a troubled interior that came out in his war stories when he'd had a few too many vodkas, and on the job, he was a perfectionist among perfectionists. He was a born cop—close to mandatory retirement, and dreading the day—and his years of experience had taught him to leave nothing to chance. Under his control, there would be no questions about chain of custody, or sloppy reporting; everything would be well organized and forensically correct.

Leaving Rivera to catch up with the others, Morrison next called back to Homicide, to speak with Kasak and Marchioni. Kasak picked up, a slightly deeper tone the only aspect that discriminated his voice from his partner's.

"What's happening, Cap?"

"Kasak," Morrison said, "I need you guys to take over a patrol arrest related to this Sutton Place incident. He's a homeless guy they picked up in the area, working Sutton Place instead of one of the train stations—probably just figured the pickings were better here."

"Can't say I blame him," said Kasak mildly. "Though if I were him, I'd get someplace warmer—I understand Fort Lauderdale has one of the largest homeless populations in the country this time of year."

Morrison cut the small talk. "Listen, this is serious. I don't want you fluffing this off, or stopping at the deli before you talk to this guy. Simmons doesn't think the guy has anything to do with what's happened here, and we need to move quick to make sure nobody starts talking like they've caught John Dillinger. I'll square it with the desk lieutenant that you guys are taking over from patrol."

"All right, Cap, we're on it."

Morrison hung up, and turned to see Sergeant Rivera regarding him with anxiety written across his handsome Puerto Rican features.

"Aw man, don't tell me the Coke boys are already on their way in," Rivera said. "It's too early for me to deal with those two prima donnas."

Morrison held back a smile. Even given how often that term was used for detectives—just the price you paid for not wearing a clip-on tie to work—Kasak and Marchioni got it the most.

"Frankie, don't worry about it," he said. "I'm giving them strict orders, and they'll follow them."

At the word "orders," Rivera visibly relaxed. The Coke Brothers were a handful, but no one who worked for Bill Morrison ever disobeyed him.

"All right, all right, you know what I want to hear," he said.

When the scene was pretty much done, Morrison got ready to head out. On the way out he stopped to talk to the cops on the scene, wishing them all a Merry Christmas and addressing them by name. He'd always had a gift for remembering names; it was one of the qualities that made him a cops' cop. Everyone liked to be remembered, from the janitor to the precinct commander, but a personal connection with their superior officer made cops want to walk through fire for him.

Offhand, one of the officers asked where the Chief of Detectives was. "I figured he'd love to come to this part of town," he laughed.

"Not on a holiday, he wouldn't," Morrison said, chuckling too. "Besides, I don't know if he's ever solved a crime, or even seen a dead body. This is obviously not going to be an easy one, and I'm sure Arndt knows the press will have more questions for him than he'll be able to answer."

He caught himself before he could say more. His hatred for Arndt was off the charts, but none of that needed to be said to the rank and file. With a few more salutations, he grabbed one of the detectives, Alexander Medveded, to ride back to "the house" with him, and they went out to his car.

Boss though he was, Morrison drove. He almost always drove; it helped him to focus and stay feeling in control. In his head, he continued the conversation that he'd just curtailed with the officers on the scene. Frederick Arndt—even the man's name was pretentious. Nine months ago Arndt had taken over for the previous Chief of Detectives, Francis Donohue, when Donohue had finally lost his battle with cancer; and since then he'd lost no time in alienating just about everyone who worked for him. No investigator himself, he'd risen on the strength of his political connections to the highest position possible in an investigator's career, and now wore his phoniness with aggressive pride, disdaining the police who worked under him. Morrison remembered hearing a story from his former partner about Arndt's promotion to Sergeant, which seemed to sum the man up perfectly. He'd been proud as a peacock, strutting around the auditorium at 1PP with his new Sergeant's stripes sewn on his dress uniform. The only problem was, they were sewn on upside-down in a V, the way the British use them. He'd already pissed off everyone else there, so they just let him walk across the stage like that; and when the PC asked him if he'd switched departments and the room erupted in laughter, he'd just glared at everyone, like *they* were the ones who had it wrong.

Detective Medveded broke the silence. "What're you thinking about, Cap?" he asked.

Morrison smiled grimly out at the traffic ahead. "Oh, you know— just some no-good, backpack and boat shoe–wearing son of a bitch," he said quietly.

"Ha! Right," Medveded said. There was only one man Morrison could be referring to, and Medveded definitely had no love for him, either.

Morrison laughed again. "Hey, you remember when we were out drinking that night, and you said—?" he began.

"How could I forget?" Medveded said. "I still think we should've done it."

"If not for the vodka, huh?" Morrison looked over at him. "God, you were so pissed at him."

"How could I not be? The asshole wanted to transfer me to Staten Island!"

"I remember."

Boy, did Morrison remember. It was hard not to look back on it with a little regret, even.

He and Medveded been drinking together, and getting pretty heated about Arndt's treatment of the latter, who was only recently back on the job after a pretty haunting experience in the Bronx that had almost gotten him killed. Arndt had been the 44th Precinct desk officer at the time of the incident, when Medveded—then an officer on the Street Crime unit—and his partner Tommy Davis had responded to a call that a woman was being held at gunpoint in her apartment. At the scene they'd heard a woman crying inside and rushed in, thinking they had the element of surprise. They were wrong. The perp, in a classic "suicide-by-cop" plan, had gotten his ex-girlfriend to call another friend over to the apartment, then tied them both to chairs, called 911 on himself and told the women to cry out when the cops showed up, and waited with his gun pointing at the door. When Medveded and Davis had burst in, he'd opened fire on them, hitting Davis in the chest and Medveded in the abdomen before Medveded was able to put him down with returning fire. Davis had died that night. But Desk Officer Arndt, as it turned out, cared less about two cops shot, than about the ton of paperwork he had to do because of it; and attempted to have Medveded transferred to Staten Island, claiming he'd violated department policy.

So Morrison and Medveded had ended up pretty well sauced at the bar by the precinct, and Medveded had made a startling suggestion: *Let's rob him.* Morrison, naturally, had assumed he was joking; but Medveded had gone on: *Come on, Bill, it'll be easy. We mask up, follow him when he goes to his car—that prick never parks near the house, he knows someone would slash his tires. And everyone knows he never carries his gun.*

Morrison had realized then that Medveded was only half-joking. It was exactly the sort of idea the Crazy Russian—as some of his fellow officers had since taken to calling him—would take seriously. Yet as crazy as the idea was, he'd been distinctly intrigued by it. He'd thought about how gratifying it would be to pull out that fucking Nantucket belt with the whales (a piece of Arndt's wardrobe he was never without) and wrap it around the guy's neck. He'd smiled to imagine seeing Arndt on the ground, his pants around his ankles, weeping—as he was known to do whenever he was under stress. It all sounded good—but he also knew it wasn't worth losing his pension over. There were too many cameras around nowadays; and besides, he had to believe that guys like Arndt always got their just deserts. Thankfully, the vodka had taken its toll on both of them, and they'd fallen asleep in their car outside the precinct.

Morrison and Medveded arrived at the precinct, having made the decision to pass on the bar tonight as they parked the car. It'd be an early morning tomorrow, and both of them lived far away—Medveded in Brighton Beach, in the same apartment he'd grown up in—so they'd also both decided to sleep at the precinct. Medveded headed off to the dorms, while Morrison walked up the back staircase towards the squad room. He knew that trying to sleep would be futile for the time being; again the bagpipes were playing loudly in his head.

Sergeant Rivera was already back at his desk, the door to his office open. Looking up as Morrison passed and recognizing the look in the Captain's eyes, Rivera got up and headed casually over to his office.

"Hey, Cap. You got a minute to talk?" he asked. This was a common enough routine with them; he didn't have anything in particular to talk about, but he knew the Captain did, and knew that asking him like this was the best way to get him to relax.

"Sure," said Morrison, and sat. The two men sat quietly for a while, Rivera taking slow sips at his coffee, before Morrison spoke up.

"Let me ask you a question," Morrison said. "You were in Vietnam, right?"

Rivera had described his experience in the military to Bill Morrison more than once, but was always ready to tell him again when the Captain was in this frame of mind. "Yeah," he said. "I was drafted when I was nineteen and a half. I had to report to Whitehall Street for the usual induction procedure before they sent me to Fort Gordon, in Georgia. I was assigned to the 25th Infantry. They sent me to advanced infantry training at one of the ugliest places in America—Fort Polk Louisiana. Tigerland. When I finished my training with a bunch of other guys, we were shipped out."

Morrison listened, and sat thoughtfully again for a moment. "All right, well, let me ask you this," he said finally. "Have you ever talked to Arndt about your time there?"

Rivera smiled cryptically. "Why do you ask?" he said.

"Oh, I don't know," Morrison said; "just a hunch of mine, I guess. I was at a dinner a while back, where he accepted an award from the Mayor for his service in Vietnam. He cried like a baby the whole time, talking about how returning vets were treated, and what an honor it was. It just—it seemed a little too over-the-top for me to buy."

"Well, he's right about how we were treated then," Rivera said slowly, "but him being in Vietnam?" He laughed. "If you ask me, your hunch is right. I'm *sure* he wasn't there."

"Why do you say that?"

"Well, I haven't been around the guy much. But the few times I *have* been around him—in fact, the last time we spoke, a couple of years ago, he'd been talking to a few guys in the precinct about being in the military. None of these guys had served, mind you. When I walked in on the conversation, I heard him say he was at the battle of Khe Sahn. Thing is, it was the *Marines* who were at Khe Sahn—Con Thien, Hill 881, I remember—and he was saying he was in the *army*. I was in the army, and we weren't there during the offensive. I asked him if he had a CIB—a Combat Infantry Badge—and he gave me a funny look, and found a way out of the conversation." Rivera shook his head. "Man, if you're going to lie about being in 'Nam, at least do your research."

"I knew it," Morrison said quietly, leaning back with a sardonic smile. He wasn't quite sure if he was satisfied or not. "You know, Chief Donohue, God rest his soul—he couldn't *stand* Arndt. Now *there* was a guy born to be Chief of Detectives. He must be rolling in his grave, to have had this guy take over for him."

"So was it just the politics that got him in?" Rivera asked.

"One hundred percent," Morrison said. "The Commissioner didn't want to appoint him—you know Harrington hated him almost as much as I do."

"Yeah, I figured that," Rivera said. He knew the answer to his next question, but asked it anyway. "Didn't you and the PC work together as cops?"

"Yeah, sure, back in the day. He was quite a cop; he took his job very seriously." Morrison's face broke out in a wide grin. "You know, before we were partners he worked Narcotics as an undercover—he had the whole long-haired biker look. One day he went into one of those old Blarney Stone Bar & Grills—you know, they have them all over the city; used to keep corned beef in the window, and all the old-time shot-and-beer guys with the spider veins in their noses hung out there. Pretty conservative places. Well, Officer Harrington walks in, looking like he just got off his low-rider, and they refuse to serve him. So he flips out, jumps over the bar, throws a bunch of hot corned beef at the bartender."

Rivera laughed. "What'd they do?"

"One of the Sergeants responded and saved his ass. They wanted him arrested—they didn't know he was a cop—but they had a problem with their liquor license, so one hand washed the other, and the whole thing blew over. They put him back in uniform after that, but he never forgot how they refused to serve him. He used to talk about how that experience showed him how it was for people to be judged by their appearance, how the blacks must suffer from that kind of prejudice, and all that. He couldn't stand to see that kind of injustice. I remember when I was real young to the job, riding in a radio car with him in the wintertime, real freezing outside. We were patrolling, and all of a sudden he tells me to stop the car. I'm thinking, *What do we got? Man with a gun? Drug deal?*—but there's no one on the street. Then I see we're outside the Blarney Stone, and he gets out, picks up one of those metal trash cans from the corner, and throws it right through their front window. Then he gets back in the car and asks me if I'm okay with it."

"That's perfect, man," laughed Rivera. "That's really perfect. So what'd you say to that?"

"I just shrugged and said, *Okay with what?* and we finished our tour. Next thing I know, he's asking the roll call guy to make us steady partners."

"Sounds like a good guy."

"Yeah, I always liked working with him. But you know, even before he moved up in politics, we lost touch. You know how it goes—you just start moving in different circles, not running into each other as much." A familiar, faraway look came over Morrison. "When Billy died—well, Harrington always had a thing about funerals, and he still went. He doesn't go to them, ever; it's not his style. I always respected him for that, for some reason. But he still went to Billy's."

Rivera nodded. He wasn't sure what to say: it seemed there was nothing to say. The silence rang between them.

"Hey Cap, it's late," Rivera said finally, looking at his watch. "You and me both ought to get some sleep." He rose to his feet. "If you'll excuse me, I'm going to head in."

"All right," Morrison said, a weary smile returning to him. There wouldn't be much room at the inn tonight. "I'm just going to try to catch a few here, I think. Shut that door after you, will you?"

"All right, you got it."

"Goodnight, Sergeant."

"Goodnight, Cap," said Rivera; and a moment later, Morrison heard his footfalls sounding quietly down the hallway towards the dorm.

4

Early the next day, Detectives and Sergeants began to roll out of the dorm for day two, hoping nothing else had come in overnight. Thankfully there was no sign of the Night Watch Squad as yet, so they knew they could take their time getting themselves together. Several detectives from the other specialty squads were already sticking their heads in to ask what the story was on Sutton Place, and though no one was talking at this point, the atmosphere was tense. Everyone knew a stubbed toe on Sutton Place could turn into a storm quickly, given a slow enough news day.

The usual parade of useless bosses, which started practically with business hours, certainly didn't help things. Whenever a case was high-profile enough to guarantee phone calls and visits from the headquarter's brass, there were sure to be a gaggle of these promotion-seekers hanging around the squad room—mid-level officials who usually spent their time in their offices reading the Wall Street Journal or watching ESPN, who were invariably drawn out by the prospect of being perceived, by the right people, to be hard at work. They were a nuisance, but not much more than that: they tended to set up shop quickly in the squad commander's office, there to remain until media attention had subsided, and were almost always gone soon after 1700 hours, when their bosses at headquarters wrapped up for the day.

But then, some of them were worse than others.

At 0930 on the dot, Chief of Detectives Frederick Arndt arrived.

Captain Morrison, who had slept poorly and should have been too tired to care, openly grimaced at the sight of the man. It was not Arndt's usual ridiculous green-tinted suit that offended Morrison's sensibilities this morning, or even his ostentatiously shined shoes, so much as his tie: a loud multi-colored "Save the Children" monstrosity emblazoned with cartoon images of people holding hands. If the irony of the tie was lost on anyone, it wasn't on Bill Morrison, who remembered when Arndt was a lieutenant and had wanted to put the fire hoses on the crowd at a rowdy demonstration, as though he were Bull Conner in 1962 Birmingham. *Save the children—!* Phony liberal sentiments or no, the man was a manipulative, self-centered asshole, and Morrison knew it—as well as he knew that Arndt was only even there because the Police Commissioner was looking for answers.

The squad held back laughter as Arndt walked self-importantly past Morrison to wait for him in Morrison's office. When Morrison had closed the door behind him, Arndt looked up from the chair he'd taken and started right in on him, clearly flustered.

"This woman on Sutton Place, Victoria Adams, is a really important person—we're going to have to pull out all the stops," he said, not bothering to acknowledge Morrison. "Overtime is approved big-time for this one. Downtown is already aware of it, and wants results. This isn't your run-of-the-mill homicide."

"Why's that?" Morrison asked disinterestedly, seating himself. It was more of a rhetorical question than anything, but he asked it anyway.

Arndt gave him an exasperated look. "She's tied to the Wilmington family," he said.

When he didn't say anything further, Morrison sighed. "More politics, huh?" he asked. "Let me guess—her family was on the Mayflower."

Arndt looked as though he'd been slapped, but Morrison wasn't waiting for him to recover. "You know, I'm getting to be pretty sick of this shit, Arndt," he continued. "*Every* homicide is important to us. We had a triple last week, and you wouldn't give me fifty cents to work with. Now it's a *really important person,* and the checkbook's open. How's that fair?"

Arndt regarded him with a cold sneer. "Well, if it comes to *fairness, I* don't think it's fair that I can't relieve you of this command right now."

"So I guess because the victim isn't a minority, this isn't just another misdemeanor homicide to you," Morrison went on, ignoring him. "You know, we got a lot of cops around here—black, white, and Hispanic— who hate that shit, and they know the rules you play by. You remember those pictures of Abbott & Costello you used to have up in your office? I was there the day you had them taken down to put up pictures of JFK and Nelson Mandela, trying to be politically correct; but I ought to tell you, with stuff like this, everyone sees through the act. We're going to do everything we can—but it won't be because she's *important,* or because it's what'll make you look good. It'll be because it's what we do all the time."

The color had drained from Arndt's face. "Watch your tone, Captain," he said quietly. "You're flirting with your career here." He smiled suddenly, his lips tight. "You have a map of the boroughs, don't you, Captain? Long Island commute? You know, you could always have a patrol-duty Captain's spot, get some nice around-the-clock work someplace far from home. They always need good captains on Staten Island, I understand."

Morrison decided he'd already listened to this long enough.

"All right," he said in a low voice. "You know what, Arndt? Go ahead. Fuck me, put me on the street—then find yourself someone better to run this squad. See how *that* makes you look. I may not be the most popular guy around the in-crowd at headquarters, but you and I both know that until you all decide you want to work hard, you need guys like me to deal with the day-to-day crap you don't want to deal with."

"Captain, you need to learn to calm yourself down," Arndt said in a patronizing tone. "You're out of control. You know, you haven't been the same since your son died."

Morrison's face went red-hot and he gripped his chair, struggling to keep the fury down. "You asshole," he said, eyes fixed on the desk, his voice a whisper of rage. "You never even went to his *wake,* much less the funeral, and you aren't going to bring him up with me now."

Even Arndt knew when he'd crossed the line. "Captain—" he began.

Morrison looked up at him, and his glare stopped Arndt in his tracks. "Listen," he said slowly. "I don't care who you are—you so much as *mention* my Billy again, you'll get a hard lesson in how we fuck someone up in this department. Understand?"

"Okay, okay," Arndt choked, his eyes tearing up at the corners. It was a strange and terrible personality trait of Arndt's, that he seemed to weep under pressure; no one had ever been able to figure out if it was a real stress response, or just another manipulative habit he'd picked up over the years. To many, including Morrison, it was utterly revolting. "I'm sorry I brought up your son. I know his funeral was very hard for everyone."

And how would you know that, you slick motherfucker? Morrison thought. Everyone knew Arndt had been in Florida the whole time, soaking up rays. But things had already gone far enough. Morrison took a deep breath.

"Look, I'm sorry," Arndt said again. "I just need a briefing, all right? The PC wants to know—just brief me on the case."

You need information, so I get an apology, Morrison thought, the rage welling up in him again. He took another deep breath to master himself before going on.

"It's a complex forensic case so far," he said through gritted teeth. "Sexual assault is usually more a crime of violent hatred than passion, as you know"—he said this last with a barely perceptible scoff—"and this was a total invasion. There are a lot of twists to the evidence on hand, but it's pretty sick stuff. Bite marks, amputations, the works. It has all the appearances of a predatory job, but we aren't sure of that yet."

Morrison spread out a few copies of photographs and lab requisitions from the case file he'd brought with him. "They got a lot of evidence from Victoria's body, as well as from the scene itself—potential DNA samples and multiple fingerprints," he said. "We'll have to wait for the results. Since it's Christmas, it'll probably take some time for the guys in the lab to come up with anything. In the meantime we're going to start with the usual suspects: husband and boyfriends. If nothing else, we'll get a sense of what her life was like. Victoria Adams was an attractive woman, and we know she was out there on the party scene. She was also married to a successful guy who travels for his job and was away at the time of her death. He's out of the country currently; we're not exactly sure where yet. He's likely either in Italy or Thailand—once we sort that out we'll have an in-person notification made to him. I should say that there aren't any clear indicators yet that he would have had anything to do with a crime like this. Now, as these photographs suggest—"

"All right, all right," Arndt said with a bored air, cutting him off. "Put together a full summary for me—I'll need it ready in two hours."

Morrison stared at him. Normally the Chief of Detectives would take notes on the information given him in a briefing of this kind; but Arndt, with his soft memory for anything he was told, was passing the buck as usual.

Just then there was a knock at the door, and Sergeant Simmons poked his head in. As though summoned, Arndt got up abruptly to leave.

"You'll have to excuse me; I'm needed elsewhere," he said curtly. "I'll be back for that report this afternoon, Captain."

Without another word, he was gone. Morrison shook his head gravely.

"Good timing, Simmons," he said.

"Yeah, thought that might save you, Cap," Simmons smiled. "Guy's not too comfortable around minorities."

Morrison laughed. "Well, thank God he's gone for now. I thought I was going to lose it. Anyway, we have work to do. What've we got?"

"Well, it turns out our victim has a place in the Hamptons and a place in Manhattan," Simmons said, handing him a few copies of property reports, "and the husband's in Italy. We've got him on a plane back today."

"Away over the holidays, huh?" Morrison said. "We have any idea whether they got along?"

"Neighbors and doormen seem to think so, along with the friends we've talked to."

"Okay. What else?"

"Well, there's some New York Post–type Page 6 stuff, but that's inconclusive so far."

"Tell me."

"Well, we've got her cell phone and email, and what looks like a book she was trying to write; so far we've got one number on her cell that pops up every day, and often at night. Seems like a writing buddy, but you never know. We'll be heading up to Rye Brook to talk to him later today."

"Him?"

"Yeah, we know it's a guy."

"Sounds like Boyfriend Time to me," Morrison mused, leafing absently through the papers on his desk. "Continuous calls at night while your husband's out of the country? Unless you're on the job, or maybe a fireman, that's interesting to me."

"Sure, sure. I'll let you know what we get out of that, Cap. You mind if I take Tina with me, from Gangs?"

"No problem—everyone else here'll be running around anyway, following up on the local stuff."

"Okay, great. I'll call you when we have something."

"Thanks. And Simmons," Morrison called after him, "send George in here, will you? I want to get him on some of these leads."

"Will do."

"George" was Detective George Hanrahan, another senior member of the Homicide Squad. His father had been a firefighter in the city, and had died in the line of duty when George was eight, leaving him to be raised by his mother. She'd made sure George had gone to college before he could even think about becoming a cop, and he'd gone all the way through a Master's in Public Administration at—of all places for a detective to have studied—Columbia. A gentle giant whose bad side even Morrison didn't particularly want to see, he was a quiet, shut-in type, and spent virtually all of his off time in the Bronx with his wife and the sheepdogs they'd gotten when they'd proven unable to have children.

Morrison looked over his "Things to Do" list, checking on the irons they already had in the fire. Phone and email records were already being processed, and a few potential suspects were due for interviews today. Compiled video footage from Sutton Place was being combed through for anything related to the incident, and the word had already been put out to other departments for similar crimes in the area. The other teams were back at the scene, canvassing whatever neighbors hadn't answered their doors the day before. The homeless guy they'd picked up seemed to be a dead end, as predicted—just another innocent person in the wrong place at the wrong time.

Morrison was Googling the Adams' Hamptons address when George Hanrahan came in, silently as always, and looked at him with his usual expression of intelligent seriousness.

"Hey, George," Morrison said. "I want you to follow up on this Hamptons property our victim owned. According to the canvas at Sutton Place she spent most of her time out there, except when the husband was off traveling."

"Sure thing," George said. "What type of place is it?"

"Oh, the usual; looks like Wayne Manor," Morrison said, pulling up the street view online. "Must have been a fortune—look at this. Beautiful place. Right on the beach, big pool, probably a full staff." He chuckled. "Not nearly as nice as my place in Levittown, of course, but hey, what is? My tennis courts are a lot bigger—they just happen to be in the public park instead of the backyard. Anyway, get what you can—have someone reach out to the Suffolk County cops for anything they might have."

"Depending on where the house is, there are a couple of smaller town departments out there that might know more, too."

"Right, I forgot about that—the Hamptons have a few departments, don't they? Let's touch them all. Actually, we might as well check the whole tri-state area. Hit them by phone, so they know we're serious—not just VICAP alerts."

"Got it. You want to call Suffolk yourself? They might respond better to your rank."

"I would, but I'm still burned over that Highway Patrol nonsense."

Hanrahan smiled. The story had gone all over the precinct. A while back, before Morrison's daughter had been on the job herself, she'd been pulled over on the Long Island Expressway for failing to signal while exiting. When she'd handed the patrolman her dad's courtesy card along with her license and registration, he'd thrown it back in her face, telling her he didn't know any captains, and written her out the ticket. The ticket itself hadn't been such a big deal, but the patrolman's disrespect for his daughter had really gotten to Morrison. It was one of those signs that things had changed for the worse, and to cap it all off, when Morrison had spoken to the guy's CO later, he'd been told that the patrolman was undeniably an asshole, but too politically connected to be punished for it.

"All right, I'll handle Suffolk," George said. "Anything else?"

"Who do we have who can talk to the FBI without having a breakdown?"

Hanrahan thought for a moment. "Well, Tommy Quinn's our unofficial liaison with the feds—he's got a kid in the ATF, so he's usually able to work pretty well with them."

"Okay. Get Detective Quinn on the phone with the feds, and you hit everyone else," Morrison said, the first signs of a dull headache beginning to creep in behind his eyes. *God, this early in the day*—*!* Kelley's was generally welcoming at the end of a shift, but today he knew it'd be particularly so. "Get everything on this Hamptons property and the owners that you can. We're already on the Manhattan property and looking for other local leads, so I'll need you guys to work quickly with the outside areas to keep everything together."

"You got it, Cap."

5

It was late in the day by the time Morrison was finally able to get away, and by then, even the short walk down the street to Kelley's seemed unfairly tedious.

The Irish pub was a decent place. Better than decent, really. Besides being the longtime regular for the precinct's detectives—the patrol cops had their own place, as was customary—it even attracted a few non-police women, which was always a nice plus. Back in the day the cops all went to gin mills—hard-drinking places with sawdusted floors, where nobody but cops, firemen, and hardcore boozers ever cared to go. Cops nowadays were different, though; they liked some atmosphere with their painkillers, and women without badges made for great atmosphere. Morrison himself was of the older mindset. Romance, he'd long felt, was a game he'd played and lost; the real good of a place like this—and as far as it went, it *was* a real good—was to push the memories to the back of his mind for an evening.

Morrison joined a group at the bar, including Sergeants Rivera, McNamara, and Simmons. As was usual for day two, everyone was still talking about the case. They were all tired; but for many of them, as busy as they'd been today, this was the first chance they'd had to go over the case collectively. The guy from Rye Brook, Rivera was just telling them, had turned out to be a bit of a dead end. He'd been a friend of the victim's since childhood, as it seemed, and had been devastated to learn of her death. He was a chef who'd published several cookbooks, and she'd apparently been picking his brain lately for advice in writing her book.

As the talk swirled around other bits and pieces of the case, Morrison looked up absently and noticed a woman sitting at the other end of the bar. She was strikingly attractive, perhaps in her mid-forties. He couldn't help but wonder what she was doing here; there was something about her that just didn't seem to fit in. Perhaps it was the way she was dressed: slightly upscale, certainly nicer than the rest of the clientele. But whatever it was, he couldn't stop looking at her.

Three drinks in, he decided he was going to talk to her. He was generally a pretty shy individual when it came to these things, but after the drinks he was feeling up to it. Downing a shot of tequila, he got to his feet, a look of determination in his eye.

"Going in, Cap?" Simmons said, with a smiling nod toward the woman. "You got a line ready?"

"We'll see," Morrison said. "Maybe I'll give her the old baby in a dumpster story—steal Rivera's thunder."

"Well, Cap, you know he swears that line works," Simmons said.

"Every time!" said Rivera, laughing.

"Yeah, but you always find the psycho pussy, the ones who fall for you and come around calling," Morrison countered. "You guys remember the time this guy's wife cut up all his clothes and threw them out on the front lawn?" Everyone laughed, Rivera included. "How're you two doing, by the way?" he asked Rivera.

"Oh, we're still together—we worked things out," Rivera said. "What can I say? She loves me."

Everyone laughed again, and Morrison wandered over towards the woman. The other three sergeants continued their conversation.

"Place is crowding up," McNamara said, looking around at the bar. The 4–12 shifters were starting to trickle in.

"Yeah—hey," said Rivera, suddenly waving to some of the newcomers.

"Those guys were on a patrol squad with me, Midtown South. Let me pull them over here—we oughta do a shot together."

He called his old friends over, and ordered them all a round. It had been a long time since he'd worked on the same squad with these guys, but back in the day they'd spent long years together, and they fell into the old rapport quickly. Rivera was thankful the shots were pretty weak—Southern Comfort shaken up with lime—as the rest of the squad were younger guys, and had given him a two-day headache the last time he'd gone out with them. He asked them how the patrol was treating them these days.

"Oh, same shit, Sarge," said one, a young officer named Devin. "We've been real busy—we were holding 92 jobs at one point."

"Not quite the same, though, right?" Rivera asked. "GPS in your cars, all your stops videotaped—man, I'm glad I'm almost done; I don't know if I'd be able to do that."

"Yeah, well, you get used to it," another officer said. "How about you guys? Heard you had an interesting homicide today."

Rivera nodded. "Yeah, definitely different," he said. "Not easy so far, either. You know how it is: it goes past day two, it's going to be rough. I wish we were on *Law & Order* and could solve it in an hour, but real detective work's a lot harder." The group laughed.

"Hey, speaking of detective work," an officer named Gray spoke up, "you hear Lou Galipoli made Detective?"

Rivera's face darkened. "He did?"

"Yeah, just the other day," Devin said.

"They gave *that guy* a gold shield?" Rivera said, incredulous. The promotion to Detective was one of the only ones the force gave out without a test, and the criteria for granting them were highly subjective.

"Tell me about it. I mean, everyone always speculates about who does and doesn't deserve that, but with him—"

"Yeah, I can't say I get that at all," Rivera said coldly. "He's a nothing cop, isn't he? Big badass, always has something to prove, terrible to people? As I recall, he's particularly weird with women—loves and hates them."

"Yeah, I'd say all that's true," Gray agreed. "He seems like a sick fuck to me. But it's pretty hard to argue with his service record—he's got a Silver Star and a CIB. I guess you have to admire that, right?"

"Yeah, I guess you do," said Rivera, frowning. "A Silver Star, jeez. Maybe I'm being too hard on him. Has he ever gone out with you guys?"

The others laughed.

"Forget it," said Devin. "He's one of those guys that doesn't have any time for you if you don't outrank him. Beat cops are nobody to Galipoli."

"Well, that sounds more like the Galipoli *I* know, anyway," Rivera said. "I've never seen him do much on the street, either—just a nasty, fake tough guy."

"I can back that up," said Simmons. "He's loaded with IAB complaints. I don't know anybody who likes working with him—I've heard a lot of guys say they have to beat him to calls just to make sure no Civilian Complaints come through."

"But with that service record—?" another young cop asked. "He must've been through a lot; isn't the guy a war hero?"

"Some excuse," said Ricky Collins, a decorated nine-year veteran who'd been working the same sector with the same partner for seven years.

"Well, it *could* be," argued the young cop. "PTSD, and all that."

"It's true, but there are a lot of guys out there with that, that don't act like he does," Collins said. "I know *I* can't stand being on a call with him. It's torture. Did you ever watch his tough-guy routine? I was glad to hear he's getting a gold shield—it'll get him off the street before we all lose our pensions behind the bullshit he does."

"Well, a Silver Star's a big deal, but I still can't believe they made him a detective," Rivera said. "You have to go through a lot to earn that badge, and all he ever did on patrol was screw up wherever he went. This has to be some political bullshit."

"I did hear Arndt had something to do with him getting made," Gray said.

"Of course," Rivera said. "It takes an asshole to push another asshole up the ladder. I'm just thankful I work for someone who won't have to take him."

"You sure?" Devin asked.

"Oh, Captain Morrison's the best of the best," Rivera assured him. "No brand-new detective's getting put in any of his squads."

"Lucky you," said Devin, standing. "Good leadership—I'd say that's worth another one! Who's in? I'm buying this time."

Meanwhile, the Best of the Best had decided to forego the baby-in-a-dumpster bullshit, and just go the direct route. The woman at the end of the bar looked up smiling as he approached.

"What's such a pretty woman doing sitting at the bar by herself?" he asked her.

"I've been waiting for you to walk over here and join me," she said.

"Good answer," he said, sliding into the seat next to her. "I'm Bill Morrison."

"Claudia Kalianis," she said, offering her hand. "I assume you're a cop?"

"Detective Captain, NYPD."

"So I can trust you, then." Another bewitching smile. "Are you married?"

"Yes."

"No problem."

Morrison was almost startled at how straightforward they'd been. He hadn't felt the need to equivocate at all with her. They'd seemed to click immediately. It happened so infrequently. *We both must need someone,* he thought; then, with a rush of exhilarating honesty, *I do, for sure.*

"So, Claudia, what do you do?" he asked, trying not to stare at her too hard.

"I'm a psychologist."

"Really! Do any forensic work?"

"All of us do," she laughed. "Didn't you know that? Just watch any

TV show or movie—we're always in the middle of some crime drama. Though it isn't far off; it is human nature that moves me."

"Is that what you're doing here, at a cop bar?"

"Might as well be! No, I'm staying nearby. I'm in town for a two-day conference."

"Over Christmas? That's rough."

"Ah, it's a living. I seem to do it all the time, so the holiday doesn't make that much difference anymore. I'm staying at the Marriott Marquis across the street."

Something about the way she'd said it emboldened Morrison, and before he knew it the words were tumbling out of his mouth.

"How would you like to spend the night with a cop?"

He hardly had time to feel stupid before she'd taken his hand and put it over hers. He felt almost dizzy with the surreality of it; it had never happened this way for him.

"Look, Claudia," he said, suddenly feeling awkward, as though he'd gone in over his head, "I don't want to give you the wrong idea. This never happens to me. It really doesn't."

"Me neither," she said softly, "but I don't care. You want to get out of here?"

"Definitely," he said.

Without a word to anyone, the two of them got up, left the bar and walked across the street. There was a refreshing crispness in the air, and Morrison felt almost giddy as Claudia entwined her arm in his.

"At this point there's no sense pretending," she said, "and since you're a cop, I'm feeling kind of safe."

"What do you mean?"

They stopped in the middle of the street. Suddenly she leaned up and kissed him deeply, passionately, before looking at him again.

"Let's have one at the hotel bar and talk, okay?" she said quietly.

He looked sidelong at her. "What are you, wanted in ten states?"

She laughed. "Not quite—but come on, let's get a drink."

They found seats and ordered a couple of drinks. With the first sip Bill's head swam; he'd already been a little tipsy before any of this had gone down, and Claudia's familiarity was more intoxicating than anything.

She gave him a coy smile. "I don't know why, but I just want to tell you about myself, and what I like," she said.

"I'm all ears."

"Just promise you won't judge me—don't say anything at first, okay?" There was a strong tone to her voice that Morrison liked. A lot. He sat back to listen.

"All right."

"Well, you know that book, *Fifty Shades of Grey?*"

"Sure."

"Well, that's amateur hour for me. Do you carry a gun and handcuffs around—like, do you have them now?"

He nodded, his eyes wide.

"I'm *really* into that stuff, but I get that not all guys are. I feel a little silly bringing it up already, but I trust you, and I don't want to freak you out. What do you think?"

"I'm—I'm good with that," he said. He didn't know what else to say; in the first fifteen minutes of knowing her, this woman had gotten him more excited than anything had in years.

"Really? That's great," she said with visible relief. "When I trust a man, I just—I need to be a certain way. I'm getting excited just thinking about it."

He smiled. "Just tell me what you want, and I'll do whatever it takes."

She leaned in confidentially. "I like to be out of control," she said. "That excites me; so do a whole lot of other ideas that I've tried, but never gone too far with because of the guys. My ex-husband left me because of this stuff."

"Really?"

"Yeah. When he filed the divorce papers it killed me—I was too embarrassed to have a deposition, so I just settled. Does that turn you off?"

"Not at all," he said. She put her hand in his again, and Morrison realized what that feeling was, stirring in him: he felt alive.

"You're amazing," she said. "I'm going to order a movie for us, if that's okay. Do you get drug tested for work?"

"Yeah, we do—random testing."

"Do you mind if I smoke around you?"

"I wish, but they clip our hair."

He felt a little embarrassed at this lie; he'd just never smoked, and had no interest in trying it. But he didn't want her to feel uncomfortable around him, and he knew most people did if you weren't doing what they were doing.

"That's all right," she said. "It's just to relax anyway, and I'm already feeling really good. Let's go upstairs—I'll show you how I like it, rather than tell you. Do you think you can walk through the lobby with your pants like that?"

Morrison followed her gaze downwards and laughed with her. He felt like a sixteen-year-old at the junior prom, but euphorically distant from it, unselfconscious.

"Well, definitely not, if you keep talking like this," he said. "We'd better go now, before it's too late."

They paid and she led him upstairs to her room. The surreal feeling of the situation was almost overwhelming, but Morrison welcomed it; as strange as it was, it felt as though he were waking up from some long, dismal dream. She put a movie on, but he couldn't have remembered for the life of him what it was. They started in so comfortably, so familiarly. There was a rhythm in the room with them, an uncontrollable excitement that built and built until they could hold it back no longer. Soon she was directing him, begging him; and it was true, she was out there with the things she wanted, but none of them were things he didn't want too, and the sweat poured down their bodies as their flesh pounded together, their hearts racing to the peak, their blood boiling on the inside, Morrison's handcuffs pulling against the bedpost until she collapsed in his arms and he followed with her, his lips seeking out her skin to taste the electricity flowing through them both.

She shivered under his touch as they lay united, the tidal wave of excitement sliding back from the shore, only in anticipation of the next.

"Bill, I—I love this so much," she said finally, her voice breaking around the unbridled passion between them. "But I know we rushed into it, and I know I'm so *different*—are you sure all this is okay with you?"

Morrison laughed slightly, as much a laugh of disbelief as anything. "I feel like I've missed out on you my whole life," he said simply. "It's okay that we moved past the standard preliminaries and introductions. There's time."

"There's time," she repeated, her smile radiant. "Yeah, there is."

"Besides, you and I aren't that different. You don't know how much I needed this."

"You and me both! We'll do more next time."

"I can't wait." He reached to the floor for his pants, chuckling to himself. "Here, let me get that—I assume you'd rather not sleep in the cuffs."

It was a real sleep for Morrison, the first he'd had in a long time: peaceful, unbroken by nightmare or discomfort. By force of habit, the ringing of his cellphone brought him instantly out of it, but after a moment's hesitation, he let it go to voicemail. It was something he hadn't done in a long time.

He looked over at Claudia, who'd awakened too and was regarding him with a concerned look.

"Your wife?" she asked. "Do you need to call home?"

"Oh, no," he smiled. "That's the one person it definitely *isn't*. I bunk in pretty often at the precinct, and anyway, she doesn't care. No, that call was from one of the sergeants I work with."

"I see. I was worried for a second there." She slid off the bed, smiling wryly. "Well, why don't we—oh, there it goes again."

Morrison picked up the cellphone, knowing he had to answer it this time. Back-to-back calls meant it wasn't just regular trouble.

"Hello?"

"Hey Cap, it's me—Rivera."

"I know who it is, man! I have Caller ID for that. But what the fuck is so important that you're calling me at 6 a.m.?"

"Look, Cap," Rivera whispered. "There's brass from all over coming in here already. I had to show up early, too. Everyone wants to know what's going on—where we're at with the investigation, and where you are."

"Okay, okay. Look, I'm—I'm not far, all right? It'll be okay—I'll be there in twenty minutes with coffee and donuts."

"All right, Cap, I'll see you."

Morrison hung up. Claudia stood in the doorway, a robe slung loosely around her.

"Is everything okay?" she asked.

"Yeah, just another day in paradise," he said, pulling his clothes together. "I have to go, though. I'm going to see you again real soon, right?"

"Definitely," she smiled. "Can you tell me what the call was about?"

"A new homicide—something beyond your typical everyday murder. It looks like there's some serious shit behind this one, some real psycho stuff."

"Well, maybe we met for a reason," she said. "I deal with psychos all the time, remember."

"A psychologist, right." He smiled back at her, excitement stirring again as his eyes took in her body. "I don't know how it could have slipped my mind."

"As long as you remember my number, I'll overlook it." Suddenly her smile turned grave. "You are going to call me again, aren't you?"

"How can you doubt it?" he laughed.

When she didn't say anything, he went over to her, taking her hands in his. "Look, Claudia," he said. "I haven't felt like a human being in so long, and last night was great for me. Of course I want to see you again. I feel like I've hit the lottery. My life—well, let's just say it hasn't been so good, and I need to get it back."

She looked deeply into his eyes. "Because of your job?" she asked gently.

"No, no—it isn't that," he said. "I just—I just can't find peace, is all. No matter what I do, at the end of the day I'm unhappy. But look," he added, gripping her hands tighter, "thanks to you, for the first time in a long time I don't have that feeling right now."

Her smile returned. "Well, as I said, maybe we met for a reason."

"I hope so," he said. "I'll speak to you later today, all right?"

"Sure." She fished a card out of her purse and gave it to him. "I'm here for this conference, but normally I'm only thirty miles away, in Stamford. You can call me at work, on my cell, at home, whatever—just call."

"All right." He kissed her, and forced himself to let go of her hands. "Believe me, Claudia, I don't remember when I ever wanted to see anyone again more than I want to see you."

"All right, Detective Captain. Talk to you soon."

6

Morrison knew Sergeant Rivera would be nervous.

The brass always made Rivera edgy, but when Morrison wasn't around, it was far worse. It wasn't only that Morrison was his boss; the two of them had a special relationship, going way back. Morrison had given him a major break early on in their days of working together.

They'd been on a gun run, first on the scene; and when they'd come up on the perp, and Morrison had shouted *Police, don't move!* Rivera had just frozen up. Who knows what it was—something left over from his days as a combat infantryman—but one way or another, it was a very close call. The perp was already cagey and was going into his waistband when Morrison ran up, punched him out, and pulled the guy's Glock out of his hand, a round already chambered. Once they'd cuffed him and brought him back to the house, Rivera had broken down in apologies and self-deprecations, sure that Morrison was going to have his ass for it, but after some discussion Morrison had given him another chance, and promised to watch over him while he worked through the last couple of years to mandatory retirement.

Now, with all the fame-seekers crowding around to get their cards punched, he was sure he'd see Rivera first of all, relieved as always to see him. But when he walked into the squad room, he was dismayed to see Chief of Detectives Arndt instead, standing in the middle of the room directing Morrison's detectives and supervisors on the investigative steps they were to take next.

Sighing, Morrison walked past the group into his office and unlocked the door. He then turned and, with uncharacteristic politeness, invited Arndt and half a dozen of his cronies to make themselves comfortable inside while they strategized. They all trooped in with him and shut the door after them.

Half an hour later Morrison emerged with a sheet of paper. The rest of the detectives in the squad room knew what this meant; the senior people had seen it happen time and time again. Whenever there was a roomful of armchair detectives coming around to involve themselves in a case—especially of the sort who outranked the Captain—they invariably had all sorts of suggestions, and those suggestions had to be followed to the letter. The thing was, they never told you *how* they had to be followed; and that was the saving grace of the whole thing.

Morrison handed the list to George Hanrahan and his partner, conspicuously explaining to them that they were not to return to the office until every one of the boxes on the list was checked off. Hanrahan and his partner knew this meant their involvement in the case would be limited, but they both knew it had to be done, and took the list without hesitation.

Once they were out the door, Morrison took everyone else into the lunchroom, away from the ears of the experts still amassed in his office, in order to develop their own plan to solve the case. He knew that despite the weight of promotions and standardized tests, his detectives possessed a wealth of knowledge, experience, and instinct that far outweighed their bosses', and he wasn't about to let bureaucracy get in the way of their work. Good ideas can come from anyone, so everyone chimed in during this session, with even the Coke Brothers listening to what the others had to say.

Once they'd come up with a good list of tasks—including some the bosses had come up with, for as Morrison was fond of saying, even a blind squirrel can find a nut every now and then—they all headed out to get the investigation underway, while Morrison headed back to his office to keep the bosses entertained.

"Hey, Cap," Rivera called to him as he passed.

"What's going on?" Morrison asked, stepping into the sergeant's office.

"Well, there's something going on in Jamaica Estates that you might be interested in."

"In Queens? What are you talking about?"

"We got another one—like we had on Sutton Place."

Morrison was taken aback. "Are you kidding? The same extreme?"

Rivera nodded gravely. "No one here knows anything yet, but yeah: it seems like we might have number two in three days. Similar profile to our other victim, too, from what I'm told—and neither of them grounders."

"Aw, shit," Morrison said. He glared at the floor, his mind racing. "That means—shit. These guys didn't just start, you know?"

"No, probably not."

"The press is going to have a field day. I hate to say this, but I'm going to have to get that asshole Arndt involved. Goddammit, and I'd just sent everybody out, too!"

"Yeah, sorry, Cap. Timing's a bitch on this one."

"It's all right—I need to see the scene first anyway. I guess I'd better get out to Queens. Who do we have left in the office?"

Morrison ducked out to look around the squad room. Alexander Medveded was still at his desk.

"Hey, Alex—grab your coat," he said. "You're coming with me. Frankie"—turning back to Rivera—"you stay here and keep the brass in my office happy."

"You got it. I'll get 'em swapping war stories—you know, the stuff they heard while they were at the range, or sitting back at the precinct desk."

"Good. That ought to do it. By the way, what squad caught the case?"

"103 Squad, Lieutenant Doherty."

"Okay, well, at least he's a decent guy."

"Yeah, the guys like him."

"All right, I'm on my way then—let me know if Arndt gets wind of this before I get back."

"Okay, Cap—I'm on top of it."

At 0745, just on the other side of a jammed Midtown Tunnel that had held him and Medveded for what seemed an eternity, Captain Morrison called Lieutenant Jim Doherty.

"Hey Jim, Bill Morrison here. How's it going today?"

"Hey Cap—not so good, and I'm guessing that's why you're calling. I read the paper yesterday; looks like we may have something in common."

"Yeah, it does. Look, I'm going to get to the point. There's no jealousy toward Major Crimes out there, is there? You think your guys will have a problem working with my squad, if we determine these are the same animals as in our case?"

"Absolutely not, Bill. It all equals out in twenty, as they say. And besides, on this one we can already tell we're going to need any help we can get."

"Okay, good. Can you count on the guys you have there?"

"Yeah, they're a great team, real professionals. We've been together a long time."

"Who've you got going on it?"

"Three sergeants and six detectives—Detective Ron Myers and his partner Kayla Barnes are already assigned, and both are real good. We've got Crime Scene here already too."

"Is it Williams and Kelly?"

"Yeah, why?"

"Good. They handled our case, and if we're right we may have the same killers connecting the two cases."

"Okay, got it. Well, I'm guessing you're interested in seeing what we've got here—when are you thinking of coming by?"

"I ought to be there in five minutes or so—the tunnel was a bitch but we're making good time now."

"Typical Bill Morrison, always two steps ahead," Doherty laughed. "Listen, I'll fill you in when you get here, all right, Cap? There's plenty to talk about."

"Sounds good. See you soon, Jim."

Morrison hung up and concentrated on the road. Medveded, characteristically tactful, stared out the window in silence. His deep empathy was something Morrison had always appreciated about the big Russian; he always seemed to know what to say or not to say. Most of the squad chalked up his uncanny ability in the interview room to his sharp tactical mind: Medveded was a World Chess Federation–certified chess master, and even during heavy snowstorms he could be found on his afternoons off clearing off a park board in Brighton Beach for a game. The kind of five-steps-ahead thinking that he employed on the chessboard was certainly a big part of his tact in interviews; if nothing else, it keenly attuned him to the thrill of out-maneuvering his opponents. But equally important was his almost supernatural ability to relate to others. Morrison had watched him talk to all types of people, from stone-cold killers to the overwhelmed mother who had shaken her colicky baby to death and tried to cover it up; playing, by turns, the roles of father confessor, Good Cop, Bad Cop, psychologist, and friend, each exactly as needed, to the person in front of him. He had an uncanny knack in reading people, and understood of his interviewees, as most others did not, the ways in which the vast majority of them were victims in their own right. He seemed to be able to make anyone feel that he understood what they'd done, and only wanted to better understand exactly when and how they'd done it.

When they arrived at the scene, Lieutenant Doherty was speaking with the duty captain to one side of the large house's taped-off doorway. Seeing Morrison as they parked, he excused himself and jogged across the street to meet him.

"Good morning, Cap," he said as they shook hands. "Glad to have you here."

"Thanks, Jim—you know Detective Medveded? Alex Medveded, Lieutenant Jim Doherty."

"Pleasure."

Doherty led them over toward the doorway, beyond which a few Crime Scene specialists were moving methodically to and fro. "Gentlemen, we're looking at one or two, more likely two, sick fucks here. No forced entry, but certainly robbery; the place hasn't got one piece of jewelry left in it. Victim's bound and tortured. Big bite-mark case. Her lips are gone—and I don't mean the ones on her face. It looks like they were done pre-mortem."

"You think these guys read about the Hillside Strangler case?" Morrison asked.

"Possibly—they definitely bagged her and brought her back to the house."

"Why do you say there's two?"

"Let me show you."

They walked in carefully, through an eerily serene-looking living room. Doherty pointed into the kitchen, where a number of the linoleum floor tiles were missing.

"Our guys were able to take some impressions from over there, of bloody shoe prints. They wanted to preserve them, so they pulled the tiles too. The prints are from different shoes, so either we have one guy who changed his shoes while committing the crime, or at least two perps."

"Got it. Hey—Williams!"

The Crime Scene officer stopped in the doorway. "Hey, Cap. You getting déjà vu around here too?"

"I was just going to ask you about that," Morrison said. "Offhand, what do you think?"

"If I had to swear right now, I'd say it's definitely the same guys from Sutton Place. The scenes are practically mirror images."

"Yeah, I was thinking that too." He turned back to Doherty and Medveded with a heavy sigh. "Well, whoever these animals are, you can bet this isn't their first time. They're definitely enjoying themselves. We're going to have to move quick, or the body count's going to grow. Jim, I'm going to have to call the Chief of Detectives."

Doherty rolled his eyes. "I should've called in sick," he said. He looked around, then added more quietly, "How did that dick get so far up the ladder, is what I want to know? He's inferior in every capacity, and his staff is no better."

"Well, you know what they say about pets and their owners—after a while they start to look alike."

"Right," Doherty laughed. "Well, I guess we'd better start putting our heads together. How do you take your coffee, anyway? Let me guess—milk, sugar, no donuts."

They both laughed. Damn the stereotype, but who didn't love a donut?

"If you're sending someone, I'll take two Boston creams," smiled Morrison. "That's my standard price for calling Arndt."

Doherty laughed again and wiped mock sweat from his brow. "Hey, thanks, man. I only have a year and a half left, and if I never talk to that guy again, it'll be too soon."

The two went over the scene in greater detail for a few minutes while Morrison took notes. Once he felt decently informed and knew the Boston creams were on their way, Morrison stepped off a little distance, took a deep breath, and dialed Arndt's cell number.

Arndt picked up on the first ring, an irritable curtness to his voice. "What is it, Captain?" he asked.

"Hey Chief," Morrison said. "We've got a second body here that looks like it's linked to our case on Sutton Place."

The irritability fled from Arndt's voice as panic took over. "What? Are you sure? Don't jump to conclusions now."

Morrison smiled in spite of himself. "Yeah, I'm sure. We have a couple of the same Crime Scene people here, and they agree."

"Oh, Jesus. This is not good, not good." Morrison could practically hear the man wringing his hands in the background. "We've got a real problem now, don't we? Okay, let's see—Jesus—where is it, exactly?"

"I'm out in the 103, Chief—Jamaica Estates, Queens."

"Another wealthy neighborhood, you mean? I wonder if—" Arndt trailed off.

"Yeah?"

"I mean, do you think it could be the Wall Street people, targeting one-percenters?"

Morrison stifled a scoff of disgust. It was incredible how quickly Arndt jumped to conclusions, and how badly. "Hey Chief, they cut the lips off this lady's vagina, and left her with multiple bite marks. I don't think they run with a protest crowd. It's a violent sex crime, and we don't even know the economic status of the victim yet. It's a pretty good bet that she's above middle income in this neighborhood, but still."

"All right. What *do* we know about her, then?"

"She's a 35-year-old female, Abigail Johnson. Looks like she lived with her husband, but he isn't at home. We're going to look for him next; apparently none of the neighbors they've canvassed have seen him for a while. Anyway, the victim's blonde, like our first victim; attractive and fit, too, also like the first. Drives a Range Rover with a baby seat in it. The kid's not in the house—"

"Jesus, you'd better do an AMBER Alert," Arndt interrupted. "We can't—"

"If you'd *wait* a second," Morrison cut in, unable to keep the exasperation from his voice. "I was going to say, the child was with the victim's ex-husband. She's okay. Now as I mentioned, the victim has multiple bite wounds, primarily around the breast area, and the same vaginal condition that we saw yesterday. We're still processing the scene, but we've already picked up footprints from at least two different types of shoe, suggesting multiple perps. I've got Lieutenant Jim Doherty with me here, and with your permission, he's going to turn the case over to us as an extension of ours."

"Do it," said Arndt. "As much as it pains me to say yes, it sounds like that makes sense here."

"Thanks for the vote of confidence, Chief."

"Anything else?"

"No, that's it for now. I'll have Doherty get me the paperwork as soon as he—"

But Arndt had already hung up.

7

Day four, and Chief of Detectives Arndt was knocking at Morrison's door.

The door was closed because it had been a late night, and Morrison was drinking a hefty dose of Jameson in his coffee to put himself right. Morrison ignored him until he went away, finished off his coffee, gave the room a hit of Ozium, and took a swig of mouthwash before heading out.

He found Arndt wandering around the squad room like a lost child, the rest of the detectives hard at work making themselves unavailable to talk to him. As Morrison approached him, he gestured toward an unfamiliar face.

"I don't recognize her," Arndt said. "Who is she?"

"I'll introduce you," said Morrison, uninterested in starting a tête-a-tête with Arndt this early in the morning. *And of course you don't recognize her, you idiot,* he thought. *She's never kissed your ass before.*

He walked Arndt over to the redheaded woman he'd pointed to. "Chief of Detectives Arndt," Morrison said, "I want you to meet Detective Tina Koreski. She's on loan from Gangs, along with two others we pulled from Robbery and Special Victims to bolster our manpower on this case."

"Nice to meet you," Tina said.

"Likewise," Arndt said with an oily smile; then abruptly asked, "How old are you?"

Morrison cringed at the inappropriate question. But Tina, young as she may have looked, was ready for it.

"I'm nine years old," she said seriously.

Arndt was visibly annoyed; as with many of their bosses, he didn't like it when the funny stuff came from inferiors. But he pushed ahead.

"So you come from Gangs, eh?" he asked.

"Yes—I've been on the job ten years," Tina said pointedly, clearly uninterested in pursuing the conversation further.

"Why don't we head into my office," Morrison suggested, holding back a laugh. Arndt agreed, and followed him in. Arndt made a face when they went in.

"Have you been drinking in here, Captain?" he asked. Apparently the Ozium hadn't quite done the trick.

"I don't drink anymore," Morrison answered. Which wasn't entirely untrue—as he liked to say, he didn't drink any more, nor any less.

"Well, in any event, we need to talk," Arndt said. "We've decided to go public with what we have."

"That's good—it's time," said Morrison.

"What should we give out, then? Did you check for other possible cases, or talk to the Bureau, or anything of that kind?"

"Of course," said Morrison. "We've done all of that, and we have some video footage. There isn't anything similar in Westchester, Rockland, Nassau, or Suffolk; but I can give you a summary on the two cases and you can decide what to give out that won't hurt the case. Remember, though, we need to hold some things back, for when we catch these guys. There's a lot of crazies out there willing to confess to something like this just to get famous."

"I'm aware of that, Captain," Arndt said tersely.

"All right," said Morrison. "I'll give you a summary in a few hours." Whatever he gave Arndt was guaranteed to be front-page material the next day, so he knew he'd have to be careful in hedging his bets. Giving up the fact that they were looking for two suspects, for instance, could be catastrophic to the case.

"Very good," Arndt said, straightening his tie. "I'll be looking for that before end-of-day."

Morrison saw him to the door and walked out to the squad room. Once the door had closed behind Arndt, the room erupted into a ripple of laughter. Medveded threw a notebook toward the door with a gesture of contempt. Even the Coke boys stood in their doorway, smiling to see Arndt gone. Morrison walked up to Tina Koreski.

"Welcome to the squad, Koreski," he said. "That was a good start."

"Yeah, I bet. I'll be in Staten Island tomorrow," she laughed.

"Maybe once all this is done," Morrison smiled back. "Now, look. I'm sure you know I pulled you from Gangs for a reason. I've actually wanted to get you on the team for a while, but didn't have an opportunity before these two homicides came along. We're lucky to have you."

"Thanks, Captain."

"Do you mind if we have a word in my office?"

"Of course."

When they'd shut the door and seated themselves, Tina spoke up.

"It's been a long time, eh, Cap?" she said.

"It has," Morrison said. "How has it been going over there for you? I haven't had a chance to check in on the Gangs squad recently."

"I can't complain—the lieutenant there takes good care of us. Still, when I heard you'd reached out for me, I couldn't have been happier."

"I'm glad to hear it," Morrison said. He'd hoped as much. "So where are you living these days?"

"I got a nice place up in the north Bronx."

"The Bronx! Weren't you in Queens before?"

"Yeah, I moved up there because of a woman I was seeing. A really good one, for a change. She works at the Northern Westchester Medical Center in Mount Kisco, in the E.R. there. She used to work at Bellevue—I met her there when I was admitted."

"So you moved up there to be closer to her?"

"Yeah." A dark look came over Tina's face. "It didn't work out, though—we were doing pretty well for a while and she took really good care of me, but you know me, I can't keep relationships."

"I'm sorry to hear it," Morrison said, knowing the feeling well.

"It's all right, shit happens."

"That it does." Morrison nodded. "Well, look, let's talk frankly here. First off, I want you to know that I'm looking out for you, and I want to make sure this goes all right for you. This is a seriously demented caseload so far, and I don't want what happened to you at the Port Authority to hurt you here."

"That's really good of you, Cap. But believe me, nothing can hurt me anymore."

"I get that," Morrison pursued, "I just want to know if you'd be all right with talking to me about that. I only heard the basics at the time; and you and I didn't really talk about it. Primarily I need to know that these cases aren't going to push you over the edge, or take you anywhere bad, but if you can talk about it, I'd appreciate that. You and I go way back, and you've been there for me in some dark times in my life. I want to be there for you too."

Koreski took a breath. "I really appreciate it, Cap. I've heard these cases are worst than most on the repulsive scale, but I'm sure I'll be okay. I wouldn't wish what happened to me on anyone; but I've carved out a little life for myself since then, and I'm better now—a lot better. As for talking to you about it, I've always known I could talk to you. I don't think I've ever had anyone treat me better than you have, and I certainly don't have any issue with telling you about it now. Maybe it'd even help me for you to hear it all."

"All right." Morrison gestured toward his cabinet. "Can I get you a drink?"

Tina laughed. "No, thanks. It's too early."

"Oh, it's never too early, kid. Remember, we have no clock around here. That's why you can get out of the job in twenty—though I hear now it's twenty-two."

"Yeah," Tina said. "I don't mind it, though; I'm really in no rush to retire. You know I had a good life after my incident. I think I'm just not that good at being happy. This girl, Cap—she was really beautiful." She smiled. "You remember when I first worked for you, and I told you I had a housemate? I think you said, *What's that?*"

"I remember," Morrison smiled.

"You were the first person on the PD that I told, and you made me feel very comfortable about it. I'll never forget that. But yeah, these days I'm thinking I'm meant to be alone. I had, and have, a need for life on the edge. Adrenaline's definitely my drug of choice, and it's the worst. Nothing is lonelier than being with someone when they aren't with you, and I don't wish that on anyone with me. But I'll bet you know about that too." She looked down at her hands. "You know, I never thought you would come back after—after your son."

"I never did." Morrison stood up, opened the cabinet, and poured a healthy two fingers of Jameson. "Here, come on. It's never too early."

"I appreciate it, Cap, but no."

"All right, then. I can't let it go to waste, though." He took a sip and sat back down. "Go ahead, Tina—whatever you can tell me."

Koreski sat back with a sigh. "So, as you know, I was assigned to the Pimp Squad when I got off probation, right after I left patrol. It seemed like I'd be a perfect fit there, at least for the short term; they wanted to grab this pimp that owned midtown Manhattan, and figured I'd be the right girl for the job.

"Well, the first time out is my only time out. I've got Sergeant Veda—holy roller on the surface, always talking about God. Turns out he was a really disturbed guy, a complete phony. Anyway, we have three two-man teams working the job. I've got a kel on, and it's tested before we go out—I'm reading five-by-five going out the door, and you can clearly hear me. So the setup is, I'm supposed to get on a Greyhound bus on 11th Avenue, pull into the Port Authority, and sit down in the terminal like I'm lost. It's like fishing for flounder in Quincy, Mass—

or in a fish tank, for that matter.

"So I get there, and everyone's hitting on me. Soon their guy comes in, big guy named Ernest the Pimp. I'm basically his specialty: runaways who hit the big city and get scared. Word was, he had a whole fleet of kids working for him, all from similar circumstances. Guess they didn't call 8th Avenue the Minnesota Strip for nothing.

"Anyway, Ernest the scumbag shows up and asks me if I want some pizza. I say yes, and we head over to Sbarro. He said he was an outreach worker, in charge of getting help to girls in the area, and asked if he could help me get home. He explained some of the dangers of being out in the big city on my own, just enough to scare a girl who was actually stuck there. He had the perfect line of bullshit; it was perfect. So I got him right where I want him—my kel's working and my backup teams are all good guys looking out for me. I feed Ernest the typical runaway story—tell him I don't want to go home, I got an abusive dad, all that stuff. He acts real sympathetic, and offers to take me to the Welcoming Center, whatever that was supposed to be. He said he'd helped a lot of other girls like me. He even asked if I had ID on me. I told him I didn't—I'd said I was fifteen already—and he said that wasn't a problem, and that the folks at the Welcoming Center could help me get an ID.

"So he tells me we have to leave the terminal, and I'm thinking I'm good: I can see one of my backup teams out of the corner of my eye, and I'm real close to nailing this asshole. All I need is an offer of a sex act, or confer to offer as they say, and he's mine. He has his friend pull this big-ass black Lincoln into the roadway at the terminal, and I'm looking around for the backup cars, and don't you fucking know it, as I'm being hustled into this car I see Sergeant Veda in one of the cars, yelling at the guys in there, and none of them are paying attention to what's going on with me."

"Wait, what?" Morrison stopped her. "What the hell could he have been yelling at them for, and why would he choose that moment to do it?"

Tina smiled grimly. "I found out later that it was because he'd found a *Hustler* in one of the cars. He was yelling at them for looking at a goddamn porno."

"Jesus," Morrison said, closing his eyes.

"So I try to back out, but Ernest shoves me into the car," Tina went on. "Now I know I'm in trouble. The team didn't see me get shoved in, and we're moving. I'm hoping the other teams spot me, and they did, but none of them moved. That was another thing—I found out later that Veda told them to hold their positions. That pervert phony born-again motherfucker told them to sit tight, so he could yell at them some more, and now no one has my back.

"The Lincoln pulls out, and no one follows us. My kel wasn't working at that point either, but I didn't know that; I'm just thinking, *No way is this fucking happening to me,* right? They got me in the front seat, and this sick fuck Ernest, he doesn't waste any time. He tells me all about how he's going to make me his fuck toy, then turn me out onto the street. So I'm like, *Okay, we got the statement we need, where the fuck are you guys?* But nobody comes to stop the car, and nobody's behind us—no plainclothes car, no radio car, nothing. They lost me. Ernest starts playing with me while he's driving, and I tell him to stop. I don't have a gun on me, or a tin—I'm just supposed to have three backup teams and a Sergeant, and I don't. I try to get out, and the guy in back grabs me by the hair. *Nice red hair, pretty girl,* he says.

"At this point I realize I'm completely fucked. Next stop is the Martinique hotel on 32nd—classic hideout spot, total dump. No one gives a shit what happens there, and you can't see any police on the block. There's a park across the street and Sanitation's picking up the garbage, so I scream when they drag me out of the car. The Sanitation guys are kicking the cans so the rats don't jump out at them, and they look right at me, with me yelling for them to call the cops. No response.

"The three guys drag me upstairs and rip my clothes off, then Ernest rapes me. The other fuck—I don't even remember his name—he sticks his dick in my mouth. At this point I pretty much wanted to die. I started to pray, wondering what the fuck I was doing there, and why

I'd trusted that moralizing piece of shit Veda. After the first two are done with me there's a third guy, and I can't even go into what that sick fuck did. They duct tape my mouth and cuff me to the bed, and I wanted to die. Sometimes I still do."

"Tina," Morrison said softly. "Are you sure you're okay with telling me all this?"

Tina shrugged. "Yeah, of course. I always talked to you. Besides, I've started; I'm not stopping now. It gets worse, if that's possible." She thought for a second. "You know, I think I will take that drink."

Morrison got up and poured one for her without a word. After a long sip, Koreski went on.

"Well, anyway, they smack me around a bit, but not bad enough in the face to damage the property, if you know what I mean. That first night I'm still praying they find me, because Ernest has already decided that this fat disgusting white guy from Scarsdale will be my first customer. Like, who would believe some money guy out of Scarsdale would even know where this fleabag hotel was, much less come to it for this?—but the guy is a freak, and he pays for the whole night. I'm still tied up when he comes in, and he does things I still don't want to talk about.

"So I'm still waiting for the troops to show up, but I'm a prisoner, and I'm really starting to lose hope. This terrible, low feeling had come over me—it was indescribable. I have to say, I truly value my freedom every day now. And I guess they had two hundred cops kicking in doors for me all over the city, and the pressure out on the street was *severe*. All the drug dealers, prostitutes, and pimps on the street were getting rousted. I was told later on, you couldn't sell a hotdog on the corner, much less crack. I can never thank Inspector Harrington enough for what he did—everything was shut down.

"At some point—fatso from Scarsdale's still having his fun with me—I hear Ernest and these mopes talking outside the room. They're getting nervous, because word's come up from the street that I'm a cop. I figure I'm dead at this point—any minute they'll come in and kill me—but they don't, and soon they're gone. At 0500 the door comes crashing in, and Cap, I was never so happy to see the boys from Emergency in all my life. I just cried and cried.

"I went to Bellevue for treatment, and that's where I met Angela. Now the whole job knows my story, or at least they think they know, and everywhere I went after that they just look at me weird. At least it felt like everyone did. I was embarrassed and depressed and there wasn't enough medication for me to take—Lexapro, Prozac, every fucking drug, till I didn't even know who I was and I couldn't drink enough. Angela helped pull me out of it. I owe her my life and my career, really; without her support I'd probably be dead. And still it didn't work out.

"Anyway, if that's what it takes to make Detective as quickly as I did, I'd say it definitely was *not* worth it. I'm just glad I didn't end up with HIV. I went to therapy for a long, long time, believe me."

"I believe it," Morrison said. "What happened to Ernest what's-his-name?"

"Good old Ernest Stanley Jackson. He fled off to Baltimore; they picked him up within a few days. They got his friends, too, in another fleabag hotel in Manhattan. Thought they were hiding out, the morons—they just went from the west side to the east side. On their way back from picking up Ernest in Baltimore, I heard they beat the shit out of him at every rest stop on the New Jersey Turnpike."

"They put him away for a good while?"

"He got twenty-five to life under the state RICO statute. All his buddies got the same."

"That's good."

"Yeah, small victories. The fat guy from Scarsdale was the guy I really wanted. He was the most disgusting animal, this motherfucker. Sweaty, fat, big rolls, real small dick. God, did I hate him—he was a rich fuck, and just, I don't know. He *paid* for me. I learned a lot about humanity and inhumanity that night, not that I really needed that type of lesson."

"So did they get him?"

"Oh, yeah. That was more vindicating than any of the rest of it.

Sergeant Devallo took good care of that one too—when he was putting him in the wagon for arraignment, he made sure to tell everyone else in the back that hey, this guy raped a young black kid. Now *that's* the way to get someone paid back."

Morrison laughed through a grimace. "It sure is. And Sergeant Veda—I'm assuming you heard what happened to him, right?"

"I heard he hung himself. I was sorry for his family, but it was hard to feel sorry for him."

"Why would you want to?"

"Well, you know…it was a lot easier to be mad at him when he didn't show any moral compass, but suicide? I couldn't believe he felt that bad about what happened to me."

"Wait, stop right there," Morrison said, holding up his hand. "What do you mean, *felt that bad?*"

"About screwing up with me. I assume he killed himself behind what happened to me."

Morrison laughed and shook his head. "Oh, no—no no, Tina, don't even think about it like that. He really did do the wrong thing by you, and his suicide had nothing to do with it. Didn't anybody brief you on what happened to him?"

"No," Tina said, her eyes wide. "I just heard his family found him hanging in his bedroom after he killed himself. Was there more to the story?"

"Oh, yes," Morrison said. "Even though it was a suicide, they investigated it as an untimely death, and they turned up a *lot.*"

"Well then! Do cut me in on it, Cap."

"It *is* my turn, I guess! And then we can get down to business."

"Deal," she smiled.

"Okay." He took a swallow of whiskey. "After your incident he got suspended with pay, you know, out on administrative leave—tie goes to the runner, innocent until proven guilty, and all that. So one day he's out at Kennedy Airport, waiting for an Aeroflot arrival; he'd apparently paid for one of those Russian mail-order brides online."

"You're shitting me. And him already married?"

"Yep. He'd told the Russians he was going to leave his wife for her. But the girl never shows up. Instead, two guys meet him at their prear-ranged spot in Long Term Parking, and explain to him that they need fifteen thousand dollars up front, so their company doesn't lose out. He explains that he already has an apartment set up for the girl in Bayside, but the guys don't bite; they tell him they have to protect her. In the end, he pays the fifteen grand and they tell him they'll meet him the next day in Bayside.

"So the next day they meet up, and tell him they'll let him know when she's in the country, and to just sit tight until then. He goes home, the jerkoff, and finds an email waiting for him, where they tell him they need proof that he's going to marry her, because he's already married and they don't believe that he really loves this girl they're supposed to bring him. For proof, they demand that he take some pictures of himself with—let's just say, without any clothes on. So what does the genius do? He sends them some real explicit photos of himself, with his goddamn face in the picture."

"What a fucking idiot," Tina laughed in disbelief.

"Oh, big time," agreed Morrison. "And these guys are good—they make him send more photos, with some really sick, sexually explicit stuff in them. These emails, you'd have to see to believe. They really got him going, telling him they need to make sure he's a real man, and can satisfy whatever her name is, and so forth. So he sends more, and a few days later they meet up in Cunningham Park and tell him they need ten thousand more."

"Jesus. Don't tell me he gives it to them!"

"No—but just wait. So Veda goes nuts, and calls the cops. A car from the 107 shows up, and Veda tells them the Russians are trying to beat him out of money. He doesn't mention the photos. The Russians tell the cops they're there to sell him a car and he won't pay, and that he'd just given them pictures of his dick. Veda freaks out, tells the cops it was all a misunderstanding, and sends them off. So now he's really fucked—the Russians tell him they want more money, or they'll show his pictures to his wife and kids."

Tina whistled. "Man. And how bad did you say they were?"

"Well, I'd say you've been through enough today—suffice it to say, they're real degrading. Anyway, so here he is, somehow still thinking there's a mail-order bride waiting at the end of this nightmare. Except now they want twenty thousand, and they're not fucking around. So he begs them to bring his bride around and swears he'll give them the last of the money from his 401(k). They actually set him up with her—she flies into Newark."

"So there was a woman after all?"

"Yeah, a really pretty one. He takes her to a motel in Jersey City, and she gets him completely hooked. The two Russian guys meet them the next day, and he turns over the twenty grand; then they tell him they want his car."

"His *car?*"

"Yeah. A Ford Explorer. They tell him just to sign it over to them right there, and they'll give him his photos back."

"You've gotta be kidding me."

"Nope. And remembering what happened the last time he called the cops, he does it."

"He *gives* them his *car?*"

"Signs it right over. His new Russian bride was very supportive of him."

"Yeah, I bet."

"Well, so then he calls a car for them, and while they're waiting, she goes to use the ladies' room. Next thing he knows, she's in his Explorer with the other two scumbags, waving at him as they drive away."

"Holy shit."

"Yeah. And it's not even over yet. They later tell him they want ten percent of his paycheck, or they'll send the pictures to his wife and Commanding Officer, and tell the cops that he sexually assaulted a woman in Jersey City. His DNA's all over her underwear, they say, and she has all the details. In that kind of a corner, what was the poor cowardly fuck going to do?"

"Oh, man." Detective Koreski was visibly floored.

"Yeah." Morrison sipped off the last of his whiskey. "Moral of the story: it wasn't you, Tina. He was a fuckhead, and he hung himself for himself. Don't even worry about it. Fucked up as it is, it's the kind of thing we see around here. Now," he said, getting up to offer her a refill, "shall we talk about your new squad a bit?"

8

C hief of Detectives Frederick Arndt tried to calm himself as he took a slow ride from One Police Plaza to the Midtown South Precinct. He could still feel the redness in his face from his meeting with the Commissioner.

Over the nine months he'd been Chief of Detectives, he'd survived pretty well on the strength of his test-taking skills, on his political connections, and on the payback of the higher-ranking officials in the department for whom he'd done so many favors on the way up. But this was different. The briefing had started well; but as soon as the Commissioner had started asking questions, everything went downhill. Arndt hadn't been prepared for questions about the plan moving forward, or whether the Medical Examiner's Office had fast-tracked its DNA tests; now he felt his ineptitude had been dangerously exposed. He'd fumbled through that part of the briefing, and stuttered with nerves. Damn that asshole Morrison, for not giving him a list of things to cover!

Yet Arndt knew better than anyone just how unqualified he was for the position he was in. Housewives watching *Law & Order* probably had a greater depth of knowledge about crime scenes than he did; it was almost a point of pride for him to have gotten as far as he had, *without* having to know it. Cops of greater ability, the Morrisons of the force, were as contemptible to him as they were obnoxious. Their kind of street-level work was beneath his ambition; it was fine for them to do, but only as long as they kept their place, and didn't get in the way of those they were meant to obey.

As a cop himself, he'd volunteered for embassy duty as often as possible, spending his shifts studying the patrol guide and avoiding grunt work at all costs. He'd made detective at a time when the city was in a fiscal crisis, after a lot of cops had been laid off and they didn't have the money to hire more, and his subsequent promotions had come along as a matter of course. He'd made himself the ideal candidate on paper, spending his indoor shifts studying and getting in close with the higher-ups. Let the other cops deal with the nightmares of work on the street—the people they'd given a break one day, turning around and murdering someone the next; the suicides they'd talk out of taking a bunch of pills, only to have them jump out the window as soon as they were gone—he had other things to think about. "Lead, follow, or get out of the way" had served him better and better the higher up he'd gone; if it was a case he couldn't handle, he could usually pass it on to someone else before any dirt got on him.

Yet now he was pretty well fucked. He'd made himself too conspicuous in the early phases of the case; and now that it seemed to have blown up into a full-scale serial killer situation, the Commissioner had him locked down for it. Ah well, he'd just have to tap the troops a bit.

His driver pulled up in front of the stationhouse, and Arndt snapped back to reality. Telling his driver to wait in the car, he took a deep breath and headed in.

He walked through the precinct house, happy as always to see his reputation precede him. Normally no one could walk past the front desk without being challenged, but they clearly knew who he was around here. Never mind the fact that no one stood at attention to acknowledge him, he thought with a little umbrage; that would change with his next promotion. He made his way straight for Captain Morrison's office and walked in without a word or a handshake.

Morrison, who'd already gotten a heads-up from 1PP about what had gone down in the PC's office, struggled to keep the grin off his face. The Captain had friends everywhere, most with the same disdain for Arndt, and he'd heard the giddy tale of the Chief of Detectives having his head handed to him by the Commissioner over and over. It would mean more work for him in the long run, but it was worth it. Anyway, the work was what he was here for.

He looked patiently at the Chief of Detectives. Arndt cleared his throat.

"Well, Captain," he said, "you've seen these two cases in detail by now; what's your take? What's our next move going to be?"

Morrison smiled. "I'm just waiting to follow your lead, Chief," he said mildly.

"Well, you have the investigations; you'll have to tell me what you're going to do with them. I know what *I* would do, but that hardly—"

"And what is that, exactly?" Morrison asked, looking hard at Arndt.

"Captain," Arndt said in a measured tone, "this is your case. I don't micromanage, as a rule."

"I understand, Chief. Let's just say I really want your input."

There were a few awkward moments of silence. Morrison was enormously gratified to see a bead of sweat running down Arndt's temple. It had obviously been a long morning for the Chief of Detectives.

"All right, Chief," Morrison said, finally breaking the silence. "Here's what we have going. We've established a taskforce, pulling detectives from the SVU Robbery and Gang squads. It's a full team of detectives we have working on this. We've expanded our canvas in both neighborhoods, and I just conferred with the District Attorney regarding a search warrant for the crime scene, just to make sure we don't lose our evidence in court."

"What do you mean?" Arndt asked. "Why would we lose it?"

"Well, you know *Mincey v. Arizona*. Or perhaps you're testing my knowledge of it?" Morrison let the tension hang for a moment, savoring Arndt's discomfort. "It was that case in the late seventies, when a cop was killed in a narc raid—they stayed there gathering evidence for a long time, but a lot of it was ruled inadmissible, since the perp lived there and they'd never gotten a search warrant. Since we don't know who's involved in our murders, and we're definitely going to want to search the scenes more thoroughly, I consulted with the DA to make sure that doesn't happen here."

"All right, good. How have the searches been going?"

"We ended up spending plenty of time at the scene, and took the bedroom carpets out in twelve-by-twelve squares. We think we'll probably get some decent samples from those—at least we hope so. We have a forensic odontologist working with us, too—with all the bite marks, we'll probably need him down the road."

Arndt nodded, obviously happy for the reminder of what a forensic odontologist did. "Of course," he said absently. "How about the husband from the Sutton Place case—any word on him?"

"Dealing with that as we speak."

"Who is?"

"Koreski and Hanrahan," Morrison said, knowing full well Arndt would have no idea whom he meant. "Listen, we all understand how serious this case is, Chief," he assured the Chief in a patronizing tone. "I can assure you, we're pulling out all the stops."

"All right, Captain." Arndt stood, again feeling sickeningly out of his depth. There had been too many blank spots for him today already; he knew he'd have to regroup himself in order to keep in control of the situation. "If everything's going smoothly, I'll be on my way. We've all obviously got a lot to do here."

"Obviously," said Morrison. He smiled and eased back into his chair. "Hey, speaking of, how was your meeting with the PC earlier? I imagine he had a lot of questions for you, but knowing you, I'm sure you were ready."

Arndt spun around, his face reddening abruptly. "Just make sure you don't slip up, Captain," he hissed. "Mine isn't the only ass on the line here."

The Chief of Detectives swung out in a rush, slamming the door on his way and leaving Morrison feeling better than he'd felt all morning.

Back at Sutton Place, Detective Koreski and Sergeant Hanrahan were meeting with the first victim's husband.

Robert Adams, as it turned out, was a good-looking, very wealthy venture capitalist. He'd been in Venice at the time of his wife's homicide, but had taken an emergency flight home upon hearing the news. His ten-hour trip had obviously been excruciatingly painful for him.

Despite an evidently high degree of personal control, he was distraught, and could think of nothing that could have led to this. He'd always felt that Victoria and he had a good, if not picture-perfect, marriage: no affairs, no suspicious friends or party acquaintances. His wife, he said, didn't even really have any girlfriends she spent a lot of time with, to say nothing of boyfriends. He gave the detectives all the information they asked for: telephone records, calendars, photographs of Victoria. Through it all they could see him trying to focus, and failing; he stared into space as Koreski and Hanrahan questioned him, and soon sobs overtook him.

The detectives trod lightly, keeping their compassion for Adams balanced with the job they had to do. There's no specific way that people, guilty or innocent, act when faced with sudden death, and certainly no right way to grill a grieving spouse; it had to be felt out. Hanrahan and Koreski were both experienced enough to know that it was impossible to rule Adams out as having been involved in his wife's murder, even given such evident suffering. But it was hard to maintain any suspicion of him. Unless he was an especially gifted actor, he was essentially non-functioning; he couldn't even understand that the clean-up of the scene was a task that he would have to handle. There were, of course, companies that specialized in such things, a list of which detectives always provided; but this was always one of the cruelest realities to deliver to the survivors of homicide victims—the news that on top of everything else, they'd have to deal with cleaning the place up themselves, invariably produced a feeling of helplessness unlike any other.

Back in the car, Koreski looked idly through the photographs Robert Adams had given them of his wife—vacation photos, holiday photos, photos of dinners and weddings and reunions—and the familiar wave of despair washed over her. So joyful, so full of life and promise. She breathed deep to master it.

9

Since Billy's death, he'd visited the Memorial a few times, always alone.

He always stayed in the St. Regis, not far from where the Memorial was—it was a beautiful hotel, and he always thought staying in a nice place would soften the pain he felt. It also had a great bar; and when he'd gotten good and drunk, he could walk two blocks to the White House and look out at its grandeur through the trees. He always hoped its beauty would elevate him, free him from his misery for a moment. Yet it seemed the nicer things were, the more morose they made him.

At the Memorial, he invariably did what every one of its visitors did: find the name of the person you'd lost, lay a piece of paper over it, and rub over it with a pencil to take an etching of the name. There were more than nineteen thousand names recorded at the National Law Enforcement Officers Memorial, but the name never took him any time at all to find. It was carved in his mind as deeply as in the wall itself.

Nineteen thousand names. Nineteen thousand, killed in the line of duty. To many it seemed an astronomical figure. Yet he had long since ceased to see it that way. Given the seven hundred thousand working in America's police departments, was it really so many? And what about the staggering rate of suicide among police officers? That was a number no wall would be built to commemorate; yet that, he knew well, was hardly less a falling in the line of duty.

He'd foregone a cab to the Memorial this time, and walked along the street towards it. As he approached the bronze lions that guarded the memorial, he noticed a thin white man in a Navy-style pea coat watching him. He realized, with the flash of instinct, that the man was contemplating robbing him, and a flood of rage ran through him. For the first time in his career, he felt the real desire to kill someone.

He knelt down, pretending to tie his shoe, and quietly removed the .38 Colt Detective Special from its ankle holster. He'd gotten the gun when he'd finished at the academy, from a little shop in Hempstead. It wasn't a sexy gun, but effective. It felt comfortable in his hand—eager for action.

The thin man moved closer. He thought he could already see the knife in the man's hand. In a moment of sublime purpose he raised the gun, pointed it at the man. Go ahead, *he said; and it was unclear whether he was speaking to the man, or to himself. The blood pounded in his ears, mingling with the sound of bagpipes, the drone of a helicopter overhead. He felt the throb of violence begging for release.*

The man took off running.

Morrison shook awake, the force of the memory coursing through him.

He'd dreamed of this encounter before. It was yet another dark moment to add to the list; yet another mental pursuer he knew he would never outrun. He sighed. At least this time he'd slept.

He rolled out of the dorm around 0700 hours, to find the squad room a scene of quiet industry. Medveded was already up and working at his desk, scouring over crime scene photos and evidence lists. Sergeant Rivera was working on his daily checklist of things to do, as he collated all the paperwork turned in by the detectives the previous night. Despite the morning's beginnings, Morrison smiled at the monastic atmosphere; it was exactly the kind of peace he enjoyed at the beginning of the day, and it was reassuring to see the task force working so smoothly, even with Arndt and his cronies overrunning the office.

He unlocked his file cabinet and grabbed the bottle of Jameson. As he was pouring himself his usual hard-day preparatory, Sergeant Simmons came into the office, his face lit up like a kid's on Christmas.

"Hey, boss," he said, out of breath. "Can I shut the door? I need to talk to you."

Morrison nodded, putting the bottle back in the cabinet. "Sure. What's up?"

Simmons closed the door. He frowned at the whiskey. "Well, first of all—Bill, are you doing okay?"

Morrison smiled. He and Simmons had known each other a long time, and worked the streets together in some very tough neighborhoods; but behind closed doors was still the only time the sergeant called him by his first name.

"Yeah, I am—you know me. I just like to take the edge off in the morning."

"I know," Simmons said. "I just—look, I know Arndt's been putting pressure on you, but everyone here knows you're the only person for this job. We'd walk through fire for you, man. We're all doing everything we can to solve this thing, and he should know that."

Morrison sighed. "Andre, he'll never know. He'll never understand what goes on in a situation like this. He doesn't have the genetic makeup. But look, you're not a man to waste words. What's really going on?"

Simmons closed his eyes and shook his head, a look of pure comic justice on his face. "Well, this is tough for me, Cap—you know I don't like telling stories. But in this case, it's just got to be told." His voice lowered almost to a whisper. "Chief Arndt is a shopping-bag guy."

Morrison almost dropped his glass. "Andre, you"—he laughed. "You've got to be kidding me."

"No, Cap. I'm not."

It was unbelievable—too good to be true. Morrison prayed it was true. "Okay, how could you possibly have heard this?"

Simmons leaned forward. "I've got this friend who's an MTA

cop, works at Grand Central. I'm sorry, Cap, but it's just—he's been breaking your balls so much lately, I had to tell you."

"Never mind that—go ahead."

"All right. So about two months ago my friend gets a call, assault in progress in one of the public bathrooms. He responds, and finds two guys in one stall: one business-type nobody standing in a brown shopping bag, and another sitting on the bowl, blowing him."

"You're shitting me."

"As God is my witness, it's Arndt. He starts crying right in the stall, like he does, and my friend tells him he needs to talk to him on the side, so the guy in the bag doesn't hear."

"Holy shit." Morrison set his glass down and laughed. "Holy shit! How could you not have told me this earlier, Andre?"

"I wanted to, Cap, I really did—there was just never a good time. Always too many eyes and ears in the office! I hope you don't think less of me for—"

"No, Andre," Morrison said, shaking his head in laughing disbelief. "No, I don't. I'm very, *very* fucking glad you told me. I don't care what anyone does in their private life, and you know that; there's plenty of terrific cops on our force that are gay. But this—Andre, this is big. It might just help get the asshole off my back, so we can solve this case."

"I hope so! Well, anyway, that's it. Just thought you should know."

"*That's it,* he says!" Morrison laughed again. "Sergeant Simmons, if you never speak another word of sense, you'll have earned your pension today, as far as I'm concerned."

0900, and a fresh pot of coffee had just been made in the squad room—probably the third since the Captain left the dorm. Most of the squad was already busy working on Sergeant Rivera's Things to Do list. Suddenly the door opened, and everyone stopped and looked over at the man who'd just entered.

Rivera was the first to speak.

"Galipoli," he said, "what are you doing here?"

"Chief of Ds told me to report here," said Detective Galipoli. "I'm part of your task force now."

"You are?" Rivera said, dumbfounded.

"Seems Arndt doesn't have much confidence in you guys," smirked Galipoli.

"Guess if he wants some innocent bystanders beaten up, he's got the right idea," said Medveded mildly, without looking up from what he was reading.

"The fuck you just say?" Galipoli snarled at him.

"Don't get too comfortable, Lou." It was Morrison, who'd heard the whole exchange from his doorway. "You won't be here long."

As Galipoli tried to come up with a smart comeback, Morrison slammed his door, furious. Arndt must be out of his mind sending him this loose cannon—even aside from his short temper and shitty treatment of women, the guy had just made detective. He picked up his phone and dialed Arndt's cell phone. By the time voicemail picked up, he was fuming, and left a message using all of George Carlin's "Seven Words You Can't Say On Television."

When he'd hung up, he heard a light knocking at the door. Morrison waved Sergeant Rivera in.

"I know, I know—the piece of shit doesn't belong here," Morrison said angrily. "Believe me, I'm working on it."

Rivera shook his head. "Look, boss, that's not what I was going to say. Hear me out."

"All right, go ahead."

"We all know the guy doesn't belong here, and that Arndt put him here to keep tabs on what we're doing. I was just going to say, don't go crazy trying to get rid of him."

"What? You're surprising me there, Frankie."

"Well, think about it! We got plenty of busywork to give him, to keep him away from the heart of the investigation. Besides, if you push too hard, Arndt might use it as a reason to take you off the case for real, and we can't have that."

Morrison gritted his teeth.

"You're right," he said. "I know you are. But I need him kept away from the details—this case is too sensitive to have Arndt fuck it up. Anything that gets back to him, he'll tell the press. You know how he is; he'll do anything to get his name out there—"

"Yeah, that's true," Rivera admitted.

"—and a press leak would be a disaster right now," Morrison went on. "So far the public doesn't know there might be a serial killer in their midst—for most of them, it's just two high-society women dead in a week. If we're going to nail these psychos, we need to keep it that way for a while."

"Fair enough."

"Anyway, I don't trust Galipoli any more than I do Arndt. You say you have busywork for him? Can we keep him somewhere he won't do any damage?"

"Sure," Rivera said. "I can have him going over phone records, or something like that."

"Great," Morrison said. "Let's put the asshole to work."

Later that morning, Chief Arndt walked into the squad room just as the other mid-level bosses were emptying out of Morrison's office. He'd been expecting pushback from Morrison based on the Captain's voice-mail, and was braced for a scene. On entering the squad room, however, he was surprised to see one of the sergeants sitting with Galipoli at his new desk, discussing an open file with him. He walked into Morrison's office and shut the door.

"Good morning, Chief," said Morrison with a friendly nod.

"Good morning," answered Arndt, a little uncomfortably. This wasn't how his new addition was supposed to be going over. He slid into the chair waiting for him. "I see the newest member of the task force is settling in?"

"Yes—thanks for sending him along," Morrison said, his voice dripping with complacency. "I know he's new to the position, but I think he'll be a great addition to the team."

"Very good," Arndt said. "I want him in on everything, understand?"

Morrison bit back a laugh. "Absolutely, Chief. Anything we have, he's open to look at—all he's got to do is ask." This was safe enough; they all knew Galipoli wouldn't know what to ask for anyway, and Arndt sure as hell wouldn't be able to tell him.

"Great. So—update me on where we are with the case."

"Well, the second victim's husband is back, and like the first husband, he's in total shock. You'll remember he was on a business trip, too."

"Of course."

"Neither one of these guys has really given us anything to hang our hat on, as far as suspects are concerned. We're still trying to make any connection we can between the two victims, but so far the only thing we have is that they both come from upper-class households, and they both like shopping at stores on Fifth Avenue—not a particularly telling fact. Home life for both seems normal: no extra boyfriends we can't take account of, or girlfriends, for that matter." Catching Arndt's quizzical expression, Morrison added significantly, "Well, you know what I mean, Chief. Different strokes for different folks, as they say. You know, we had some guys go over to Grand Central and Penn Station to talk with the MTA cops—"

"Why would you do that?" Arndt asked sharply. "Do we have any reason to think the victims had been through there?"

"Oh, just, you know—if you think there might be a hidden back-story, it never hurts to check in those places. Even if it's rich people we're talking about. Everybody's got secrets. Don't tell me you've never heard of the things people do around there?"

"I'm afraid I haven't," Arndt said, a tremor starting at the corner of his eye.

"Oh, bizarre shit," Morrison said, enjoying himself. "The public restrooms are a playground for freaky stuff. You know, my guys actually talked to several MTA cops who said there are guys who walk around the stations with big shopping bags, looking for someone who might be interested in hooking up. They go to a stall, and one guy stands in the bag while the other guy sits on the bowl. That way, no one can see there's two guys in there. Can you imagine that?"

"That's—I can't see how it's relevant," Arndt said weakly.

"No, you're right," Morrison said. "Still, it's interesting stuff, for us cops. We have to seek these things out, to keep the job fresh. You understand."

"Yes, of course." Arndt stood up abruptly. "If that'll be all, Captain, I'll be on my way."

"Sure," Morrison said, smiling. "I'll see you again soon, eh, Chief?"

Something in the way Arndt walked out made him think otherwise.

Rivera broke the news to Detective Francisco Garriga. He'd drawn the short straw, and would be the first partner assigned to work with Galipoli.

In many respects, Garriga would've been everyone's first choice for the assignment anyway. He was an all-American tough guy of Cuban descent, 5'8" but hard as nails. He'd served in the Marines for ten years before joining the force, and still very much bore the "once a Marine, always a Marine" mentality of loyalty and team spirit. He'd also been a Golden Gloves champ back in the day, and had fought for years on the NYPD boxing team. As a veteran both of the military and of the NYPD's gang squad, he had zero tolerance for bullshit, and could sniff out a poser from a mile away. Morrison and Rivera were interested to see how Galipoli's war-hero status would hold up with Garriga as his partner.

Having introduced the two, Sergeant Rivera handed them a list of things to do.

"Here you go, gentlemen," he said. "Don't come back until it's finished."

"Yessir," said Garriga smartly. As they started for the door, he turned to Galipoli. "You got a pad and pen in your pocket there, rook?"

Galipoli shook his head peevishly. Garriga pulled them up short.

"Seriously?" he said. "Would you go into combat without your weapon? Don't you know a detective's most valuable tool, besides his mind and intuition, are his pen and pad? Jeez, man, get with the program." He opened a supply closet and handed Galipoli a pad and pen, looking at Rivera as though to say *Where'd you dig this guy up?*

As Rivera chuckled, Garriga tossed the new detective a set of car keys. "Here ya go, rook," he said. "Let's see if you know your way around this city."

Towards the end of the day, Morrison closed his door and dialed Claudia's number. Even the sound of her phone ringing made his heart a little lighter.

She picked up, a laugh in her voice. They talked for twenty minutes or so, and planned her next visit to New York. She understood the demands of his job meant he wouldn't be able to get away for a while. Unlike many other women in Morrison's life, however, she was okay with it. Morrison could hardly believe it, but she seemed to have the same attraction to him that he had to her: it made her willing to accept whatever of himself he was able to give her.

After he hung up, Morrison looked around with a sigh. The night was winding down, with no new developments on either case and no new Arndt sightings for hours. Happy hour, as far as he was concerned.

He gave Pat McNamara a call to see if the sergeant wanted to get a drink with him at Kelly's. McNamara was still by Penn Station, so Morrison drove over to pick him up.

"Hey, Cap," said the sergeant, jumping in.

"Hey, Pat," Morrison said. "Shall we head over to Kelly's? Nothing like whiskey to get that Penn Station smell off of you."

"Funny you should say that," McNamara smiled. "I was just thinking, I don't even smell things anymore on this job. You remember when you were a rookie, and you'd practically gag at some of those calls? I haven't done that in years—practically don't feel anything in this job anymore."

"I know what you mean," Morrison agreed, shaking his head. "Why do we do it, do you think?"

"Honestly, for me, it's the only thing I'm good at."

"Yeah, I guess that's true of me too."

McNamara looked hard at him. "You know, I've been meaning to ask you," he said. "You doing okay, Cap?"

Morrison said nothing.

McNamara went on. "You know the guys love you, right? They really do. They know you care, and they know you've always got their back, and they love you for it."

"I know that," Morrison said wearily. "You know I know that." He sighed heavily, a look of intense frustration suddenly crossing his face before he went on. "The question is, are any of us okay? We're all burnt. Look at O'Dell: guy survived Vietnam, then he gets sent out to search for bodies in the Rockaways after that American Airlines flight crashed, right after 9/11. He doesn't talk about it—hell, none of us that were there really talk about either of those days. But he isn't right. None of us are. Tina, Medveded, me—none of us are right."

McNamara nodded silently.

"We're all the same," Morrison went on. "That's why no one likes cops. How could you do *this,* and have people like you?" He gestured strangely out the car window. "That's why we only get along with each other. How many friends do you and Gina have that aren't on the job?"

McNamara thought about it a minute. "None," he said.

"Yeah, well, me neither," Morrison said. All at once, his face brightened. "Though I met a pretty nice woman the other night, when we were out."

McNamara smiled too. "I wondered about that. Is that where you disappeared off to?"

"Yeah. I don't know, I feel kind of different about her. I feel different *because of* her. She was out there, but it felt good. It felt spontaneous. I felt *alive* with her."

"You going to see her again?"

"Yeah, I am. I think I'm going to try to work on it. Maybe try to keep that happiness going."

"That's great, Cap." McNamara looked out the window. "How's—how are things with your wife, anyhow?"

Morrison made a noise, something between a cough and a laugh. "Oh, the same old," he said. "We don't ever talk about our son, and she blames me for what happened."

"Do you need to talk about him?" McNamara asked.

"Sometimes," Morrison said. "But when I do, I talk to myself." He gripped the steering wheel, his jaw tensing. "You know, I blame myself for his death, too," he added abruptly. "I know I always will."

The silence hung between them. Outside, passersby surged through the lurid light of shopfronts, an anonymous mass.

"I mean, how many cases did we do last year? I don't even know." Morrison's voice sounded faraway, preoccupied; it was as though he were talking to no one. "And it isn't like it used to be, nothing like that, but we still get the most gruesome shit. Look at these homicides we've been dealing with. Who *does* this shit? And how do you leave your family at home and go to work, when your work is dealing with *that?*"

"I don't know," said McNamara thoughtfully, "but I also don't know what I'm going to do when it's over."

The radio chatter suddenly picked up with the shouts of an officer on the other end. *10-13, shots fired, officer down, 44th and Broadway*—Morrison and McNamara could hear the gunfire in the background.

The car turned smoothly and quickly, as though imbued with a life of its own. Not a word passed between the two men, but a certain tense clarity had entered between them, as between two surgeons in a trauma unit. They knew it was unlikely that any ambulance had been called; police transport each other, and prefer not to let anyone else touch their wounded until absolutely necessary.

When they arrived, the scene was all too familiar. A uniformed cop was being hustled into the backseat of a radio car, ready to leave for Roosevelt Hospital. A young black man lay on the ground, in handcuffs though evidently dead. The sight, smell and sound were the same as they always were: dumped cars, flashing lights, blood, burnt rubber.

Morrison grabbed one of the cops who'd been helping to load the injured officer into the car.

"How is he?" he asked.

"Gunshot wound to the head, boss," said the other cop. He was covered in the wounded officer's blood, and seemed close to shock himself. "It looks pretty bad."

"Okay, let's get him to Roosevelt," Morrison said, gesturing to two other officers on the scene. "What happened?"

"Not sure yet; we know the perp shot him with his own gun."

Morrison gestured toward the cuffed body on the ground. "And him?"

"Shot down by the responding officers. He's dead."

"God, does he have to go to Roosevelt?" McNamara asked idly as the others drove off. "I hate it there."

Morrison shrugged helplessly. It was the closest hospital to the scene, and besides, for a cop, no hospital was good enough when another cop was down.

"What's the cop's name?" he asked.

"Tong—Nguyen Tong. First-generation Vietnamese. His dad was a cop too. One of those cops directing traffic in Vietnam, with the white helmets—they called them White Mice."

Morrison looked around grimly, foreseeing the same miserable routine playing itself out. The uniformed bosses would be all over the scene soon. All the cops who worked with Officer Tong—and many who didn't—would be in the hospital overnight, crowding into the hallways outside the emergency room, praying, anxiously awaiting any word. Though Tong wouldn't need it, they'd all offer to give their blood for him; it was a symbolic gesture, and one that helped to relieve the feeling of helplessness they all felt when one of them was in trouble.

Morrison felt the old subliminal screaming hatred come over him. It was an irrational rage, a rage simply at everyone who wasn't a cop, but it went hand-in-hand with the intense feeling of brotherhood on the force that incidents like this brought sharply into focus. At times like these he would think of everyone he'd ever heard make the familiar claim that the police were public servants, that it was taxpayer dollars that paid their salaries. *Take a look at that cop,* he thought, *and tell me if you're paying enough. Tell me—*

McNamara patted him gently on the arm.

"Come on, Cap," he said quietly. "This isn't our place anymore; if they need us here, they'll tell us. Let's get over to the hospital, huh?"

Morrison nodded and walked back over to the car, his heart heavy and the bagpipes blowing loud.

10

Morrison's detectives were gathered for Sergeant Rivera's daily briefing on their daily assignments. The tension in the squad room was palpable. A week had gone by since their case's second homicide, and the task force seemed to be no closer to solving the two cases than they were the first day.

It was a familiar axiom to most police departments that cases left unsolved after four days were in for the long haul. This had been a more pointed statement back when most homicides were committed by victims' acquaintances; since the eighties, when crack hit the streets, homicides had become increasingly difficult to solve, due to the frequency with which murders were perpetrated by people the victims had never met or had much of anything to do with, outside of proximity or connection to the drug trade. But serial-killer cases were harder still in this respect; these were the cases where the connection between victim and killer was often altogether nonexistent.

"Galipoli and Garriga," Rivera called out, passing photocopied sheets to the two detectives. "Here's a list of all the big Fifth Avenue stores we haven't hit yet. I want you guys to bring pictures of both victims with you, and hit every one of those shops to see if anyone working there recognizes either of them. We need to know if they remember anything about who might have helped them, or if anyone approached them in the store, to see if we can pick up some common link between the two."

"You got it," said Garriga.

"This is bullshit," Galipoli muttered under his breath.

Morrison, listening at the back of the room, slammed his door open. "Galipoli, in my office—*now,*" he said.

Galipoli shrugged back at him. "What'd I do?" he asked casually.

"Just get in here," Morrison said. "We're going to discuss it in private."

Galipoli stood and headed over, snickering as Morrison shut the door behind him.

"You think this is funny?" Morrison barked. "Well, let me tell you something, pal: you're a detective, and a brand-new one at that. Believe me, there's absolutely *nothing* you ought to be laughing at around here right now, if you value your job."

Galipoli stepped into Morrison's face until he was standing toe-to-toe with him.

"Captain, let me tell you something," he said, the same insufferable smirk still on his face. "I've been here a week now, and all I get are bullshit assignments. Go out and canvas this location, go check for cameras at that location. I'm not even getting to read the whole case folder; just the little bits and pieces that Rivera gives me at the morning briefing. But look, I'm not stupid. I know you guys are having team meetings without me, and that's fucked up. I've got the right to know just as much as anyone else, and—"

"Sit the fuck down, Galipoli!" Morrison suddenly shouted. Startled for a moment out of his cocky pose, Galipoli took a seat.

"Now listen," Morrison went on, "because *I'm* going to tell *you* what you have a right to in this office. This isn't a schoolyard, or a Young Republicans meeting, or some other bullshit place where you get to have your say. This is a detective squad; and here, I'm the boss. That means, what I say goes. You get to know exactly what I want you to know. You aren't the case detective here, you're here to assist, and if that means you get one shitty assignment after another, guess what? You're going to go out and do it, and be glad you're getting to do anything at all. You don't *ever* question an assignment given to you, especially on a case like this. As far as you know, the stores we're sending you to could provide us with the only possible link between the victims in this fucking case. And let me say another thing," he said more intensely, "just because I know what you're thinking right now. I don't give a shit *who* you have backing your assignment to my task force. I really don't. If I think your presence is going to hurt this case, you'll be gone in a heartbeat. You get that? The chief can only cover your ass so much. You have a lot of talented people around you, so rather than putting on your tough-guy prima donna act, you ought to try to learn something from them."

Galipoli glared at him, a bright redness suffusing his face. "I'm as good as any of those people," he seethed.

Morrison laughed in his face, then leaned in close to the furious detective. "You wouldn't make a good pimple on one of their asses," he said.

"You're never going to know how wrong you are," Galipoli said strangely, the smirk returning at the edge of his mouth.

"I'm sure I won't," Morrison shot back. "Now get your partner and get the fuck out of here."

Galipoli stood and stormed out, grabbing his jacket on the way out of the squad room. Amid the restrained laughter of the others, Morrison called after Garriga.

"Hey Francisco," he said. "Make sure all those stores get covered, whether he likes it or not."

"You know it, boss," Garriga replied.

"Thanks. And Garriga," Morrison added, "just be careful out there, huh? We've got to deal with him for now, but I don't trust that guy."

"No worries, boss." Garriga waved back at him with a broad smile. "I got him."

A short while later, Detective Medveded poked his head in at the

Captain's door, a manila folder in his hand.

"Hey boss, you got a minute?" he asked.

"Sure," Morrison said, gesturing him in. "What's up, Alex?"

Medveded sat. "Well, I've been going over this case, and something's been bothering me about the two scenes," he said.

"What do you mean?"

The detective opened up the folder. "Well, look at these photos from the first scene at Sutton Place."

"Okay, sure."

"What do you see?"

"I see the victim: mutilated, some torn and scattered clothing, some potential DNA evidence, not much more."

Medveded flipped ahead through the folder. "Okay. Now look at the second scene we discovered in Queens, and tell me what you see there."

"Same thing: mutilated victim, torn clothing, some evidence of the victim being bound. Multiple cigarette butts, shoe prints on the carpet. So what are you thinking?"

"Well, unlike the first scene, this one takes place in multiple rooms, right? Doesn't it seem to have been more chaotic than Sutton Place?"

"Sure, I guess you could say that."

"Well, Cap, I think there's a good reason for that. I think the one in Queens was committed first, before Sutton Place. At Sutton Place, they're better at their craft: no cigarette butts left behind, no shoe prints, et cetera."

"You may be right. Can we get confirmation from the medical examiner? If they can pinpoint the time of death for both our victims, it might help us down the road to catch these guys."

"I'll talk to them. We need to check with the lab guys anyway, to see if any of our fingerprint evidence has turned out."

"Great. Thanks, Alex."

As Medveded went out, Morrison mulled over this new information. The glimmer of hope it contained wasn't much, but the change of direction could be good for the case. They'd been spending so much time on the Sutton Place murder, thinking it'd been the first; if Medveded was right, this would involve quite a shifting of gears.

The office phone rang. It was Detective Hanrahan.

"Hey, Cap," he said, his voice urgent, "we may have gotten a break here."

"Yeah? What've you got, George?"

"Well, me and Tina went back over to Sutton Place to do some additional canvassing, and see if there we saw anything out of the ordinary, right? So as we're working the block, we noticed a camera on the corner of 59th Street and Sutton Place, on a building we had no record of talking to before today."

"All right, good. And—?"

"So me and Tina get the building's super and ask him if anyone from the PD had spoken to him, and he says no. I figure it's a stretch, since it's a couple of blocks from the crime scene, but we ask him if he has the video saved from the night we're thinking our murder took place. He tells us his video's saved for sixty days—most of these buildings overwrite before thirty, you know, but this guy's a tech guy. So he takes us into his office and sits there with us for a few hours, reviewing the footage, and based on what we saw, I think we have our victim walking towards her building alone."

"You sure?"

"We can't be one hundred percent, because it's dark and the video is a little grainy, but we think it's her. We also got what looks like two guys exiting a black car from the opposite corner, walking behind her."

"No shit?"

"Yeah, a couple of preppy types. Not sure if they followed her all the way home, but what's interesting is, several hours later we see these same two guys going back toward their car. They're in an awful hurry and they look all disheveled, like they'd been in a fight."

Morrison was ecstatic. "George, this is great work! Don't tell me the video has a time and date stamp on it—?"

"Yep, as a matter of fact, it does, boss," Hanrahan said. "We already have a couple of copies. And there's more, too—when these guys get back in their car we get a shot of their license plate. It's blurry, but we can see it isn't a New York plate."

"Oh man, that's awesome news, George—really great news. Let's get the video over to our guys in the lab and see if they can enhance what we have there. We'll also need to pull a couple of teams to go back over all the video in the area, now that we have a possible timeframe—we could easily have overlooked something before. Great work, you two."

He hung up, beaming in spite of himself. Two moves in a day—this was great! He called Rivera in.

"Frankie, I just spoke to Hanrahan—we need to get the Coke boys and McNamara's crew over to Sutton Place right away."

"I'm already on it, boss—I was on the phone with Tina just now, getting the same briefing," Rivera said excitedly. "Hey, this could be it, huh? Nothing like hard-nosed detective work to get a case solved!"

"Well, let's not get ahead of ourselves—we don't even know for sure if this is our victim, much less if these two guys actually followed her. But yeah, it's great work. And Frankie," Morrison added, his voice lowering, "let's keep this under wraps. We don't need Galipoli or Arndt screwing this up just yet."

"No problem, boss. We'll keep it close."

Towards evening, Morrison was still riding the high of the day's new discoveries when Garriga breezed in, alone, and asked tersely to speak with him. He waved the detective in, and without a word Garriga slumped in the chair in front of him. It was only now that Morrison saw the frustration on his face.

"What's going on, Francisco?" Morrison asked. "You okay?"

"Sure, sure," Garriga began abstractedly, then stopped. He looked hard at Morrison. "Look, boss, you know this isn't something I'd ever do normally, but I can't work with this Galipoli guy another day."

Morrison was surprised. "Why, what happened?"

"Ah, Cap, you know I'd rather not—"

"I'm going to need to know, Detective," Morrison insisted.

Garriga blew out a long breath. "Well, it's been all day, really. It started pretty much when we left here. I thought he should drive, so I got into the passenger side, and I was barely inside with the door closed when the fucker steps on it and speeds off. Real dick-swinging bullshit kind of stuff. So I said, *Hey, Lou, slow down, we don't need to get in an accident,* and this guy tells me to go fuck myself."

Morrison smiled. "Okay. So what'd you do?"

"I told him to pull the car over and get out with me, so we could settle things. I walked over between a couple of buildings, and he followed me. I tell him, *Look, man, I need to explain something to you. Nobody talks to me that way.* And this asshole, he starts trying to step to me, getting all big in my face and telling me to stop lecturing him."

Morrison's smile grew wider. "Let me guess. You hit him with a good solid right."

"Two lefts *and* a right," Garriga corrected him. He looked up quickly. "But look, Cap, it wasn't like I knocked the guy out. I just needed him to know he needs to show me some respect."

"It's all right, Francisco," Morrison laughed. "I had a feeling something like this might happen, and I knew you'd be the right man for it. How'd he take it?"

"Not good, Cap, that's the thing. There was no apologies, no talk, no nothing—he just gets back in the car with all this rage in his face. The guy's not right, boss. He really isn't. We didn't say a word to each other all day after that. Look, you know I'll do anything for you—it's just—is there any way you can assign him to somebody else? I just think it's going to get ugly if we keep working together, and I don't want that on my hands."

"Don't worry about it, Francisco—you've put in your time. I'll figure out someone else to pair him up with."

Garriga was noticeably relieved. "Thanks, Cap. I really appreciate it." He rose. "I'm going to head out, if you don't need anything—?"

"No problem. It's been a big day, for a lot of reasons; I'm about ready to turn in too. Have a good night. Oh, and Detective?"

Garriga stopped in the doorway. "Yeah?"

Morrison smiled. "Thank you. I really mean it."

"All in a day's work, Cap," Garriga laughed on his way out.

11

Bill Morrison blinked awake and rolled out of the bunk. It had been almost a week since he'd been home; thankfully, it was a situation he was used to, and he always kept extra supplies in the office. After a quick rinse in the shower, he checked the time—just after 0700 hours. Time enough for a call with Louise Donohue and a visit to her husband's grave before the day's work began. Normally he would have preferred to drive out and visit Louise in person, but with the case running as it was, and with her living up in Stamford now to be closer to her family, it was a bit of a stretch.

He spoke to Francis Donohue's widow often; and in keeping with the Chief's last wishes, he still made it a point to visit her every month or so to make sure she was getting along all right. At least, that's how Morrison framed it for himself, though really, the two of them had suffered through their losses together, and speaking with her was as therapeutic for him as it was for her.

The conversation over the phone with Louise was grounding and normal, exactly the sort of thing Morrison looked forward to about talking with her. Her voice bore the same weary tone his had since his son's death, and with the same layer of comfort from the rest of the family prospering. Her kids were grown up now with families of their own, and were doing well. Her daughter had moved out West to raise a family, and one of her two sons had recently left the force with a disability, at which Louise secretly rejoiced. Morrison told her about Claudia, and the chemistry he'd already felt with her. There was no judgment or demand for logic in Louise's response; she understood immediately, complications and all.

When they'd talked for an hour or so, Morrison excused himself with the usual transparent excuses. He never told Louise when he was going to visit Francis's grave, but he always suspected she knew somehow; perhaps it was his imagination, but on those days their signoffs always had a knowing undertone to them.

He had realized the night before that he'd spoken a bit flippantly in telling Garriga he'd be able to find someone else to partner with Galipoli. He now realized that the alternatives were very few. All of his senior people were already paired up in teams that worked well together; it would be crazy to interrupt that working rhythm, especially in the middle of a case like this, just to saddle one of them with a guy whose integrity he already had serious doubts about. The odd person out, he'd realized, was Tina Koreski. He wasn't happy about putting her—of all people—with a guy like Galipoli, who he'd already heard had problems with women; but if he didn't want Garriga losing it with the guy, he didn't have much choice. Besides, he told himself, Tina was a strong woman, with more than enough fortitude to kick Galipoli in the ass if he got out of line with her.

On his way out, he left a note for Sergeant Rivera: *Sorry to do this to you, but I need you to tell Tina she's going to be paired with Galipoli moving forward. She won't be happy, but tell her I need her to do this for me. If she needs to talk to me, tell her I'll be back later.* He thought a moment, then added, *By the way, talk to Garriga and see if he's gotten any impression of Galipoli's military experience. I forgot to ask him about it yesterday, and I'm curious what he thinks.*

Saint Raymond's Cemetery, in the Throgs Neck area of the Bronx, was the only Catholic cemetery in that borough. In 1932 it was used as the meeting place between Charles Lindbergh and the kidnapper who'd taken his son, a fact on which Bill Morrison never failed to reflect during his visits there. It had been called "The Crime of the Century"—an abduction for what was at the time an enormous ransom. Despite the paying of that ransom, at this very cemetery, the kidnapper (or kidnappers, as many had suspected) had murdered the infant child anyway, and deposited his remains to be discovered six weeks later. Quite a shame—but not the only one Morrison associated with this place.

Morrison passed row after row of headstones on his way to the grave he was there to see. Massive as the cemetery was, he'd long since moved past the need for a site map. Step after step, his feet found their way automatically; and soon he stood before the familiar tombstone.

Francis P. Donohue—Loving Father, Devoted Husband, Outstanding Policeman.

Morrison stood, bowing his head in reverence for a moment of silence. Then he spoke to his friend and mentor, casually and openly, as he always did—as though the Chief were standing there with him, as, in some way, he was.

They'd graduated from the same academy class, despite Donohue being a few years older—everyone else had called him the oldest rookie on the job. Donohue had spent four years in the Navy working on submarines, then a few more as a dockhand in Boston, before the force had called him. He was a true Southie, but being unlikely to find a job in Boston, he'd started in the Stamford PD where, being unknown around town, he was scooped up immediately to work as an undercover narcotics officer. Soon he was on the statewide narc squad, working the worst streets in Hartford, Bridgeport, and New Haven.

Donohue had always hated that people thought of Connecticut simply as a quaint place full of covered bridges. He liked to remind people that where he worked, the police union had a billboard on I-95 that said *Welcome to Dodge City! Where the politicians dodge questions, and the people dodge bullets.* A lot of people thought that billboard was funny, but not Francis Donohue; he knew firsthand that they had the crime to back it up. He'd been stabbed in Bridgeport, shot at in New Haven, almost run over in Hartford. He'd even been beaten by the police, when they didn't realize he was an undercover.

After several years in Stamford, he'd been called by the NYPD when they were rehiring after the layoffs ended in '79, and Morrison, a young cop at the time, had learned the investigator's craft from him. It was Donohue who had encouraged him to study and make sergeant. It was Donohue who had impressed upon him that that was the way to chase the bad guys without doing so much grunt work, and had showed him how to keep on the right side of the brass without sacrificing integrity.

Now the man was gone, and there was no replacing him. A pang went through Morrison; for an instant it seemed as though the memories of his son and Donohue had merged. All these parts of him, lost forever—how much more of himself could he lose, and still be himself at all? How much longer could he bear to be the one left behind?

Shaking the thought off, he kissed the top of the headstone and returned to his car.

The weather wasn't as brutal as it could be for January, especially with the windows up and the sun beating down through the windshield; but it was a shock as always to get back out after the long drive back. Morrison was scarcely out of the car, rubbing his hands together in front of the stationhouse, when he saw Tina Koreski walking up to him.

"Cap, can we talk?" she asked.

Well, no surprises there, he thought. "Look, Tina, I know you're not happy to have to work with this guy, but I need you to do it. It's for the good of the team, believe me."

She waved him off. "No, no," she said. "I'm not going to complain, boss. I understand you're in a tight spot with him, and I'm definitely not happy about it, but I'm a team player. I'll do what I have to do. I just wanted to talk about it for a second."

Morrison's relief vanished in the strangeness of her tone. "Of course. What's up?"

Koreski's expression was uncertain. "Well, you're going to have to forgive me for saying this, but—uh—well, have you noticed how he looks at our victims' photos?"

Morrison was surprised at this. "No, I haven't," he said. "Why do you ask?"

"I guess I didn't either, before I was partnered up with him a bit ago," she said, "and I know I haven't really been around him long enough to pass judgment, but I could swear he almost looks like he enjoys seeing how they were tortured."

"Enjoys?"

"Yeah. I mean, I've watched Medveded stare at the same photos for hours, but that's different—you can always tell he's bothered by what happened to these women. But not Galipoli. I swear I thought I saw him smile while we were going over the photos in there, and someone was talking about what it must have been like for the women."

"I've heard he's got a pretty sick outlook," Morrison said, "but that's a pretty extreme idea. Granted, I have no use for the guy, but what exactly are you saying here?"

Koreski looked embarrassed. "I don't know," she said. "Maybe I'm passing judgment too quickly."

"If you mean it, you can tell me, Detective. I take this kind of thing very seriously."

"No, I'm sorry, Cap. Forget I said anything. I just—none of us like the guy, is all. But like I said, I'm a good soldier. I'm not going to complain about it."

"Thanks, Tina. I know I can count on you. Just keep me updated, will you?"

"Of course, Cap. I will."

12

Fifteen days had passed since the last homicide on their case when Captain Morrison got the call. His instincts had spoken again as the phone rang, and became stronger as he drove over to the scene. This, he knew with a sinking feeling, was victim number three.

Northwest corner of 63rd and Third Avenue—another nice building in an upscale neighborhood. The building was beautiful, really: sixteen stories, fancy lobby, aging doorman. The victim had lived on the fourth floor.

Just outside the elevator, he met Sergeants Rivera and Simmons talking to two patrol cops.

"Well, boys, what do we have?" he asked.

Sergeant Simmons gestured toward the cops. "They tell us that one of the maintenance people had gotten a call from the Children's Assistance Society, saying our victim hadn't shown up for work and wasn't responding to texts, calls, or emails. The maintenance guy went up to knock on the door and found it propped open, with no one answering the knock. They aren't allowed to enter apartments without permission, so he called the super, and the super found the victim."

"Where are these guys now?"

"We've got them at the stationhouse. Medveded's talking to them."

"That's good."

One of the patrol cops jumped in. "They swore to us that they never went inside," he said.

"That's good, too. If we get any prints that match theirs, they'll have a lot of explaining to do."

Two Crime Scene officials walked out of the apartment, carrying large paper bags. Not Williams and his partner this time, Morrison noted, but these guys were no less capable. "Hey, fellas," he said to them as they passed. "Give me the rundown, will you?"

"Well, boss, we have one female, white, late forties. Not a bad-looking woman, judging by the photos in the apartment; though it's tough to tell otherwise, at this point. Seems to have been bound and tortured. Massive bite marks on her body, and missing the lips from her vaginal area. Looks like the sick fuck bit them off."

Morrison nodded grimly. This was getting to be too familiar. "How much longer do you guys need before we can get in?" he asked.

"Give us another half hour, and we should have everything we need."

"All right. Does it look like they tried to cover their tracks in any way?"

"Yeah. The shower was still dripping, and her hair was wet—it looks like they took her in there to get rid of some trace evidence. Stupid fucks left towels in the bathroom, though—we bagged them. There should be some good hair and fiber evidence on them."

"Okay, thanks," Morrison said. "Let me know if you guys find anything else unusual before you wrap up."

"Will do, Cap."

Morrison turned back to his sergeants. "Well," he sighed, "this is our third now. People are going to lose their minds when this hits the press." A weary thought crossed his mind of the additional pressure on its way from downtown. His task force was already stretched, and pulling double shifts tracking these psychos; he was going to need more help. He shook the thought away for the moment. "What are we doing here so far?"

Rivera reviewed his notes. "We have a canvas of the building done, Cap. Seems this one is at least somewhat different from our other victims: she's a social worker. According to Crime Scene, she's got a Master's degree hanging on the wall in there. Her name's Jennifer Burnett—48 years old, according to paperwork in the management office. They have no emergency contact listed, and the doorman says she lived alone. She kept to herself for the most part, though every now and then she went out to one of the local bars. No forced entry, so either she knew her attacker, or they pushed in behind her. Based on the call from her job and what Crime Scene sees inside, it looks like she's been dead a couple of days."

"All right. We're going to need to interview all of the doormen—who knows what the other shifts might have seen."

"Bad news, boss," Rivera answered. "Seems they only have a doorman until 2300 hours. The building cut back just before the holidays, to save some money."

"Jesus," Morrison muttered.

"The good news is, we have video of the lobby area," Simmons said quickly. "One of the guys is downstairs now trying to secure a copy, so we can go through the last week to see what our victim's habits were. Hopefully these guys were stupid enough to come through the front door."

Morrison smiled. "Well, let's hope; we definitely need a break here. Do we have anyone checking the surrounding area for cameras? Are there any parking garages in the area where they might have parked?"

"The Coke Brothers are checking that out now," Rivera told him.

"Okay. It's a new timeline; let's get on it. If you gentlemen will excuse me, I'm going to have to call the Chief and let him know about all this—I'm sure this'll be interesting."

The call with Chief Arndt was mercifully brief. The Chief's concern, as always, lay more with his career than with the victims; but tonight, fortunately for Bill Morrison, there was a major political benefit that

Arndt apparently couldn't afford to miss. *One night to come up with a game plan,* Morrison thought.

The press was already out in front of the building when he walked back up the block. One of the reporters, recognizing him, ran up to stick a microphone in his face. Before the reporter could get a word out, Morrison pushed the microphone away with a terse "No comment," grabbing one of the uniformed officers to stand watch over the entrance.

Back on the fourth floor, Morrison's people were huddled in the hallway. Rivera seemed excited.

"Boss, hey, glad you're back," he said. "Listen to what Kasak and Marchioni got."

He looked toward the back of the group, where the Coke Brothers invariably settled. True to form, there they were, trench coats and all. Both of them always wore trench coats with belts, no matter what was happening; it was a common joke that if they had to get to their guns it would take ten minutes just to untie the belts.

"What's up?" Morrison asked.

"Well, we found a few cameras on the block," said Marchioni. "Most of them aren't much use—old systems, grainy footage, you know the drill. But one of the buildings just had a new system put in, and the building manager really knows how to operate it. We took a look at the footage for the last four days, and we have what looks like a similar car to the one on Sutton Place, with a partial plate."

"Terrific," said Morrison. "Anything of our perps?"

"Yeah. They're two white guys, or maybe the second guy is light-skinned Hispanic, both well dressed, like in the first video. We don't have them with our victim, but they exit the car around 2325 hours two days ago."

Morrison clapped his hands together. "Okay, now we're making progress! What's the car?"

"BMW, looks like; with Connecticut plates we're thinking."

"Anything else?"

Kasak spoke up. "Well, similar to the first video we had, we got them hustling back to their car about three hours later. Their clothes are definitely messed up—not the way they were when they got out."

Morrison turned to Rivera. "Okay, make sure someone does a lawman search on that partial plate. Tell whoever does it that it's possibly a BMW—that ought to help limit the vehicles that come back. This could be the break we're looking for, boys."

Not long thereafter, Crime Scene wrapped up, and Morrison and his people entered the apartment. The body would be present, under guard as usual, until the Medical Examiner's morgue wagon showed up for it. Back in the day, that would have meant hours, due to the number of homicides; these days, the detectives sometimes ran into them on their way out.

"Cap," Rivera pointed out, gesturing at the livid bite marks around the corpse, "these guys, they're big biters, huh? Look, it's the same as the last one—bit her vaginal lips clean off."

"Yeah," Morrison agreed. "They really upgraded the torture on this one, though."

"We're a lot better on the forensics this time, I think," Rivera went on. "Crime Scene said they think we have some good DNA on the carpet. She has drag marks, too, look—they gave her a bath before they dragged her in here."

"Yeah, Crime Scene mentioned that," Morrison said.

"Well, they're smart, but not real smart. They took care to wash her off, but they just dropped more transfer evidence by moving the body around. Crime Scene's taken multiple prints off the floor and bathroom walls."

"Good."

"Look at the rug burns—the small stab wounds—the lips," said Simmons with a grimace. "That's some real heavy-duty suffering. Man, I want to get these guys."

"Yeah, they're animals all right," Rivera agreed.

Morrison noticed something. "Hey guys, any of you seeing what I'm seeing with these bite marks?"

The others all looked closely. Leo Kasak was the first to see it.

"Looks like two different people did the biting this time," he said.

"Exactly. The one guy, our original biter, had a smaller mouth. These other marks definitely show a wider spacing between the teeth, no? I mean, I'm no dental expert, but they're clearly different sizes."

The others agreed. It looked like the second guy was getting more and more into participating in the torture.

Morrison's stomach growled. For the first time, he realized none of them had eaten all day; they'd all been too absorbed in gathering information from the crime scene and its surrounds. He told the team to meet up at Luigi's—a favorite hole-in-the-wall Italian joint, with a room in back where they could talk about the new developments—and stepped out to call Claudia.

"Hey, handsome," she said. "How's your day going?"

"That's a long story," he chuckled. "Are you still coming to the city tonight?"

"Yeah, just got a little tied up today—no pun intended!" They both laughed. "Honestly, I can't wait. I've already booked my room for two nights. Are you okay with staying over tonight?"

"Of course. I should be by around eight—or actually, better make that ten," he added, glancing at his watch. "We've actually just had a new homicide in our series."

"Oh, shit. Are you sure you don't need to stay there? We can make it another time, if you want."

"No no, I need to see you," he said. "Even for a few hours. As long as you don't mind coming in."

"All right," she said. He could hear the smile on her face. "Get there when you can—I'm walking out the door now. Can't wait to see you!"

13

Luigi's was a fixture for Morrison and his team. They'd come here for years, and nothing had changed. The décor was nothing to write home about, but the food was great, and it was always private enough to talk there. Morrison and Francis Donohue had spent many a night here, talking over cases in the back room; Donohue had always stressed the importance of breaking bread with his team, of making them feel like family.

Morrison grabbed a table in the back and ordered food for everyone, along with a Miller Lite and a shot of Jameson for himself—he'd have to keep it on the lighter side for Claudia later. Like modern-day Knights of the Round Table, his team filed in and found seats: three of his sergeants and most of his detectives.

Morrison started in. "Okay, people. We have three homicides now: all women by themselves. From what you've seen, do you think these guys stalk their victims, or are they randomly selecting them?"

Everyone began to bandy around their various opinions on the matter, but when Alex Medveded spoke up, the rest of the table went silent.

"These guys have hit twice in the 19th, and once in Jamaica Estates," he said. "I think they're familiar with these rich neighborhoods, but not with the victims themselves. Based on this, and on the car we think they're driving, I believe they come from affluence themselves—children of privilege, if you will. As to whether it's random or stalk-based, I think it's both. I think they have *territories* they're stalking, like a shark does. It doesn't matter what fish they find in that territory, but once they find it, they do their homework."

As he finished, the rest of the table nodded in agreement. He'd put it very succinctly.

Morrison held off his response. A few dishes were being brought to the table—Morrison had ordered family-style—and the Captain raised his beer for a toast.

"To Chief Francis Donohue: may he rest in peace," he said. "If he were still alive, he'd be sitting here with us."

They toasted, and for a moment the conversation passed into fond reminiscence. Rivera talked about how the Chief had once spent three hours with him after the end of a case, just talking to him about his family life and the struggles he was going through at the time.

"At some point I'd asked him, *Chief, don't you need to go home?* and he just smiled at me and said, *Frankie, I've got Louise, the best woman in the world, and she'll have dinner on for me at 0300 if that's when I get there.* Man, he really loved her."

"He was no one to fuck with, either," Sergeant Simmons added. "He was a tough man, nerves of steel. He used to buy dope from anyone and everyone in the street. He was such a white boy, freckles all over his face—they called him Pinky, you remember that? He was a great undercover."

"And a serious Irishman," McNamara threw in. "I never saw the man miss a St. Paddy's Day parade. He held on a long time with that cancer, too—you know what happened to his kids, Cap?"

"They're all doing pretty good," Morrison said. "I actually just spoke with Louise; she says they're well."

"You guys keep in touch?"

"Oh, regularly. You know I promised Francis I would, when he went into hospice care; I would've done it anyway, though. She's a good friend, a real sweet woman. Pretty much Francis in another body. You can really trust her."

"Nothing like our new chief, huh, boss?" Rivera said with a smile.

Morrison laughed. "Yeah, nothing like him." He finished off the Jameson. "You know, just between you all and me, Francis and I had a lot of talks about that. He really hated Arndt—had no respect for him."

"That makes more than a few of us," Rivera said, and the table laughed in agreement.

McNamara raised his glass again. "Well, let's drink to getting this collar while he's on vacation," he said.

Everyone laughed and raised their glasses, but Morrison demurred. "We shouldn't get to talking about collars just yet," he said, "but here's to a successful outcome soon, anyway."

They toasted again. Detective Jeffrey O'Dell, a tall, tough-framed Vietnam vet who'd joined the force just today, returned the talk to the case.

"I know we have a partial plate from the street cameras but it doesn't appear to be a New York plate," he said. "Based on what I was told, it might be Connecticut; but there are several other states whose plates look like that. I've got a book of plates back in my office; if I can't figure it out from that, I'll go to Arty Annouer over in Auto Crime—best motor vehicle guy in the history of the department. I'd bet he knows more about cars than the rest of us put together. He can probably lock us in on a make and model too, if you'll let me show him the video."

Morrison nodded his approval as O'Dell went on.

"And I know I'm new to the group, but I just wanted to say thanks to you, Captain Morrison, for bringing me on this case. I'll give you a hundred and ten percent until this thing is solved."

"We're glad to have you," Morrison answered, "especially now that we've got three on the books. We're going to need all the help we can get on this one." He turned to Tina. "Koreski, any thoughts?"

"Well, one question, Cap: our first two victims had husbands who were travelling at the time of their murders. Could there be a possible airport or airline connection here?"

"The third one's single, though," Kasak said. "There was no connection to air travel there; really the only thing they've all got in common is that they were home alone."

Morrison nodded. "Simmons?"

"I'm taking a hard look at all the databases, and working with the FBI to see if we can connect this MO to anything elsewhere," he said. "Based on what we've seen, it seems reasonable to suspect that these guys are carrying a rape kit of some kind. We've found traces of similar materials at all three scenes, and though they're pretty common household items—rope, tape, lube, et cetera—the materials are identical, suggesting that they're carrying them around with them."

"And the MO?" Morrison pressed him. "Do we have anything yet on that?"

"Well, I did find one through Quantico. They had this guy in Florida twenty years ago, they called him the Palm Beach rapist. He had a whole tool belt with all this shit: knives, pliers, the works. He was a nipple man, though."

"Where is he now?"

"Still working on that, Cap."

"All right. What else are we still missing, people?"

"Commonalities between victims," McNamara said. "We've still got a few avenues left to check. I've got Tina here and Lou working on that."

Morrison noticed that Tina averted her eyes at the mention of Galipoli's name. Fortunately, the hotheaded detective had had some prior commitment tonight, saving Morrison the necessity of figuring out how not to invite him. He wanted to know what Tina was thinking, but sensed that now wasn't the time.

"Well," he said, changing the subject, "I heard from the PC's office, through Arndt, that the case came up at comp stat this morning, and not in a good way. Now that there's three, I'm sure my ass will be going downtown tomorrow to talk to the PC directly." He looked at his watch—2130. Time to meet Claudia. He stood up. "Listen, they've got my card here, so everybody stick around for coffee and so forth—I've got something to take care of tonight, so I'll have to see you all in the morning," he said. "Let's all dig deep on this new information, okay? We're going to get these guys."

14

Morrison made great time from the restaurant, and had soon arrived at the hotel. He paused to collect himself before heading into the bar; but all that went out the window when he saw her. Claudia was sitting at a corner table, legs crossed, in a tight-fitting black cocktail dress. She looked incredible—sexy, classy, and comfortably familiar all at once. As he crossed the room toward her she looked up, and a beautiful smile lit up her face.

He grinned ear-to-ear in return, feeling helpless and silly at the sight of her. He couldn't believe the warmth that came over him, just from seeing her sitting there. He slid into the seat beside her—across the table wasn't going to work for him tonight. They leaned in, and unselfconsciously exchanged a kiss that would have made a teenager blush.

"Hello, darling," she said, her voice uneven with passion, when they sat back, their arms still around one another. "Have you missed me?"

"Claudia," he said, and faltered. "Claudia, I have to tell you: no woman has ever gotten so much on my mind, or made me feel so wanted—so satisfied—so—"

"Horny?" she laughed. "I certainly hope I make you feel that, or this is totally unfair."

"God, definitely," he laughed back. "You drive me completely fucking wild. But when I see you, or hear your voice, it just—it washes away all the worries." He paused to look her deeply in the eyes. "So yes, I guess you could say I've missed you."

"I know," she said quietly, her smile deepening. "You do the same for me."

They talked a while over the details of their day. Morrison was again amazed at the easy familiarity between them; as different as their jobs were, they each seemed to understand the other perfectly, and see immediately through all the nonsense that kept other people at a distance from them. Claudia's psychological mind was as capable of engaging with the twists and turns of Morrison's work, as he was of working through the details of hers. At one point, remarking on this, she smiled.

"You know, I don't think I've ever met someone so grounded in reality," she said. "It's a rare quality, believe me! Don't take it the wrong way, but I've already got a nickname for you."

Morrison laughed in surprise. "I won't be! What is it?"

"You're my Bullshit Remover. It's so refreshing, how cut-and-dried things can be with you. You laugh, but it's a very new thing for me. There's always so much more doubt about things like this! But from that first moment with you, it's just been—different. I feel you with me all the time."

"I know what you mean," he said. "I feel the same. I know I've said it to you before, but I'd pretty much given up on ever feeling like this again. I know we're moving fast, but it doesn't seem wrong to me at all." He smiled at her again. "I guess it doesn't hurt that the sex is so good, huh?"

"Not at all," she laughed. "I've never felt so free with myself."

"Me neither. You bring the animal out of me, and I love it. I've enjoyed sex in the past, but usually once it was done, the drive and desire were gone too—even the need for closeness wasn't there anymore. I feel like I can't get enough of you; the sex just feels like one way of getting that closeness."

She squeezed his hand, signaling for the check. "I know it's been a long day for you, but I think I need to get some of that closeness before anything else happens," she said. "Forgive me, but I've been looking forward to this for days."

It was all they could do not to rip each other's clothes off on the elevator ride up.

Once inside Claudia's room they embraced savagely. The thirst for each other's flesh overwhelmed them. Their clothes flew off haphazardly, scattering over the indifferent hotel furniture.

Morrison no longer needed a script from Claudia. Something in him had risen to her demands as though to an invitation, and he knew that what he wanted was what she wanted too. He pressed her hard against the bathroom door, kissing her neck from behind as his arms encircled her. When her hands came together over his, he gripped her wrists together in one hand, raising them above her head while his other began its search over the rest of her body. Her response was immediate and eager; already her tension was near its breaking point. His fingers went everywhere, testing the limits of her pleasure until she moaned for release, arching her back against his hardness behind her.

But he was in no hurry. When he felt she was at the edge he pulled back, still holding her hands in his, and pulled her over to the bed, holding her there while he reached for his jacket pocket. She smiled as he pulled out a handful of silk ties.

"Someone's a quick learner," she breathed.

"Guess I've been waiting for the chance," he said.

He pushed her back and tied her hands together, looping the tie over the post at the top of the bed. Spreading her legs, he tied one ankle to each corner. When he'd finished he stood back and looked at her, her long, beautiful body stretched across the bed like an offering. She looked up at him hungrily. Now he was in complete command of her, and she loved it.

He began to lay soft kisses along her forehead, working his way all the way down her body to her feet. He wanted to kiss every inch of her;

and from her reaction, she hadn't had too many men take their time with her this way. She was already crazy with desire, straining against the ties in all directions.

"Please," she said again and again, her body finishing the request. But again he backed off.

Picking up his jacket again, he retrieved a bottle of massage oil from the inside pocket. He poured some out onto her feet and legs and slowly massaged her, the rhythmic motion of his hands forcing her into calm submission. He worked up to her breasts and arms, always coming tantalizingly close to where she was readiest for him, but moving on when she twisted against him.

By the time he returned to her inner thighs she was moaning, begging him to enter her. This time he gave in to the temptation a little, sliding his fingers deep into her as he continued to tease her. She was breathing heavy now, overcome with ecstasy and anticipation. It was enough; and with increasing intensity he pulled her to her climax, kissing her hard and allowing her panting excitement to carry him with it to the edge.

He unlooped her hands from the bedpost and pulled her down the bed toward him. She arched her hips up and shuddered as he drove deep inside her, catching the wave of her orgasm. She put her hands around his neck to draw him closer, deeper, and he felt the suddenness of his need as it caught up to hers, moving them faster together until they came in unison, beyond all sense swearing love for each other as they collapsed into the sheets.

The alarm woke them earlier than either of them would have wanted, but Morrison had another long day ahead of him.

They kissed, laughing together at their situation. They'd awoken in the same position they'd fallen asleep in, in each other's arms with one of Claudia's feet still tied to the bedpost. Morrison moved down the bed to untie it, awkwardly venturing on an apology. Claudia put her finger to his lips.

"No sorries between us, my love," she smiled.

He smiled back, caressing her face. She looked up at him, and again he was overwhelmed by the sight of her.

"Claudia," he said, "I don't think I can exaggerate how you make me feel. You are my meaning, my joy. You balance things for me. I can feel you steering me to happiness and lust and ecstasy and contentment that I've never felt before." He looked deeply into her eyes. "Thank you, for all you are—and for being there waiting for me that first night. It was a miracle for me, it really was."

She looked back at him profoundly. "Bill, I watched you from the moment you walked in that night," she said. "It wasn't normal for me, and I can't explain it, but watching you told me so much about who you were. I saw how you treated the people you were with, and the people who stopped by your table to talk to you; you were obviously someone of importance to all of them, but you never acted differently towards any of them. You treated everyone equally, and made them all feel at ease. I wanted that ease, too—I could see the way people fall in love with you."

He laughed. "Well, not everyone," he said.

"You're wrong," she insisted. "They all do. Some are probably afraid of it, because you could easily usurp them, but deep down they're enamored with you: with your ability to communicate with people, your open manner and receptiveness. I've been thinking about it a lot, and trying to find a way to articulate it; I think love is ultimately the best word for it. It may seem like a strong word for it—"

"No," he said quickly, then faltered, unsure what to say next. "No, I see what you mean."

"Well, it's how I feel, too," she went on. "The way you talk to me, make love to me, it's all so fluid and unbroken, so natural, like one soul flowing through all these interactions each day. I always know what I'm getting with you—you're always you. It sounds ridiculous, but believe me, it's absolutely priceless. You make me want to be myself too, and make me feel totally confident that I'm going to be accepted for who I am. I love you for that, Bill."

The words had come out completely naturally; and before he knew it, Morrison was echoing them.

"I love you too, Claudia," he said. "It may be crazy for us to be saying it so quickly, and with everything else going on, but it really feels right to me."

She nodded her agreement, and for a while they lay silently together, basking in the excitement of the bond between them. Morrison stilled his nerves, forcing himself to enjoy the moment a little longer. He knew the peanut gallery was going to be all over the office today, what with the new developments with the case; he'd have to be there early to be on top of things beforehand.

But all that could wait just a few minutes more.

15

Staying over at Claudia's hotel meant a short ride to the precinct this morning; Morrison had that to be thankful for. The day, he was sure, would not prove so merciful. Though they'd parted in hopes of seeing one another again that evening, he was almost certain the day's events wouldn't allow it. He knew he was lucky to have had one night of relief; two was unheard of in times like these.

He switched between News Radio 88 and 1010 WINS to hear what the media was saying about their third murder, and for the first time he heard the phrase "possible serial murderer loose in New York City." *Well, that does it,* he thought. The news radio stations tended to be pretty mundane, as they had to get everything out in a very short period of time; the more sensationalistic, ratings-seeking TV news stations would hardly be so terse.

He walked into the office to find Medveded and Rivera talking over coffee. Rivera looked up at him anxiously.

"Cap, have you seen any of the news?" he asked.

"Yeah, I heard it on the radio," Morrison answered. "Bet they're having a field day with it, huh?"

"Sons of bitches," Medveded said bitterly. "They don't give a crap about how hard this is on us, or anything about the victims' families—they just want to scare the shit out of people. Nothing like a good tragedy to rope in the viewers! Go ahead, spill all the beans to make a story—why not call up the murderers and give them our home addresses while they're at it?"

"Well, nothing we can do about it now," Morrison said. "The genie's out of the bottle. Still, they don't have everything we have, so we need to stay focused. Frankie, make sure we stay on top of the video guys, and press the guys on the lawman search to get that car ID'd. Once we get the car, we will have a pretty good shot at our guys, I bet."

"I'm all over it, boss. We should have the car down before this afternoon."

The information came in much faster than Rivera had predicted. It was hardly 0900 hours when Detective O'Dell walked into Morrison's office.

"Boss, I think we got the car," he said.

Morrison sat up in his chair. "Yeah? Go on."

"Well, I spoke to my guy in Auto Crime, Arty Annouer, and we got about fifteen hits on the lawman search. He walked me through what we had, and narrowed it down to one vehicle: it's a black 2009 BMW 650i, Connecticut plates."

"Nice, high-end," Morrison said.

"Yeah, that does narrow it down. It looks like this kid has money—or at least he comes from a family that does."

"'Kid'?"

"Yeah. Registered owner of the car is Adam Rutherford, male, white, twenty-one years old. Lives in Greenwich, Connecticut—looks like with Mommy and Daddy. Only child, from what we can see so far. We found his Facebook account; I've got Tina out there right now, using a phony profile to try to friend him. We want to take a look at his photos, and anything else he might have posted."

"Great," Morrison said. "What else?"

"Well, he's never been arrested—no prints on file of any kind. We've found a few photos of him through a Google search. Looks like he attends Boston College, but we're still trying to run that down to make sure."

"Boston College, huh?" Morrison said. "You know what? Let me call Louise Donohue—I think one of her kids went there. She may also have connections in the Boston PD that we could use."

"Still, huh?"

"Oh, sure. Cops stick together, you know that. It's a brotherhood. I'm sure any old friends of her husband's there would have stayed in touch with her, especially given the man Donohue was."

"Well, give it a try; anything helps."

"We have anything else?"

"One thing. Pretty interesting, really. When we did the Google search on this kid, we kept seeing one other guy in the pictures we found of him. He's in almost all of them."

"You don't say. Maybe our perp number two, huh?"

"Exactly. We don't have a name yet, but hopefully if Rutherford friends Tina we'll be able to get something from his Facebook."

"Terrific. This is great, Jeff." The phone rang. "Excuse me, will you? Let me handle this call, and I'll get everyone together on this."

"Absolutely." O'Dell ducked out as Morrison picked up.

"Good morning Bill, it's Tommy Johnson in the PC's office."

"Hey, Tommy," Morrison said, his stomach tightening. "What's going on?"

"The boss wants to see you in his office at 1000 hours," Tommy said. "He wants to discuss this latest homicide with you."

"All right. How's he holding up with all the media stuff?"

"Oh, fine. He just told me to get you down here. You know how he is—he's tired of getting half the answers from Arndt."

Fair enough, Morrison thought. "Sure, Tommy, I'll be there," he said.

When they'd hung up, he called out to Rivera.

"Frankie, let's get everyone in the kitchen," he said. "I need to speak to them right away."

"Okay, let's go around the room," Morrison started. He looked at Tina. "First thing I want to know is from you, Tina: have you gotten this guy to bite on your friend request yet?"

Tina lit up like a utility infielder who just got a pinch homerun. "Absolutely, boss," she said. "I put the request in, and not ten minutes later he accepted it."

"Great. What have we got?"

"Well, the guy's a real piece of work. His whole Facebook is a self-admiration shrine. I can't believe how much shit people put on there now. We got confirmation that he goes to Boston College, and lives in a dorm on campus. His roommate there is a lifelong friend, a guy named Brian Anderson."

Morrison looked over at O'Dell, who was nodding. "You got it," O'Dell said. "Anderson matches our second guy from the video by height and weight."

"Bingo," Morrison said. "So what do we have on this Anderson guy?"

"Another kid of privilege," O'Dell said. "His parents also live in Greenwich, in a house slightly smaller than Rutherford's—a humble 15,000 square feet." A murmur of laughter went around the room. "He's another student at Boston, as Tina said; no criminal record on him either. And something else from Rutherford's Facebook account: we have a few pictures of the two of them at an event here in New York City, on the night of the Sutton Place homicide."

"Okay," Morrison said, clapping his hands together for emphasis. "You all know the drill at this point. We need to focus on these two guys, either to close the ring around them as suspects or to rule them out. Anyone else?"

"I've already reached out to the Greenwich PD," said Sergeant McNamara. "I have a contact there from a homicide course I did a couple of years ago. Hopefully they'll be able to help us."

"Great. Have your team pack their bags; I'm going to have you guys head out to Boston. We need to get more on these guys, and fast. These guys make any moves, I want you on them. Get me some evidence that we can test for connections to the crime scene—cigarette butts, coffee cups, anything."

McNamara was already standing, along with the rest of his team. "We all have a change of clothes in our lockers; we'll head out now," he said.

"All right. O'Dell," Morrison said, turning to the tall veteran, "you're our point man on anything and everything we pull up on these guys. Put it all together for us. Go as far back as you need to—hell, get me their kindergarten graduation photos if you can. The rest of you, get anything you can to O'Dell." He stood, putting on his coat. "I'm headed to the PC's office—I want everything we have before I get there. Rivera—?"

"You got it, Cap. I'll call you on your way."

"All right. I'll call Louise Donohue on the way, too—she may have a useful connection or two for us." Morrison took a deep breath. "Let's hope these are our guys."

16

"**G**ood morning, Captain Morrison."

Irene, the PC's executive assistant, had been there as long as Morrison could remember, and had to be one of the best gatekeepers in the history of the department. She'd held off all of the top brass at one time or another—no one got past her without an appointment. Tough as nails, that little old lady.

"Commissioner Harrington is back early," she told him with a pleasant smile. "You can go right in."

"Thanks, Irene."

Morrison opened the door. The Commissioner was sitting at his desk, but stood to greet Morrison when he came in. Morrison had seen him make top people squirm in meetings many times before, and he knew from the look on the PC's face that this would not be one of those days.

"Good morning, Commissioner," Morrison said respectfully.

"Bill, we go too far back for formalities behind closed doors," Harrington said warmly. "You know that."

"Indeed we do, Commissioner," answered Morrison with a smile. His respect for the city's top cop was too great to allow him to slip into first names; Robert Harrington had been Police Commissioner for two mayoral terms, and had been an outstanding cop for his entire career before that.

"Suit yourself," laughed Harrington as they sat. "Well, Bill, give me the rundown on what we have going on here."

"Well, boss, in the last twelve hours we just got a huge break," Morrison said. "We now have two white male suspects: Adam Rutherford and Brian Anderson, early twenties. They both come from Greenwich, Connecticut, from wealthy families. This is all still fairly fresh, so we don't have everything we need just yet, but I can give you what we've got. Neither of them has ever been arrested—not even a traffic ticket that we can find. No prints on file, so AFIS means nothing right now. One of them owns a BMW that matches the one we have on video from at least one scene, possibly another. We are into one Facebook account, and have photo evidence from it that they were in the city on the night of the homicide on Sutton Place. I have a team, led by Sergeant McNamara, already on the way to Boston College to conduct surveillance, develop any information they can on these guys, and recover DNA samples if possible."

"Is that Patrick McNamara?" Harrington asked.

"That's right, Commissioner."

"Good man—no one's better at surveillance."

"I agree, sir."

"All right, what else?"

"Well, I'm told the timeline of our homicides coincides with the school's holiday break, so there's more plausibility that these are our guys. We have a few selfies of them from Facebook; my impression is that we have a leader and a follower. I just spoke with Sergeant Rivera on the way here, and they've found a few articles about Rutherford saying that he turned down a scholarship to Harvard so he and his buddy Brian Anderson could go to Boston College together. Seems they're inseparable—which should make it easier for us to find them both."

"Okay. Is that all we have?"

"Yes sir, for the time being. I'm hopeful we'll have a lot more within the next several days. Obviously, we're still running down some other leads, until we close the loop on these guys; I can't ignore those other avenues. But this is our biggest lead."

"Bill, I'm going to be frank with you," Harrington said. "The city's starting to panic on this one. The mayor keeps reminding me how serial killers are bad for tourism—as if I need to hear that. We need to stop these homicides, now."

"I understand, Commissioner. We're working around the clock on it."

"I trust you, Bill. I just wanted to speak to you in person about this. I've been getting such a runaround from our illustrious Chief of Detectives, I felt I needed to talk to someone I have faith in, for a change."

"Thank you, Commissioner. But since you brought him up," Morrison added, "I wanted to let you know: Arndt just dropped a guy onto the task force, Lou Galipoli—new detective. All my people get a bad vibe from this guy, so I've marginalized him within the task force, but I'm afraid that won't last, since he's Arndt's boy. I'm worried that the efficacy of our work could be jeopardized, especially with the media now involved."

"I understand," Harrington said. "I'll keep Arndt out of your hair for now."

"Thanks, boss. It means a lot to me."

"Sure thing, Bill. Just keep me up on this as it develops. You have my cell. If we get another break, call me right away."

"I will, Commissioner."

When Morrison got back to the squad room, he found Rivera, Medveded, and Koreski going over all the variables in their case folder, updating the case flow chart. The chart was not the sort of thing the general public ever saw, and certainly nothing like they used on *Law & Order;* it included everything from a timeline of the victims' movements prior to their deaths, to gruesome crime-scene photos, to whatever information they'd managed to glean from Rutherford's Facebook page so far. Tina had even pinned up a photo of the two suspects from their Greenwich private high-school yearbook—they looked like two little preppy angels.

"Frankie, have we heard from McNamara yet?" Morrison asked.

"Yeah, they made it to Boston," Rivera told him. "Found the car parked on the street. They're set up on it until they see either of these guys."

"Nothing yet, though?"

"No, not yet. It's a big campus you set them to wander around—three campuses, in fact, and about 14,000 students."

"I know, I know. I just have a feeling, that's all. They didn't hook up with Boston PD yet, did they?"

"No, boss—they took a couple of undercover cars from Narcotics, and aren't talking to any of the locals until you give them the green light. One team went to Greenwich to check the homes out; the other's in Boston, sitting on the car."

"All right. Time to be patient, I guess."

Just then, Morrison's cell phone rang.

"McNamara," he said as he picked up, smiling at Rivera on the way into his office. "What's going on?"

"Well, Cap, I think I'm on one of our guys," he heard McNamara say in a low voice. "The shorter one—Anderson. I'm not a hundred percent on it, but I've got one of my guys helping me follow him anyway."

"Good. And the rest?"

"Back on the car still, in case Rutherford comes around."

"What's Anderson doing?"

"Seems like he's just hanging around the campus," McNamara said. "Doesn't seem like he's in any rush to get to class, that's for sure. Though it is late in the day; he might be done. He also seems like a bit of a social misfit—he doesn't make eye contact with any of the women on campus, but he tries to look up their skirts when they walk past."

"That's got to be our guy," Morrison said. "Holy shit, that easy, huh?"

"Yeah, how's it feel to be so smart?" McNamara laughed.

"Damn lucky," Morrison said. "Well, listen, don't get made—remember, we need some good DNA or fingerprint samples from these guys. That may be our only way of tying them to the crime scene. Keep me posted."

"Will do, Cap. Talk soon."

Morrison hung up and leaned back, letting the rush sink in. Today was just getting better and better. It looked like he was even going to have a few free hours tonight. He picked up his cell phone again and dialed Claudia.

"Captain Morrison, the Bullshit Remover!" she answered. "How's your day going, my love?"

"A lot better than I thought it was going to," he said with a pent-up laugh.

"Yeah? That's great!"

"Believe me, it is. How do you feel about spending two nights in a row in my excellent company?" He realized, as he said it, that he was actually apprehensive of how she'd respond—how could such good luck last? But her response was immediate.

"Absolutely!"

"Great," he said, trying not to sound too relieved. "I ought to be done around seven, I think, if you want to meet me. What do you say we hit the Capital Grille, over here?"

"Oh, I love that place. Be warned, though, if we go there I'm going to make you try a pineapple martini."

The thought brought a smile to his face. "Baby, I'll try anything you want me to try," he said, shaking his head bemusedly.

"I'm going to hold you to that!" she laughed.

17

orrison parked out in front of the Capital Grille, where he could keep an eye on the car. It was an old work habit that died hard; not only was he responsible for the department car, but he was proud of driving it. He felt it to be symbolic of the job that, for all its complications, had kept him going through the years, and saved his life at least as many times as it had risked it—one of the few things that had ever made him feel completely at ease with himself.

Now, entering the restaurant, he found one of the others waiting for him. Claudia was at the bar, drinking one of her aforementioned pineapple martinis. Morrison gave her a kiss on the cheek, and signaled to the bartender.

"I'll have another of the same," he said, smiling at her.

"You won't regret it, I promise," she said. "So how did your day end out? As good as you were saying before?"

"Yeah, it was a good one. One of my teams managed to get a tail on one of our suspects, so hopefully our case will be making strides soon. But let's talk about you first—I really miss you when I'm not with you—I want to know all about you."

"I know what you mean," she said. "But that's a big question! Where should I start?"

He wasn't quite sure. "Well, you've said you have the same feeling I do, that this is a big break for you, that you've had a bad history with relationships—you were married before?"

"Yeah," she mused, toying with her glass. "Angelo. I don't know why; he was the biggest mistake of my life. I think I was just getting older— I mean, not really that old, but thirty, you know—I think I was just afraid I'd miss out on being married. It was a big deal for me growing up; there's a lot of pressure to get married in Greek families like mine."

"Was he Greek too?"

"No, but that didn't matter to my family. They were just relieved that I was getting married. My parents really wanted me to have a big wedding, especially my dad, so we did—"

"Big Fat Greek Wedding, huh?"

She laughed. "Yeah, just like that, except not all good. Mostly bad, really."

"Why so?"

"Oh, Angelo was a jealous man—really over-the-top jealous. I couldn't move. I couldn't breathe. He had to know my every move. When I was a little girl in Astoria, I had a Greek teacher who'd come to the house on Wednesdays—oh, of course," she said as his eyes widened, "there was *no way* I wasn't learning the Greek language. We're a very proud people! Well, this teacher would use my parents' phone to talk to his wife, you know, constantly asking her questions. *Where did you go today? Who were you with?* Very possessive. Anyway, Angelo reminded me of that teacher. But he started to change—or at least I finally started to notice it. I overlooked everything for a long time to keep my family happy."

"How do you mean, he started to change? He got more possessive?"

"No, that stayed the same; he just got more distant. I think he never wanted me, but he didn't want to look bad either—he had an old-fashioned Italian family, so in a way we both got married for the wrong reason. But the change was really obvious. At first he wouldn't come home. I thought he was off playing bocce; he was in lots of clubs.

Then he started spending all his time on the Internet, talking to his friends. He was in the computer field—that was his business—so at first I assumed it was research he was doing. I later found out he was talking in chat rooms."

"To other women?"

"So I assumed! But then I came home early one day and his computer was on, and I looked. He was talking to other men."

Morrison nodded. "I see."

"I was shocked," she said. "All that time I thought it was me!"

"But that's not the worst thing that could happen, I guess," Morrison said. "At least you knew it *wasn't* you."

"Yeah. We were both hurt, but we were both relieved to stop living a lie, too. It wasn't really all that bad; it just went on for a long time, for how unhappy it made both of us." She took a sip of her drink. "Anyway, your turn, Silent Detective. Why's your life so fucked up?"

"Oh, mine's a long story."

"I've got all night." She smiled. "Well, not *all* night. But you know what I mean. Besides, they haven't even shown us to our table yet."

He laughed. "Well, it wasn't so dissimilar, I guess," he said. "Except I was married to what I thought was a really spectacular woman—had everything you could want. We had two great kids together. It's kind of sad, but I remember the day I figured out she was cheating on me."

"Oh, I'm sorry," she said, grimacing. "What happened?"

"Well, when I was a young cop there were two guys—old timers, as we called them, or hairbags. That was a nickname we had for guys with time on the job who wouldn't leave. They used to talk before roll call; and when they talked everyone would listen, you know, out of respect. You just shut up. One of them had been at Guadalcanal, and the other was at Iwo Jima, and they used to argue over which of them was tougher. It was kind of like being in a history lesson—they'd argue about their beach landings, their combat tours, everything. But they were good to each other, and both very typical of that era, with wives they'd been married to for a long time. They'd all go on vacation together down the Jersey Shore way, before Snooki and that bunch turned it into a sideshow.

"Anyhow, one day I'm talking to another young guy, and sort of complaining about how my life was going, you know, in a general way, and brought up how my wife had been acting. I was even joking about it, talking about this country song by Ronnie Milsap, *There's A Stranger In My House.* So the old-timers were sitting in the back of the stationhouse, and I didn't even realize it, but they'd stopped talking and were just listening to me. They'd never spoken to me before—I was too new for that—but all of a sudden one of them says to me, *Hey, kid. I overheard your conversation—did your wife, by any chance, recently go shopping and buy a bunch of new bras and underwear?* I was real surprised and I go, As a matter of fact, she did. And he asks, *Like, all of it?* And he was right there, too—she'd pretty much replaced everything. *Go home,* he says. *Your wife's cheating on you.* And I was totally floored, because I knew the old fuck was right."

"So what'd you do?"

"Well, so I start questioning her, and her answers weren't adding up. When a person lies to someone close to them, especially if they're cheating, their plans get very contrived. The amount of detail they give you goes way beyond a normal conversation. It's similar to an interview with a suspect; they're trying to give you so much detail, you won't check it out. But the devil's in the details, as they say. When something really happens to someone, they remember it that way forever. When they make it up, it changes every time they tell it.

"So one day she tells me she has to go to JFK to pick someone up for her boss from a Wings West commuter flight, Boston to New York. Unfortunately for her, I was a cop, and I knew the story sounded like shit. At the time, JFK didn't have any commuter flights; those were all out of LaGuardia. So I got a little crazy."

Claudia looked sideways at him. "What do you mean, crazy?" she asked.

He laughed. "I just mean, I went a little overboard on surveillance.

I got a copy of our phone bill—back then they printed out all your calls—and I noticed that whenever I was working, which was a lot, she would spend hours on the phone with one number in particular."

"So did you bring it up?"

"Well, not yet; I kept my mouth shut. Then one night she was going out to see a band play, and I was supposed to be working but surprised her by taking the day off. So we go to this place, and—well, when you've been a cop for a while, you get these instincts. This band isn't my kind of thing, and it certainly isn't hers, but there's this guy in the band, and the way they look at each other, I knew right away it was him. So on the way home, we're both drunk, and I pull over and tell her I have someone else. She tells me she does too—*I'm so sorry this happened,* she says. Then I tell her I really don't have anybody, and that I never wanted anyone but her, and she knew she was caught."

"God, that sounds awful. What'd you do?"

"What could I do? I said all the usual stuff, called her a lying fuck, et cetera. I wanted to punch her in the head, but I couldn't. She asked if we could start over; I was so stupid, I thought she meant it. I agreed to work on things, but I couldn't get past this guy from the band. So a few days later, thinking things are worth another try, I decide to bring her flowers at her office—she was an assistant principal—and I walk in the office and who do I see sitting outside her office typing, but the guy from the goddamn band."

"No way."

"Yeah. He was her assistant. It all clicked. I told him that I needed to talk to him, and she went totally crazy. She was crying all over the place, not because she felt bad, but because she was afraid I'd hurt this asshole."

"And did you?"

"No, no. I took him for a ride and told him I should put a gun to his head. That was it."

"That's good. What happened with her afterward?"

"Oh, we stayed married, even renewed our vows. It was a waste of time. It wasn't long before I caught her again. This time the rug burns on her back gave it away."

Claudia couldn't help but laugh. "I'm sorry, I just—she sounds terrible."

"Oh, she was—and this time she really showed it," he smiled. "She didn't want to look bad in front of her parents—it was already her second marriage, so she was determined not to have it be her fault if it ended. So she tried to make me out to be some sort of nut."

"Really? How?"

"She started moving things around, even changed where I kept my socks. I even thought I was going out of my mind, just like she wanted everyone else to think. So I was suspicious again, and got a friend of mine who was a private investigator to hook up my home phone to a recorder. I thought I'd catch her that way, but this time she was ahead of me, and I never found any conversations with the new guy. Those were bad days—I couldn't help being suspicious of her, and I thought I was losing it. I finally caught her when our kids recognized the guy at a baseball game. She'd been calling the guy Stephanie around the kids, so they wouldn't blow it with me that she was spending time with a guy; and one day we're at a ballgame and the kids recognized him and start pointing him out, saying *Look, Mom, it's your friend Stephanie.*"

"Oh my God," Claudia laughed again. "I almost feel bad for her, that's so ridiculous."

"Oh, believe me, I was never so relieved in all my life. I missed putting the kids to bed, but it was for the best."

"I'm sure. And what about them?"

"My kids? They turned out to be really good people, both of them. My son went to Princeton—hell of a ballplayer, too. He got a tryout with the Phillies a while back. My daughter took the breakup hard, but she came through okay, too. She actually followed in my footsteps, and is a detective up in Hartford. She's great—I talk to her pretty much every day, just to tell her to have a safe tour and all that. I'm proud of both of them, really proud."

"That's great." Claudia touched his arm. "And besides your son—the one you lost—you have a daughter with your wife now?"

"Yeah, Nadia. She's sixteen. She's doing well—as well as sixteen-year-olds do, anyway. She does well in school. I feel bad about being away as often as I am, with the job and all, but I think she's used to it. And ever since Billy—I just—"

He faltered, looking uncomfortably at the bar. His son's name had run through him like ice water. Claudia leaned in closer.

"It's all right," she said simply. "We don't have to talk about it right now, if you don't want to."

"I just don't want to scare you off with it," he said abruptly. He held her hand in his, suddenly unable to look her in the eye. "I do want to talk to you about it, Claudia—about everything. And everyone has a bad side, I know that. I don't know, I guess I just want you to know a little about that side of me now, before we—before you get in too deep."

At a mention of his name, Morrison turned. A host was standing behind him with menus, ready to bring them to their table. He turned back around to find Claudia smiling deeply at him.

"You're a little too late there, darling," she said. "I'm already in the deep end of this pool." She finished her drink and squeezed his hand. "Now come on, let's eat."

18

Three days after surveillance had begun in Boston, Morrison, Rivera, and Medveded sat looking over a group of photos taken of their two prime suspects. So far the team had a number of photos of Adam Rutherford and Brian Anderson, both separately and together—running from the college to Fenway Park, working out in the campus gym—and the dynamic between the two men was clear. Rutherford came across as the obvious alpha of the two: he was taller, better looking, and possessed of a false bravado that seemed to play off of his friend's lack of confidence. The shorter, slighter Anderson carried himself with a much more cautious air.

"Looks like we have a leader and a follower here, huh?" Morrison said.

"Definitely," Rivera agreed. "Rutherford's taller by a few inches, better looking—smarter, too. He wasn't bullshitting on his Facebook page about Harvard—he was offered a scholarship there, but turned it down. Anderson seems to have gotten into BC through connections."

"Ought to be useful when we get to talk to these two," Morrison said, looking over at Medveded. "Are we any closer to pinning them down?"

"Well, it's still hard to get a match between these photos and our crime-scene videos," Medveded admitted, "but we're close. And we're almost a hundred percent on Rutherford's car being near that one scene."

"How's DNA recovery going?"

"Not great. Any potentials we've had so far were contaminated by others before the team could recover them."

"We'll keep trying. Are they hard to track?"

"Not particularly," Medveded said. "They seem to be hanging around campus pretty exclusively—the car hasn't moved since our team spotted it, and these guys don't seem to be big on public transportation."

"What about your connection through Louise Donohue, Cap?" Rivera asked. "Did you find out anything from the Boston PD?"

"I found out that they haven't had anything close to our cases," Morrison said. "And that goes for both homicides and sex crimes. I put McNamara in touch with them, though; we should see what he says. We ought to ask him about the DNA samples, too—we have a lot of good DNA from our crime scenes, and we ought to go for the DNA match if we can get it."

"I'll get him on a conference call now," Rivera said, reaching for the phone.

McNamara picked up on the first ring. "I was actually just going to call you guys," he said. "We have some good news here."

"Let's hear it," said Morrison.

"Through campus security, we were able to get a couple of our team in to work out alongside our suspects in the gym," he said. "A bit tough for the older guys, but we were able to keep a real close eye on our two boys."

"That's great," Morrison said. "Were you able to pick up any DNA samples there?"

"Yeah, we were. We got a couple of swabs off the elliptical machines after they used them. Also, the geniuses both had water bottles with them, and they threw them out right in front of Hanrahan. Hopefully we'll be able to take some good DNA off them, possibly prints as well."

"Excellent. We still need more, to make sure we can rule out contamination, but that's a good start. Do you need any extra bodies to help you out?"

"Maybe. Hanrahan's on his way to New York with those samples for vouchering and processing, and we could always use a few spare eyes if you've got 'em. We've all been running sixteen to eighteen hours a day, with one guy staying on the car after we put these guys to bed, so I'm sure it wouldn't hurt."

"Okay, we'll send you two more," Morrison said, gesturing at Rivera to make a note of it. "How about those Boston PD guys I put you in touch with—have you spoken with them?"

"Yeah, I have; they've been very helpful. These guys have been going to a Mexican restaurant near their dorm every night since we started, and the Boston PD know the place—they set us up with the manager, and hopefully we'll be able to get some additional samples off of them the next time they're in."

"All right, McNamara, keep it up and stay safe. We'll send you those other guys ASAP. Don't go talking about the Yankees or anything in the meantime."

"Oh yeah, we found that out real quick," McNamara laughed. "Good way to get a whole bar to turn on you in a hurry. Take it easy, fellas."

Seconds after they hung up, the phone rang again. Rivera picked up and listened a few moments, a look of concern furrowing his brow.

"Okay, where?" he asked, giving Morrison a familiar look as he took notes. *Fuck,* Morrison thought. *We've got another one.*

Rivera hung up with a deep breath, and Morrison knew his fears were realized. "Looks like we've got one at a brownstone in Gramercy— Twenty-First and Park," he said.

"Goddammit," said Medveded quietly.

"What the fuck!" Morrison exploded, furious. "Our guys have been on these two in Boston for three days!"

"Well, let's go check it out," Rivera said. He grabbed his coat. "They backed right out, so we don't have much detail yet."

"All right, yeah," Morrison said. "No sense jumping to conclusions, right? I'll call McNamara back on the way."

When they arrived at the scene—a nice brownstone typical of the quiet, moneyed neighborhood of Gramercy Park—Crime Scene was still arriving, so they had to wait a while before entering. But when they did, Captain Morrison immediately found his suspicions confirmed—but in a disturbingly uneven way.

The scene inside was eerily similar to that of the first three. The similarities were stark: even the same types of rope and tape were used as previously. Yet, though the victim had not been tortured as keenly this time—there were no bite marks on her body—her murder appeared to have been more violent. The other three had had their faces left untouched, but not this one: her model-beautiful face was distorted in places by livid bruises. Her nails were all broken, as though she'd had a chance to put up a real fight against her attacker before he'd gotten her tied up—another difference. Also, with her long, black hair, she didn't quite fit the blonde or dyed-blonde profile of the previous victims.

"You think we might have a copycat killer here?" Morrison asked Rivera, after he'd instructed Crime Scene to bag the victim's hands for DNA collection.

"Could be, Cap. Hard to say, though. Would that be better, or worse?"

"I don't know," Morrison said. "Either way, it's bad—and it's my ass on the hot seat. Check with McNamara—let's see what he says about our Boston guys. I want to confirm they were there all night."

"I just hung up with him. He says to give him twenty minutes."

"Okay," said Morrison, running his hand through his hair in frustration. "How many people do we have working right now?"

"Besides the ones in Boston, we're only missing two—Galipoli and Koreski."

"Okay, get everyone we can on this, now. We need to know everything about this victim, ASAP. I don't like the way this looks, Frankie," he added. "I don't think this is our guys."

"You think we got *another* set of psychos running around now?" Rivera asked.

"I don't know. But I do know the press is going to have a field day with this one, and the PC's going to have to make a statement, so we'd better have something for him. Arndt's going to be looking for any way he can to throw us under the bus." He grabbed Medveded to join them. "And listen," he told them quietly, "I need you guys to say *nothing* about a possible copycat, understand? That thought stays with the three of us. This includes the rest of the task force. Got it?"

Medveded and Rivera nodded.

"Christ, do you think we should have picked up the guys in Boston sooner?" Medveded asked.

"No, we had no cause," Morrison sighed. "We would have just tipped our hand before having to let them out again."

Before they left the building to brave the media circus already gathering outside, Morrison dialed McNamara again.

"Hey, Pat," he said, "can you tell me if there's any way these guys went for a ride last night?"

McNamara sounded stressed. "Well, we didn't see the one car move, but we still haven't found the other car—the one registered to Anderson."

"Tell me we sat on their dorm all night," Morrison pressed him.

"We did, but there are multiple ways in and out. Their pattern seemed to have them leaving through the same door every day, but it's possible we could have missed them. Does it look like we have the same stuff at this new scene?"

"Sort of," Morrison said, "but it doesn't feel right. There are no bite marks or lips taken, and the victim's been beaten real badly. It just has a different feel. You got the DNA from those two in, right?"

"Yeah, O'Dell called a little while ago—it's all in."

"Okay; let's see what we have, then. I need those lab results *yesterday*. And let me know if you see either of those guys this morning—it's important, for all of our sakes, that we didn't lose them in Boston last night."

"Yessir." McNamara cleared his throat. "Cap, if there's any trouble—I just want you to know I take full responsibility for this. I don't think we missed them, but if we did, I know it's me who should go down for it."

"Well, I appreciate it," Morrison said, "but let's not go jumping on our swords just yet. Just give me the information on those guys' whereabouts as soon as you have it—our asses may well depend on it."

19

On his way back to the stationhouse, Morrison called a meeting with his task force. But before he could enter the squad room, he was met by a very flushed and visibly worked-up Chief of Detectives Arndt.

"Captain, I want you in your office, now," he commanded, and stormed back inside.

Morrison followed him in, gritting his teeth in frustration. It was exactly what he had been hoping to avoid—at a time like this, Arndt wouldn't be here for answers, but for the opportunity to take Morrison down a notch that he'd been awaiting for so long. And though Morrison would usually give as he got with the Chief, without the information he needed, he knew he didn't have a leg to stand on. He took utter responsibility for his command, and if his team in Boston had let two serial killers slip past them, he had this last girl's blood on their hands. *My days as head of this task force may be numbered,* he thought grimly as he closed the door.

Arndt didn't wait for him to sit down.

"Captain, can you tell me what the fuck you think you're doing here?" he shouted. "I thought your team was supposed to be surveilling our suspects 24-7. Now we have another murder—what are your guys doing up there, sleeping in their cars?"

"Chief, we're not sure yet whether—"

"Exactly—not sure! Not sure who's behind this murder; not sure where our suspects from the previous murders might be; not sure what his men are doing; not sure of *anything* we need to be sure of, it seems! Can you tell me why someone so completely clueless ought to be running a squad in the first place, Captain?"

A knock on the door saved Morrison the indignity of answering. The squad Principal Administrative Assistant, Tamika Edwards, poked her head in.

"What is it?" Arndt barked at her.

"The Commissioner's on the phone for Captain Morrison," she said.

"Put him through—*I'll* talk to him," Arndt snapped. He picked up the phone. "Hello, Commissioner, Chief Arndt here. Yes. Yes, I understand, but—all right, of course. Yes, Commissioner, I'll take care of it. No problem. I'll be there in fifteen minutes."

He hung up and glared at Morrison.

"This isn't over," he said. "I'll be back."

He stormed out. A few minutes later, Tamika knocked again. Morrison picked up the phone wearily.

"Hello, Commissioner. Sorry about that."

"It's all right," Harrington told him. "But look, Bill, we need this—we need it really badly. Have we gotten anywhere on the two guys in Boston?"

"Yeah, we just got possible DNA and some fingerprints delivered to the lab this morning."

"That's good. How much time do you need to confirm a match?"

"Well, based on the severity of the case, and if everything goes right, and if they put us ahead of everything else—"

"All right, Bill, I get it. How long?"

"Four days, generally."

"I'll give you three," Harrington said. "And before you ask, that's how long I'll be able to keep Arndt in check. After that, I won't be able to hold him back. Understand?"

Morrison felt a chill go down his spine. The PC was putting his own neck in the noose in place of his. If another serial homicide turned up in the next three days, whatever happened to Morrison, the media would do Harrington ten times worse. Morrison thanked his lucky stars again for giving him such a standup man for a Commissioner.

"Thank you, Commissioner," he managed. "I won't let you down."

"I know you won't, Bill. Talk soon."

Morrison emerged to a squad meeting already in progress. Everyone was there with the exception of McNamara and his team. McNamara was on conference, listening in from the field. The room went silent as Morrison joined them.

"Don't stop on my account—let's keep this going," he said as he sat.

Sergeant Simmons spoke up. "Okay, where were we? Right—we now have some possible DNA from our suspects, as well as fingerprints, so right now we need to make sure they jump to the top of the list for testing."

"We at least have results from the previous three murders," Rivera said. "The lab has confirmed they're all from the same suspects."

"I think we all knew that from experience, wouldn't you say?" Morrison said. "I'm not sold on the fourth yet, but I'll call the Medical Examiner about that. For now, we know it's the same two guys—let's hope they're our two. McNamara—?"

"I'm sorry, Cap," McNamara said. "I know it's my fault, but we can't lock these guys in last night. They're here now, but the trip to Manhattan doesn't take that long, and we just can't say for one hundred percent that they were here all last night."

"It's all right, Pat, I get it. Surveillance is a tricky business. Just stay with them for now, right?"

"Definitely, Cap. With the two extra bodies, we've got them blanketed."

"Good. That'll be all, Sergeant," Morrison said. When McNamara had hung up, he turned to the rest of the group. "Now listen, everyone: we have a three-day reprieve from the PC. Get that? *Three days.* After that, we will *all* be pretty well fucked—and I include myself and the PC at the top of that list. It's like in baseball: if the team's having a losing season, the managers are the first heads on the block. So I want all the stops pulled out. Favors, prayers, acts of God—everything. We need to get everything lined up and ready to move the *minute* we get the results back. If you don't know what that means for you, ask Rivera or myself. Andre, get on the horn to the DA's office—we already briefed Stan Rosenthal in the homicide bureau. Make sure the DA has everything we've got, and tell him we're just waiting on the lab."

"Yessir, will do."

Galipoli, apparently fed up with the proceedings thus far, spoke up loudly from the back.

"What the fuck were these guys in Boston doing, anyway?" he raged. "Why couldn't they just stay on these fucking guys the way they should have?"

"It's a complicated situation, Galipoli," Simmons said, trying to calm him down. "There were a lot of exits to the dorm, and—"

"No, that's bullshit," Galipoli said. "We're having to pick up the slack for them, and it's bullshit! They're there for surveillance; they dropped the ball. That's all there is to it."

"Okay, that's enough," Morrison said. "If you want to have that as a private conversation, go ahead, but this isn't an encounter group. We're solution-finders here, not finger-pointers, Detective. I know you're new to the squad business, so you need to understand how this works: it isn't a one-man show. We're a team, and we leave the criticism to people outside this squad—believe me, there are plenty of them."

"But all they were supposed to do was—" Galipoli started.

"*Enough,* I said!" Morrison shouted. "Galipoli, you can see me after this meeting's done. Everyone else, you know what you have to do. Get to it!"

The task force dispersed to their separate tasks. Galipoli followed

Morrison sullenly into the Captain's office, and closed the door after them. He opened his mouth to protest, but before he could begin Morrison had unhooked a framed document from the wall and handed it to him.

"Read that," Morrison said.

Galipoli looked at it. It was a rather famous quote from Theodore Roosevelt, the so-called "Man in the Arena" passage:

> "It is not the critic who counts; not the man who points out how the strong man stumbles, or where the doer of deeds could have done them better. The credit belongs to the man who is actually in the arena, whose face is marred by dust and sweat and blood; who strives valiantly; who errs, who comes short again and again, because there is no effort without error and shortcoming; but who does actually strive to do the deeds; who knows great enthusiasms, the great devotions; who spends himself in a worthy cause; who at the best knows in the end the triumph of high achievement, and who at the worst, if he fails, at least fails while daring greatly, so that his place shall never be with those cold and timid souls who neither know victory nor defeat."

After a few minutes Detective Galipoli looked up from the quote at Morrison. His expression was inscrutable—an angry, confused blank.

"What is this supposed to mean?" he asked.

Morrison stared at him, and shook his head. "If I have to tell you what it means, then you're in the wrong place, Detective."

Galipoli tossed the frame on Morrison's desk in disgust. "I've been saying that since I got here," he said indignantly.

Morrison leaned forward. "Now, you listen to me, pretty boy," he said. "You may have other people fooled, but not me. I may be a team player at heart, but I can recognize special, and you aren't it—at least not in the right way. You know, there's no one who wants to work with you in this whole department—*no one*. That's something special, but these are good people, and it doesn't speak well of you. And your reputation for heavy-handedness is only part of it. I've been watching you, Galipoli, and I've seen the way you act while you're working this case. I don't know whether it was your time in the service, or what, but I don't like how you look at those case photos, and other people have noticed it too."

"You don't know me," Galipoli said. "None of you know shit about me."

"That's exactly my point," Morrison said. "You're not *present*, Galipoli. You stare off into space during meetings, and the first time you open your mouth, it's to criticize your fellow teammates. I know you have a service record, and I respect that; through everything I've tried to give you the benefit of the doubt. But this is a team—more of a family, really—and you need to get with the program."

"Thanks, but I already have a family," Galipoli sneered, "and this team of yours can't even do their job right. Now you done with me, Captain, or do you have more quotes to show me?"

"All right, asshole," Morrison said. "I see you aren't listening. If this weren't an all-hands-on-deck situation, hooks or no hooks, you'd be gone; and that's exactly what's going to happen, as soon as we get it cleared up. Now get the fuck out of my sight, and try to change my opinion of you."

20

L ater, Morrison stopped by at the Medical Examiner's Office to speak with the head of the DNA laboratory there.

James Fernandez was a retired FBI agent and scientist who'd come to work in the New York Medical Examiner's Office about ten years ago. He was one of the best FBI guys Bill had ever worked with over the years—meticulous, patient, and, most importantly, easy to get along with. He'd been a friend of Morrison's for years now.

When Morrison walked in, the tension must have been visible on his face. Fernandez welcomed him in with a concerned expression.

"Bill, are you okay?" he asked, almost immediately once they were inside.

"Yeah, I'm fine," Morrison answered, none too convincingly, "but I need a favor."

"Anything you need, you know I'll do my best."

"I know it." Morrison grimaced. "It's about the DNA for my case."

"Bill, aside from the latest murder, your Crime Scene samples have been ready for several days now," Fernandez said. "We ran everything through the DNA Databank and CODIS already—no matches. Didn't your guys tell you that?"

"Yeah, they did," Morrison said. "I actually need something else.

My guys just dropped off some possible DNA from two suspects up in Boston. Have you seen it yet?"

"No, not yet."

"Well, I need that material tested and run against my previous stuff, and I need answers within the next three days."

"Three days?" Fernandez looked away, blowing out a long breath. "Bill, you're, uh—you're asking a pretty tough one here."

"I know, Jim, I know—and *you* know I wouldn't ask you if it didn't matter. My career depends on this."

Fernandez thought a moment, then nodded. "Okay, Bill—okay. No guarantees, but I'm going to really try to pull a rabbit out of my ass on this one for you."

"Thanks, Jim. I mean it, I really owe you one."

Fernandez laughed. "Well, do you really? You know, Bill, you're a fucked-up guy, but I remember when my son had his problems, and Amy and I both remember what you did for him. Do you?"

Morrison did. Some years back their son had come back from Iraq with a lot of demons and a new drinking habit, and had gotten picked up out of state, acting like a lunatic. Morrison, still in the midst of the turmoil surrounding his own son's death, had called in a favor to keep the guy out of jail, picked him up, and driven him off to the crayon farm himself, with Ricky screaming in the back of the car. Ricky had hated him at the time, but it had been a turning point in his life: now, after a lot of successful therapy, he lived on Staten Island with a family of his own and a very happy life.

"Well, that's what friends do," Morrison said simply.

"It was a lot more than that, to Amy and me," Fernandez said. "You were the only one there to show him any compassion, and I'll always owe you for it. If I have to stay all night every night to get these samples done on time, I will."

"Thanks a million, Jimmy. That's going to be critical for me. Now I just have to get Stan on board."

"Rosenthal? Why would he be any trouble?"

"He wouldn't; it's the case. I'm just going to need a little speed on processing it, is all."

"Wow, they really have you on the hot seat with this one, huh?"

"Man, you better believe it."

"Well, count on me, Bill. I'll do my best."

On his way out, Morrison dialed up Assistant District Attorney Stan Rosenthal.

Stan was another old friend, a straight shooter from way back who'd worked on countless cases with Morrison and his team. Morrison knew his help would be as indispensable as Fernandez's in this situation; he'd need both men's help to take the case down quickly enough to satisfy the powers that be.

"Stan Rosenthal, Manhattan District Attorney's Office—how can I be of service?"

Morrison smiled. As long as he'd known Stan, the ADA had answered the phone as though he were brand-new to the job.

"Hey, Stan, Bill Morrison here," he said.

"Hey, Bill, good to hear your voice," Rosenthal said affably. "I was wondering when I'd get this call."

"I'm sure you were. Stan, I'll cut to the chase: I'm in real need of your help."

"So it sounds, my friend. I just hung up with Sergeant Rivera a few minutes ago; sounds like we've got a real winner here. Let me put it together here: two rich kids from Connecticut are your primary suspects. Your guys have surveillance footage from the area around the homicide, and have two guys who fit their physical description, but it needs to be enhanced to lock them in. On the other hand, we're sure the car in at least one video is the one registered to one of our suspects. We have matching DNA in the first three cases, but the results for number four aren't in yet, nor have we confirmed matching DNA from the suspects yet. We've had them under surveillance for a few days now, but we aren't quite sure if they were in Boston during number four, as we didn't have eyes on them overnight. Am I missing anything?"

"Only the hard part," Morrison said.

"Okay, what's that?"

"I've been given a three-day reprieve from the PC to get this done, and after that you'll be dealing with a new task force commander."

"Oh, really?" the ADA said in a low tone. "Well, I guess that explains the call the DA got from your Chief of Detectives earlier today."

"What?"

"Yeah, Arndt called the big guy upstairs, who in turn called me. Thankfully the DA likes me, so he let me know that Arndt wants your head on a stick, and mine too, if possible, since he knows I'm a friend."

"Shit," Morrison said. "I should've expected he'd try to jam us up. So what'd the big guy tell him?"

"He told him the office of the District Attorney was here to protect the judicial system and wouldn't impede the investigation or slow the process for anyone." Rosenthal laughed. "In other words, he politely told him to fuck off."

Bill breathed a sigh of relief. "Thank God for that."

"Yeah, well, we have enough problems as it is," Rosenthal said. "Honestly, can the ME's office have those suspect samples done and compared to the crime scenes in time?"

"Well, hopefully; I just spoke to Jimmy Fernandez—he's a good friend—and he said he'd do everything in his power to make it happen."

"That's good news. Calling in your favors today, huh, Bill?"

"You know it."

"How about the fingerprints?"

"Those are at our lab for processing. We could get that match back even sooner, with any luck."

"All right." Rosenthal cleared his throat. "Listen, Bill, this case is still going to be tough, without statements from these guys. The forensic evidence is definitely really good, *if* it turns out to be them—but a statement would seal the deal."

"I know. We're already making plans to snatch them up in Boston as soon as we get anything back."

"I figured you would be. Let's just be sure we do this right, okay? Let me know when things come through from the lab, and if you can get them to make a statement in Boston, I'll make sure I'm standing by to get arrest warrants done so they can hold them there without any hangup."

It was what Morrison had been waiting for. "Stan, you're the best."

Rosenthal laughed again. "I know I am," he said, and the two hung up.

21

Back at the stationhouse, the clock was ticking.

This was the worst part of the job: the waiting game. Word from the forensic lab, word from the Medical Examiner's Office, word from McNamara in Boston—until they heard from one or another of these, virtually nothing could be done but sit there and sweat. Morrison felt like an inmate on death row, waiting for the Governor's pardon—and equally unsure it would ever come.

Suddenly, Sergeant Rivera pushed open the door to his office.

"Cap, you got Captain Johnson from the lab on the phone for you," he said in a rush.

Morrison grabbed the phone. "Send it in," he said.

The phone barely had a chance to ring. "Give me some good news, Tom," Morrison said.

"What—no good morning, Bill?"

"Come on, Tom, don't break my balls; you know I need this."

Captain Johnson laughed. "Sorry, Bill, I know," he said. "I think you'll like this, though. We got prints off both your bottles, and they match some of what we recovered from the first three crime scenes."

"Bingo!" Morrison shouted in exultation, almost dropping the phone. In ten seconds, he'd just gone from death-row inmate to king of the world.

Rivera, still standing in the doorway, pumped his fist in silent relief.

Morrison recovered his composure. "Thank you, Tom—thank you."

"Thought you'd appreciate that," Johnson said. "We're still working on number four, but three gives you something to tag these guys on."

"That's terrific, Tom. If you'll excuse me, I have another couple of calls to make."

"I figured you would, Bill. Talk soon."

"Definitely. Thanks again, Tom."

Morrison hung up, and turned to Rivera. "Get me Stan Rosenthal in the DA's office, and get the team ready to travel. We're going to Boston."

"Hell yes." Rivera beamed. "I'll put him through in a second."

"Hey, Bill, what's the news?" Rosenthal asked when they'd gotten hold of him.

"We've got a fingerprint match on both suspects. They were at the crime scene."

"That's fantastic!"

"Tell me about it."

"And the DNA? How about that?"

"No word yet—hopefully we'll have it by tomorrow."

"All right, the fingerprints will do for now. So what's your plan?"

"I'm going to take a team up to Boston today, and speak to these two."

"All right. Wow, that turned around quick!"

"As it does."

"As it does, is right. Well, that's great news, Bill. I'll prepare arrest warrants and be ready for your call."

"Thanks, Stan."

"You know, it couldn't have come at a better time, either—your boy Arndt came by a little while ago, ranting and raving about you again."

This time Morrison could laugh. "Oh, did he?"

"Yeah, I guess he wasn't satisfied with how his call with the DA had gone. Man, that guy really has it in for you!"

"Well, he's going to be disappointed to hear this, then. Thanks again, Stan—I gotta go."

"No problem. Good luck in Boston—we'll be waiting on your call."

As Morrison hung up, he heard the door to the squad room swing open. As though on cue, in walked Chief of Detectives Arndt with a stiff, businesslike air. He slammed Morrison's door shut behind him.

"Captain, I need to speak to you, now," he said.

"Okay, Chief," Morrison said. "What is it?"

"You're relieved of command," Arndt declared.

"I see," Morrison answered. "And on whose authority?"

"Mine," Arndt smirked. "Frankly, I've had enough of your bullshit, Captain. You've been abusing your people, and that is intolerable."

Galipoli, Morrison thought with disgust. *Of course he'd complain to Arndt.* But one thing at a time.

"Well, Chief, if that's what you want," Morrison sighed.

"It most certainly is. I take abuse of personnel very seriously."

"Sure, I understand. I mean, I was just getting the team ready to go to Boston to pick up our serial-murder suspects, but you seem like you've made up your mind."

Arndt froze. "What—what are you talking about?" he stammered.

"Well, I just got off the phone with the lab, and we have multiple print hits on our suspects. We were heading out to grab them today."

"What suspects?" Arndt asked, confused.

"Well, obviously it isn't important," Morrison said. "If you'll excuse me, I'd better get started on cleaning out my desk, for whoever's taking my place."

"All right, stop, stop," Arndt said. "You're not relieved—only, why wasn't I briefed on this sooner?"

"We only got this break within the last hour," Morrison explained. "Why do you think I haven't acted on it until now?"

The Chief's mood changed instantaneously. "I knew you could do it," he said ingratiatingly. Morrison could already see him itching to call the PC and pat himself on the back. Morrison glared at him.

"Well, first of all, I *didn't* do it," he said through clenched teeth. "A task force of talented men and women did it. It's *teamwork*, Arndt— something men like you and your boy Galipoli never seem to understand."

Arndt wasn't listening. He turned and walked out of the office, already dialing his phone. "I got them, Commissioner," they heard him saying as he walked out. "Yes, that's right. Can you hold off on the press conference? We're heading up to Boston to pick them up now."

Once he was gone, the detectives in the squad room had a good laugh at his expense. Morrison came out to join them, but suddenly felt a nauseous feeling run through him. He sat, feeling a tingling running down his arm as he did. Sergeant Simmons walked in, just in time to see him putting a hand to the tightness in his chest.

"Hey Cap, you okay?" he asked. "You don't look so good."

"I'm fine," Morrison told him, waving him off. "Just some chest pain. I probably just need a drink."

"I'm serious, man, maybe you should get to the hospital," Simmons insisted.

"No chance," Morrison insisted. "We've got to get to Boston and grab these two—I'm *not* missing out on that. Besides, Winston Churchill worked through a heart attack, and if that's what I'm having, I'll be fine. My kids are covered. But just so you guys know," he added to the rest of the room, "if I do go, I want an Inspector's funeral. Remember that. If I don't get one, I'll haunt your asses."

"All right, all right," Simmons conceded.

As Morrison was getting the task force together for a briefing on their way out to Boston, Tamika put through a call from Commissioner Harrington. Morrison picked up, glad to have good news.

"Bill—do we have these guys?" Harrington asked.

"Just about," Morrison said. "We've got positive print hits on both subjects, putting them at the scene for the first three murders. We're still waiting on the DNA. I'm about to brief my team before we head up to Boston."

"So you aren't ready for a press conference just yet?"

"No, Sir, we aren't."

"Glad I called, then," Harrington said. "I have Arndt flipping out, telling me he's got the guys and calling for a press conference ASAP."

Morrison laughed. "Typical. No, we need to get to Boston and talk to these guys first—hopefully we'll get some statements to tie them up nice and tight."

"All right. Bill," Harrington went on, "you said your print evidence tied them to the first three murders. Do you think these guys are responsible for all four?"

"Still up in the air," Morrison said. "I can tell you this, though: if the fourth isn't them, we may have a problem. No one outside of this taskforce knew about the stuff they'd used in the other three murders, so unless these guys told someone else what they were doing, or one of them did something on his own, I'm at a loss right now about it."

"Okay, well, let me know the minute I can release something—the mayor and this city want answers."

"Of course, Commissioner. You're my first call, once these guys talk. I've got the best interview people in the world going with me, and we've got search warrants going through for Greenwich and their dorm rooms."

"Good. Tell all your people thank you, from me. We'll have a Jameson when this all goes down. I miss the good old days—my whole life's so political now. And listen, call me on my private line or cell phone. I don't need Arndt any more involved in this than he is already."

"I understand, Commissioner."

The two old friends hung up, and Morrison emerged to get his team briefed.

The whole group was ready to go—Simmons and Rivera, the Coke Brothers, Tina Koreski and her unlikeable partner Galipoli, Garriga, and Medveded. Everyone knew his role, and was prepared for a long couple of days. It would be important to try to get an incriminating statement out of one or both of their Boston dirtbags; courts couldn't always be trusted with mere forensic evidence, and in the case of guys like these two—no prior records, wealthy families, well educated—a steadfast profession of innocence could still be a serious problem.

Morrison brought Koreski with him in his car, and their four-hour ride began with a lot of talk about the case. He was pleasantly surprised at how much detail Tina had absorbed about the case; he'd never doubted her ability, but it was clear she'd come a long way since joining them. It wasn't long, though, before her talk turned to another familiar subject.

"I gotta talk to you about this Galipoli guy again, Cap," she said. "I know you've gotten a lot of complaints about him, including from me, but—"

"Let me guess," Morrison said. "You can't work with him either?"

"No, Cap, it isn't that. I know he's got a service record, and I'm trying to give him a chance. But the way he's been with this case, it's just been really scary. I mean, he actually scares me—especially with what I've been through, I've kind of got a sixth sense about people, men in particular."

"I believe it. So what do you mean, the way he's been? Like, with how he looks at the photos and stuff?"

"Yeah, that, and some of the comments he's made."

"Such as—?"

"Crazy shit. Like, talking about the victims, he'll say they must have really pissed these guys off, and that they were lucky because it might have been worse. He's said a few things that even made it sound like he admired what they did. Fucked up stuff, Cap. The guy just isn't right."

Hearing his own words echoed back to him gave Morrison pause. "How does he act towards you, Koreski?"

"Oh, like a total douchebag. I mean, he's so self-absorbed, all he talks about most of the time is himself; but he still thinks every woman wants him, me included. He even had the balls to tell me, *Hey, you may be into women, but I know you'd love to get me in bed.* Arrogant son of a bitch."

"Has he made you feel threatened?"

"Not particularly yet, outside of the way he talks about our victims.

But I could see it turning real fast."

Morrison considered. He knew he had to take at least some of this with a grain of salt. The guy was definitely an asshole, and probably a bit fucked up from his time in the military; but realistically, it was a pretty slim chance that *any* cop—no matter how much of an asshole he was, or how bad his PTSD—could admire what had been done to their victims. Still, coming as it did from his team, Morrison had to take it seriously.

"I'll pay more attention to his actions," he said finally. "Once we sew this case up and we don't need the extra manpower, we ought to have a better shot at getting rid of him. For now, though," he added, "let's focus on grabbing these two in Boston. I have a feeling that'll solve a lot of our problems at once."

22

Morrison and his team arrived in Boston around five. Traffic wasn't quite as bad as it was during rush hour in New York, but it was close. When they were within city limits, he called Sergeant McNamara to ask him if there'd been any movement.

"None at all, boss. Our guys came out to grab some stuff from the local store, but they've been cooped up inside ever since."

"All right. We have every exit covered, right?"

"Absolutely—the extra guys you sent made a big difference," McNamara confirmed. "Everything's covered this time. And hey, I've been speaking to a Detective Lieutenant from District D-14 of the BPD—really good guy—his name's Francis Donohue! Can you believe that, boss? What're the chances, huh?"

"He must be smiling down on us from above," Morrison smiled. "Is he the one helping us out on this?"

"Yeah, one of them. But you'll be meeting with Lieutenant Wayne Polk—he's all set to meet with our team at their Brighton location, at 301 Washington Street. He also hooked us up with the Boston College PD, and they'll be at the meeting too. They've really helped us out with making sure we had places to do our surveillance from without standing out like a sore thumb."

"Great. And you? Can you break away for the meeting without hurting our coverage at the dorm?"

"Sure, Cap, no problem. I'll meet you there in twenty minutes or so."

Morrison pulled up in front of the D-14 stationhouse, just a minute ahead of the rest of his team, and smiled at what he saw. The outside looked about as different from a New York stationhouse as it could have. The building was a welcoming, tan brick structure, with a wide granite staircase leading up to the front door. Above the door protruded a white second-story porch, surrounded by a white railing; and all around the building was a nearly block-sized lawn of nicely manicured, picturesque grass.

"Far cry from what we're used to, huh, Cap?" Koreski asked.

"I wonder if they'll send out a butler for us," Morrison joked.

Once he and his team were through the front door, though, they saw enough similarities to the stationhouses back at home to feel at ease. The interior was worn and battered-looking with use, and the desk supervisor on duty looked like he was having the kind of day that most patrol supervisors were used to. At the moment he was wearily answering the questions of a pair of young officers who seemed as though they had yet to find their way to the locker room, much less the streets of Boston. It was a pretty universal annoyance for desk supervisors; the academy could only teach recruits so much, after which point the responsibility almost always devolved on the desk supervisor on duty. As a result, they tended to become surlier the longer they worked the desk; and it was clear to Morrison that this supervisor had been doing it a long time.

As Morrison approached the desk and held out his shield, a look of relief passed over the supervisor's face. He dismissed the two young cops immediately.

"Good day, boss," Morrison said, showing the customary deference. Although he outranked the supervisor, he was in their house.

"Good day, Captain." The desk supervisor smiled, immediately recognizing Morrison's New York accent. "What brings the NYPD up to Boston?"

"We're here to see the detective squad commander."

"No problem—up the stairs, second door on your right."

Morrison and his group headed up the stairs into the detective squad room. Now this was what he was used to. People in suits, jackets off, sat all around the room, busily working on computers and talking on the phone, dealing with their case loads. One man looked up from his computer, and stood to greet the captain.

"Detective Lee Sherman," he said, offering his hand. "Can I help you guys?"

"Captain Bill Morrison. One of my sergeants, Pat McNamara, has been talking to your boss—is he in?"

"Sure, come this way."

Detective Sherman led them into a briefing room, and had them take a seat. In a few minutes, a tall, powerful-looking man entered the room. Morrison and his people began to stand, but he held up his hand.

"Please, don't get up for me—you guys must be tired after your trip up," he said affably. He extended a hand to Morrison. "Captain Morrison? Lieutenant Wayne Polk. Nice to meet you."

"Same here," Morrison said. "We really appreciate your help on this one."

"No problem. Always glad to get a couple of psychos off the street. From what I've heard, these guys have been a real pair for you, huh?"

"Yeah, they've definitely made our lives miserable for a while now," Morrison agreed. "I'm just glad they didn't do anything up this way as well."

The door opened again, and Sergeant McNamara walked in. Lieutenant Polk greeted him like an old friend.

"Pat! Glad you could make it," he said. Morrison made a mental note to thank McNamara later. The police fraternity was always open, but out-of-town visitors' behavior still always determined the level of cooperation they received, and it was clear to Morrison that McNamara had done an excellent job of keeping on good terms with their Boston allies.

Lieutenant Polk sat and turned back to Morrison. "Sergeant McNamara has fully briefed me on what's going on," he said, "and I wanted you to know, I've requested the assistance of the BPD Special Operations Division. I know this is just going to be a voluntary request to bring these guys back to the stationhouse, but if things go badly, it's always nice to have the guys in heavy vests ready to help out."

"Agreed," Morrison said. "If we can get them to come out voluntarily, that'll be enough for me—I'd just rather not have to go in after them, with all the other students inside."

"All right. We'll leave that to you guys; McNamara says you have an idea of how that'll go down. How about warrants?"

"Our ADA, Stan Rosenthal, has got arrest warrants drawn up for both of them. He's holding off on presenting them to the judge, in hopes that we can get statements out of them voluntarily."

"Okay, great. We'll follow your lead—we'll make sure we have guys covering the whole dorm while you pick them up. I assume you'll be stationed in the lobby?"

"Yes, that's the plan."

"You think they'll come quietly?"

"I think so. We have reason to think they're probably going to try to play it cool, so if we pick them up casually they may come back without any trouble. They've gotten over the system their whole lives; hopefully that cockiness will work in our favor this time."

"Well, then, you just let me know what you need, and I'll make sure it's there." Lieutenant Polk smiled. "It sounds like these are definitely your guys, so let's make sure they don't go anywhere we don't want them to."

Back at the BC dorm, all of the entrances were indeed well covered by the time Morrison and the rest of his team arrived. Morrison had occasion again to appreciate the BPD's help: both his people and a number of Boston detectives were stationed inconspicuously around the whole building, and even with his trained eye, Morrison had to have a few of their surveillance spots pointed out to him.

Lieutenant Polk had been true to his word. Two blocks away, a BPD SWAT team was standing by in a tactical vehicle, and sharpshooters had been deployed to the roofs of two adjacent buildings, just in case. Morrison was hopeful that they wouldn't be necessary, but knew from experience that the Lieutenant's precautions were completely reasonable. Chance favored the prepared mind, as Morrison was fond of saying; and with every suspect—especially two whom they suspected of such heinous crimes as these—you had to expect the unexpected.

The hope was for one or both of the suspects to exit the dorm, where a group of NYPD and BPD detectives would approach them and try to persuade them to come back to D-14 voluntarily. Although no mention of a firearm had been made during any of their investigations, these two were suspected of being a couple of the most violent preppies ever to don an alligator shirt, and nobody knew what a knock at their dorm-room door might bring about. A lot of perps did extreme things when they found they were being brought to justice for the crimes they'd committed, and in a dorm setting, there was no telling how many people these two could hurt if they decided to go out in a blaze of glory.

After several hours had passed without movement on the part of their suspects, the decision was made to try to lure one or both of them out to Anderson's car. Pat McNamara was the best voice actor among them, so he made the phone call to their room. Someone picked up on the second ring.

"Hello," McNamara said, in a remarkably subtle Indian accent. "This is Dr. Patel from the Boston Health Department. Is this Mr. Brian Anderson?"

"No," the voice on the other end replied flatly. "This is his roommate."

"Do you know where Mr. Anderson is right now?" McNamara asked.

"Sure, he's right here—hold on."

McNamara gave a thumbs-up—both suspects were in the apartment.

"Hello?" Anderson's voice sounded nervous.

"Mr. Anderson, this is Dr. Patel from the Boston Health Department," McNamara went on. "We need to see you as soon as possible. We have had one of your girlfriends here with a serious venereal disease, and it would be in your best interests if you could come in right away."

"What? What do you mean, serious?"

"I'd rather not discuss it with you over the phone, Mr. Anderson."

McNamara could practically hear Anderson quaking over the phone. "Is it—is it AIDS?"

"Again, Mr. Anderson, I'd really rather not talk about it over the phone. We need to see you in person."

"Okay—okay. I'll jump in the shower and be right down. What was the address?"

As McNamara read off the address, the rest of the team went quietly into action. Fifteen minutes later, they were waiting in the dorm lobby as both Anderson and Rutherford came out of the elevator. Before they could exit the lobby, a few of the detectives approached them.

"Brian Anderson and Adam Rutherford," one of the BPD detectives said, "I'm Detective Manchester. We'd like to talk to you about something, if we may."

"We're on our way somewhere. What's this about?" Rutherford asked, in an almost condescending tone.

"We just want to talk to you about some criminal activity in New York City—it shouldn't take long."

This was the do-or-die moment. If the two refused to cooperate, the detectives would have to take them into custody, and things could get ugly really fast. Anderson looked over at his friend; there was no way *he* was going to make the decision on his own. Rutherford took the lead.

"No problem, officer," he said, his tone dropping into a practiced smugness. "We'll help out any way we can."

The two were separated, and taken to D-14 in different cars.

On the ride to the stationhouse, both were read their Miranda rights, despite not being under arrest yet; Morrison didn't want to take any chances. It was another critical moment, as one of the pro-visions offered them the use of an attorney, but once again, neither Anderson nor Rutherford disappointed. Both waived their rights, and were willing to talk.

Morrison had decided in advance that Alexander Medveded would be the first to talk to Anderson, while Rutherford would be left with Kasak and Marchioni. Medveded always preferred to work alone in these situations, as he took a more cerebral approach to the interview process, and didn't want to have anyone else there to distract or derail him. The Coke boys, on the other hand, invariably worked as a pair, playing off of each other in a classic good-cop-bad-cop partnership.

As Morrison later learned, the two car rides were very different for their two suspects.

Adam Rutherford was actually rather chatty with Tina Koreski and the BPD's Detective Manchester, with whom he rode back to the stationhouse. Perhaps it would be better to say he chatted *at* them than with them, as Koreski remained quiet through the whole ride to keep her New York accent to herself for the time being. He went on for a while about who his family was and who they knew—greasing the skids, as he seemed confidently to expect, for his eventual release.

Brian Anderson, on the other hand, was extremely quiet; and Detective Medveded, who rode next to him, observed his eyes welling up a number of times. Anderson turned his head a few times, stifling his sobs under coughs or clearings of the throat, but it was already far too late for these shows of emotion to go unobserved. Alexander Medveded's chess match with this opponent had already begun.

23

By the time Alexander Medveded stepped into the interview room at District D-14, Brian Anderson had been expertly prepared. On top of Medveded's silence in the car on the way over, he'd instructed the BPD detectives to bring Anderson past the holding cells, where the overnighters were being held. That spectacle was enough to scare anyone: cells crammed full of sick, angry people, deranged with hostility and screaming at anyone who passed. For a quiet little rich white boy like Anderson, it had been sufficient to get the tears flowing again.

Now, like a conductor before a performance, Medveded paused outside the interview-room door, took a breath, and went in. Before he could even sit down, Anderson opened his mouth.

"Look, it's not like it's my fault," Anderson blurted out. Medveded was a little disappointed; he hadn't even touched a chess piece yet, and his opponent had already revealed his primary weakness. But none of this made it onto the detective's face. With a casual nod, made without looking in the suspect's direction, he slowly sat down.

"I completely get it," Medveded said gently, favoring Anderson with an empathic look, "and I want you to know that I appreciate your cutting to the chase. It's going to be a lot easier to help you that way. If you were to ask me, I'd say you look like a bit player in all this."

"All—this?" Anderson said, catching himself.

"Yes, all this," Medveded said patiently.

"I don't know what you're talking about," Anderson backtracked. "What is it exactly that you want to ask me about?"

This time Medveded allowed his disappointment to show. "Come on, Brian," he said. "You know as well as I do, what this is about. The women, Brian."

"What women?"

"Well, let's start with the one on Sutton Place in Manhattan, shall we?"

Anderson sat quietly, refusing to speak; but Medveded could see the horror of that night playing itself out behind his eyes.

"Look," he said, moving his chair closer to Anderson's side of the table, "I can tell it upset you. It's obvious that it did. I've seen a lot of killers—all ages, classes, and colors—and I can see you're no killer. But you're going to have to meet me halfway; that's why we separated you guys, so we could get a straight story from you. I can help you out here, believe me; and with the truth out in the open, I think we can get past what happened together—because you are *not* the guy who started this. Am I right?"

Anderson sniffed and looked down at the table, despondent. "Yeah, that's right," he said finally. "Adam was the one—it was Adam's idea."

"Right, that much is obvious," Medveded said dismissively. "When did he get the idea to do this?"

Anderson sat quietly again, silent tears rolling down his cheeks. Medveded touched his hand. Anderson recoiled.

"Why would I talk to you?" he said, suddenly vehement. To his surprise, Medveded laughed, shaking his head pityingly.

"Look, why do you think *I'd* want to talk to *you*?" he asked. "The investigation is already over. Do you think we came to your dorm *not knowing* what had happened? Not a chance, Brian. But we need to give everyone a chance to speak for themselves—especially in a situation like this one, where there is more than one person involved, and it's all too easy to pin everything equally on both of them. If you don't think that's how it went down—like *I* don't—you need to hear both sides of the story. But look, Brian, if you trust Adam that much, by all means, don't speak with me, and whatever he tells us will be what happened. I believe you, when you say it isn't your fault—I've seen too much to disbelieve you. Adam is obviously a nasty guy, and he obviously has a problem with women. But taking it for granted that he was in charge, when did this—thing—of his start?"

Anderson looked at him hard. "Did Adam speak to you already?" he asked.

"He's talking to one of the other detectives. I don't imagine they're having a great time with him—I believe you're telling the truth, but it's hard to believe Adam's capable of it. He's a good-looking, tall, young guy, and he's always gotten over. It's easy to see that he hasn't really *had* to learn honesty."

Anderson turned his eyes back to the table, but his face had taken on a new expression. Medveded knew his next move would put Brian in check, so he played it carefully.

"Come on, Brian," he said. "Are you going to put up with it again? How many times in your life have you been blamed for something that was all his idea?"

Anderson looked up at him, a different kind of hard passion blazing in his eyes. "Not this time," he said. He shook his head. "Not again. It doesn't work for me anymore."

"That's why we're here," Medveded said. "Take your time, Brian. Start from as far back as you need to."

Anderson wiped his face with his hands, and looked away again. "We've been friends since we were kids," he said. "He's always pushed me around. This thing—well, we always take our Christmas breaks together. We've done that for as long as I remember. This year we started out in Cancun, but we had six weeks off, so we made a stop over in La Jolla, you know, California?"

"Of course," Medveded said patiently.

"So we stop in this little grill along the road, in San Diego," Anderson went on. "Old Town. You know where I'm talking about?"

"Yeah," Medveded said. "A lot of rich people there."

"Exactly. Anyway, we were having a few drinks at the bar, and there's this woman on the other side. Looking at her, you could tell she had money. Good-looking, blonde hair, big tits, a little older but well put-together. Turns out she lived in a place right by the PCH. So Adam decides to start talking to her. He walks over, usual Mr. Big Shit stuff, and she blows him off."

"Is that how it began?"

"Yeah. I mean, she *really* blew him off. Like, made him look like two cents in front of a bunch of people. He was really pissed off. So he comes back over to where I'm sitting, and goes, *Come on, we're out of here.* I figure, okay, whatever he says—guy's obviously pretty embarrassed. So we get outside and jump in the car, and Adam can't stop talking about what a bitch she is, and how he's going to teach her a lesson, she doesn't know who she just fucked with, et cetera. We must have sat there another hour in the car, him just blowing off steam."

"Okay."

"So then she comes strolling out of the place, looking like she'd had a few too many. She gets in her pretentious little fucking two-seater Porsche, and we follow her out of the parking lot. I figure he's just going to fuck with her a little while she's driving, but he just stays behind her all the way to her house."

"He followed her home?"

"Yeah. We watched her pull into her driveway. She looked wasted—she stumbled through her front door. We watched her house for a little while, then Adam decided she was home alone." Anderson's expression darkened as he looked back at Medveded. "He decided—not my idea—*he* decided we were going to knock on her door."

"And you? What'd you say?"

"I was really scared. I was like, *Adam, what the fuck are we doing here?* He just told me to shut up and follow his lead. We banged on her door—it must've taken her five minutes to answer it." Medveded noticed that Anderson's voice had fallen into a distant monotone. "When she got to the door, she was still in her clothes, but she looked really drunk. Adam started talking to her, and grabbed her arm. She wasn't as wasted as we thought. She remembered Adam from the restaurant. She asked him why he was at her house, and he said that she'd left her credit card and we stopped to drop it off on the way home. She said I thought I took my card. She turned to check her purse, and that was when Adam pushed her inside. He started choking her. She kicked him in the balls, and tries to run down the hall. Adam tells me to grab her, so I chase her down the hall and grabbed her hair and pulled her down. She started screaming, and Adam ran over and covered her mouth with his hand. She was wearing a real short red dress and he pulled it up over her waist. She bit him on the hand, and he lost it. He tore her underwear off and stuffed it in her mouth to stop her from screaming. That's how he started." Anderson paused, his face a mask. "Can I have some water?"

"Of course," Medveded said, moving swiftly to the door to call for a bottle of water. He knew this moment was critical—he needed to keep Anderson talking, and give him as little time as possible to think about what was happening. "Water's on the way, Brian—can you remember what happened next? I know sometimes it's hard to remember—"

"No, I remember fine," Anderson said. Medveded noted just the subtlest hint of braggadocio in his voice. "She started to calm down—I guess she figured she couldn't fight her way out with both of us holding her down. Adam had this look in his eyes—he didn't say much, but I've seen that look before, and it always ended badly. It was never this bad before, though. He took the underwear out of her mouth, and started asking her questions about where she kept her money and jewelry in her house. She said she had a safe in the basement, and we could take everything she had. She starting telling us her husband would be home at any minute, but looking around the house it didn't seem like anyone else lived with her. She was crying, totally scared. I went to check the closets and there were no men's clothes anywhere. Adam called her a lying bitch—*First you bite me, and then you lie to me,* he says—and that's when he really went crazy. He had me hold her, and he went into the kitchen. He ripped out all the drawers, and came back with a plastic supermarket bag. He put the bag over her head and took off his belt, and started to choke her with the bag over her head. He kept tightening and releasing his belt, to kind of control her breathing."

"Did you ever try to stop him, or leave the house without him?"

"No," Anderson said. "He's my best friend, even though he was acting crazy. And I couldn't leave him alone."

"I understand," Medveded said, betraying no emotion. The son of a bitch had just locked himself in as a willing accomplice.

One of the Boston detectives came in and handed Medveded two bottles of water. The interruption came at a good time; the flow of the interrogation was undisturbed. Medveded handed Anderson one of the bottles, and cracked the other open.

"Cheers," he said, raising his bottle with a slight smile.

"Cheers," Anderson replied, returning the smile.

No remorse there, Medveded thought. No one who felt any compunction for having done something like this could smile, much less return a toast, during their confession. It was as surefire a tell as the so-called "sleep of the guilty," when suspects fell fast asleep on the hard wooden benches in their cells almost as soon as their cell door had been shut.

"Right—so go on, what happened next?" Medveded asked.

"Well, we dragged her into the basement with the bag on her head. She looked terrified, but in a weird way I think she liked it. You know, one of those freaky chicks."

"And how many times did you have sex with her?"

"None. I mean, I guess I did, technically. But I didn't even want to do it at first—I even tried to take the bag off her head. Adam told her to blow me, and pushed her face at my crotch. I was afraid that she might bite me, but Adam had the belt around her neck and told her if she bit me, he'd kill her. Like a dog on a leash. They tend to do as they're told—it was kind of cool. She was good. I came down her throat and all over her hair. She was a freaky bitch—I'm telling you, she kind of liked it. I got a bit scared, because of all the CSI shows talking about DNA, but Adam said not to worry, because we didn't have any on file."

"And did he have sex with her too?"

Anderson gave a short, scoffing kind of laugh. "He tried, but he was having a little problem," he said. "Probably because he'd drank too much."

"So he couldn't get an erection," Medveded said.

Anderson laughed out loud.

"What's so funny?" Medveded asked, smiling along with him.

"Oh, just the word *erection*," Anderson said. "I just don't hear it much, and it makes me laugh. But yeah, he couldn't get an erection."

"Did that make him more angry?"

"Yeah, a lot more. He told me he wanted to get some jumper cables, and went into another room in the basement to try to find some."

"What did you do while he was gone?"

"Nothing, really. I just held the belt and made her crawl around on all fours like a dog, you know, just trying to keep her scared. He came back in and said he couldn't find any cables, but that these would do, and he held up a pair of pliers and a box cutter. She started screaming again, and he stuffed her panties back in her mouth. He tried to get it up and fuck her again, but it just wasn't happening, so he starts telling her it's her fault, because she's such an ugly whore, and starts biting her all over. He told me that if I wanted to be even with him I better do the same, and I didn't want to, but I did. He had the gag in her mouth and watched her face while he pulled at her pussy with the pliers. It was brutal, man; I couldn't really stand it. He really started biting her, really frantic, and I wanted to go. He tried to fuck her one more time and he just couldn't, and he lost it and cut off her lips. She passed out and I got some water and threw it on her and tried to revive her. We moved her to the couch; she was bleeding real bad. Then he put the bag over her head and made it so she stopped breathing. I didn't do that—he did that."

"That was our understanding of it, too," Medveded said evenly. "What'd you do while he was killing her?"

"I went upstairs to look for money, to make it look like a robbery. We got about four hundred dollars."

"Four hundred and forty, by the receipts we pulled up," Medveded said, making up a number.

Anderson shrugged. "I don't know; could have been," he said dismissively. "Anyway, when he was done Adam put the box cutter in her hand and wiped it off with a paper towel, and we got out of there. We got a room at some shitty little motel, cleaned up, and got out of California."

"Right, well, that makes sense with what we knew about the La Jolla incident," Medveded said, making sure his voice was edged with just the right tone of impatience. "The others are a bit more complicated, I expect."

"Not much," Anderson said with a slight yawn.

"Well, let's talk about that next," Medveded said calmly. Inside, it felt as though he was exploding. Not only had he just taken a confession on a crime none of them had been aware of, but he could sense Anderson's prideful detachment from the crimes he'd committed, and behind the impenetrable front of Medveded's empathy, he hated the young murderer. It was inexpressibly difficult, this part of the job—sitting in a room for hours with a person so reprehensible, they made you sick; listening to them recount horrific acts with cold indifference, all the while acting as though what they were saying was the most normal thing in the world to you. But Medveded had mastered it.

Anderson sat quietly a moment. Before he could get too into his thoughts, Medveded leaned in.

"You know, Brian," he went on, "we've seen a lot in this line of work, and in the grand scheme of things, what you did there? It wasn't so bad. Obviously, it was mainly Adam's doing, this whole thing, and your part in it was completely secondary—but besides that, you know, I get it." He dropped his voice to a confidential whisper, looking toward the door. "I mean, I know what it's like to grow up wealthy; I grew up in Lake Success, over in Long Island. Always had money in my pocket. And did *I* get respect from women? No. And why? Because deep down, they're all bitches, my friend." Anderson smiled slightly, nodding his head in agreement. Medveded continued. "Far as I'm concerned, they *all* deserve a little of that. You can't take it as far as your friend Adam did, but that wasn't you. And you said she enjoyed it—didn't you say that?"

"Yeah, I think she did," Anderson smirked.

"And the others?"

"Harder to say, but yeah, I think so."

"Well, I've got news for you, Brian," Medveded said, nodding. "They almost *all* do. It's not talked about, but it's true. Trust me, I've seen a lot of these types of cases, and I'm sure that if *you* thought they were enjoying it, it's because they were. But I'm getting off-topic," he said, allowing himself to appear the slightest bit flustered. "What happened when you guys got back to Boston?"

"Well, Adam got obsessed with what had happened in San Diego. I mean *obsessed*. He even went online and was researching murder and sex crimes from the past."

"So was that when you guys planned the New York murders?"

Anderson held up a finger. "*I* didn't. That was all Adam—he just kept telling me about all this stuff he was reading about, and what a rush it had been back in California. I didn't like how it had ended, but he said it'd be different. He kept saying the next woman would be better, prettier, sexier—he said we'd make sure she was someone who'd excite him."

"So tell me about the first," Medveded said.

"The one in Queens," Anderson said thoughtfully, to Medveded's secret gratification. So the Queens woman *had* been the first, as he'd suspected. "That was really similar to the San Diego one, actually; at least in how it started. We'd gone to see the tree in Rock Center that day. When we were leaving, driving down Fifth Avenue, this cute blonde cuts us off. Adam beeps at her, and she flips him the bird"—Anderson raised his middle finger demonstratively—"and suddenly it's like déjà vu all over again. Here we are, following this broad all the way to Queens. I know the area okay; I've got a few relatives in Jamaica Estates.

"So anyway, she pulls into her driveway. Her house is completely dark—no sign of life. Adam parked around the corner, near a house under construction, and we walked back to her house. We're waiting out front, kind of talking about what's going on—I just wanted to make sure it didn't go as far as the last one, but Adam was really getting excited—and she opens the front door. I think she was throwing something out. She was pretty startled; I mean, we were standing *right* in front of her door. She tried to slam it on us, but Adam was really fast, and I helped him, and together we were too strong." Anderson got a strange look. "We've always been a team, him and me. I mean, he was in charge of all this," he was quick to add, "but it's hard to stop helping someone when you're so used to it, you know?"

"Of course I know," Medveded said. "How do you think these police-brutality things happen, where there's more than one cop involved? You get one bad guy, doing one bad thing—how does anyone else go along with it? It's the camaraderie. You work, or live, or go to school with someone long enough, you can't just turn on them when things get complicated; it's just human nature. But please," he said, forcing another friendly smile, "go on."

After two and a half more hours of interviewing, Brian Anderson had confessed to four murders. One more to go, and Alex Medveded would have done his job to the absolute best of his ability. Not that he hadn't already; looking on from the next room, a number of detectives were all but taking notes on the techniques he'd been using. The man was an absolute artist—he'd been so convincing in the course of the interview, some of his own colleagues had caught themselves wondering whether he didn't have a side of himself he'd been hiding from them all along.

"So, Brian," Medveded was saying, as patiently and deliberately as in the beginning, "we have the woman in La Jolla, one in Jamaica

Estates, one on Sutton Place, and one on 63rd Street in Manhattan. I really appreciate your cooperation in telling me all this; it's going to be crucial in the case against Adam, and in helping you however we can. Now we just have one more to talk about: the woman from Twenty-First and Park Avenue South."

Anderson looked at Medveded like he'd suddenly sprouted a second head.

"What are you talking about?" he asked.

It was the closest Medveded came to betraying surprise in the whole interview, but he kept his composure. "Come on, Brian," he insisted. "We've really had an open communication between us over the last several hours. I feel like we understand each other really well. Don't tell me you're not going to tell me about this one, after all that?"

"I swear, I don't know what you're talking about," Anderson said, shaking his head vehemently. "We only did the ones I told you about—nothing else."

Now came the second real surprise for Detective Medveded: he felt instinctively that Brian was telling him the truth. Perhaps Adam had done this one on his own—? He decided to take Anderson's word, and feel out that possibility.

"Don't you think Adam could have done it without you? I mean, from what you told me, he was never able to perform while you were there anyway; you even said you'd started calling him Dead Dick, after the one in Queens."

Anderson laughed. "Yeah, that's right—he was a dead dick mother-fucker, all right. But I don't think he'd have done it on his own; I mean, I'm sure he *could* have," he caught himself, "but I just don't know when he would have done it without my knowing. I can't remember the last time we weren't together. When'd it happen, anyway?"

"Three days ago," Medveded said immediately, knowing the rapport he'd built with Anderson was worth infinitely more than the "*you* don't ask the questions, *I* ask the questions" stance a lot of cops would take.

"No way," Anderson said. "We haven't left Boston for a week."

"All right, I believe you," Medveded said, meaning it. His mind was racing. "Listen, Brian, can I get you something to eat? I know we've been at it a long time."

"Sure—I'm pretty hungry," Anderson agreed. "Something good."

"Sure—whatever you want," Medveded said. After everything Anderson had just given up, he'd buy him a goddamn steak dinner if he asked for it. "I'm going to grab someone to order for you; think about what you want in the meantime. And Brian," he said on his way to the door, "I think you appreciate that I've said some stuff in here that I would rather not have spread around. You know I'm here to help you; can I have your word that you won't repeat what I've said to you?"

Anderson smiled. Medveded could practically see the wheels in his head turning around the leverage he thought he had.

"Absolutely, Detective," he said. He put up his right hand in mock sincerity. "I swear it."

"Great. We're going to return you to the holding cell in the meantime, if that's all right with you."

"Of course." Anderson's face was conspiratorial, the face of someone used to being an accomplice.

Medveded let himself out. When the door closed behind him, he gestured to one of the BPD cops standing by.

"You can move him back to the cell," he said. "I'm done with him. Let's get him something to eat—just get him whatever he wants. Let's keep him comfortable and on our side for the time being, until we nail down his friend."

Medveded headed over to Polk's office, where Morrison was waiting for him.

"Well? How'd it go?" Morrison asked, knowing very well how it always went with Medveded.

"We got him, Cap," Medveded said. "He gave up everything."

"Incredible," Morrison said, marveling as much at the detective's modesty as at his superlative ability. However many hours in a room by himself with a sociopath, and the guy was still saying *we*. Consummate team player, that was for sure.

"One problem, though," Medveded added. "They didn't do the one in Gramercy."

"Are you sure?"

"Definitely."

"All right—well, shit." When Alexander Medveded was sure, there was no room for doubt. "Who the hell did it, then?"

"I don't know, and I'm pretty sure these guys won't be able to tell us," Medveded said. "But if we have a copycat still running around in New York, Cap, the clock's ticking."

24

While Medveded's interview with Anderson was underway, preparations were being made a few doors down for a very different line of questioning. As Adam Rutherford was led into his interrogation room, Captain Morrison was holding a last-minute briefing with the Coke Brothers when Tina Koreski walked in.

"Cap, can we talk about this?" she said. "I really want to talk to this guy. I wanted it before we got them, but since the ride back to the stationhouse, I'm convinced it's the right thing."

"Why do you say that?" Morrison asked.

"He wouldn't shut up on the ride back—he was trying to get all suave and sophisticated with me, talking all kinds of shit. I think that's going to be his weakness here."

Morrison turned to Kasak and Marchioni, who, as usual, had been standing there the whole time without saying a word.

"Would you wait outside the office for a moment?" he asked them.

They nodded placidly and walked out without dispute, secure in their assignment. For Morrison to hand over the interrogation to Koreski was unheard-of; it would be like swapping out a ten-time all-star for a utility player in a Series game.

"Tina," Morrison said once the door was closed, "we both know what happened to you. I wouldn't ever want you having a meltdown from someone bringing back those memories, but we *really* can't risk it happening now. This case is just too important for all of us."

Koreski was visibly struggling to hold back her anger. "Captain," she said carefully, "I'm not that woman. I can handle this, I know it. I need you to trust me on this."

"Of course I trust you. But even aside from all that, I already told the Coke boys that they'd get the first shot at this guy. I can't take that away from them; you know that."

"But if—"

"Enough," Morrison said firmly, holding up his hand. "Kasak and Marchioni get him first. If they struggle with the guy, you'll get your chance."

"All right," Koreski said through clenched teeth. Morrison opened the door and poked his head out.

"Okay, boys," he said to the two waiting outside. "Let the games begin."

Leo Kasak was the first to enter the room. The shorter of the Coke boys was nevertheless imposing. Built like a brick wall, he had the street-smart toughness to back it up. His family had come over from Poland to settle in the Greenpoint section of Brooklyn, where many Polish immigrants had settled before them; and he still remembered the late nights outside of bars on Humboldt where, as a young man, he would sit and watch as men brought their disputes out to settle them in the street. Back then they didn't use guns or knives, or even their fists; they quite literally used their heads. Squaring off outside the bar, they'd run head-on at each other like stags, slamming heads until one or the other of them couldn't get back up. Once the dispute was settled, they would invariably return to the bar together and buy each other a drink, with as little talk afterward of retribution as of post-concussion syndrome. In this old-fashioned atmosphere of honor and raw power, Kasak had come into his own, and it was easy to see him applying the philosophy still.

His partner, detective Michael Marchioni, was right behind him.

Mike was slightly overweight and balding, though he never seemed willing to accept the fact. He liked to say he had a receding hairline, and went to great lengths to keep what little hair he had left slicked back in an '80s tough-guy style to match his pencil moustache.

Like the rest of their shtick, the Coke Brothers' hardline persona had proven rather slow to adapt to changing times. They were certainly the oldest detectives on their Major Crimes squad, holdovers from the era of the Son of Sam and two-thousand-homicide years in the city. Legends in their own minds, they were extremely resistant to change—a fact that, for men who'd come into their own as cops during a time when the blackjack was a way of life, was sometimes a problem in a community that no longer accepted police brutality as part of the job.

Yet as Morrison knew—and as they continued to prove to their detractors—Marchioni and Kasak were generally quite good with the background details. They developed their cases slowly, often using tactics unique to themselves; but when they struck, it stuck. For this they were well known throughout the department, and beyond. Some called them the Old Bulls—a nickname that had its origin in a joke Bill Morrison sometimes told to explain them to newcomers. *An old bull and a young bull are sitting on a hill, overlooking a herd of cows. Let's run down and fuck one of those cows, the young bull says excitedly; to which the old bull calmly replies, Let's walk down and fuck them all.*

They found Adam Rutherford sitting comfortably in the interview room when they entered. He looked up at them with a smug smile when they sat down, and both could tell immediately that Rutherford would be a tougher nut to crack than his friend down the hall.

Kasak was the first to speak, in the agreeable, old-friends-reuniting tone with which he began every interview. It was the easiest way to size up a suspect, and invite them to reveal any weaknesses or tells that might give the interviewer leverage. For now, Marchioni sat silently beside him, notepad at the ready.

"Hello, Adam," he said. "I'm Detective Leo Kasak, and this is my partner, Mike Marchioni. We'd like to talk to you today about some things that happened recently in New York City."

Rutherford shifted in his seat, pulling himself back from the table where he'd been leaning. The Coke Brothers took mental note: it was tell number one.

"Ask away detective," he said confidently. "I have no problem answering any questions you might have. Though I'm not sure what you'd want to hear about from me, unless it's what parties I've attended there, or how many girls I've fucked."

Kasak smiled, unshaken by the ugly turn in Rutherford's tone. "So, you do visit New York City, then?" he asked, maintaining his civil tone.

"Sure. Doesn't everyone who's anyone visit it?"

Answering questions with questions was usually a stall tactic, making time to think of what to say next. Kasak made note of that, too.

"And you'd say you usually visit the city to party?" he asked.

"Yeah, like I—"

"Have you been to Sutton Place, over the past several months?" Kasak asked quickly, throwing Rutherford off-guard. Rutherford looked away. Marchioni scribbled something on his notepad.

"Where's that?" Rutherford asked obliquely. "I've never heard of it."

"Upper East Side. You know—lots of pretty women, known for nice buildings with expensive price tags."

"I don't know, I guess I might have been."

"That's a pretty nice car you have," Kasak said, changing topic.

"Damn right it is," Rutherford said under his breath.

"I'm sorry?"

Rutherford smirked. "I said yes, it is."

"How long have you had it?"

"Couple of years now."

"Got it new?"

"Of course. You think I'm buying used?"

"Does anyone else ever use it, besides you?"

"What are you, crazy? No one touches my things. That's why they're mine."

"I see," said Kasak. "So when you visit the city, where do you go?"

"I don't know—we just tool around looking for cool things to do."

"'We'? Who's we?"

"Myself and Brian Anderson, the guy you have in the next room."

"How long have you two been friends?"

"As long as I can remember, pretty much."

"And do you often visit the city together?"

"Whenever I'm there, I'm there with him."

"But you don't let him use your car."

Rutherford gave a little laugh. "Like I said, Detective, he's always with me. He never needs to use my car, because I'm the one driving us. Aren't you listening?"

Kasak returned his smile, striving to keep down his disgust. This kid was going to be tricky.

"All right," he said evenly. "Fair enough. Let's talk a little about the places you've visited in the city, shall we?"

Bill Morrison watched with concern through the two-way mirror of the interview room. It had been an hour already, and Rutherford hadn't slipped up once—a fact that was obviously beginning to wear on his interviewers' composure. The pace of the interview had accelerated noticeably, and particularly with Marchioni, it was starting to look as though the Coke Brothers' old-school patience was about to give way to their old-school ruthlessness.

Morrison cursed under his breath. Why hadn't he had Medveded do this guy? He'd known Rutherford was going to be more difficult to break; what the hell had he been thinking? Alex had the patience to play cat-and-mouse for hours; Leo and Mike—as good as they were—were more likely to lose it with this rich punk and his attitude. He'd have to keep a careful eye on things; if Kasak and Marchioni got too aggressive, Rutherford could shut down and ask for a lawyer.

Kasak had had a folder sitting in front of him through the whole interview so far, which several times had attracted Rutherford's eye.

Now Kasak opened it, taking out a few photos and placing them on the desk in front of Rutherford.

The first was of Abigail Johnson, the woman from Jamaica Estates. It wasn't a crime-scene photo, but one taken from her home, showing her before she'd ever met her killers.

Rutherford looked at the photo for a long moment before shaking his head.

"Nope, never seen her," he said flippantly.

Kasak placed additional photos on the table—of Victoria Adams, the woman from Sutton Place, Jennifer Burnett from 63rd Street, and Giovanna Palmiere from Park Avenue South. All of them were beautiful women, with bright, sunny smiles. Both detectives noticed that Rutherford barely glanced at the last photo before he answered again.

"Sorry to disappoint you," he said. "I don't know any of these broads."

Marchioni had had enough. Slapping his notebook face-down on the table, he picked up the folder and drew out a few more photographs—this time crime-scene pictures of the same women after their gruesome murders. He spread them out unceremoniously in front of Rutherford.

"Maybe this'll help you remember them, you fucking animal," he snarled. "This is how you last saw them, after you had your fun."

Rutherford stared back at him, the smile gone from his lips but still dancing maddeningly in his eyes.

"I'm sorry, Detective," he said. "I really don't know what you're talking about."

"The fuck you don't!" Marchioni shouted, slamming his palm down on the table. Kasak looked over at his partner with a silent warning, but Marchioni was too pissed off to notice it. He gestured at the pictures in disgust. "You know, you must be one sick motherfucker to do that. *Real* sick. And you think you're getting *away* with it?"

"This *conversation* is starting to bore me," Rutherford said evenly. "If you aren't going to put me under arrest, I think I'm—"

He was cut off by the noise of the interrogation-room door swinging open. Morrison leaned in to talk to the two detectives.

"Can I speak to you both outside for a moment?" he asked in a stern tone.

Kasak and Marchioni stood stiffly and walked out. Morrison had hoped Rutherford's ego would be flattered enough by this display of internal conflict that he'd stick around for the next round, and it was. Rutherford leaned back in his chair, smiling triumphantly.

"See you later, suckers," he scoffed.

Marchioni turned back toward him with a murderous look in his eyes. Morrison grabbed his arm.

"Mike, that's enough," he said, pulling the door shut behind them.

"Wish I had a goddamn bottle of Coke right now," Marchioni grumbled.

25

Detective Tina Koreski opened the door and went in.

Rutherford was holding the photos of the victims, flipping through them nonchalantly in an apparent effort to show indifference toward whoever was here to speak to him.

"Like what you see?" she asked as she sat.

Now he looked up, startled for a moment by the feminine voice. In an instant he'd recovered, and gave her the elevator eyes.

"I do, now that you're here," he said cockily.

She smiled coyly, beginning to gather up the crime scene photos in a distracted way. "I'm flattered; I don't normally appeal to everyone's taste."

"Yeah, well, my taste isn't everyone's."

She didn't follow up with the obvious question, but held his eyes for just a moment, long enough to make him think his comment had interested her in a decidedly non-professional way.

"Adam," she said, appearing to brush off whatever thought had been going through her mind, "I want to apologize for the behavior of my colleagues. That wasn't how this was supposed to go; this is meant to be a friendly conversation."

"I'm glad they sent in somebody friendlier, then," he said, not taking his eyes off her.

She looked up at him again, pretending to be momentarily mesmerized by his charms.

"Well," she said more slowly, "I think they maybe just don't understand people like you—"

"What do you mean?" he interrupted.

"Well, just someone *with* it all: I mean, you have money, and power, and looks"—she appeared to catch herself in a smile—"I mean, most of the people we talk to aren't, uh, quite so—"

"I get it," he said, smiling. This was obviously what he was used to: insecure girls who stroked his ego and went weak in the knees when he paid them any attention. "Well, it's nice to meet you, Miss—"

"Tina," she blurted out; then seemed to recover. "Koreski. Tina Koreski."

"Tina," he said. "Lovely to meet you. You seem so *young* to be doing this, Tina."

To cover her repulsion, she giggled a little and looked away, playing with her hair. "I mean, I guess," she said. "This is sort of a trial run for me—"

"A trial run?"

"Yeah, I guess so."

He looked at her warily. "Doesn't sound like they're taking this very seriously."

"Well, I mean, it's not like you're under *arrest* or anything. Then it'd be different. And besides—" She faltered a bit, then gave a *What the hell* kind of laugh. "I sort of asked."

He smiled again, and she knew his ego was hooked.

"Okay, Tina," he said, giving her the up-and-down again. "Is it *Officer* Tina?"

"Detective," she said.

"Wow, okay—Detective." He raised his eyebrows. "Does that mean you still carry handcuffs?"

"Of course," she laughed, then lowered her voice as she met his eyes again. "Day and night."

"All right then, *Detective* Tina," he said, "what do you want to talk to me about?"

She appeared to shake herself back to the job at hand. "Well, right *now*," she said with a breath, "these women." She nodded toward the pictures left on the table.

"Ugh, *these* bitches again," he said languidly. "Well, go ahead."

"Bitches?"

He sighed, catching himself. "They just *look* like bitches, is all; the type of women I've met a million of. That type of women, they never get me. Not many of them do, though—not like *you* seem to." He smiled again, obviously used to this sort of thing working.

She smiled back. "Well, if you had to pick one of them out as most attractive, which would it be?"

He laughed. "What kind of a question is that?"

"Just *answer* it," she said with a flirty laugh.

He looked at the photos again and picked up victim number four, Giovanna Palmiere.

"I don't know about *most* attractive, but I can tell you, *this* one sure isn't my speed." He tossed the photo aside.

"All right, down to three, then. Which one?"

"I don't know; they're all pretty much the same to me."

"Seriously? You're telling me you don't find *any* of them more attractive than the others? Don't you have a type?"

He laughed, thinking he'd drawn her out. "Not in these photos," he said; then added, "in this *room*, maybe." Thinking he'd made her speechless with so brazen a come-on, he let it hang for a moment before going on. "To be honest with you, they all look like nasty, snobby bitches to me. I wouldn't kick them out of bed, but none of them really do it for me."

"All right," she said. "I mean, you have to admit, they're beautiful women."

"Sure, they're fine," he said. "That shirt you're wearing is doing more for me right now, though."

She looked down, acting surprised, and went to button the top buttons.

"No, no," he said, "leave 'em. You look great."

She pretended to be flattered and sat up straight again, leaving the buttons undone. This guy was going to be putty in her hands.

"Let's talk about something else," she said coyly. "What do you like to do when you come to the city?"

Morrison and the Coke Brothers watched from the other side of the two-way mirror. None of them could believe what was happening. Certainly none of them would be capable of interrogating anyone in this fashion. Yet they were all impressed. Unorthodox as it was, Tina's improvised method had already brought out a few very interesting statements from Adam Rutherford—including an offhand mention of 63rd Street as a place where he'd parked his car, and an admission that he'd been to Jamaica Estates, apparently to visit a friend whose last name and address he couldn't recall—and through it all, she hadn't missed a beat. Better still, despite her traumatic past, even Rutherford's most insulting comments and egregious pick-up lines had failed to throw her off or make her visibly uncomfortable; she'd somehow managed to weave them seamlessly into the increasing flirtation between them. And after hours of it, she still showed no sign of slowing.

"So, can you remember the last time you were in Manhattan?" she was now asking.

"Oh, I can't remember the exact date, but it was a Wednesday."

"Can you remember roughly the date range?"

"January—somewhere between the second and the tenth."

"Did you come alone?"

"No, Brian came with me."

This statement put both of them in the city during homicide number three. Tina brushed over it with a flirtation. "No lady friends?"

Rutherford bit. "None that I can remember."

"Good," she said faux-self-consciously. "And how about before that—do you remember when you were there last?"

"We were in around Christmastime."

"Do you remember what days, specifically?"

"Let's see: we came down just before the twenty-fifth, and were there for a couple of days."

Another bingo. This put both of them in the city during the Sutton Place and Jamaica Estates murders. The guy wasn't getting any less cocky, that was for sure. Koreski remembered from her training that a lot of serial killers believed they were smarter than the police—or anyone else, for that matter—and often derived enjoyment even from getting caught, in that they were able to push the envelope with their adversaries just a little more.

"How about after that last time in January—did you visit the city after that?"

"No, that was the last time we were there."

She noticed that he was looking again at the pictures spread out on the table, including the more gruesome crime-scene photos. It wasn't lost on her that he invariably spent more time looking at those pictures than at the ones taken of the victims before they were killed. It seemed to her the appropriate time to start giving him some hardball questions—they'd just have to be gone about very delicately.

"Tina," he said, interrupting her train of thought, "I need to use the men's room, if that's all right with you."

"Of course," she smiled. "I'll have someone escort you."

"You could always escort me yourself," he suggested with a sleazy smile. "You know, hold it for me."

She laughed lightly, looking down in an effort to appear charmed. "I'd love to, but I don't think my boss would appreciate that," she said. "Just give me a sec; I'll grab someone for you."

She stepped out to ask two of the BPD detectives to escort him. When they'd brought him to the restroom, Morrison emerged from the next room where he'd been watching the interrogation, and called her out into the hallway.

"Tina, you're doing great in there," he said quietly.

"Thanks, Cap—that means a lot, coming from you."

"Forget me," he chuckled. "Kasak and Marchioni can't stop talking about how well you're working this guy."

Koreski smiled. "For real?"

"No bullshit. They'll probably never tell you, but I wanted to let you know. You're gaining some serious points. And by the way," he added, "here's some news that might help you. Medveded got the other guy to confess to everything—including a homicide in La Jolla, California, months before they started their killing spree out here."

"Are you kidding me? *California?*"

"Yeah. We already spoke to San Diego PD, and everything Brian told us matches one of their unsolved homicides to the letter."

"Unbelievable. I'll definitely use that—thanks, Cap. I'd better get back in there."

"Yeah, go ahead. Keep up the good work, Detective!"

She went back into the room and waited for Rutherford to be brought back in. *La Jolla, California—!* She'd have to be careful with how she played *that* particular hand, but it was undoubtedly information she could use.

After a much longer interval than she'd expected, Rutherford reentered the room, and the two detectives closed the door behind him.

"You know, I missed you in there, Tina," he said in an oily voice when he'd sat. "It wasn't the same without you. You should've *come* with me."

He winked as this last emphasis passed his lips, and a sudden lightheadedness came over Detective Koreski. Where had she heard that before—? At once it hit her. That filthy hotel room. They were the very words *he'd* said to her, that fat, disgusting pig from Scarsdale, as he pressed his weight down on her, the cheap bedcovers scratching against her face…

With an effort, she snapped back to the present.

"Listen," she said, striving to keep the flirtatious edge in her voice,

"All jokes aside, I have to ask you something."

"No jokes here," he said, still smiling. "Go ahead, Tina."

"You've said these women look like bitches, and I believe it," she said, lowering her voice to a whisper. "Based on our time together today, I think I see what the problem was."

"Yeah? And what's that?"

"You're not a man to be disrespected, and they disrespected you."

Adam Rutherford sat stock-still, the smile still hovering on his face in an eerie mask of self-satisfaction.

"Now look, this is between us," she went on. "When you went to the bathroom I told them we were done. I'm supposed to be finishing up with you now. Just tell me, because I need to know: am I understanding you right? Just yes or no; you don't have to say anything."

After what seemed an eternity, he gave just the quickest hint of a nod.

She moved her chair closer to him. "I knew I did," she said quickly, as though in a rush of excitement. "I felt it when you came in. You're not a man to be fucked with, are you, Adam?"

"No, I'm not," he said, the smile unmoving.

"No, it's obvious," she said. "I almost wish I'd been there, for—but we don't have to talk about that, if you don't—"

"They didn't know what hit 'em," he whispered proudly, his eyes gleaming.

She was almost too shocked to respond. Fortunately, the energy of her performance kept her going.

"Of course they didn't, the stupid bitches," she said with a little laugh. "They didn't know the first thing about a man—what you do, what you need."

"Are you saying *you* do?" he asked.

"Come on, Adam," she said, her voice sultry. "Of *course* I do. I know all *sorts* of things men need."

"Yeah? Big words, Tina."

"When we get out of here, I'll show you. I do know how to find you, you know."

"Yeah, I bet you do," he smirked. "Crazy little bitch, aren't you?"

"The craziest," she said. "Bet you didn't think some of us were cops, huh?"

"No, I *know* some of you are," he said. "I've got first-hand experience."

Yeah, I'm real sure, you little shit, she thought. "Well, you don't need to try to make me jealous," she said. "I'm above that bullshit. But you *have* to tell me—I have to know—which was the best?"

"The best?"

"Yeah, the best," she insisted. "*You* know—the most fun, the most... *right*. The Queens bitch looks like she was the most stuck-up one, to me."

"Completely stuck-up," he agreed. "Living in that big house, driving a fancy car—all that, just because she spread her legs for some rich guy like me. She didn't know shit about having money, or power—none of it. Absolutely no respect."

Koreski couldn't believe it. After hours of dancing around every detail, he'd opened up like a fire hydrant on a hot day. Thrilled, she pressed on. "But was the older one better? The one on Sutton Place? I'd assume she'd have at least known better."

He sneered. "Right, you'd think. But no—stupid whore. But we had fun with her." He sounded as though he'd forgotten she was there. "She deserved it. The other one, she didn't do anything, but what the hell? The women in that neighborhood are all the same."

"You mean this one," Koreski said, pointing at the victim from 63rd Street.

"Yeah, her," he said dismissively. "Just the wrong place, wrong time, really—for her, I mean. Brian and I were exactly where we wanted to be."

"And this one?" she said, pushing the last photo toward him, of victim number four. "Another rich bitch, like the others?"

"Oh, I don't know," he said. "I've never seen that one."

For an instant her confusion got the better of her. "You mean—you didn't kill her?" she asked.

It was a slight slip, but the effect on Rutherford was catastrophic. In an instant his eyes went dark.

"You fucking *bitch,*" he snarled.

"What—?" she began.

"You fucking *lied* to me, you little bitch," he said. "You're no better than any of these whores!"

He swiped the photos off the table in fury. Instinctively her eyes went after them as they flew aside. Another error. As quick as lightning, his hands shot across the table. His right caught hold of her wrist as it came up; his left wrapped tight around her throat.

"You little bitch—you nasty little lying *bitch!*" he shouted through gritted teeth, bearing down hard on her windpipe.

The door flew open with a crash. But before Morrison and the Coke Brothers could get through the doorway, Koreski had gripped Rutherford's left wrist with her free hand, and twisting her body suddenly to the side, she pulled him bodily over the table. As he straightened his legs to get them under him, she moved in close and brought her knee up squarely into his balls.

Rutherford gave a choking noise and doubled up, his hands flying open. Koreski slipped backward, out of his grasp, and in an instant Kasak had slammed him face-down over the table, and held him down while Marchioni cuffed him.

"You can't—you can't fucking arrest me," Rutherford was gasping.

"You bet we can, motherfucker," Marchioni said, straightening him up.

"You dumb pieces of shit," Rutherford said. His face glowed a horrible red. "You're fucked, totally fucked. My family will have me out of here before you finish your paperwork. And you"—he glared at Koreski—"you're going to see me again, you fucking cunt!"

"Yeah, well, don't hold your breath for that, asshole," she said, her voice ragged. "When you finish your time in New York, there's some folks in La Jolla who'll want to talk to you."

Rutherford stared at her, a look of dawning horror coming over him. It obviously hadn't occurred to him that his lifelong friend could have given him up.

"It's all right, pal," Kasak said, moving him along. "Lady-killer like you? You'll be real popular in prison, I have no doubt about it. You try your tough-guy tactics on the guys you meet there—I bet they'll be real impressed."

Marchioni shut the door after them. Morrison helped Koreski into a chair.

"Tina, are you okay?" he asked. "Did he get you bad? Christ, the little shit moved quick."

"I'll be fine, boss," she said hoarsely, rubbing her throat. "I *am* fine. I'm sorry I fucked up—I didn't—"

"Fucked up?" Morrison repeated, incredulous. "What the hell could possibly make you think you just fucked up?"

"I just—I didn't get into detail about any of the murders with him. I meant to, I did—it just—it got out of hand too quick."

Morrison had to laugh. "Tina, you've got to be kidding me. You got the guy to admit to three murders, and he tried to choke you right in front of us! You did a fantastic job. There was a point where I didn't think he'd break, but you kept on him, and he did. And when he started—classic bragging bullshit—you just gave him enough rope to hang himself. It was very well done, Detective. Very well done."

Kasak poked his head in the door.

"Cap, we've got ADA Rosenthal on the phone," he said.

"All right, thanks. Let's get out of here, Koreski—I'd say you've been in this room long enough."

He walked out. As Koreski followed after him, she passed the Coke Brothers in the hallway. To her astonishment, Kasak gave her a smile and a wink, and Marchioni nodded respectfully.

Tina Koreski beamed inwardly. It was probably the closest thing to a pat on the back a young detective had ever gotten out of the two of them.

26

Bill Morrison picked up the phone in elation.

"Stan, great news," he said. "After a whole goddamn day in interviews, we just got statements out of both of these animals!"

Stan Rosenthal laughed. "Well, congratulations, Bill—but I knew you had them ten minutes ago."

Morrison's blood suddenly ran cold. "Come again?" he asked.

"I got a call from Chief of Detectives Arndt about ten minutes ago. He said you had statements from both suspects, and told me to drop the arrest warrants." When Morrison didn't say anything, Rosenthal went on. "He made it sound like you'd called him, Bill—are you saying you haven't?"

"No, Stan, I haven't," Morrison said, screwing his eyes shut in rage, "but I have a feeling I know who did."

"Hmm," Rosenthal said, his voice uncomfortable. "Then I guess you didn't give him the name of the arresting officer either, for the warrant application?"

"No, I didn't. Let me guess—Detective Lou Galipoli?"

Stan was silent on the other end for a moment. "Yes," he said finally, "that's the name I have."

"That's bullshit, Stan—you've got to change that, right now."

"I'm sorry, Bill, it's too late. I already submitted it to the court. I thought you wanted it right away, to make sure these guys didn't get any wiggle room."

"No, I understand," Morrison said, holding down his frustration. "It's not your fault. Listen, Stan, I need to try and sort this out, all right? I'll talk to you later."

Morrison hung up the phone, having just gone in seconds from total jubilation to total dejection and anger. At just this moment, Sergeant McNamara walked into the office.

"Cap—you okay?" he asked. "You look like someone just pissed in your cereal."

"Pat, can you believe the balls on this fucking guy?" Morrison said.

"Not sure what you're talking about."

"Galipoli had Arndt put his name on the arrest warrants."

"You mean he took the collar?"

"Yeah. Christ!" Morrison slammed his fist on the desk. "The guy's a piece of shit, but I can't believe that even he would do something so selfish. This is a goddamn task force, with a lot of people on it who broke their asses, yourself included. You guys deserve this arrest, not him—the guy did next to nothing on the case! All he did was force us to juggle people around, because no one could work with him. This is really bullshit."

"Jesus, that's really lousy. Sorry, boss."

"Not as goddamn sorry as he's going to be when he walks in here."

As if he'd been awaiting the word, Louis Galipoli strutted back into the Boston squad room, proud as a peacock.

"Galipoli, get in this office!" Morrison shouted.

All the heads in the squad room turned as the Captain's voice boomed down the hallway. Even Galipoli's smirk faltered for an instant, before returning with a vengeance. He brushed past Tina Koreski, giving her a slimy wink as he passed that made a disgusted chill run down her spine.

When he'd gone into the office, Morrison slammed the door with such force that the whole wall shook. Everyone in the outer office started to look for the exit. Even the Bostonians got up to take a walk.

"How dare you," Morrison said through his teeth.

Galipoli said nothing, but kept on smirking at him.

"You think this is funny? You—who have done absolutely nothing of significance throughout this entire case—you call your buddy Arndt and steal the collar from the detectives who worked their asses off for it, and you think it's fucking *funny?*"

"I don't know what you're talking about," Galipoli said. "You can't prove I did anything."

"Can't prove—! Arndt called in the goddamn warrants with *your* name on them before I'd even talked to the fucking ADA!"

Galipoli snickered. "Hey, it's not my fault the Chief recognizes talent."

"You motherfucker," Morrison seethed. "I should suspend you on the spot."

"For what?" Galipoli laughed maddeningly. "You have nothing on me. I didn't call the Chief—if you have evidence that I did, show me. Otherwise, quit yelling and let me do my job."

Morrison was beside himself. "Your fucking *job?* Let's get something clear, Galipoli: you have *never* done your job around here. You aren't cop enough to shine the fucking *shoes* of anyone in this taskforce. Understand me? *Barney fucking Fife* made a better cop than you! You've made a whole career out of your supposed military heroics, but listen up, punk: nobody other than Arndt and a handful of sycophants like yourself believe they're even true. The rest of us see through the act. You're a phony—we all know it, just like I *know* you called Arndt. Do you know how I know that, Galipoli? Because he's your *only* goddamn friend around here. No one else can stand working with you, because outside of kissing political ass, you're an insufferable fucking prick." Galipoli's smirk remained, but his face immediately reddened at the insult. Morrison went on. "But you know what else? You're a special kind of prick, the worst kind—you're an *incompetent* prick, who still thinks he deserves all the accolades. That's you in a fucking nutshell, Galipoli: incompetent and stuck-up. The fact that you think you deserve to make this arrest tells me everything I need to know about you. Well, the bullshit stops now: I'm taking you off this task force, effective immediately."

Galipoli fixed him with one of his trademark blank stares.

"Are you finished, Captain?" he asked after a long silence. "Because I have two prisoners who need to be brought down to Boston Supreme Court for processing."

He turned and walked out, leaving Morrison alone in his fury.

Morrison caught himself back from shouting after him, and instead picked up the phone and dialed Commissioner Harrington.

"Commissioner," he said when he got hold of him, "I'm sorry to bother you in the evening."

"No problem, Bill, I'm up," Harrington said. "I just spoke with Chief Arndt, actually, and was going to call to congratulate you on the great job your people did up there."

Morrison's heart sank. Like the little weasel he was, Arndt had already called the Commissioner before Bill had had a chance to derail his and Galipoli's little scam. "Commissioner," he said, "did Arndt tell you who was making the arrest?"

"Yes, he did—Lou Galipoli, isn't it? He said the detective did a great job, and really deserved it."

"He's a liar," Bill blurted out. "The guy's a piece of garbage who's done nothing but cause me heartache since he was assigned here. I can't—"

"All right, now, Bill—calm down, you're going to give yourself a heart attack."

"I'm sorry, Commissioner. It just isn't fair to the men and women who broke this case. They deserve this arrest, not him."

"Well, I get your frustration," Harrington said, "but from what I understand, the arrest warrants are already dropped, and this guy Galipoli's name's on them. I'll make sure your people get the proper recognition from the department, though—for now, just let it go."

"Bob, this isn't right," Morrison said. His emotion surprised even him; he never called the Commissioner by his first name. "Can't you do anything to stop it?"

Harrington's voice was apologetic, but firm. "I know what it means to you, Bill, but it's too late. I'm sorry, really I am. Believe me, this won't go unnoticed—nor does the outstanding work your people have done. Listen, when you get back to the city, come to my office. We need to talk."

"All right, Commissioner, I will."

"Speak soon, Bill."

The Commissioner hung up, leaving Bill Morrison with the dial tone.

Sergeants Simmons and McNamara were standing on the steps of District D-14 when the first news truck pulled up. In seconds, another truck arrived, followed by two more. The two detectives watched as, like piranha in a feeding frenzy, their crews jumped out and vied for the best spot to get the money shot of the two suspects being led out.

"Oh, boy," McNamara said quietly. "The circus is in town."

"How the hell did they find out so fast?" Simmons asked.

"Galipoli," McNamara said simply. In a few words, he explained what the Captain had told him a few minutes earlier.

"Jesus," Simmons said, hanging his head in disgust. "Well, we'd probably better go tell the Cap they're here, huh?"

"Yeah, let's go," McNamara said.

When they walked into the squad room, Morrison and several others were already looking out the window. In the time it had taken Simmons and McNamara to climb the flight of stairs, another five news trucks had arrived, and were putting up their transmission towers for the live feed.

Morrison turned from the window and called in all of his people—or rather, all but one, who was busy primping for the cameras. His heart was heavy as he spoke.

"Listen," he told them, "I want you all to know how grateful I am for all of your hard work. Everyone in this room did a fantastic job, and I'm proud to know you all." He took a breath, then went on. "Unfortunately, none of you will be taking this arrest. Detective Galipoli has been credited as the arresting officer, per Chief Arndt."

The room hung in a stunned silence for a moment. It was clear this was none of Morrison's doing, but the egregiousness of Arndt's decision shocked everyone. The Boston officers shook their heads in sympathy for their New York comrades, feeling the full sting of the unfairness at hand.

Alex Medveded was the first to speak.

"Well, I'm glad," he said, his Russian accent just barely showing through his weariness. "I'm too tired to have to deal with these two piece of shits anymore."

There was a ripple of laughter as one by one, the rest of the room echoed his sentiment. Tina Koreski got up with a smile, walked over, and wrapped her arms around Morrison in a huge hug.

"We all love you, Cap," she said. "Making the arrest on a case like this doesn't mean anything. We all know who did the work, and you're the one who gave us the opportunity to do it."

Morrison felt his apprehension replaced with an overwhelming gratitude. "You guys are incredible," he said. "I should've known your incredible work ethic would show through even in this ridiculous situation. You're a remarkable team—a remarkable *family*—and I really appreciate it." He turned to where Lieutenant Polk was standing. "I particularly want to thank you, Lieutenant Polk, and all the men and women of the Boston Detectives, for your help, your hospitality, and your friendship. Know that you're all officially members of our extended family, and if you ever need anything in New York City, we'll be there for you."

There was a light hubbub of *Hear, hear*s and handshakes around the room, interspersed with a few good-natured Red Sox/Yankees jabs. When they quieted, Morrison spoke up again.

"Now, the sun's coming up"—he added, pointing out the window to the Boston skyline, glowing with the day's first light—"and I, for one, am ready for breakfast. Obviously, Galipoli's going to do a walkout for the news people—"

"Yeah, little shit's off doing his hair for 'em right now," scoffed Rivera.

"—but I think I'm going to skip that, head out the side door, and get a bite to eat before we hit the road. I've heard good things from our Boston friends about the chicken and waffles over at the Hen House on Massachusetts Avenue. Anyone want to come with me?"

As one, the whole room rose.

"Well then," Morrison said, smiling, "let's get going."

27

Bill Morrison rode back to the city alone. Uncharacteristically he left the AM/FM and police radios silent, and let the hum of the highway keep him company for a change. Despite how well his team had handled it, the bittersweet ending to the Rutherford-Anderson arrest had left a decidedly bad taste in his mouth, and it had taken his second phone call to lift his mood.

His first had been to Louise Donohue, making sure she'd be home for his visit; he wanted to thank her in person for her help with the BPD. Unfortunately she'd been on her way to the airport, heading out to see her daughter, so Bill had given her the good news and his thanks over the phone.

The second call was to Claudia, and just hearing her voice was enough to lift his spirits. It was euphoric, talking to her; the only dark feeling was the doubt that she could possibly feel the same. He told her about their success with the case, and now it really *felt* like a success; she made him feel heroic, appreciated, right with the world. She was free tonight—she was *always* free for him—and so glad he was coming back.

He'd hung up and driven in elated silence for fifteen minutes, his foot heavy on the gas and his mind racing with excited possibility. It seemed the world had turned around for him, as it always did after he spoke with her; it seemed he was ready for anything. The world he wanted would come to *him*—and as if on cue, his phone rang again.

"Bill," the voice said when he picked up. "James Fernandez here."

"Hi, Jim—guess you heard the news?" Morrison said.

"I did! Congratulations on your arrests. That's not what I'm calling about, though. I have the results from the DNA screening."

"Great—we get a match on our guys? Tell me you have good news for me, Jim!"

Fernandez laughed. "Well, let's just say the DNA samples your guys recovered from these two in Boston tested out to be some of the best numbers *ever,* as far as probability goes. Anderson tested out 1 in 150 million, and Rutherford's 1 in 175 million."

"You'll have to translate for me—what are you telling me?"

"I'm telling you that for three of these homicides, you've got a better chance of hitting the lottery two times in the same week than these not being your perps."

"Terrific!" Morrison caught himself. "Wait—you said three? Not four?"

"That's part B," Fernandez admitted. "Sorry to tell you, but neither of these guys' samples match any of the evidence from number four."

"All right," Morrison sighed. "I'm not too surprised, but I'd held out hope for the city's sake. Thanks for the update, though, Jim—sounds like we've really got a rock-solid case here. I'm going to have Sergeant Rivera come by your office first thing to pick up those results."

"No problem, Bill. I'll talk to you soon."

Morrison just had time to reach Rivera before he pulled into Claudia's driveway.

It was the first time he'd been to her Stamford home, a good-sized one with a neat front lawn and a deck just visible out back, overlooking the water. The other details of the place were quickly lost beside the little blue note he found taped to the front door, with lipstick lips imprinted across the fold, and several small hearts scribbled across the front. He

opened it, and his heart jumped at the three words he found there:
Come to me.

Trying the door, he found it open. Just inside, he found a trail of rose petals strewn across the floor, leading up the stairs. He smiled, tossing his jacket across the railing and loosening his tie as he went up toward the second floor. He could hear music playing softly down the hall, and followed it.

He pushed open what was obviously the bedroom door, letting his tie drop to the floor as he did. The room was half-darkened, with an enticing smell of jasmine in the air.

Then he saw Claudia, and he felt his heart jump in his chest.

She was sitting in a large armchair in the far corner, wearing a black leather corset, thigh-high stockings, and what had to be five-inch black stiletto fuck-me pumps. Neither of them said a word as she rose from her seat slowly and came toward him. Morrison had already begun to unbutton his shirt, and stripped it off without taking his eyes from hers. Her eyes screamed to him what she wanted, and he knew he wanted it too.

He kissed her passionately, and as she closed her eyes he grabbed her by the throat, suddenly dragging her across the room towards the bed. Pushing her down roughly, he flipped her onto her stomach, pulling his belt from his pants in the same motion. He slipped one end through the buckle and tightened it around her wrists. Slipping the loose end through a notch in the headboard, he slid down her supine body, kissing up the back of one leg, then the other, purposely avoiding her bare skin as he moved from her thigh-highs to her corset. She moaned softly against the bedspread as he moved up her back, kissing against the laces and blowing through them against her skin. He propped himself up on his elbows and slipped his hands beneath her to massage her breasts through the leather of the corset, his weight pressing down on her. She arched up against him and turned her head to speak to him, her voice rough with desire.

"Please," she begged, "take me now, Bill—I need you inside me—"

He reached one hand up to grab her hair gently, but firmly; and pulled her head back to whisper in her ear. "All in good time, my love," he said. "But I want to savor you before I devour you, and right now, I'm getting what *I* want."

His words surprised and sent shivers through her; and with the thrill of having found the perfect partner for her deepest desires, she gave herself up to his control.

Bill Morrison awoke to find the bed empty.

How long had he been asleep? He checked his phone for the time—it wasn't late. Thankfully, tired as he was, he hadn't slept through to the next morning. His clothes were missing, and there was a soft terrycloth robe hanging from the hook on the back of the bedroom door. He wrapped the belt around his waist and headed downstairs, a strange, delicious smell wafting up to meet him.

Walking into the kitchen, he found Claudia there in a matching robe, just closing the oven.

"I was wondering where you'd gone to," he said, smiling.

Claudia smiled and came up to kiss him on the lips. She softly bit him as she pulled away.

"I thought you might be hungry when you woke up," she said. "Please, sit—I've just taken it out."

"You're amazing," he said, laughing in disbelief. "You didn't need to cook for me—we could have gone out."

She put her hands on her waist in a mock pout. "No *way* am I making you take me out for dinner, when I am perfectly capable of feeding my man."

"She's beautiful, sexy, understands me—*and* can cook?" He laughed again. "What did I do to deserve this? Thank you—I don't know what it is, but it smells wonderful."

"It's a traditional Greek dish called *pastitsio*—consider it Greek lasagna. And if you love me like I love you, that's all the thanks I need."

"Well, I'm head over heels in love with you, so I guess I pass."

"Right answer," she smiled, pouring each of them a glass of wine. "Let's eat."

They sat side-by-side at the table, their legs touching as they ate. The food was incredible, and Morrison realized as he ate that he couldn't remember the last time he'd had a home-cooked meal. Kathleen hated cooking, and had long since given up on making the effort for him.

"You know, Claudia, I could get used to this," he said when they'd finished. "You might be in trouble."

She laughed. "I was counting on it!" she said. "My mother always said, feed a man with love, and he'll love you for your lifetime."

"Well, I can't make any promises for *your* lifetime," he joked, "but I can sure imagine loving you for mine."

She wrapped her arms around his neck to hug him close. He felt a wetness against his cheek, and realized her eyes had teared up with happiness.

"I trust you, completely," she whispered. She picked up her wine glass and refilled it with the last of the bottle. "Come out to the deck with me—it doesn't seem too cold tonight."

They stepped out onto the deck, and nestled into a chair together, sharing the glass between them. There was no conversation—just touching, kissing, closeness. When the glass was empty and they'd gotten cold, Bill rose with her in his arms and carried her in, her arms wrapped tightly around him, her breath hot against his ear.

As he carried her back up the stairs again, their hearts beating faster together, Bill Morrison had the strange realization that he felt closer to normal than he remembered ever having felt. It was indeed a feeling he could get used to.

Who knows? he thought. *Maybe I'll make it all the way back.*

28

The following day passed in a blur.

It started off with an early call from Arndt, and it was a testament to Morrison's newfound good mood that it only made him roll his eyes to talk to the man. Arndt, who hadn't heard the news about their third murderer likely still being on the loose, was again ready and eager to have Morrison off the task force; but being informed of this little hitch in things, was equally quick to retrace his steps before hanging up in a huff.

After his second wonderful home-cooked meal in God knew how long, Morrison left Claudia and drove back to the city. He stopped quickly at the stationhouse to make sure their case's follow-up materials were being handled properly, then went out on the rounds to thank the first responders from each of their crime scenes in Manhattan and Queens, and let them know the news of Rutherford and Anderson's arrest. The bond between the patrol division and the detective squad was indispensable; and no one knew better than Morrison how crucial such positive reinforcement and follow-up was in keeping that bond tight and morale strong. Every officer appreciated being appreciated; and if the principle was lost on some of the force's higher-ups, it had never been lost on Bill Morrison.

Later in the evening, once he'd finished for the day with his errand of gratitude—it would continue until he'd visited each of the relevant precincts' late-night roll calls as well, but that could wait for now—he and Sergeants McNamara and Simmons headed over to Kelley's to join the rest of the team for a small celebration. He'd called the owner earlier to ask him to put the team's drinks on his tab for the night; they'd more than earned it already, and with a potential copycat killer on the loose, would continue to earn it for the foreseeable future.

Kelley's was too small for the whole team to sit together at one table, so they all intermingled throughout the night. Galipoli, predictably, was nowhere in sight. It occurred to a few of the team that no one had ever seen him out with *any* of the cops he'd worked with.

At one point in the evening, Morrison made his way over to a table where Sergeants Rivera and McNamara were sitting with Detectives O'Dell and Garriga and another longtime cop named Timothy Morality, the irony of whose name had never escaped him. Morality, who'd been McNamara's longtime radio-car partner, was regaling the others with stories from back in the day, before McNamara had made the big time.

"This guy was always the foil," Morality was saying, laughing. "It was just too easy to get his back up. I remember this one fishing trip that we went on, when we were both new recruits. Tommy Burke—"

"Oh, come on, Timmy," McNamara groaned, putting his head down. "Not that story, man."

"No, no, Timmy," Morrison said with a smile, pulling up a chair at the end. "By all means, go on."

"Gotta obey the superior officer, eh, Pat?" Morality laughed. "Well, as I was saying, before I was so *rudely* interrupted: Tommy Burke—he was precinct club president back then—he told us about this great fishing trip out of Captree Piers on Long Island. May 2nd, 0500 hours—we were going for flounder, as I recall.

"So the morning of the 2nd, Pat picks me up at 0300 for the drive out to Captree, we grab a coffee and a bagel, and hit the road. It's a long drive, and when we finally get to the slip where the boat's supposed to be, it's empty. Pat asks some old-timer standing off to the side if he knows where the boat's at, and the guy just laughs and says *That boat ain't been here in ten years!*"

The others laughed.

"Some good old-fashioned rookie hazing, huh?" Garriga asked.

"Well, sure," Morality said. "At least, that's what Pat's thinking. And man, is he *pissed!* He gets himself real worked up, ranting and raving, cussing up a storm about Tommy Burke messing with us, pacing back and forth on the edge of the dock. And just then, the boat next to us in the slip blows their air horn, and *this guy* gets so startled, he falls right off the edge of the dock into the water!"

The others cracked up, slapping McNamara on the back good-naturedly.

"Well, that's when Tommy and damn near the whole precinct come out onto the dock," Morality went on, "everyone hooting and hollering while Pat's trying to climb back onto the dock. I put my hand out to help him up, and he looked up at me with the most *priceless* face—"

"I'd just realized he was in on it the whole time," McNamara said.

"Oh, God, it was perfect," Morality said, wiping his eyes. "Just perfect. Laurel and Hardy—that was us, eh, Pat?"

"It sure was *that* day," McNamara smiled. "But come on, Timmy, tell them the rest. You gotta give me some credit here!"

"Okay, okay. Truth be told, Pat was a good sport about the whole thing," Morality went on. "And he felt a *lot* better when he ended up winning the pool for the biggest fish—two hundred bucks! He bought the whole bar later that night, when we got back."

"Class act," Rivera said.

"It certainly was," Morality admitted. "I don't know how he is with you guys, but back then, it was a grand gesture. Tommy Burke was always the guy buying, back then." He drank off the rest of his beer in a gulp. "Gentlemen, I'd better be getting on my way," he said, rising. "It's been a pleasure, truly it has."

"All right, Timmy Immorality," McNamara said, rising for a bear hug with his former partner. "Take good care, all right?"

"And you, big shot," Morality said.

When he'd gone, the others looked around at each other, their hilarity settling. Morrison could see that past exploits hadn't dominated all of the evening's talk. As the others looked on expectantly, McNamara turned to him to open up the conversation.

"Cap," he said, clearing his throat, "since these guys are all veterans, and still involved with the military through various organizations, I asked them to dig into that matter we spoke about. I thought you might want to talk it over tonight."

"Great," Morrison said. "You all know, of course," he said to the others, "this has to be of the utmost confidentiality. If you'd rather not do it, I completely understand."

The other three nodded their heads silently. Nobody was bowing out.

"All right, then," he said. "All of you served our country—two in the Army and one in the Marines, right?"

Garriga, sitting between O'Dell and Rivera, gave the other two jabs to the ribs. "That's why they call it 'The Few and the Proud,'" he laughed. "Most folks have to settle for the Army."

"Oh, sure, it's real selective, with guys like you in there," Rivera laughed back. "Were you a steer or a queer in boot camp?"

"All right now," Morrison said, knowing this kind of ribbing could continue all night. "Serious business, now."

O'Dell's face grew serious. "Cap, I served proudly in the Army, and still have family in the service. I want to make sure this guy is for real, and I have no problem calling everyone I know who can help us. If we're wrong, okay; but if we're right, I want you to know it'll probably open up a pretty huge can of worms."

Morrison understood exactly what he was talking about. If their suspicions about Galipoli were correct, the question of how he'd slipped past the applicant processing system and made it this far on the job could take them all the way up the ranks.

"I understand that," he said curtly. "I'm willing to deal with those developments. Now how do you suggest we go about it?"

"We'll need to start by getting his DD-214, which should show all his deployments," O'Dell said. "Then we'll need to track down some people from his old unit and see what they can tell us about him."

"I've got a friend in Applicant Processing who might be able to help with his original folder," Garriga said.

"Yeah, me too," nodded Rivera.

"Good," said Morrison. "Let's start by talking to them."

"I assume we're going to be keeping this to ourselves?" O'Dell asked. "No Internal Affairs?"

"Yeah, I want to stay away from Internal Affairs for now," Morrison said. "I'd like for us to clean up our own house here, as much as possible."

"Then let's try our friends one at a time," Rivera said. "That way we won't attract attention with it. You guys talk to Garriga's friend, and if you strike out, we'll call mine. She's good with computers."

Pat McNamara snickered knowingly. "She still talks to you? I thought you two had a falling out."

"Yeah, she was mad for a while," Rivera admitted, "but who can resist this face?"

They all laughed.

"All right, guys," Morrison said. "I'll leave the first round to you. Anyone who gets any information, make sure you call me right away. I don't care what time it is—*call me*. I have a bad feeling about this guy, and I hope I'm wrong, but if I'm right, we need to know as soon as possible. Now I'm going to grab another drink. Anyone need anything?"

The others didn't, so he made his way to the bar alone. He'd just ordered when he felt a big arm around his neck and a kiss on the top of his head.

"Hey, Cap!"

It was Simmons. He was obviously wasted—surprising, considering that Simmons never got drunk normally.

"Boss, you're the best," he slurred, loosening his hold on Morrison's neck. "Everyone who ever work' for you loves you, man."

Morrison laughed. "I know, Andre. And it's mutual—you guys are my family."

"You see? Thass what I'm talking about. You really care about your people, we can tell. We can all tell. Thass what keeps this team so tight." Simmons made a web of his fingers and clenched them together demonstratively, concentrating hard on them. Then he leaned in close, suddenly serious. "Everyone except that fuck Galipoli," he said vehemently. "*That* guy's no team player."

"I know it, man," Morrison laughed, rolling his eyes at the constant theme but not wanting to expose his own suspicions too far. "He's just different. I don't know, though—maybe it's his time in the service."

"Ha! Well, it ain't that," Simmons scoffed. He lowered his voice. "It sure ain't that. Cap, his time in the service is bullshit—Dave O'Malley said so."

"Oh yeah?" Morrison said, perking up. "What'd O'Malley say about him?"

"Well, it was a few weeks ago," Simmons said, nodding somberly. "Dave was stopping by the squad room after an arrest, and Galipoli, that fuck, he's juss talking about 'mself—talking up his time in the military, what he done there, you know, putting the res' of us down for not serving, that kind of thing. He didn't see Dave when Dave came in, so Dave just stands there, listen' to him for a few minutes. He was in the air cavalry, you know—the patch with the horse on it and the stripe across it, like that guy from *Apocalypse Now*, Ronnie somebody—"

"Right," Morrison said, eager to hear the point. "And what'd Dave say?"

"Dave said the shit Galipoli was saying was all wrong. He told Lou he was *full-of-shit*"—he emphasized these words with jabs of his finger against his palm—"about his tour of duty in Iraq. He said that, right to his face."

"What'd Galipoli say?"

"Well, thass the funny thing," Simmons laughed. "Galipoli didn' say anything—he just got up and walked out the room, like he just got caught lying to his parents or some'm."

"You don't say," Morrison said, feeling a thrill of vindication. "That's interesting—I may need to talk to O'Malley about that."

"Oh, yeah, you should," Simmons said. He tapped his ear. "He'll give you a *earful!*"

"Thanks, Andre; you may have made my night."

"All in a day's work, Sir—!"

Simmons made an attempt to stand up straight and salute, tipping comically to one side in his eagerness. Both men laughed.

"How're you getting home tonight, anyway, buddy?" Morrison asked, holding him up.

"Oh, I'm takin' a cab tonight, don't worry," Simmons assured him. "I don't want to ride no subway like this—definitely no car."

"I'm glad to hear it," Morrison smiled, and meant it. In the past, cops generally got a pass if they were pulled over for driving with a few in them; but there'd been far too many tragedies as a result, and those days were long gone.

"Oh, sure," Simmons slurred. "Fact, I think it's just about time for me to get going—I'm startin' to feel a bit buzzed." They laughed again.

"All right, then, Simmons," Morrison said, helping him with his coat. "Get home safe. And thanks again for the info about Galipoli—I'll be sure to check that out."

29

Tina Koreski was already in the office the next morning when Morrison emerged from the bunk room at 0800. The celebration at Kelley's had gone late, and aside from Medveded, who was always early no matter what, Morrison was surprised to see anyone there on time. Detectives' days generally don't end on time, so their starting times had a bit of leeway too. But Koreski was bright-eyed and bushy-tailed, and got up to follow him to his office.

"Hey, Cap, before everyone comes in, I'd like to have a quick word with you, if I might," she said.

"Sure, Tina, come on in," he said, filling his coffee cup on the way in. He reached into the file cabinet behind his desk for the bottle of Jameson, thought about it, then put the bottle back unopened. Maybe Claudia really *was* making a difference. "What's up?"

"I just wanted to thank you for the other day," she said, "for giving me a shot."

He smiled. "I think I should be the one thanking *you* for the other day," he said. "You said you had a feeling about Rutherford, and you were right. I should've listened to you the first time, and given you the first crack at him—I don't think anyone else could have gotten him to talk the way you did."

"I appreciate that, Cap—it means a lot to me that you felt I did a good job. You know, I actually surprised myself that night; there were a couple of times I wanted to puke just being so close to that piece of shit. But I was surprised—I held it together."

"That's an understatement, Koreski. You impressed everyone that night. And I'll admit," he added, "I'm glad the sicko gets to suffer the indignity of you taking him down physically on top of that. It's typical of these cowards who prey on the weak—they talk a big game when they think you're weaker, but when they're faced with someone who can handle themselves, they crumble like *that*." He snapped his fingers. "And you really handled yourself well, Detective."

She nodded. "Thanks, Cap," she said quietly. "It means a lot."

"Good. Now get back to work, will you?" he said good-naturedly. "We want to make sure these assholes don't see the outside of a prison for a good long time."

"Yes sir," she smiled on her way out.

Despite the general good mood that prevailed over Rutherford and Anderson's arrest, the day moved along at a pretty hectic pace. Everyone was working on one aspect of the case or another—banging on computer keyboards, putting in phone calls, and meticulously going over each and every Detective Follow-up Report produced throughout the case. The two suspects would eventually be extradited from Boston to New York to face charges, and as always, every *i* in the case file needed to be dotted and every *t* crossed before it could be brought to the District Attorney for court preparation.

With the suspects behind bars, the city was able to breathe a sigh of relief. Captain Morrison, on the other hand, was far from relaxed. The evidence against their guys having committed the fourth homicide was very compelling, so he'd tasked Detective Medveded—whose paperwork was long since done—to revisit everything they had on it, particularly those aspects it shared with the first three murders that were reported on in the media. The similarities were striking; and if it turned out that these details were nowhere to be found in the public record, they might readily assume their third killer had had some more intimate connection with the crimes or their perpetrators.

Morrison wondered if they'd missed something. Had they pressed those two in Boston hard enough on a possible third suspect? He was sure Anderson would have told Medveded everything he knew, but Rutherford was another story—he only lost his cool long enough to implicate himself; once he'd calmed down, he'd kept his mouth shut. Even given everything he'd told them, there was no way of knowing what he hadn't—*if* he'd known. The more disturbing implication was that if it *hadn't* been done by an accomplice of the other two, the crime may have originated with a stranger who simply had access to the case—in other words, someone on the inside. Morrison's team was good, one of the best; but no matter how strong the gag order is, cops talk—especially to fellow cops—and who knew who'd talked to whom.

He was shaken out of the thought by a hurried knock at the door. Rivera poked his head in.

"Cap, we got another one," he said. "Female, late thirties—she didn't show up to work today, and her coworker went to check on her and found her dead with the apartment door open."

"Fuck," Morrison said. "Where?"

"Thirtieth and Park."

"Shit—that's only nine blocks from the last one. Not good, Frankie. Who do we have who isn't busy right now?"

Rivera shook his head. "Nobody," he said, "but Koreski, Medveded, and Garriga are heading over to the scene already."

"All right, let's get out there, then," Morrison said, grabbing his jacket. "I'll drive."

The building on Thirtieth was a small one, only four stories, set back about seventy-five feet from Park Avenue South. It had a four-foot-high wrought-iron gate leading to the front door. As they pulled up in front, Rivera pointed to a building across the street.

"Doorman over there," he said. "Maybe we'll get lucky, and the guys on *that* door will have seen something. I'll head over and talk to the guy on duty now, see if he can give me the name of the overnight guy for now—I doubt our copycat would have worked in daylight."

"All right, sounds good," Morrison agreed. "Grease 'em if you have to. I'll see you up there."

He headed through the iron gate and was greeted at the front door by a uniformed officer, who pointed him up to the second floor. The door to the street-facing apartment was ajar. Morrison found Detective Williams from Crime Scene in the hallway, bagging evidence.

"Well, hello again, Otis," Morrison said. "What have we got here?"

"A mess, to start with," Williams answered. "Whoever did this likes doing it, and definitely *doesn't* like women. Even more so than the others, I mean."

"What do you mean?"

"Well, by her photos, this girl was a really good-looking woman, and you wouldn't be able to tell by looking at her now. This guy messed up her face *bad.*"

"One of our other cases was similar," Morrison said. "You didn't get that one. Now I think of it: when you finish up, would you mind looking at the homicide from Twenty-First and Park Avenue South for me? I'd be interested to hear what you think."

"Yeah, of course—I heard about that one, but never saw what they recovered. If it'd help you, I'd be glad to."

"Thanks," Morrison said. Normally his own taskforce would be in charge of any comparisons between crime scenes, but he knew Williams was meticulous in his work, and might see something his own people had missed after so much immersion in the case. "I know you're still in the middle of processing the scene, but what else can you tell me about it right now?"

"Well, we found her bound with some rope, similar to the other scenes we'd processed on the Boston guys. We've also collected some hairs from the victim's body that don't look like hers. She's got some skin under her nails, too—looks she put up a good fight. I can't imagine this was a quiet incident; if anyone else was home while she was being attacked, I'm sure they would've heard something."

"Did you see any bite marks, or any other kind of physical injuries?"

"No bite marks, but plenty of injuries."

"What type of injuries—anything with her lower half?"

"No," Williams said. "It mostly just looks like she met a boxer—lots of bruising all over, like he used her as a heavy bag. Like I said, this guy's a real animal."

"All right. Thanks, Otis—let me know when we can get in there and look for ourselves."

Morrison met up with his team out in front of the building. They'd completed their initial canvas of the building and block for anyone who might have seen or heard anything in reference to the murder, and were comparing notes as Morrison walked out of the building.

"Okay," Morrison said, clapping his hands. "Do we have anything yet that might be useful?"

Detective Garriga flipped through his notebook. "Yeah, I got one guy—an older gentleman who lives two doors from the victim's residence. He says around 0100 he'd taken his dog out for a walk; he said he usually doesn't walk his dog so late, but he was howling and he thought he needed to go—"

"Come on, Francisco, get to the point."

"Just giving you what the guy told me, boss! So anyway, as he's walking out his door, the street's fairly dark. Not much of a moon out last night, and the streetlight near his house has been broken for a few weeks. He hears some commotion near where the victim's house is. He isn't quite sure which doorway, but he says he sees a pretty big guy and a woman on the steps leading into one of the buildings—could be the victim's doorway, but he's not sure. He says she seemed a little intoxicated, by the way she was hanging onto the guy."

"Did he get a closer look at them?"

"He said he didn't walk off his stoop, and waited for them to go inside before he took Trevor for his walk. Trevor's the dog."

Morrison stared at him. "Yeah, I kind of figured that one out. Anything else?"

"Not really—he said when he was walking past the victim's house, he saw someone close the window in the front of the apartment. He said he only noticed it because it made a squeaking noise as it was being shut."

"Did he get a look at who shut the window?"

"He said he didn't, but he did say he heard a man's voice saying something like *We're going to have some fun.*"

"Jesus. Do you think he's giving you everything?"

"Yeah, boss. He was an older guy—very cooperative. He wasn't holding back."

"Okay, great. Anybody else get anything?"

Medveded and Koreski shook their heads. As Morrison was about to speak, Rivera came walking up to them from across the street, a smile on his face.

"I might have something," he said. "Not great, but it's better than nothing."

"Go ahead, Frankie."

"The guy working the day tour was really helpful," Rivera said. "He got the night doorman on the phone for me, and the guy told me that somewhere between 0030 and 0130—he isn't sure of the exact time—he saw a dark-colored sedan park just off the corner of Park Avenue South, I guess just down there." He pointed down the block. "He said a guy got out of the driver's-side door and proceeded to *drag* a woman, who could barely stand, out of the passenger seat. He could hear them talking, and he said the guy was saying some pretty nasty stuff to the woman. He says he's used to people passing by his building, especially at that time if night, talking all kinds of shit to each other, but this was different."

"How so?"

"He said they were only on the street for a few minutes, but the whole time this guy was talking, the woman wasn't saying a word—like she was unconscious."

"If he saw the guy again, does he think he could recognize him?"

"No—he said that side of the street was dark, with the trees in front of the house and one of the streetlights out."

"How about the car, we get anything on that?"

"No, he didn't pay it much mind. Once they were inside, he went back in his building."

"Okay," Morrison said. "We got two people who saw something, which is good, even if neither one can identify anyone; we have a time frame to work with. I want you guys to do a canvas of Park Avenue South, and see if there's any video that might have picked up the car for a possible make, model or plate number. I'm going to stick around here, in case Crime Scene finishes up soon."

The other three detectives nodded somberly, and started off silently down the block.

30

The first news truck pulled up a few minutes later. Morrison shook his head, wondering again how they'd found out so quickly. He did have his suspicions.

He paused for a moment at the door to tell the uniformed cop to move the yellow police tape and increase the size of the crime scene. Before he could get back inside, the first reporter was upon him, sticking a mic in his face.

"Is this the work of a copycat killer, Detective?" the reporter asked.

Morrison was taken aback for a moment, then quickly shook his head. "No comment," he said, retreating into the vestibule.

Once inside, he got out his phone and dialed Chief Arndt.

"Chief," he said curtly when Arndt had picked up, fighting back his frustration. "Did anyone in your office use the words 'copycat killer' today, by any chance?"

"I have no idea what you're talking about, Captain—and watch your tone," Arndt answered. Something in his voice told Morrison he'd just caught a man with his hand in the cookie jar.

"Well you know, Chief, a reporter just asked me about the copycat killer," he said. "Wherever he heard it from, it's not good that the information's out."

"Now, calm down, Captain," Arndt said. "It'll be fine. You'll just have to step up to the plate a little. Assuming you're the right man to lead the taskforce, I mean."

"What are you—" Morrison snarled. Arndt hung up on him.

Morrison hung up, fuming. He knew Arndt was the one leaking the information to the press; he had to be. It was just like him to put his own connections ahead of the integrity of a case. The press was going to have a field day with it, previous arrests be damned.

The detectives from Crime Scene walked out past him.

"We're finished, Cap," Williams said to him. "Looks like our copycat is at it a—"

"Hey, Williams, you mind not using that word?" Morrison interrupted him irritably. "The media's already starting with it."

Williams shrugged. "Sorry, Cap, I'll try to keep it down—but it definitely looks like the same guy or guys as before. I called the other team that handled the other murder you'd mentioned, and ran a few things by them; they confirmed the items we recovered all appear to be the same as the ones used a few blocks away."

"Jesus," Morrison said. "Well, thanks for looking into that for me. And don't mind me—it's just shaping up to be a tough day. I didn't mean to take it out on you."

"No worries, Cap, I know the story. *What have you done for me lately,* right?"

"Yeah, exactly. Thanks, Otis—be seeing you."

Morrison was interrupted on his way into the apartment by his cell phone ringing. Rivera, Garriga, and Koreski were just returning, so he waved them into the crime scene as he picked up. Jeffrey O'Dell was on the other end, his voice excited.

"Sorry to bother you, Cap, but I may have something here on the Galipoli thing," he said.

This got Morrison's attention. "No problem; just give me some good news," he said.

"Well, I'm not sure if this is good or bad news—it's probably a little of both. I made a connection through applicant processing, thanks to Sergeant Rivera's girl Helen Rosario. Helen was great—she probably saved us twenty steps and a boatload of time digging on our own. She was able to pull Galipoli's applicant file for us."

"Okay, and—?"

"The file says he was in Operation Iraqi Freedom, and according to what she had in the file, he did get a Silver Star."

"Hmm," Morrison said, a bit disappointed. "Well, I guess I was wrong about this guy, huh? Maybe he's suffering from PTSD after all."

"No, no, Cap, that's the thing," O'Dell said. "I think you might be right about him after all."

"Go ahead."

"So, according to Helen, it doesn't seem like he completed a tour of duty."

"What?"

"Yeah. It looks like, when he was being hired, his investigator didn't follow up with the military about his service record. Helen was able to hook me up with the investigator, who—thankfully—is still on the job, down on Jay Street in Brooklyn. We avoided the whole *I won't talk to you 'cause I don't know you* runaround thanks to Helen, who did a three-way call and introduced me. Turns out we had a few guys from the job in common—remember Michael Belmont from the three two? They're neighbors up in Yonkers."

"So what'd the guy have to say?"

"Well, he didn't remember the case until I told him Galipoli had won a Silver Star in the war, then it all came back to him. He was hesitant to talk to me once he knew which case it was, but when I told him why we were looking into it, he opened right up. Basically, he knows he dropped the ball. He had several military contacts he says he should've called during the investigation, but once he saw the Silver Star in his folder he figured there was no need to. Thankfully Helen was still on the phone, and he told her that his notes should be in the folder. Sure enough, she digs through the file and in the back are a couple of names and numbers of the guys he didn't call. I promised him I wouldn't make him look bad, but I'm not sure if that's going to be possible."

"Okay, but so far we just have an applicant screwup; tell me you called some of those numbers back."

"One was all I needed. Sergeant Gonzalez—local guy, lives up in Mount Vernon. He's still involved with the military, as a reservist. I told him who I was, and that I was interested in talking to him about Lou Galipoli, and he laughed and said it had been a long time since he'd heard that name. It didn't seem like he had a lot of respect for him. We talked a little about our military experiences, and I told him about my time in the 9th Infantry and in Vietnam. He told me about being severely wounded in Anbar Province, and his road to recovery. Seems like that's one of the reasons he doesn't like Galipoli—he didn't want to say too much on the phone, but he was shocked to hear he was a cop, much less a detective. He actually thought Galipoli had been court-marshalled and dishonorably discharged. When I told him about the Silver Star, he said—and I quote—*No way; it must be a different guy we're talking about.*"

"Now we're talking," Morrison said. "What else?"

"I'm afraid that's all I've got for right now—Gonzalez was at home with his kids and couldn't talk. He's willing to meet me tomorrow, though, to tell me everything he knows about the Galipoli he knew."

"Tomorrow?"

"If you can spare me for the day."

"Yeah, I think so—I have everyone else working hard on the murder."

"That's what I figured. Glad I was right! I told him I'd meet him in the morning in Mamaroneck, at this little Irish pub. I'm going to bring a photo of Lou with me, just to make sure we're talking about the same guy—he says he can't believe it is."

"Terrific. Nice work, Jeffrey. Actually," he added, suddenly feeling one of his hunches pressing at the back of his mind, "I think I'd like Sergeant Rivera to go with you too. I know we're all busy with this case, but I have a feeling this'll be worth it. Besides, it's just for an afternoon."

He'd long since learned to listen to these feelings, however unaccountable; they were the silent voice of professional instinct. "You think this guy will be all right with that?"

"I don't see why not; Frankie gets along with everyone. Besides, he's ex-military too, which might help."

"All right. I'll tell him. Let me know what you come up with, all right?"

"Yessir. We'll see what he says."

Back at the precinct house, Morrison parked in his usual spot out front. He felt extremely tired—his whole body was exhausted. *I can't believe this nightmare is continuing,* he thought. He'd felt so good just a few days ago; now he could feel himself falling back into the usual malaise of depression, accompanied by an acute pain in his chest. He'd felt the chest pain before. But this time, even he had to admit it was worse.

He walked into the squad room, and Sergeant Simmons looked up with concern. Right away he could see something was wrong.

"Cap, are you okay?" he asked.

"I'm fine," Morrison said, shaking his head. "Nothing a shot of Jameson won't cure."

Simmons stood up and headed Morrison off, not giving him the chance to go into his office.

"Come on, Cap," he said firmly. "We're taking a ride."

Too tired to argue, Morrison complied.

Without delay, and almost without further conversation, Simmons herded him into his car and drove him down to Beth Israel Hospital, on Sixteenth Street. When they were there, he marched his Captain straight into the Emergency Room. Typically for New York, the lobby was packed, and Morrison grimaced in dismay. Most cops believe that if you want to get sick, just visit any busy emergency room—and Morrison was no exception to this prejudice. But Simmons wasn't hearing it. He walked right into the back with Morrison, sat him down on an empty gurney, and asked for the head nurse.

There is much in common between nurses and cops; they often seem to share a kindred spirit. Both groups deal with people at their lowest points in life, and are often misunderstood by the people they're trying to help. Everyone in an emergency believes their case is the most important, and to such a person, someone for whom emergency is routine—for whom it is part of their job to prioritize emergencies objectively—can easily come off as aloof, or even cold. Only the professionals who deal with such emergencies daily can fully understand the heart that lies behind the professional manner. That said, though, a heart attack in progress was a high-priority emergency, no matter whom it was happening to; and Simmons was afraid that was exactly what Morrison was experiencing.

In a few minutes, a tall, pretty Hispanic woman, who by her actions was clearly in charge, came out from behind the central desk. She scrutinized Morrison closely.

"How can I help you?" she asked Simmons.

"I think my Captain here is having a heart attack," Simmons said. "He's having chest pains now."

The head nurse grabbed another nurse, and together they moved Morrison into a small area surrounded by a privacy curtain. As he was changing into a hospital gown, Morrison winced.

"The pain is pretty acute, huh?" the head nurse asked him.

"Nothing I haven't felt before," he lied. "I'm sure I'll be fine—I don't need any of this fuss."

The head nurse raised an eyebrow. "Let me be the judge of that," she said. "You just lie back here. My name's Nancy Dominguez."

Morrison lay back on the bed. "Bill Morrison," he said, wincing again as he raised an arm to gesture toward Simmons. "The worrywart over there is Sergeant Simmons."

"Well, if you are having a heart attack, you're lucky he's got some sense in his head," she said. "Now lie back! You cops always think you can tough it out. Trust me, we can do this the easy way, or the hard way." Smiling, she held up several tie-downs for him to see.

"Phew, okay, okay," he said, lying back. "Lady, you'd make a good interrogator."

"I know it," she said. "If I didn't enjoy what I did so much—!"

Simmons smiled at the pretty nurse. "You could interrogate me anytime."

She looked him up and down with a smirk. "Honey, *you'd* give me everything I wanted to know in five minutes," she laughed.

"That'd be a long night for Andre," Morrison joked. All three laughed, and Morrison winced again, worse this time. The nurse quieted them down and began a preliminary examination.

Three hours and two doctors later, the diagnosis came back. Morrison, as it turned out, was suffering from a severe anxiety attack, brought on by stress at work and exacerbated by drinking. The ER doctor prescribed him some time off and a course of Xanax. Morrison accepted the diagnosis quietly, having absolutely no intention of taking either.

Having dressed, he walked out of the ER unit to find Sergeant Simmons in deep conversation with the head nurse. Simmons looked up at him.

"You ready to get going, Cap?" he asked.

"Yeah, let's go," Morrison said. Nancy handed Simmons a slip of paper.

"Call me anytime," she said as Morrison pulled Simmons toward the door.

Outside, Morrison gave Simmons a questioning smile.

"I have a heart-attack scare, and you go after the head nurse?" he asked.

"What can I say?" Simmons laughed. "She likes the same kind of music I do."

31

Morrison rolled himself out of his bunk, headed to the shower, and hoped this day would be better than the last.

Sergeant McNamara was emerging from the shower as he went in. Before he could duck inside, McNamara hollered out to him.

"Hey, Cap! You see the paper this morning?"

Morrison dropped his head, already aware of what he was going to see. He went back out to the squad room, picked up the paper, and sure enough, there it was.

COPYCAT KILLER LOOSE IN NEW YORK!

Thank God for journalistic integrity, he thought, flipping to the story inside. It was even worse than the headline—nothing better than fear-mongering for the general public. He dropped the paper on the desk in disgust and retreated to the shower for five minutes of peace.

Meanwhile, in Mamaroneck, Detective O'Dell and Sergeant Rivera were waiting outside the pub where they'd arranged to meet Sergeant Gonzalez. The seasons were finally starting to turn to early spring—one of the best parts of living in the tri-state area—so they opted to wait outside in the cool, fresh air rather than inside the musty pub. They watched as several cars and SUVs came and went, with no sign of the Sergeant.

Finally, an older-model Ford pulled up, and they could both tell from the look of the driver, when he got out, that their rendezvous had arrived. Though he was dressed in civvies, his clean-cut appearance and almost at-attention walk gave him up for a military man. Rivera extended a hand.

"Sergeant Gonzalez," he said. "I'm Frankie Rivera. Thank you for your service."

The other man smiled. "Ernesto Gonzalez," he said, shaking Rivera's hand. "You know, I'm not too used to being thanked for that."

"I know how you feel," Rivera said. "Jeffrey here and I—Sergeant Gonzalez, Jeffrey O'Dell—we were both Vietnam guys, so we get it. Hey, at least they don't spit on you anymore, right?"

"That's true," Gonzalez said. "I guess times have improved that way."

Laughing, the three of them made their way into the pub. It wasn't much on atmosphere, but at this hour it was quieter than most diners. They chatted a while about their respective military experiences and their reception on coming home, encouraging the bond of shared experience they had already between them; then, once the coffee had been refilled, they got down to the matter at hand.

Jeffrey O'Dell opened the manila folder he'd had sitting on the table in front of them since they arrived, and turned a photo of Lou Galipoli towards Gonzalez.

"Yep, that's him," Gonzalez said immediately, anticipating O'Dell's question. "I still can't believe the guy's a cop, though."

Rivera glanced over at O'Dell. "Well, Jeffrey and I were hoping you'd elaborate on that a bit," he said. "What exactly do you know about Louis Galipoli?"

"Where do you want me to start?"

"I mean, we'd appreciate you telling us everything you know about him, so wherever you want to start would be fine."

"All right," Gonzalez said, with absolutely no hesitation. "I'll start by saying that he's the biggest piece of garbage I've ever met."

Rivera and O'Dell laughed. Gonzalez looked at them, his smile stony.

"I mean that," he said quietly.

Rivera nodded. "I know, it's nothing we haven't heard, believe me. It's just—well, they're pretty strong words for a guy who was awarded a Silver Star."

Ernesto Gonzalez looked as though he'd been slapped.

"There is no way *this* guy"—he stabbed a finger roughly at the photograph—"won a Silver Star."

"I know it's hard to believe," O'Dell said, "but it's in his military records—we looked up his applicant folder from when he was coming into the department."

Gonzalez shook his head, adamant. "I don't care what paperwork it's on—I cannot believe *he* did anything that would be even *remotely* close to deserving a Silver Star. Absolutely not. This guy was on his way to a court martial during our time at Camp Falcon!"

"Court martial?" Rivera asked, his eyes wide.

Gonzalez sighed. "You guys really *don't* know much about Louis Galipoli, do you? Okay, I'll start at the beginning, then. When I was a Staff Sergeant, he was assigned to my platoon; and from the first day, I could see there was something off with this guy. I mean, the *first day*. And it didn't take long for my instincts to be proven right by his actions, either.

"Being the platoon commander, I didn't hang out with the rank and file all the time; but pretty soon after he came on, several soldiers of African-American descent came to me to complain that Galipoli was a racist. You know how it is—as soldiers in a combat zone, you tend to rib each other in ways that back home might not be considered appropriate. So at first, I thought that might be what was going on here. I talked to the guys about it, then sat down with Galipoli to talk about what the boundaries were when it came to the platoon, and what I would tolerate. I should have seen it during that first interview, but I didn't."

"Should have seen what?" O'Dell asked.

"His attitude. He could have cared less about the brotherhood of being a soldier, or that his life might depend on his platoon mates, or any of that. He was completely callous toward what anyone else thought. Anyway, like I said, I should have started a file on him then, but I gave him a bit of play, since he was new. It was a big mistake.

"The next incident involved a female soldier named Eleanora—pretty woman, could have been a model. Women in the military have changed since back in the Vietnam days, you know—back then, most if not all of your enlisted females were nurses. Nowadays they work in a lot of positions, and they end up working closer to combat than in the past. Anyway, Eleanora came to me to complain about Galipoli. She's African-American too, so at first I thought it was the race issue again; but no. Once again, he'd gone way beyond anyone else with the comments, this time of a sexual nature. She told me he wouldn't leave her alone—and not in the usual stupid *I want to be your boyfriend* kind of way. This was more in a degrading, chauvinistic way. The things he'd said were really vile, really disgusting.

"He never physically did anything to Eleanora—probably because she was a tough cookie who would have shot him if he tried anything—but he was unrelenting, and was moving toward stalker status before she brought it to me. This time I didn't hesitate. He was written up and ended up in the stockade after Lieutenant Lyons was done with him."

"Sounds like a real piece of work," Rivera said. "But so far, it doesn't sound like he was much more than mouth."

"Well, that's what I thought, Sarge," Gonzalez said. "But wrong again. That was only the beginning. He wasn't out of the stockade for more than a week when another female soldier named Cynthia came to me. She was another good-looking woman—but when she walked into my tent, she was a mess. Took me half an hour to calm her down before she could talk. When I finally got her to tell me what was wrong, she told me Galipoli had just tried to rape her in the showers."

Rivera turned his head in disgust. "Are you shitting me? He tried to *rape* another soldier, and he ends up getting a Silver Star?"

"Now you know why I don't buy it. Anyway, this time we had some physical evidence: Cynthia had bruises on her face from where Galipoli had slapped her around. He really beat her up. The only thing that stopped him raping her, apparently, was that another soldier walked into the shower, and he ran off."

"Did the other soldier see who it was?" O'Dell asked.

"You bet he did, and he spoke up about it too. So I had the MPs bring Galipoli before Lieutenant Lyons again. Obviously this one was going up the chain, so I sat down and did a file on the incident, and delivered it to the Lieutenant myself."

"Can you remember when this all happened?" Rivera asked.

"Absolutely—October 6, 2006."

Rivera's eyes widened. "How do you remember that specific date?" he asked.

"Oh, that's a day I'll never forget," Gonzalez sighed. "Later that night we got hit with enemy mortar fire. Blew the base to hell. I took some shrapnel to my left side—I'm lucky to be alive. They airlifted me out, along with a few other soldiers who got hit that night."

"Do you know what happened to Galipoli after the attack?" O'Dell asked.

"Well, I'd *thought* he was court martialed, but now it sounds like he wasn't. I didn't follow it after that. I was hurt pretty bad—I spent the next two years coming back from my injury."

"What about Lieutenant Lyons? Have you seen him since you were injured?"

Gonzalez nodded gravely. "He got it worse than me that night. His tent was right next to a munitions truck that took a direct hit. He was killed in the explosion."

Rivera and O'Dell were silent for a long moment before Rivera spoke.

"What would you say," he said slowly, "if I told you it was Lieutenant Lyons who signed off on Galipoli's Silver Star?"

Sergeant Gonzalez stared at both of them, dumbfounded. *"What did you say?"*

"That Lieutenant Lyons signed off on—"

"I heard you—it's just—it's impossible," Gonzalez stammered, furious. "Lieutenant Lyons was going to recommend a court martial for this piece of crap, not a Silver Star. It has to be a mistake. Listen," he added intensely, "I don't know how it happened, but it's bullshit. Complete bullshit. If he's anything like the Galipoli I knew, that guy ought to be in jail."

Rivera and O'Dell nodded. "Do you have anyone we can talk to about what happened to him?" O'Dell asked.

"Yeah, definitely," Gonzalez said. "I have a couple of contacts who were also at Camp Falcon; they must know what happened to Galipoli. Rich Dyer, particularly—he'd be a good man for you to talk to."

"All right, make sure to get that to us," Rivera said. "We don't buy the guy's story either, but we're having a hard time making anything stick."

"A Silver Star," Gonzalez said. "That's absolutely unbelievable. You know, I was thinking of becoming a cop, now that I'm done with military service—but with guys like that on the force, I don't know!"

"Well, don't let him put you off," O'Dell said. "If we can get any of this verified, he won't be there for long."

"Let's hope not," Gonzalez laughed. "He's a dangerous customer to trust with law and order, that's for sure. I mean, the thought of him earning any sort of *medal*—it's just insane! And Lyons signing off on it—! That sounds like forgery to me; forgery, or some kind of enormous mix-up. I mean, the guy had absolutely no team mentality, no thought for anyone else, no—"

"Same Galipoli, all right," Rivera sighed. "If you gentlemen will excuse me a moment, I've got a phone call to make. I have a feeling the Captain will be interested in hearing this."

32

Captain Morrison had a restless night's sleep.

The events of the past several days—culminating in Sergeant Gonzalez's information about Galipoli—were really getting to him; and he was struggling for the peace to sleep for one more hour before the squad room started to buzz again.

The door to the bunkroom opened. Someone was standing in the doorway, backlit and indistinct. Morrison sat up in his bunk.

"I hope you have a good reason to barge in here, whoever it is," he said.

McNamara's voice drifted across in an urgent whisper. "Sorry, Cap—it's me, Pat, and yes, it is important."

"Christ, is it another homicide?" Morrison asked, his heart racing.

"No, Cap," McNamara said. "It may be worse than that. Can you get dressed? We need to talk out of the office. I'll wait for you out front." And turning into the light, he was gone.

Morrison scrambled to get dressed, wondering as he did what could be going on that Pat McNamara couldn't even talk about here. Whatever it was, it couldn't be good. *So much for another hour of sleep,* he thought.

When Morrison exited the front door of the precinct, McNamara was sitting out front in an unmarked car with the motor running. Morrison saw Sergeant Simmons sitting in the backseat. Somehow the sight made him more anxious than before. He jumped into the front passenger seat, and they peeled away from the curb as if they were heading to a 10-13.

"Pat, tell me—what the fuck is going on?" Morrison asked.

"Just give me a few minutes to park, Cap," McNamara said, "and we'll show you what this is all about."

Morrison had never seen his sergeants act like this before, so he quelled his curiosity a moment and went with it. At this time of the morning there was little traffic, and after a quick drive they'd reached the Westside Highway and West 34th Street. They pulled into a quiet parking lot close to the water. For an instant it flashed through Morrison's mind that if they were gangsters, this was when the guy in the backseat would put an icepick in the back of his head. Thankfully, he knew that wasn't the case; though from the others' demeanor, what he was about to hear seemed as though it might make that scenario seem less painful.

Once they'd parked, McNamara turned to him.

"It's in the trunk," he said resignedly. "Let's take a look, shall we?"

Morrison realized he was now completely in the blind. What the hell could be in the trunk of the car that had these two sergeants so distressed?

When they were all standing behind the vehicle, McNamara looked one way, then another, then swiftly opened the trunk. There, in the otherwise empty trunk, sat a small black knapsack. Sergeant Simmons reached in, pulled it towards the edge, and opened the zipper to expose its contents.

Morrison's eyes grew wide as he saw it.

"A rape kit?" he asked.

"Yep," McNamara said. "And a pretty carefully put-together one, at that."

So it appeared to be. At a glance Morrison saw rope, tape, lube, a knife and sap gloves—special gloves with lead sewn into the fingers. He looked up at the two sergeants.

"Please don't tell me we forgot to voucher this stuff from one of the crime scenes?" he said.

"No, boss, we didn't forget," answered McNamara. "This didn't come from a crime scene."

Morrison was confused. "Well, where the hell did it come from, then?"

McNamara took a deep breath, then spoke quickly. "We had to put one of the cars into the shop for maintenance," he said, "so I had Garriga take it over to the garage in Queens. He dropped off the car, and as he was leaving, one of the mechanics called him back over to the car—he'd seen this bag on the floor under the backseat. He hadn't seen it before because the interior's black."

"Jesus, you don't mean—"

"Yeah. Garriga brought it back from the shop, and when he got to the squad room he opened it to see whose it was. As soon as he saw this shit, he put on rubber gloves so as not to contaminate anything. He also found a pair of panties that looked like they had been ripped off of someone. We had him package those up and deliver them to the Medical Examiner's Office for any possible DNA. He also found a pair of men's shorts and a shirt—looked like workout gear—so we had him take that in as well."

"Okay," Morrison said slowly, trying to process everything. "So how the *fuck* did this bag get in the back of a police car?"

"We can't be sure of that," McNamara said. "But what we can tell you is the last person to sign out the car the night before."

Morrison stared at him, the blood dropping out of his face. "Who?" he asked, with a sickening certainty that he already knew the answer.

"Lou Galipoli."

Morrison closed his eyes, the nauseous rush of horror mixing with the sense of everything coming together.

The tape and rope used by their copycat, and by the two guys from Connecticut.

The facial bruising of the last two victims—easily accomplished with sap gloves.

The information from Sergeant Gonzalez.

Tina Koreski's hunches, and his own.

The way they'd seen Galipoli look at their crime scene photos—interestedly, admiringly, *proudly*...

"Who knows about this?" Morrison asked.

"As of right now, only the two of us, you, and Garriga," Simmons said.

"Okay," Morrison said. "This guy is obviously a sick fuck, but we've got to tie this all together and make sure we're right. So far, we have an intense hatred for his attitude, a story from when he was in the military about a possible rape, and this rape kit. It may seem like enough, but it isn't. We can't say one hundred percent that it belongs to him—only that he'd signed out the car last. We need more information to take him down. I don't like the idea of a rapist and killer on the job, but if he is one, we need to make sure he goes down hard."

The other two nodded gravely as he went on.

"Now, this is going to collapse on us within the next twenty-four to forty-eight hours, so we need to act fast. I already have Rivera and O'Dell meeting with another military contact today, and you tell me we have the clothes from this bag at the ME's office. Now we need to put some surveillance on Galipoli—and I mean *right away*. We also need to grab a sample of his DNA somehow, for the comparison. Ideas?"

"He smokes like a chimney," Simmons said. "He's always putting his butts in those periscope things out front of the precinct."

"Great. I want you to *quietly* empty those things out, and let's have someone make sure no one else uses them until he does. In the meantime, grab his coffee cup off his desk, get his tissue if he blows his fucking nose—whatever we have to do, *get it done*. I don't have to tell you guys how this goes. McNamara, get the detectives we can trust the most, and get surveillance going on him right away. We can't afford another homicide now."

Later, Morrison was back at his desk, the tension boiling in him. Detective Kasak stuck his head in the door.

"Chief Arndt on the phone for you, Cap," he said.

"Tell him I'm not here," Morrison growled.

"You got it," Kasak smiled. "Where should I tell him you are?"

"I don't know, whatever you want—tell him I took my goddamn grandmother to the zoo. I just can't talk to that asshole right now."

He heard Kasak return to his desk and pick up the phone. "Captain Morrison took the day off to bring his grandmother to the zoo," he heard Kasak saying as Tina Koreski walked in and closed the door.

"Next in line?" Morrison said, his mood slightly lightened.

Koreski looked determined. "Cap, Sergeant McNamara just told me what's going on, and asked me to do surveillance on Galipoli."

"Okay, so?"

"I think I have a better idea."

By this point, Morrison knew Koreski's methods had more than earned his consideration. "Let's take a walk," he said. "I'm a little hesitant to speak about this in the office."

They headed around the corner from the precinct house, to a little hole-in-the-wall diner a few blocks away where they had a small, closed-off private section they let cops use to talk. Once their coffee was on its way, Koreski leaned in.

"Cap, I know we don't have enough yet to nail Galipoli for the copycat," she said. "I think if we really want to get him, we need to catch him red-handed. Based on what we have so far, even if we got a match on the DNA a high-priced lawyer might be able to get him off—you know, convince a jury that there was contamination of the evidence, or try to say that we framed him. We haven't exactly kept our dislike of the guy to ourselves."

"Yeah, that's true," he admitted. "So what's your plan?"

"The guy's been asking me to go out with him since he got to the taskforce. He always told me it would be between us—he wouldn't want anyone in the squad to know we went out, stuff like that. Why don't I say yes?"

Morrison couldn't believe his ears. "Tina, I can't let you do that," he said.

"Why not? This is the best chance we have of nailing this sick fuck. And if he isn't the guy, the worst thing that happens is I get stuck listening to him rave about himself all night long."

"And if he is? You'll be in exactly the same situation you were in undercover, all those years ago."

"Not at all," she said coolly. "I'll have *you* in charge this time, and backup I can trust. That makes all the difference in the world."

Morrison considered. Koreski had certainly demonstrated her toughness to him. She might also be right; if Galipoli was the copycat, they'd need every ounce of positive evidence against him they could get, and his treatment of women was his weakest point. On the other hand, backup or no, it was extremely risky; if Galipoli was the one who'd perpetrated the last two murders, there was no telling what he could do, or how quickly he could do it, if he thought he'd get away with it.

Morrison looked at Koreski. Her eyes were steady, focused.

"Come on, Cap," she said again, unshrinking under his glare. "You know I can do this, and we haven't got time to think it over all day."

He knew she was right.

"Okay," he said. "But we're going to have you wired, with at least three backup teams."

"Great," she said steadily, with an air of having thought it all through. "I want Kasak and Marchioni as my primary backup. I trust them, and I know they won't let me go."

Morrison smiled. "Careful what you wish for, Tina—you just might get it."

"I'm counting on it," she said. "And if you're in charge of it, I know it'll go fine." She rose to her feet. "Hey, I'll see you later, okay,

Cap?—Medveded and I are on night surveillance."

"Okay, Koreski," he said. He watched her on her way out as he signaled for the check. It was a strange effect; she looked so small, so vulnerable, but at the same time so self-contained. It seemed to him he'd never seen someone look so sure of themselves before.

God, I hope I've made the right decision, he thought.

33

"**I** don't know what the hell I'm gonna do with myself when I retire," Frankie Rivera said, shaking his head. "I mean, how does a guy go from seeing all the crazy shit we've seen, to sitting at home watching reruns of *Barney Miller?*"

He and Jeffrey O'Dell were on their way up to Cold Spring, and in the course of their exchange of memorable moments from their work on the force—fairly typical cop talk, though pretty hair-raising by civilian standards—he'd gotten around to lamenting the little time he had left on the job before he had to go.

"I mean, *no* one understands us the way we do," he went on. "That's got to be the hardest part of leaving the job behind—the people."

"It's the hardest part of the job as it is," O'Dell put in.

"Absolutely," Rivera agreed emphatically. "I remember going to parties with my wife's company—as soon as everyone hears you're a cop, they all want to tell you about their experiences with one. Most of the time they ask questions about TV shows they've seen—*Do you guys really beat people in handcuffs? Have you ever shot someone?* They don't know what a good cop's job is really about, how much time we spend running around trying to put the goddamn bad guys in jail. There's no family life; that's why so many of us get divorced! We miss every holiday, every birthday—"

"Every anniversary," O'Dell said.

Rivera squinted his eyes, his lips curling up in a smile. "Oh, those are the worst," he said. "They never let you live those down."

"Never," O'Dell agreed. "I remember this time, we were going to a wedding upstate, my wife and me. My wife's sister is getting married, right? Little town. I know I got a long ride home afterwards, so I have a couple of beers. Not enough to get me drunk—though this was back in the day when drunk driving wasn't the hot topic anyway—just literally a couple. And don't you know, on the ride home my wife starts giving me shit about why can't I be more like her sister's new husband? *He* comes home every day at five. *They* spend every weekend together. No mercy, this breaking my balls. I started to feel like Charlie Brown listening to the teacher."

"I've been there," Rivera snickered.

"Well, so anyway, after a bit I turn to look at her to make a point, and a fucking deer bolts out in front of the car."

"Oh, man. What happened?"

"She screams, I swerve to miss hitting Bambi, and we run off the road into a ditch and knock down a tree."

"Holy shit! Was everyone okay?"

"Oh, sure. More than okay—still fighting! The cops showed up, and me and her were still fighting like cats and dogs, screaming at the top of our lungs."

Rivera laughed. "Incredible," he said. "The cops good to you guys?"

"Very good. They weren't too happy when they first got out of the car, but when I identified myself they couldn't have been nicer. They took me and my wife to a local diner to get us to calm down while they were doing the report—they even bought us coffee. That wouldn't happen nowadays."

"Yeah," Rivera sighed, with the feeling of every older generation of cops that the younger generation of cops was no good.

They pulled into town. Cold Spring, a little town about an hour or two up the Hudson from the city, looked like the archetypal American town—Main Street, quaint little clapboard houses, American flags on every other telephone pole. They passed a few antiques stores and restaurants, family-owned businesses by the look of them. It was a refreshing change from what they were used to.

At the dead end of West Street by the water, they found a small blue compact sedan with a man sitting in the driver's seat. He waved to them, rolling down his window as they pulled up alongside the car.

"Sergeant Rivera, I presume?" he asked.

Rivera nodded. "That's me," he said, "and this is Detective O'Dell." He and O'Dell showed their badges.

"Great," the man said. "Captain Richard Dyer. Pleasure to meet you both. Follow me, if you would."

They followed him out of the park to a place called the Hudson House Inn. When they'd parked, they found Dyer at an outside table at the far end of the porch, seated with his back to the street. He was everything they'd expected to see in an officer of the United States Army: tall and lean, with short, almost crewcut-style hair and a calm, steady gaze. They'd done some looking into his background before their trip, and found numerous personal testimonies to his character along with a number of service medals.

"I know you guys like to sit where you can see who's coming toward you," he said amiably, "so I left those for you." He gestured to the two chairs on the opposite side of the table.

"That's much appreciated," Rivera laughed as they sat. "It would've been distracting otherwise."

"I know the feeling," Dyer said. "Now, how can I help you gentlemen?"

Rivera got right to the point. "We'd like to ask you a few questions about Camp Falcon, and some of the men and women who served under you."

Dyer nodded thoughtfully. "Well, don't get me wrong, I loved serving my country," he said, "but I have to admit, it's been a long time since I heard that name, and since I left active-duty service, I haven't stayed in touch with too many of those people, either. I don't mind saying I'm trying to forget some of that past."

"I understand," Rivera nodded. "But I thought you were still in the service."

"No, I left. I'm in the reserves, but now I own my own business—computer IT."

"All right," Rivera said. "Well, whatever you can remember will be helpful, I'm sure. For starters, can you tell us anything about Lieutenant Gerald Lyons?"

Dyer smiled fondly. "Ah, Jerry was one of the finest men who I ever served with," he said. "Got his CIB—er, sorry, Combat Infantryman Badge—"

"Oh, that's all right," Rivera assured him. "Both of us are former military."

"Oh, all right. Well, he got his CIB his first week on the ground. Real soldier's soldier. He wanted to go to Ranger school at the end of his tour, but he never made it home."

"What happened to him?" asked O'Dell.

"We took a mortar attack at the base," Dyer said quietly. "He was one of three killed. Four others were wounded."

"I'm sorry to hear it," Rivera said. It was clear the Captain was still troubled by the loss. "Can you tell us when exactly the lieutenant was killed?"

"Sure," Dyer said without hesitation. "That was October 6, 2006." When the other two sat in significant silence, he went on. "It was a pretty widely known date. It was all over the media—so many false reports about what happened that day."

"I'm sure there were," Rivera said. "And what about Louis Galipoli—does that name ring any bells for you?"

Dyer's face darkened. "It sure does," he said. "That man was one of the loudest, most undisciplined soldiers"—he shook his head—"strike that, *human beings* I've ever known."

Rivera and O'Dell nodded. It seemed Galipoli's way of winning friends and influencing people hadn't worked for him in the military, either.

"I see," Rivera said. "Well, besides that general statement, what can you tell us about him?"

"Oh, he was bad news from day one in Camp," Dyer said. "One complaint after another. The icing on the cake was when he tried to rape a female soldier." He nodded as the other two exchanged glances. "That's right, despicable but true. I don't remember her name, unfortunately. She was lucky that someone walked in on them; otherwise she'd have been raped."

O'Dell leaned in, deciding to go for the main point. "Captain, I know this is going to be a tough question," he said, "but in your opinion, how does a guy like that go from being on the block for a court martial to being awarded a Silver Star?"

Dyer favored them with the incredulous look they'd come to know well. "*What?* You must be crazy," he said with a laugh. "There's no way he was put in for a Silver Star! The guy was the most useless individual ever to serve in our military. He was well on his way to being drummed out of the service. Silver Star—! He wasn't even allowed outside the wire! All the non-coms were afraid to take him out; they thought he'd frag one of them."

O'Dell took some papers out of his folder, including a copy of the commendation write-up for Galipoli's Silver Star.

"Can you take a look at this and tell us what you think?" he asked.

Captain Dyer carefully looked over the paperwork, shaking his head.

"Conspicuous gallantry," he mumbled in disbelief. "This guy was a coward—a disgrace to the uniform. And signed by Lieutenant Lyons—! Absolutely impossible. This is a fake, I'm sure of it—a total fake. Look here: it was written on the day Lieutenant Lyons was killed."

The two nodded. Neither of them had missed the connection. "Do you think it's possible that Galipoli forged the lieutenant's name on this commendation?" O'Dell asked.

Captain Dyer picked the papers up again and looked over the signature line. "Well, this is going back some years now," he said, "but I don't recall his signature looking like this. I couldn't swear to it, but I'm pretty sure that's not his signature. I'm guessing this guy is the reason you wanted to speak to me about Camp Falcon, then?"

"Yes, sir," Rivera answered. "We're trying to verify some things about his past."

"He wanted for something?"

Rivera cleared his throat. "Actually, he's a detective in the NYPD now."

"A *detective?*" Dyer repeated. "Man, you guys must have really lowered your standards to let *that* guy aboard. He's a maniac."

"You don't need to tell me," Rivera said. "But let me change topics a moment. What can you tell us about Ernesto Gonzalez?"

Dyer blinked. "He's a great soldier, and a better man," he said. "He's one of the few people I have kept in touch with over the years, though I haven't spoken to him in a while now. Don't tell me he's mixed up in something too—?"

"Not at all," Rivera said. "We just spoke to him yesterday. He's the one who gave us your name. He said he wrote Galipoli up for most of his complaints, including the last one for attempted rape, and also said that Galipoli was brought to Lieutenant Lyons's tent shortly before the attack that killed him, and—"

"Stop right there," Dyer said, raising his hand. "Are you telling me that on October 6th, 2006, Galipoli was with Lieutenant Lyons *during the attack?* If that's what you're saying, how could he not have been injured?"

"I'm afraid I don't have an answer for that," Rivera said. "I wasn't there. But I do have a somewhat sensitive question for you. Once the attack was over, did you see Lieutenant Lyons's body?"

Captain Dyer looked down at the floor, the color draining slowly out of his face. He sat stock-still for a moment, breathing deeply.

"Are you all right, Captain?" Rivera asked gently.

After a moment, Dyer looked up again. "Talking to you today has brought back a lot from my past that I've tried to keep there," he said. "Jerry Lyons was one of my closest friends in the military. The day he was killed was extremely difficult for me, and one of the primary reasons I left active duty."

"I understand," Rivera persisted, "but did you see his body the night he was killed? Believe me, Captain, I'm only asking because I have to; it's very important, possibly critical, to what's going on right now."

The captain looked directly into Rivera's eyes, his own welling up with tears.

"No, I didn't," he said finally. "I saw the body bag he was in, but I never opened it. I couldn't. Maybe that sounds weak to you, but he was my best friend."

"It's not weak at all," Rivera said, shaking his head. "We've each been in the same position, many times." He waited a moment before posing the most difficult question of all. "Captain," he said, "do you think there's any possibility that he—that Louis Galipoli may have killed Lieutenant Lyons after the attack started, and used the attack to cover it up?"

Captain Dyer sat breathless for a long time, his eyes searching sight-lessly over the tabletop.

"Oh my God," he said quietly. "He killed Jerry Lyons. This piece of crap killed him, and because I couldn't look at his body, the moth-erfucker got away with it."

O'Dell and Rivera's eyes widened. O'Dell began to say something, but stopped himself as Dyer went on.

"The non-coms all told me he was capable of fragging them," he said. "I never believed it was actually possible, but it all makes sense now. The guy was on his way to being court martialed, and because of a freak attack at the wrong time, he was able to kill my best friend, destroy the paperwork for his court martial, and replace it with this bullshit Silver Star commendation." He slapped the paper in disgust. "I'm sorry, guys, but we have to stop here. I have to notify the CID—the United States

Army Criminal Investigation Command," he explained, forgetting in his passion that his listeners were military men. "They'll want to talk to you guys—this is serious shit, gentlemen. God, thanks to me he could have gotten away with it!" He stood abruptly, shaking his head. "Listen, I'm sorry I can't give you more, but this is mind-blowing for me right now," he said. He took out his phone. "I just need to get in touch with someone at the CID—I need to talk to them right away."

"It's all right," Rivera assured him. "You've been very helpful, really. I'm just—are you sure you're going to be all right, Captain?"

"Oh, I'll be fine," Dyer answered, with an effort. "I just have to make sure this gets put right. This means a lot of work! They're going to need to get in touch with Jerry's family to exhume the body, have an autopsy done—this is no simple matter." He shook hands hurriedly with the two detectives. "I'm really sorry to go like this, gentlemen," he said, "but I think you're in a position to understand my concern."

"We certainly are," O'Dell said, looking over at Rivera. "And anyway, don't worry about it—from what you've told us, it sounds like we're going to have some work to do ourselves."

34

The news from Rivera and O'Dell was the last straw, and Captain Morrison instructed his top three sergeants to call an emergency meeting of select members of his task force. The meeting was scheduled to take place at Luigi's—this was a matter too sensitive for the precinct at large—and Morrison waited apprehensively at their table in back for his team to file in.

The first to arrive were McNamara and the Coke boys.

"What's going on?" Leo Kasak asked Morrison as they sat. Morrison looked at McNamara.

"You didn't tell them?" he asked.

McNamara shook his head. "I figured it was best held for when we were all together," he said.

"All right, then," Morrison said. "Sit tight, boys; I don't want to have to go over all of this twice."

The remainder of the group—Rivera, Simmons, O'Dell, Garriga—showed up within the next few minutes. Koreski and Medveded, out surveilling Galipoli, were conspicuously absent.

As the team seated themselves, an air of somber mystery restraining their usual high-spiritedness, Morrison felt a swelling of camaraderie mingling with his apprehension. Everyone around the table, sergeant or detective, was someone he trusted with his life. Now he would have to trust them with Tina Koreski's as well.

He cleared his throat.

"All right, listen up, everyone," he began. "Some of you know why we're here, and others don't, so I'm just going to go over everything with you. Ultimately, I'm going to ask you to be involved in something that you might not want to get involved in, and I want you to know that if you're uncomfortable with it, I understand, and I won't fault anyone for dropping out. I don't expect everyone to agree with what I'm about to tell you; it's a difficult thing even for me to bring up, especially because it may involve one of our own.

"As you all know, since the Boston boys' murders, we've had a copycat killer running around the city. We've all been particularly struggling to figure out how this person had access to certain information regarding those early crime scenes that wasn't released to the press. As we have discussed before, there were really only two possible explanatory scenarios. One was that Anderson and Rutherford had told someone else about what they'd done. The other was that it was someone on the inside—someone within the department. Since the arrest of those two psychopaths last week, and their denial that anyone else was involved, certain information has come to light that leads me to believe, very strongly, that we have a serial murderer on our team."

The table was eerily quiet. Everyone remained completely focused on Morrison, waiting to hear the name spoken. Under the intensity of their gaze, he felt the full weight of what he had to tell them.

"I admit, this is very difficult for me," he continued at length. "I've always considered the police to be the good guys, as you all do, and given the benefit of the doubt to our brotherhood at every opportunity. The fact that we're all even here should demonstrate my conviction that our information is reliable. I'm sick to my core with what I have to tell you, but it needs to be said: Louis Galipoli is our copycat."

The silence deepened into shock. Despite the universal dislike of the new detective, no one could believe—could even *want* to believe—that one of their own could commit the atrocities they'd seen. Kasak and Marchioni stared at Morrison, confounded; they knew he wouldn't bring up such a thing lightly.

"Jesus," Kasak said finally. "I always knew the guy was a jerkoff, and no one could stand his egotistical attitude, but to think he's a rapist and a murderer—man, that's pretty hard to deal with."

Bill Morrison raised his hands to quiet the murmur of agreement that ran around the table. "I know," he said. "Believe me, I know. I've really been struggling with this myself. And once you hear what some of us already know, you can make up your own minds as to whether it's the right conclusion or not. And I want to stress again that at that point, you can bow out if you want to."

Next he had the other members of the squad tell the group what they'd discovered over the past few days. Sergeant Rivera started off with the information they'd collected from the military personnel they'd spoken to. He recounted Gonzalez's and Dyer's allegations of attempted rape and murder, pointing especially to the connection between Galipoli's slapping and punching his intended Army victim in the face, and the severe facial bruising they'd found on their copycat victims. He also mentioned, to the horror of the team, Captain Dyer's suspicion that Galipoli had killed his former lieutenant to cover up his wrongdoings.

This information was followed by the discovery from the car. Francisco Garriga explained what he'd found inside the gym bag, and each item described raised the pitch of anger around the table. When he mentioned the last item, the sap gloves, Kasak and Marchioni leaned back from the table in disgust.

"I don't know about any of you," Mike Marchioni blurted out furiously, "but I'm in. Whatever you want us to do, Captain—I'm in. And I know I speak for Leo and myself when I say, give us the word, and we will fuck this guy up. Beating on women—! This piece of shit isn't a man, he's a monster, and he needs to be stopped."

"Absolutely," Kasak agreed. "Give us ten minutes alone with him!

No backing out here, Cap."

Around the table his sentiment was echoed to a man. Everyone felt the same; no one was backing out of the assignment, no matter what it was. Morrison was touched, but hardly surprised; good cops can never stand bad ones. There was no "blue wall of silence" or tolerance for a cop who could do such a thing; a cop who crossed that line was no more than a disgrace to the job.

Again Morrison raised his hands to quiet the table.

"Now you all know how I've felt, these past few days," he said. "It's a hard and unusual position to be in, to wish your professional instincts were incorrect, and have them proven right anyway. But there's still some room for error here; and we can't act until we're a hundred percent certain that Galipoli's the copycat. As compelling as the evidence is, we need to be patient and put together a solid case against him, before we charge out of here to grab him. That's where the plan comes into play."

Rivera was waiting for this. "Okay, Cap," he said. "What's the plan?"

"You may have wondered why Tina and Alex aren't with us this evening," Morrison said, to a ripple of nods around the table. "They're currently conducting surveillance on Galipoli. I've discussed my plan thoroughly with them already, and they're in full agreement with it. But they're going to need your help to make it work.

"So far, we've been lucky, and Galipoli's been tied up in court processing the Rutherford/Anderson case," he continued. "Karma's a bitch: his hijacking of the arresting-officer commendation has actually worked in our favor. As of an hour ago, he's been at home; he's scheduled to come into the precinct tomorrow morning for regular duty."

"Excuse me, but what about the radio car?" O'Dell asked. "Won't he be suspicious if he comes back and doesn't find his bag there?"

"We've returned the bag, with all its contents except the panties and shorts," Morrison explained. "Those are with the Medical Examiner's Office; hopefully he won't notice they're missing until too late.

"Now, we're going to be playing a dangerous game of spider and fly, boys," he went on, "and we can't risk him catching onto us until we've got him. Based on everything we know about him, Galipoli has used his supposed charm on the women he's attacked; tomorrow we're going to turn the tables on him. Tina Koreski's going to be our spider. Before you ask, she's the one who came up with the idea; I was hesitant to allow it, but she wants to catch him as badly as any of you do, and her thinking is sound. Galipoli's been after her since he met her on the taskforce: asking her out, telling her it'd be their little secret, et cetera. If he asks tomorrow when he comes back, as we have reason to think he will, she's going to say yes.

"We think his insistence about it being kept secret from the squad goes further than the usual professional reasons. To put it mildly, we think he has plans for Tina beyond the typical first date. Now I want to stress this: if we're right, and he is our copycat killer, Tina is going to be in serious *danger the whole time she's with him.* This means we all need to be on point in keeping her safe. Some of you may know she was let down before; that cannot, that *will* not, happen again. She's asked that Leo and Mike be her primary backup team."

The Coke brothers looked surprised.

"She asked for us specifically?" Kasak asked.

"It was her one condition for doing this," Morrison said.

Kasak and Marchioni nodded. Despite the gravity of the situation, they were unable to keep their pride from showing through.

"We won't let anything happen to her, Cap," Marchioni said. "We swear it on our lives."

"I know you won't," Morrison said. "That's why I agreed to any of this. Now, everyone else will also be out on the street during this operation—*except* Alex Medveded. After his interview of the one guy in Boston, Galipoli has been talking to him more and more: telling him how much he admired his work, how well he handled all the gory details, and so forth. Alex has been playing along with him ever since, and he believes he may have Galipoli suspecting that he, too, is into the shit those psychos did."

There was a murmur of disbelief around the table.

"Look, Medveded's great, no doubt about it," Simmons said, "but this is pushing it for me."

"I agree," Rivera said. "You have to be a complete idiot to talk to the cops, if you really committed a crime."

"An idiot, or an egomaniac," Bill Morrison returned. "You can't underestimate the lengths a person like this will go to for their ego, Frankie. Anyone they can get to appreciate how smart they are, and how they fooled the stupid cops for so long—they'll do it. Think about the worst serial killers: so many of them ended up talking, for that reason alone. Galipoli might not be dumb, but he's definitely got an ego, and in all likelihood he's hankering for some recognition."

There was a general assent to this last; if there was anything Galipoli had in spades, it was ego. Morrison went on.

"All right, now, what do we know about the two victims in the copycat case? They both were killed in their own apartments. So we figure, if Galipoli does ask Tina out, and he is trying to push things, he'll want to get them back to her place at some point during the evening. Accordingly, Sergeant McNamara's had a friend in TARU wire up Tina's apartment for both audio and video. She'll also be wearing a kel, starting in the morning, to capture any conversation between her and Galipoli. Remember, every conversation she has that day will be recorded for evidence purposes—so don't say anything stupid."

The tension at the table finally broke a little as the others laughed.

"Yeah," Simmons said, "maybe that means Garriga will let up for a day on his Jack Nicholson impersonation from *A Few Good Men*—'You want me on that wall! You need me on that wall!'"

The group laughed out loud as Garriga blushed. Once a Marine, always a Marine, he'd been known to stand on a desk and recite the entire scene in its entirety, playing both roles.

Morrison, smiling, quieted them down once more. "Okay, people," he said, "here's how it's going to go for the rest of you. Rivera and O'Dell, you guys are backup team number two. I want you on Galipoli, as soon as he leaves the precinct. McNamara and Garriga, you're team three, with ears on the kel. Simmons, you're with me for team four. Remember, we don't know what's going to happen—we could all be wrong, and just spend a quiet night listening to them having dinner together. But I strongly doubt it.

"The most important thing, obviously, is Tina's safety. I can't say this enough: *we can't lose her.* If they end up back at her apartment, the second we have enough to lock him in, we go through the door. I'll have the ram with me. Everyone is to wear a vest—Kasak, Marchioni, that means you—and bring flashlights as well. We know there'll be at least two guns in the house if they go there, and if he's capable of shooting his army lieutenant in cold blood, don't think he won't shoot us in the heat of the moment. Tina has a safety word in case things are getting too hairy and she wants to pull the plug early—in which case, presuming it's outside, Sergeant Simmons will approach them as though he'd just seen them by chance, so as to not give the operation away. The code word is *pumpernickel.*"

O'Dell laughed. "I thought a safe word was supposed to be something easy to slip in!" he said. "What's she going to say—*I love the color of your eyes, they're just the shade of pumpernickel?*"

The rest of the table joined in his laughter. Yet there was a shade of nervousness underlying it, now that they knew the plan. Despite their strategy's simplicity, they all knew how messy things could get either way. If Galipoli was the copycat, anything going otherwise than as planned could give him the opportunity to kill again. If, on the other hand, he wasn't the copycat, and found out he was suspected, a world of shit could fall on all of them. Both scenarios were nightmarish. Still, the job had to be done.

"All right," Morrison said, rising. "I'm going to speak to a waiter; they've been kind enough to leave us to our business so far, but we should eat while we're here. We're going to need to be rested and ready tomorrow. If Tina gives me the green light, we all know what we're doing tomorrow night.

"Let me just add," he concluded, "that I truly appreciate all of you standing with me on this one. I know this could mean all of your careers if it goes wrong, as it could mean mine. Thank you. No matter what happens, I'm proud to stand beside all of you."

"We're with you, Cap, whatever happens," said Rivera. "Now go light on the bread, will you? I don't like to feel too heavy when I'm running a sting on one of my serial-killer coworkers."

The others laughed as Morrison went off in search of the waiter.

35

The next morning, Bill Morrison was at his desk before six. As usual, Sergeant Rivera was the next one in, not counting Medveded. Morrison had wanted Medveded and Koreski especially fresh for today, so he'd had Garriga and O'Dell relieve them on surveillance the night before; but typical for Medveded, he was already in the office this morning, reviewing the notes he'd been making since the arrests in Boston on his conversations with Galipoli.

Morrison watched Medveded through his office window. *The chess master at work,* he thought. Not even six in the morning and the guy was already mentally sizing up his opponent. Morrison smiled to himself. He knew he'd made the right call on that one, at least.

Tina Koreski showed up next, having spent the last hour getting set up with the kel. McNamara was already waiting outside in a surveillance van, ready to capture her every word. She'd made sure to dress normally, but Morrison's practiced eye noticed an extra button open on her shirt, showing just a little more cleavage than usual.

Morrison suppressed his many second thoughts about the operation, knowing they needed a smoking gun to ensure their case against Galipoli couldn't go up in smoke. The man himself would probably stroll in between eight and nine; he was never one to be early, but never late enough to get him any grief over it. That gave Morrison a couple of hours to review his own notes and get his thoughts in order. If Galipoli was the copycat, it would certainly cause some trouble with the other two arrests; thankfully he hadn't actually been involved in the case in any tangible way—his only connection had been through his friend, Chief Arndt—so it might be possible to prepare for that contingency, too. In any event, Morrison hoped the solution he'd prepared would work.

As expected, Louis Galipoli wandered in around eight-forty. Morrison watched him come in, with a heightened sense of disgust at the man's arrogance. It was unfortunate that other heads would likely roll if he turned out to be their copycat—particularly that of his initial investigator, who'd likely just been in the wrong place at the wrong time—but Morrison certainly wouldn't mind seeing Chief Arndt take some serious heat for this one. It had been on his say-so alone that the pretentious asshole had been put here in the first place, behind which decision lives may have been lost. He turned as Galipoli strutted by, to conceal his disdain.

Galipoli, for his part, had other things to look at. Almost immediately upon his arrival, he had his eyes on Tina Koreski. He had definitely noticed the extra button; you could almost see his face light up like he'd hit the jackpot.

Koreski played it cool; she didn't want to come across as too anxious by approaching him—she normally avoided him overtly whenever possible—so she made her way into the squad room kitchen, banking on the enjoyment he'd shown previously for cornering her there. Galipoli had always taken every opportunity to get her alone there, standing wide in the entryway to force her to make contact with him as she left. Today, she knew, it would probably make her skin crawl to touch him. It occurred to her that if everything went as planned, he'd have plenty of chances to touch her later, and the thought made her shudder.

Galipoli, true to form, wasn't ten seconds behind her.

"Hey, beautiful," he said, sidling up next to her so he could stare down her shirtfront. "I see you're giving them some fresh air this morning."

She ignored him, busying herself in washing her coffee cup.

"Come on," he insisted. "Don't tell me you didn't do that for me. I'm sure Boston's made you think at least a *little* about what you have in front of you—?"

Koreski closed her eyes, imagining McNamara listening from the van outside. Guy probably wished he had a bucket to puke into.

"Come on, Lou," she sighed, playing along, though with restraint. "You're the same egotistical man as always."

It was perhaps the first time she hadn't cursed at him after a comment like the one he'd made, and he didn't fail to notice. He moved closer, and when he spoke again, his voice was softer, more earnestly insinuating.

"Tina, you know you want me," he said. "What's the problem with admitting it? No one else is gonna hear you."

Despite her revulsion at the situation, Tina had to suppress a laugh thinking of McNamara on the other end of the wire. She turned her face away from Galipoli to hide her reaction; it came off as evasiveness on her part, which he took up like an encouragement.

"Hey, I can be quiet about it too," he said breathily, moving still closer.

Normally this would have been the point where she would have gotten rougher in brushing him off; but not this time.

"Look, Lou," she said quietly, allowing her voice to falter just a bit as she looked around. "It's not—all right, yes, if you have to know, you looked pretty impressive walking those guys out in Boston."

For an instant she worried she'd given up the game, his expression seemed so surprised. But then, as quickly, he recovered.

"Yeah?" he asked, the cockiness in his voice tempered with a wheedling note of self-deprecation. "That turn you on, just a little bit?"

Again she hesitated, long enough to put the idea of an internal conflict in his head. "Lou, come on, don't—" she said with a light laugh.

"It's okay," he said with eerie tenderness, reaching out and touching her hair. She fought down the urge to break his fingers, instead closing her eyes just for an instant to let it happen. His hand slid down towards her shoulders and upper back.

"Lou, not here," she protested in a whisper. "People might walk in—then what'll we do?"

It was the opening he'd been waiting for.

"So why don't you let me take you out tonight?" he asked, in a voice barely louder than her own. "Nobody here has to know anything—it's strictly between you and me, babe."

"I don't know, Lou. I—"

"Look, it's not like we're going to be on this bullshit task force forever anyway," he said petulantly. "The case is done, those idiots are in jail, I'm moving on to better things. What's the problem? I'm not telling anyone, if that's what you're worried about."

It took everything in her not to lash out at him, but she was in it now. "You just—you have to promise not to, Lou," she insisted. "You know no one here likes you, and I don't want to get any shit from anyone for going out with you."

"Of course," he said, flashing that oily smile again. "Only you and I need to know this night ever happened."

The words fell slowly from his lips, and she caught at them carefully. *This night?* The son of a bitch was already convinced she was in the bag.

"All right," she said. "I'll go. Just get off my back about it, okay?"

"I don't think you'll be saying that later," he joked sleazily. "Why don't I pick you up at your place, and we can have a drink before we go out?"

Uh-oh, she thought. *That's the last place I want to start the evening with this guy.* She thought quickly. "I won't be going straight home after today," she said. "I have an appointment at the beauty parlor after work."

"Come on," he protested. "You're beautiful just the way you are."

"If it's a date, I'd rather look my best," she said lamely. "Look, it won't take long. We can meet up in Manhattan, have a bite to eat, and see where the night takes us. Okay?"

For an instant, he didn't seem pleased by this at all. For the second time she worried she'd scared him off; but then, as if by magic, the smile suddenly returned.

"All right honey, anything you want," he said. "Give me the address of the place where you'll be, and I'll meet you nearby."

She quickly scribbled an address on her pad, tore it off, and handed it to him. He glanced at it briefly, almost angrily, then abruptly turned and walked off without another word.

When he'd gone, she closed her eyes and breathed a sigh of relief. Her heart raced, her palms were sweating. It flashed through her mind that she'd likely humiliated Galipoli by turning down his suggestion of meeting place; she prayed again that her backup team would be there for her later whenever he decided to make her pay for it.

She headed to the ladies' room. Once inside, she shut off the kel for a moment's privacy, and stood looking into the mirror.

Beauty parlor? she thought to herself derisively. Who the hell used that term anymore? Even her own mother would say "salon." *God, I'm such an idiot,* she thought.

She hoped she wasn't doing something more drastically idiotic still. The door was still open; she could back out. The Cap had told her time and again that no one would think less of her. How could she have volunteered for this, anyway, after what happened to her before? Had she forgotten? The years of therapy, the nightmares, the memories she'd spent years working to put in their place—all of it piled up in front of her now: the horror of helplessness, the silent panic of getting in over her head. She couldn't deal with that happening again. And it *could* happen again—

"No," she said out loud. She threw cold water on her face, tried again to breathe deeply. "Come on, girl, you can do this," she went on in a whisper. "This won't be like last time. Kasak and Marchioni are watching your back, along with a handful of other guys who'd kill for you." She fixed her hair and dried her face, forcing her nerves to settle. "It's going to be okay."

Besides, a voice at the back of her mind insisted, *you're in too deep to back out now.*

36

The rest of the day flew by in an anxious rush.

The backup teams all found reasons to leave early, in order to be set up on Koreski well before her scheduled rendezvous with Prince Charming. Morrison, left alone with them, tried not to watch Galipoli, but found it impossible; the way the man looked at her was enough to make anyone uneasy. When Koreski finally left he building, Morrison imagined it was almost as much a relief for him as it was for her.

Twenty minutes later, Galipoli took off—a conspicuous difference from his usual routine. He was never the last person in the squad room, by habit. He was obviously being careful to maintain a clear separation between Koreski and himself in Morrison's eyes. Morrison played along, keeping his head down over the case he was pretending to review. With a glance in his direction, Galipoli grabbed his jacket, shut his desk drawer, and without a word, was gone.

Morrison reached immediately for the radio sitting next to him in its charger.

"It's show time," he said to the waiting teams. "Let's talk status. Team one, how're we doing?"

"All good, Cap," came Kasak's voice over the radio. "We've been on Koreski since she left the office. We're parked down the block from the salon now."

"Okay. Team two?"

"Standing by to follow Galipoli now," O'Dell said. He and Rivera were out front in a car they'd borrowed from the impound lot, so as not to draw attention to themselves. "Sergeant Rivera points out that the car he's driving matches one of our descriptions from the last homicide: dark sedan, looks like a patrol car."

"Good to know. Team three, how about you guys?"

"We're down the street from the salon now, mixed in with the commercial vehicles," Garriga said. He and McNamara were in a tinted-out surveillance van, with McNamara in back listening in on Koreski's kel.

"Okay," Morrison said. "Simmons, I'm sitting tight for a minute— I'll be down to join you when Galipoli heads out."

"Copy that," said Simmons, from his position in the precinct parking lot.

"All right, keep alert, everyone," Morrison said, grabbing his jacket.

Down in the lot, in a far corner from the access ramp, Simmons watched a shadow coming down. *Morrison,* he thought. He put his key in the ignition.

A sudden feeling stopped him. *Was* it Morrison? He waited a moment to be sure.

To his surprise, it was Galipoli who came around the corner instead. Simmons shrank down in his seat quickly, keeping one eye on Galipoli and thanking his lucky stars that he'd parked at an angle and distance where he couldn't have been seen. What the hell was the guy doing in the precinct lot? Was he on to them?

Galipoli looked left and right as he approached one of the squad's unmarked cars. As Simmons watched in amazement, he produced a Slim Jim from his jacket sleeve, and expertly popped the lock with it. *If he'd left something in one of the cars, why didn't he just bring down the key for it?* Simmons wondered idly; then, in a cold flash, he remembered the bag with the rape kit. He stiffened as Galipoli reached into the backseat.

Jesus, he thought. If he opens it and finds those things missing—oh, Jesus.
Galipoli *was* opening it.

Shit, he's going to see! You gotta get out there and do something, so he doesn't—

Just then there was a flash of headlights and a marked patrol car drove down the ramp. It was likely just a car that needed a fill from the precinct pump; but it may have saved their whole operation nonetheless. Simmons breathed a quiet sigh of relief as Galipoli shouldered the bag, smoothly as a cat burglar, and headed back up the ramp, whistling as he went.

"Team two, Lou's on his way up to you," Simmons said into the radio. "He had to grab his party favors."

"Yeah, I see—we've got him coming out now," said O'Dell. "We were wondering what he was up to down there. He have a near miss? He looks like he's in a real hurry to get out of here."

"Yeah," Simmons said. "Motherfucker'd just about opened that bag, when a patrol car came down. Let's hope it's thrown him off his game for the moment."

"Well, he just tossed the bag in the trunk without looking in it, so it looks like we're good for now," said O'Dell.

"Let's hope that luck holds up long enough for us to nail this lunatic," said Morrison, who'd been listening in.

"All right, he's moving," O'Dell said. "We're tailing him over toward Ninth Avenue."

"Great, I'm heading down," Morrison said.

Simmons had brought the car to the top of the ramp to wait for him. "Well, Andre," Morrison said as he jumped in, "I guess our investigative instincts have just been validated! He just had to have that bag back, didn't he?"

"Guess he did," Simmons said, shaking his head. "Son of a bitch even broke into a cop car to get it."

Morrison looked at him in disbelief.

"Broke in?" he asked.

"Yep—Slim Jimmed the door like a pro."

"Christ," Morrison said. "The guy's got balls, I'll give him that. Well, I wish we had the DNA back from those panties and shorts to shut him down hard, but this'll definitely do for now—the bag's enough to do away with any of *my* doubts." Morrison took a deep breath. "Now we just have to make sure the rest of this goes off without a hitch."

Detective Tina Koreski was the only customer in the salon.

The stylist's conversation hadn't taken much of the edge off; if anything, it had only made it more difficult to keep her focus. She'd promised Captain Morrison that she'd be all right, but since she'd left the precinct, it had been a constant struggle to keep the panic at bay. It did no good to remind herself that this time was different, that this time she would have the best help she could have; her mind continued to race with ugly scenarios, in spite of her.

She'd already gotten the text from Morrison that Galipoli had returned to the car on his way out for the rape kit. In a detached sense, that was a good thing, since it meant they didn't need to have any more compunction about accusing him unjustly, and could focus on getting the evidence they needed to draw the noose tight around his neck.

On the other hand, it really did mean she was walking right into the lion's den.

She was brought back to the present by the stylist removing the towel from around her neck.

"This ought to get your attention," she said. "Voila! You're done."

"Wow, just like that, huh?" Koreski said. "Let me see."

Koreski looked in the mirror, smiling. She couldn't help but admire the work the stylist had done. She wasn't normally a woman who spent much time at the salon; hell, she hadn't even known what to call it when she'd spoken about it earlier! She'd had to have one of her friends tell her where this place was, and call to make the appointment for her.

"It looks great," she said, and meant it. *It damn well better!* said a voice at the back of her mind. A simple wash, cut, and dry had cost her two hundred dollars. Now she knew why she didn't go to these places normally. She'd have to make sure Galipoli wouldn't be the only one to enjoy the results.

Standing, she fixed her blouse, again reopening the extra button to make sure Galipoli got a good view of the merchandise. She checked her makeup one last time in the mirror, and handed the stylist a tip.

"I hope your date goes well," the stylist said.

"That makes two of us," Koreski said, making one last effort to smile on her way out the door.

Now that he had his things back, Lou Galipoli was feeling more at ease as he pulled away from the precinct. Soon he was cruising up Sixth Avenue, on his way to the address that Tina had given him for the salon. He felt anxious and wanted to get there early, but not so early that he'd be waiting long. He knew from experience that the longer you stuck around in one spot the more likely it was that there'd be someone who'd remember you.

He had fake plates in the trunk, but didn't have a place to stop and put them on without being noticed; he'd have to wing it. He didn't like doing that normally—too many variables involved—but the temptation of finally getting that bitch alone was too much to back away from.

He'd known his charm would work on her in the end—it always did—but he felt a special sense of satisfaction in knowing it had this time. A policewoman, snatched from the very task force that, unbeknownst to them, was already looking for him—had anyone ever pulled off anything so audacious before? And under the open disapproval of the whole team, too—! But that was the force of his charm, especially with women, whom it tended to affect in a very different way than it did men. They might put on the same show of disliking his attitude, but in the end he was a man who got what he wanted, and all women wanted that, however inconsistently they showed it.

Of course, he couldn't have her showing that kind of inconsistency tonight, so he'd come prepared with another sort of charm to exert on her: a nicely balanced cocktail of Xanax and Rohypnol—"the predator drug," as he enjoyed hearing it called around work—mixed with a drink and re-bottled just for her. The combination of the two had always seemed to him to work better than either on its own—keeping a victim on the edge for a longer time, it made it easier for him to take his time and enjoy himself.

He passed the salon and found a spot to park halfway down the block, making sure to put himself somewhere fewer bystanders would be, but where she'd be able to see him clearly when she came out. He couldn't have her calling him to find out where he was; in order for everything to go off smoothly, there had to be no trace of them meeting.

Right on time, he saw her emerge from the salon. A new flush of pride ran through him to see her; it was a big change, and she'd done it for him. He was also happy to see the pretense of the tough detective dropped. Now she looked the way he liked them to look, like a young girl in a beauty pageant: dolled-up but slightly out-of-place, unsure, out of their element. Helpless.

He stuck his hand out the window and waved cheerfully. She saw him immediately, and walked up the block toward him with a nervous step. *Walk into my parlor,* he thought elatedly, and greeted her with a big, winning smile.

37

Tina Koreski approached the car under the watchful eyes of Kasak and Marchioni, who'd been following Galipoli's every move since he'd pulled up. They snapped several photos of the two of them as she opened the door to get in.

She slid into the seat and shut the door behind her, unconsciously crowding over as close to the passenger-side door as she can.

"Hello, honey," he said, looking her over with a leer. "You weren't kidding about that place—you look amazing."

Her eyes wanted to roll back in her head, but she restrained herself to smile. "Thank you," she said. "I'm glad you like it."

He leaned in closer, and she feigned distraction to turn her head away from him. "So what have you got planned for tonight?" she asked, in a voice perhaps a bit too loud. *Don't blow this, Koreski,* she thought to herself, and turned back around to look at him.

He was showing a Cheshire-cat grin that he must have thought charming, but which, under the circumstances, almost made her gasp in revulsion. "Don't you worry, honey," he said. "I've got something very special in mind—something I'm sure nobody's done for you before."

The words cut through her like a knife. Galipoli, she remembered, had been new to the task force too; he didn't know about her past. *Play it off,* she thought.

"I can't wait," she managed. "I love surprises. And I think it's sweet that you've planned something out for me." She smiled, warming to the act. "It seems so uncharacteristic."

"Oh, I'm full of surprises," he said.

"I see that," she laughed. "And everyone said you were such a douchebag! I should never have listened to them."

She couldn't help taking the jab at his ego, and it cut deep. *Too deep,* she realized, as his eyes suddenly darkened.

"Of course they would think that," he said. "Those pathetic fucks, hiding behind their badges! Of course they're jealous of someone with options—someone who can think for himself!" He glared at her, his face caught in something between a proud smile and a snarl. "None of them have ever tried to figure out for themselves what a real man is capable of," he added in a strange tone.

She reached across the car and rubbed his shoulder. "Hey, simmer down, tiger," she said, forcing the words through a flirtatious smile. "You're the one I'm with tonight, remember?"

His smile returned with an eerie suddenness.

"Of course I am," he said. "There's no question there." He reached into the backseat and brought up a small cooler. "And you're right—tonight's about us, not those jerkoffs. Let's get this party started, shall we?"

He pulled two bottles from the cooler.

"I didn't figure you for a beer girl," he said, opening her bottle and handing it to her. It was a bottled margarita. *Well, no wonder you're wrong,* Koreski thought, *having never been in a bar with any of us.*

"This is perfect," she smiled, happy to have him back under control. "Thanks."

"My pleasure," he said lightly. He opened a beer for himself. "What shall we drink to?"

"To our little secret?" she said, raising her bottle. *The guys in the van will enjoy* that *one,* she thought.

His grin widened. "Our little secret," he agreed; and with genuine smiles, the two toasted.

A few blocks away, parked with Simmons, Morrison was feeling a bit better about the operation.

Team one, the Coke boys, hadn't lost Galipoli's car once; nor had Rivera and O'Dell, who'd been leap-frogging with them to make sure it always remained in sight. Morrison had also been on the phone with Garriga throughout, getting constant updates on the conversation; eventually he'd simply had the detective turn up the volume so he could hear it for himself. McNamara had pointed out that Tina had sounded a bit stiff towards the beginning, but under the circumstances, it was completely understandable. And besides, she sounded much more at ease now, and in control. Even her voice and speech patterns seemed much more relaxed.

"She sounds like she's eased into the role, anyway," Morrison thought out loud.

"Completely," Simmons agreed. "Sounds like she's really putting on a good act—even *I* think she likes the scumbag."

"Well, we'll hang back for the moment," Morrison said. "Two close tails is enough." He addressed his teams over the radio. "Any of you guys with eyes on them, want to give me an update?"

"Just sipping their road sodas together in the car," O'Dell said. "Still driving around aimlessly, seems like. Real proper date."

"She still going with it?"

"Definitely a convincing performance on her part," O'Dell confirmed. "He just reached over the seat and grabbed her arm, and she's sliding closer to him. I don't know how she's keeping from punching him in his fucking face, with that obnoxious grin of his."

"Hang on," Morrison said, listening closer to his phone. He could hear Galipoli talking in the background, over McNamara's radio. "Garriga, what was that last?"

"He said, *There, isn't that better? Come on over, I know you want me*," Garriga said. "Cocky fuck."

"Yeah, well, see how that—"

"She's got her head on his shoulder now," O'Dell said. "She's looking—okay, wait, he's going through her bag. He's just taken something out. Think it's her phone—yeah, he just kissed the screen—he's putting it in his jacket pocket."

Morrison's nerves jangled at the urgency in O'Dell's voice.

"He's going through her purse now," O'Dell went on. "She's not stopping him; she looks really out of it."

"Neither of them's saying anything, Cap," Garriga said quietly over the phone, a note of alarm in his voice.

"Fuck," Morrison said to Simmons, his heart pounding. "He's drugged her."

"You think so?" Simmons asked. "We didn't have any evidence of drugs in the previous—"

"Yeah, I know," Morrison snapped. "He's changed it up for her." He picked up the radio again, but Marchioni's voice came through, interrupting him.

"Team one to team leader," Marchioni said.

"Go ahead, team one."

"He's picked up speed," Marchioni said. "We're still on him, but yeah, they're really moving now."

"Stay on him," Morrison almost shouted. "Where does it look like they're headed?"

"West Side Highway," Marchioni said. "Yeah, just reached it. Northbound on the West Side."

"Where the hell's he going?" O'Dell asked. "He's tearing ass—they heading to the Bronx, or what?"

"Just don't lose him, any of you," Morrison said again. "Run him off the goddamn road if you have to—*just keep on him*. Let's head up to Tina's, Andre," he told Simmons. "I have a feeling he's heading to her place. Maybe he just got it off of her ID. The others can tell us if he changes direction."

"Cap, he's talking again," Garriga was saying. "You catch that?"

"I missed it—what'd he say?" Morrison asked, after listening for a moment.

"He said, *Looks like you've had a bit too much to drink,*" Garriga said, "*but you'll feel better when we get you home.*"

"That confirms it," Morrison said, his heart sinking. "Team leader to all teams: be advised, Detective Koreski's been drugged. I think Galipoli's bringing her to her place in the Bronx, but keep your eyes on him in case anything changes. Simmons and I will meet you there. In the meantime—" He faltered. "In the meantime, remember: no losing that car. Let me know of any and all movements."

And pray he doesn't do anything to her before they arrive, he thought to himself.

38

Tina Koreski wasn't completely out of it, but she was close.

Long since, the words she wanted to say had stopped coming to her lips. Before her self-control had dropped away she'd had a moment of horror; but as suddenly as it had arisen, it had sunk down again below the surface of the vast drowsiness that had enveloped her. Now her thoughts held together no better than her words, coming together only to swim apart again before she could make sense of them.

She tried to push herself up. Feeling her stir against his shoulder, Galipoli snickered and patted her head condescendingly.

"It's all right," he said, reveling in her utter powerlessness. "Don't worry about it, baby. You're in for the time of your life." Exiting the highway and heading down a residential street, he checked his GPS. They were less than half a mile from her house.

"It's going to feel so good when I fuck you hard," he said absently, almost angrily.

The harsh words brought a moment of clarity to Koreski's semi-conscious mind.

"Wha—what'reyou—talking—" she began to slur.

Suddenly, her head rocked back in an explosion of light and pain as Galipoli slapped her in the face, hard.

"Shut the fuck up," he snapped. "From now on, you only need to speak when I tell you to, get it?"

The slap had knocked her away from him, and now she slumped in her seat. He tried half-heartedly to pull her back toward him, but she was dead weight. She sobbed quietly, pain ebbing hotly through her nose and cheek. The car seemed like a black hole, with blurred lights flowing around it on all sides, all blackness below and behind her, and *him*, the darkest center of the hole, talking absently somewhere beside her.

"That's right, bitch, cry," he was saying. "Cry, like all the other little bitches do. You all think you're so high and mighty, sticking your tits out for everyone to see—but no touching! No touching!" He gestured with his hands, his voice echoing in her ears as he chanted in a mocking falsetto. "Looking down your nose at me—*fuck you!* I have to keep showing you cunts who the man is, but fuck it—I've shown others, and I can show you, too." He wiped his mouth with the back of his hand, the motion bright and sudden. "Before tonight's done, you're goddamn right you're going to show me the respect I deserve. You're going to beg me for your miserable, stuck-up bitch life. You ready for that, bitch? I know *I* can't fucking wait."

"We've got to stop him now," Simmons said, listening along with Morrison to Tina's kel on speakerphone. "We can't let this psychopath get inside with her."

"We'll get him," Morrison said. "Just wait a second. Team leader to all teams," he said over the radio. "We're a few minutes away from Koreski's place. Be ready to take him down when he arrives—I want him as he's heading up the front steps."

"Copy that, team leader," answered Marchioni. "We're still on the car; we'll park across the street from him as soon as it looks like he's stopping."

"Same here," O'Dell said. "We're about a minute away."

Simmons was confused. "We have enough on him already, Cap," he said. "Why don't we take him now?"

"Just trust me, Andre," Morrison said tensely. "This is making me nervous too, but I know what I'm doing here."

"Okay, he's parking," Marchioni said quietly. "We're pulling into a driveway across the street to get in position."

"We're right behind you," O'Dell said. "We'll pull over and stay in the car, to make sure he doesn't spook."

"What's happening?" Morrison asked.

"He's going around to the trunk," O'Dell said. "He's opening the trunk—he's got the gym bag. He's opening the passenger door. He's got Tina; looks like he's got to carry her."

"Okay, bitch," came Galipoli's voice over the kel, eerily quiet. "Let's get going."

"The Coke boys are outside their car, across the street," O'Dell said. "Galipoli's got Tina—he's pulling her down the street towards her place."

"Waiting on your signal, Cap," Kasak whispered.

"We'll be there in fifteen seconds," Morrison said.

"Cap, he's almost to the steps," Rivera's voice came through suddenly.

Morrison's patience broke. "Take him down!" he shouted into the radio. *"Do not let them get inside!"*

It was all the Coke brothers needed to hear. Neither of them had all-out sprinted in fifteen years, but nobody would have known it who'd seen them bolt from cover and race across the street. At the same time the doors to Rivera and O'Dell's car exploded open as they too flashed down the block, leaving the doors open behind them.

Galipoli, just pulling Koreski up the first steps to her building, was just reaching in his pocket for the keys he'd taken from her purse when he was startled by a ferocious yell from behind him.

"Police! Don't move, motherfucker!"

He spun in alarm, one hand reaching instinctively for the gun in his waistband. Before he knew what was happening, a mass like a thick sack of bricks slammed into him, knocking him off-balance. Powerful arms wrapped around him in an inexorable bear hug and Kasak had him off his feet, twisting him away from Koreski's limp body as Marchioni bolted in to catch her. Struggling one arm free, Galipoli tried to swing an elbow at Kasak's head. Kasak ducked under the blow, swung Galipoli around and dragged him to the ground, where in another instant Rivera and O'Dell had his arms pinned and had secured handcuffs on him.

Galipoli's gun had fallen to the ground in the scuffle, and Rivera kicked it into the grass before reaching down to pull a second from Galipoli's waistband as Morrison and Simmons ran up.

"I imagine this one's Tina's," he said, holding up the gun. "And neither one of them in a holster, huh? Just like the petty street thug you are, Lou—it's too bad you didn't blow off your balls with one of them."

"Hey, hey," Galipoli was gasping. "What the fuck are you guys doing?"

"You know exactly what we're doing, asshole," Marchioni said, looking down at him in disgust, "and you're damn lucky we're not doing worse."

"Bullshit," Galipoli managed. "You're making a mistake. We're on the same job—we were—we were on a fucking date!"

"Yeah, well, that may be true," Morrison said, "but we happen to know very well what type of shit counts as a date to you. The woman's unconscious!"

"She—we were drinking—"

"Save it for your statement, Lou. You already know your rights, so we're not going to bother. Frankie," he said, "Simmons and I are going to get Detective Koreski to the hospital. You and O'Dell, get this piece of trash back to the stationhouse. Mike, Leo, call up the local precinct for a patrol car to sit by his car until department tow shows up, then head back to the house. I'll have McNamara and Garriga follow us for the time being, and we'll all meet back there." He looked down at Galipoli, who'd been sent into a sullen silence, and shook his head. Galipoli's face registered little, but Morrison had seen his hands tense up when he'd mentioned his rights. *Typical bully,* he thought—*a big bad tough guy as long as he's in control; but the second he's backed into a corner, the real coward comes out.*

Now to see what Alex Medveded would make of him.

39

It was convenient that Morrison and Simmons were already in the Bronx. Cops always knew the best hospitals in the city, and the borough's Montefiore Hospital was right at the top of the list. Still, Morrison found himself as concerned as ever. Koreski was still very much out of it, and despite their interruption of Galipoli's plans, there was no telling what effects his assault might already have had on her. Drugged victims, especially those with a prior history of trauma, had died under similar circumstances before.

They entered the hospital through the area usually reserved for ambulances, to cut their wait. The initial admissions process could wait—there'd be plenty of time for that later, once Koreski was being taken care of. A security officer approached them as they passed through the first set of automatic doors, then nodded in understanding when he saw their badges, still hanging around their necks from the takedown. He pushed a wheelchair under Koreski to receive her as Simmons set her down.

Luckily for them, it was an unusually slow night in Emergency. Seeing them approach with Koreski in the wheelchair, a nurse walked right over.

"What's happened to her?" she asked, looking Koreski over for wounds. Usually when cops were rushed in like this, it was because they'd been shot or stabbed.

"Not the usual, but maybe as bad," Morrison said. "She's been drugged—we don't know what with. Seems like a tranquilizer cocktail, but we believe her assailant had planned to kill her, so it could really be anything."

"All right," the nurse said, gesturing over an orderly to wheel Koreski into a room. "I'll have a doctor in to see her immediately."

Morrison watched her go with a sinking feeling of helplessness. Simmons put a hand on his shoulder.

"Best hospital care in the city, Cap," he said softly. "Come on. Let's leave them to their work."

Morrison nodded wearily. He had to make a call to Stan Rosenthal anyway; they'd need the ADA's help to secure search warrants for Galipoli's car and residence, and it would take a minute to bring him up to speed with their investigation.

"All right," he sighed. "If you need me, I'll be out on my phone—it's high time we make this thing official."

Louis Galipoli sat in the back of Rivera's car, trying to ignore the cuffs biting into his wrists.

"You're sure we can't take these off, guys?" he asked. "It's not like I'm going to run on you—*I* know I didn't do anything, so I have nothing to run from."

"That may be," Rivera said, "but it's not for us to make that call. You know—Cap's orders. I'm sorry."

"Of course," Galipoli said with an understanding smile. "I get it. Just thought I'd ask."

Yeah, keep smiling, motherfucker, Rivera thought. Before the arrest had gone down, Morrison had arranged beforehand with him and O'Dell to go soft on Galipoli on the way home, so they might have a shot at getting something out of him later. Predictably, Galipoli had switched on his oily charm almost immediately, and had been pestering them the whole way home to take his cuffs off, open the window for him, and so forth. That was the way with guys like him: never quite believing they were in the wrong, they always felt they could talk their way out of whatever shit they'd gotten themselves into. When they couldn't, delusion was usually sufficient to fill the gap; this one was just willing to carry those delusions to other, extremer lengths.

When they arrived at the station, Kasak and Marchioni were right behind them. In accordance with another prearranged plan, Rivera pretended to take a call from Morrison so he and O'Dell could hang back, handing Galipoli off awkwardly to the Coke brothers to bring inside. He saw Galipoli snicker at their apparent lack of cohesion; Rivera could practically hear him congratulating himself on being the center of so much attention. With any luck, the ego boost would loosen up his tongue.

Kasak and Marchioni brought Galipoli to the rear door. Marchioni draped his jacket over his shoulders to hide the cuffs.

"Might as well preserve your dignity while we can," Marchioni muttered.

Galipoli said nothing, but grinned inwardly in surprise. He couldn't recall a single time either of the Coke brothers had spoken to him before tonight, especially with that kind of consideration. And the rear door, too—! Perhaps his charm *was* breaking through.

"You know, I appreciate that," he said, as they marched him up the stairs. "But you know, you *could* just take the cuffs off of me—I'm not going anywhere."

Kasak and Marchioni kept quiet. As they brought him into the squad room, he decided to try again.

"Come on, guys," he persisted. "Take them off—or could you at least loosen them a bit? They're on really tight." He faltered on the shorter detective's first name. "Kasak?"

Kasak looked over at his partner in mock deliberation.

"I don't know, Mike," he said. "Should we take 'em off?"

"Fuck him," Marchioni said sternly.

On cue, Medveded emerged from the kitchen. On seeing Galipoli in cuffs, he feigned shock.

"What the fuck's going on here?" he asked the Coke boys. "Why's Lou in cuffs?"

Galipoli looked quickly from Kasak to Marchioni.

"He's under arrest," Kasak said. "You know that."

"Yeah, but he's still one of us," Medveded said, as though explaining something to a small child. "Surely you don't think he's going to run off?" He moved toward Galipoli. "Here, let me get those off," he said quietly.

"What the fuck do you think you're doing?" Marchioni said, putting out a hand to stop him. "You aren't taking those off—this guy's a fucking animal."

Medveded pushed his hand away slowly, his face an impassive mask. "He's *one of us,*" he insisted again. "And you know as well as I do that those cuffs aren't doing anyone any good. These old-fashioned ideas of yours"—without taking his eyes from Marchioni's, he removed Galipoli's cuffs and tossed them on the nearest desk—"aren't always the right solution. Now we're going to wait in the kitchen—aren't we, Lou?—until the Captain returns."

Galipoli smirked at Marchioni.

"That sounds fine to me, *Alex,*" he said. "You see that I'm cooperative; lead the way."

"We don't know how long the Captain's going to be," Marchioni objected gruffly.

"It's all right, Detective," Medveded said, waving him off. "I'll take responsibility for him."

Having set the scene, Medveded walked ahead into the kitchen, placing one hand casually in his pocket and turning his back to Galipoli as he went. There would be no interrogation room or notepad handy for this one—that'd set off red lights even for someone as dense as Galipoli—and having already established a bond with his opponent, he wanted to reinforce it at every opportunity. Besides, Kasak and Marchioni were right outside, and if Galipoli attacked him, the small blackjack in his pocket was more than ready.

But Medveded was sure he wouldn't. Galipoli was a coward, and at this point, likely eager for any inside indulgence he could get. And Medveded planned to indulge him as much as possible. Since the operation had begun he'd been reviewing his notes, listening in on the radio and communicating with Sergeant McNamara about everything Galipoli said to Tina while they were alone, committing the salient details to memory in case he had opportunity to use any of them during their "casual" conversation.

Now the chessboard was set, and the real game could begin.

Once they were in the kitchen together, Medveded shut the door behind him, giving Galipoli a "just between us boys"–style wink as he busied himself with fixing a coffee.

"If you think I'm going to talk to you, you can think again," Galipoli said, the smile still on his face.

Medveded looked at him sideways. "Did I say anything about talking? Relax. You want any coffee?"

Galipoli nodded, rubbing his wrists. "Yeah, sure."

"How do you take it?"

"Light and sweet—like my women," Galipoli scoffed.

Medveded chuckled lightly as he slid the cup across the table.

"You know, it's funny you're so suspicious of me, Lou," he said. "If anyone here could understand you, it's me."

Galipoli snickered. "How do you figure that?"

"A few reasons," Medveded said vaguely, "but mainly because nobody else would try. I don't know if you know it, but I've been the one to speak up for you on a few occasions—the other guys pretty much all think you're an asshole."

It was the second time Galipoli had been reminded of this fact, and it nettled him deeply. Medveded watched him stare at the table, his indignation overpowering his sense. *It doesn't even occur to him that the two people who've told him that tonight might be the people who hate him the most,* he thought.

"I mean, *I* don't," Medveded said. "But then, I haven't always gotten along with all of them either."

"Fuck them," Galipoli sniffed. "They're morons. I don't care what anyone thinks of me; I know who I am."

"That's good," Medveded said approvingly. "It's not a common quality, especially among people in this line of work." He leaned in over his coffee. "You know, Lou, I don't miss much," he said.

"What's that supposed to mean?" Galipoli demanded.

Time to take a chance. Medveded glanced at the door ever so quickly—just long enough to let Galipoli see he was doing it. "Only that I've seen your work," he said, "and I'm impressed with what you've done since you got here."

Galipoli eyed him warily. "Thanks," he said.

Medveded smiled knowingly at him. There it was—the weak point. In that moment, Medveded saw how Galipoli would crack. It would take a long time and a lot of statements as vague as that one to bring him around, but Medveded was going to get a statement out of him.

Some games, you just had to play right up to the clock.

Back at Montefiore, Morrison was hanging up from speaking to Sergeant Rivera, who'd called him for an update on Koreski as soon as the Coke boys had gotten inside with Galipoli. He was happy to have had good news to give him.

Tina was going to be all right. They still didn't know what Galipoli had given her, but a few final tests were being administered to figure it out. In the meantime she'd been given fluids to flush out her system, and the drug's effects seemed already to be lessening. Simmons was waiting outside her room, along with McNamara and Garriga, who'd arrived not long after they had.

Seeking out the nurse who'd helped them, Morrison took a moment to tell her how grateful he was for her and her staff's help when they'd arrived. He handed her his card, and told her that if she or they ever needed anything, they could call him. It wasn't the most common offer from Bill Morrison, but he meant it sincerely.

Now, returning to the hallway with the others, he heard a faint voice from inside.

"Cap, are you there?"

At a nod from the nurse, Morrison entered and slid the curtain aside. Koreski, pale and weak-looking but none the worse for wear, burst into tears as he, McNamara, Simmons, and Garriga all moved in to hug her at once.

"I'm sorry I'm crying, guys," she said, smiling through her tears. "It must be the drugs."

"Not at all, Tina," Morrison said. "We're just glad you're all right."

"Incredible job tonight, Koreski," Simmons said. "We're all really impressed."

"Still, man," Garriga said, "I don't think Pat and me ever want to listen to an operation like that again! Had us on the edge of our seat."

Koreski laughed. "Where's Kasak and Marchioni?" she asked.

"They're back at the stationhouse with Galipoli," Morrison told her. "Rivera and O'Dell are there too."

"Right. Alex having a crack at him?"

"Yeah." Morrison smiled, though still concerned. "Listen, Tina, seriously: are you okay?"

She nodded. "Cap, I'm better than okay," she said. "I was a little nervous for a minute there that you guys might let me down, but I'm glad to have had the fear, just to have it proven so wrong. For the first time in a long time, I'm feeling trust again—thanks to you and all the guys, especially Leo and Mike. I owe them a big hug when I see them."

"They'll be glad to see you," Morrison said.

"Well, look," she said, "I really appreciate having you all here, but shouldn't you guys get going? This is too important to have you guys sitting around the hospital with me."

"Are you sure?" Simmons asked.

"Yeah, I'll be fine. Get back to work and make sure that piece of shit doesn't see the light of day again."

Morrison smiled at her proudly.

"When she's right, she's right," he said to the others. "And I promise we will," he added, letting go of her hand. "Still, we don't leave our own alone. Pat, I'm going to have you stay with her; I'll ride back to the house with Garriga and Simmons."

"Sure thing, Cap," McNamara said.

"Rest up, Tina," Morrison said, rising to go. "You take as long as you need to feel better—there's no rush. Hell," he laughed, "for all we know, Alex might still be working on the guy when you get back."

40

It had been three hours already.

It wasn't a long time to listen by anyone's interview standards, especially Medveded's—it seemed no time was too long for him. But it was pretty unbelievable that Galipoli had been able to talk about himself for so long. He was his own favorite subject, far and away. Anyone listening might have thought he was being interviewed for the Nobel Prize—*if* they could stand to listen to him for that long. It was a big if; Morrison and the others listening out in the hallway had long since taken to standing shifts.

Still, Medveded, who knew Galipoli was just an ego for whom no audience was enough, kept his patience as he played Galipoli piece by piece, gradually breaking down his defense of the king. Slowly but surely, it was working. Under his careful ministrations, the conversation had developed into the friendly banter of two old friends.

"I mean, it's got to be tough," he was saying now, "having that much attention all the time. Especially from women—I can't even get a fucking woman to look my way."

"A lot of guys can't," Galipoli said dismissively. "Women are bitches, that's why."

"That they are," Medveded agreed, "but still, you've got to have them eating out of your hand. You're tall, you've got good looks—hell, you're a goddamn war hero!"

"Yeah, well," Galipoli said, with mock humility.

"They've got to be throwing it at you," Medveded went on. "That type of shit is exactly what women want. It's what men want, for that matter."

"What the fuck's that supposed to mean?" Galipoli snapped suddenly, his expression ugly. "I ain't into guys."

"That's not what I mean," Medveded backtracked. "I just mean, guys must be jealous of you. Again, something I don't envy you for. I'm not a jealous type, so other guys' stuff doesn't bother me—I know I've got things going on for me too. But—"

"Well, why do you think the rest of this shit task force hates me so much?" Galipoli burst out. "They couldn't shine my shoes, and they know it. Just look at tonight! These assholes think I need to *force* women to do the things they do with me. It's bullshit! They all beg me for more."

It was an obvious opening, but Medveded let it slide. Every bread crumb Galipoli dropped would lead him to the truth eventually.

"Speaking of which," he said, "where the hell are those guys? I told them I'd stick around until they got back, but I wasn't planning on being here all night. Do you want anything to eat? I'm starving."

"Yeah, that'd be good," Galipoli said. "I could go for a burger."

"Sounds good to me," Medveded said. *Anything to keep you in the chair, and not asking for an attorney,* he thought. He found a menu and put in the call, making sure to get Galipoli whatever he wanted. Some perps talked more easily when they were fed, and Medveded had a feeling Galipoli was one of them.

As they were finishing up, Medveded made his first move toward the king.

"I want to be honest with you about something," he said, "but I need you to keep it to yourself."

"Course," Galipoli said, barely concealing his interest. "What's up?"

Medveded cleared his throat. "I can't *stand* that fuck Morrison," he said quietly.

Galipoli almost choked on his food.

"Come on!" he said loudly, laughing in disbelief. "Don't bullshit me—"

"Hey, shut the fuck up," Medveded hissed, glancing at the door again. "I'm not telling you so you can send it around."

"Sorry, man," Galipoli said, his smile still wide. "It's just, I thought you two were tight."

"*Everyone* does," Medveded said. "Especially him. And I'd prefer it to stay that way, if you don't fucking mind."

"Sure, sure," Galipoli said. "Sort of a friends close, enemies closer kind of thing?"

"*Exactly,*" Medveded said, nodding profoundly. "Exactly. I'm not a stupid man; I have ambitions like anyone else. I'm not planning on sticking around this phony operation forever. You got to play the game, you know? That's why Morrison's stuck here—he can't keep his act down long enough to move on. The way he talks to Chief Arndt—"

"I know what you mean," Galipoli interrupted, leaping at the bait. "Arndt might be a punk, but he's up top, and he recognizes a good thing when he sees it."

"I've never really talked to him much; he a good guy to know?"

"Definitely—definitely." Galipoli looked at Medveded with a sideways smile. "I mean, I wouldn't be here if it weren't for him."

"What do you mean?"

Galipoli laughed. "You don't think one of these other assholes would have recommended me for a shield, do you? They wouldn't know good policing if it walked up and kicked their ass for them."

"No no, I see what you mean," Medveded said. "Still, you didn't have to grease the wheels on that? I mean, most guys, that's how they end up getting it these days," he added casually, as though bribery were a natural part of the job. "I remember I had to pay a fortune for mine."

"Oh, I kicked him a *little* something," Galipoli sniffed. "That's just the industry—even the high-ups who recognize talent have to get something out of it for themselves. But it wasn't much, in the long run. So yeah, he's a good guy to know. Him and Dave Cook—he's another guy who keeps his friends close."

Medveded hadn't been expecting a reference to the City Councilman, but he was smarter than to let it show. "Cook, out of Brooklyn?" he asked, playing dumb.

"Yeah, District 43 in Bay Ridge," Galipoli said. "Where I grew up."

"How'd *he* help you?"

"Well, honestly, the war hero thing has its perks," Galipoli smiled. "When I first got on the job, Arndt took me under his wing. He's kind of looked out for me since then, sort of treated me as his project. Anyway, he had me get involved with all these fundraisers for politicians over the last few years. I never had any money to donate—you know, on a cop's salary—but I'd go with him a lot, and he introduced me to a lot of people. Most of them are phony fucks, as you'd guess. Real snooty motherfuckers. Once they knew I wasn't a donor, most of them wouldn't even talk to me."

"So why was Cook different?"

"Well, so Chief Arndt takes me to his office one day, last year. He was up for reelection. Real nice guy, for a change. Once he hears I'm from his district, he couldn't be nicer. Tells me he'd love to have a war hero on his campaign committee, you know, start showing up to events and so forth—"

"What'd he pay you?" Medveded asked bluntly. Galipoli looked surprised. Medveded rolled his eyes. "Come on, man," he said. "I've been doing this for a while. Just haven't found any opportunities lately. What'd he give you, a couple hundred per appearance?"

Galipoli laughed, his pride getting the better of his discretion once again. "A couple hundred? That's chump change," he said. "He gave me a G every time, sometimes more."

Medveded whistled low, as though impressed. "You weren't worried about it blowing up on you?"

"Fuck no," Galipoli said. "It's what I deserved. Besides, Arndt told me Dave could be trusted. I could put you guys in touch, if you want—it couldn't hurt to talk to him."

Medveded feigned interest. "I mean, the extra money must've been nice."

"Damn right it was. Down payment for my car, right there."

Medveded's mind raced. Corruption in the department was rare nowadays, but where it did exist, it almost always went up the ladder. He decided to test the extent of Galipoli's knowledge.

"Even so, I guess your envelopes weren't as good as Arndt's," he said.

"Are you kidding?" Galipoli laughed. "No way. *No way.* Say you're a politician, and you're in a situation—imagine the kind of help the Chief of Detectives can give you."

"Sure, but—"

"Look at it this way, man. Sometimes Cook would ask me to deliver Arndt's to him, so one time I opened it up. I wasn't doing anything with it—just looking. There was ten grand in there. *Ten fucking grand.* Cash. Tax-free. Think I'd say no to *that* every couple of months?"

"No, I guess not," Medveded laughed.

"No is right, my Russian friend," Galipoli said grandly. "I'd jump at the opportunity."

Medveded jumped at his, to bring the conversation back around to the homicides.

"Man," he said. "I'm learning something today. I haven't had the balls to take that kind of chance in my career."

"You want the reward, you gotta take the risk," Galipoli pontificated.

"Yeah, yeah, I know," Medveded agreed sheepishly. "But look—women are a different story, right? You have a natural ability there. You got a secret, or what?"

"Like you said, it's natural."

"I mean, it must be. I've seen Tina staring at you when you were at your desk—"

"Tell that to those motherfuckers!" Galipoli exploded, gesturing towards the door.

"I'm sure she'll tell them herself," Medveded said calmly. "I mean, it was pretty obvious. She didn't think anyone saw her, but I did. Girl eyed you like a ham sandwich. I swear, half the time I caught her looking at you, she looked like she was about to start touching herself under the desk."

This got a rise out of Galipoli. He leaned forward, suddenly interested.

"I *knew* that bitch was into me," he hissed under his breath. "It's the same with all of them. They all act high and mighty when other people are around, but deep down they're all just bitches in heat. I get them alone, I can't keep them off of me."

"Yeah?" Medveded asked, hesitant to commit more in case Galipoli was baiting him.

"Oh yeah," Galipoli said with a faraway look. *No baiting there,* Medveded thought. *It's chest-thumping time.* "You should have seen Tina tonight," Galipoli went on. "Little fucking minx."

"What happened?"

"Well, consummate gentleman that I am, I pick her up from the salon," Galipoli said, eager to tell his side of the story. "Once she gets in my car, she can't keep her hands off me. I'd brought a couple of drinks along so we could get started early, so we drank those, and man, that chick was ready to go. She didn't even want to wait 'til we got to her apartment. She's got her head on my shoulder, you know, kind of distracting me while I'm driving—I was like, *Slow down, honey,* but she couldn't hold herself back. She wanted to blow me right in the car."

"Unbelievable," Medveded said, and meant it. "I would never have known that about her."

"Oh yeah, she was pretty freaky," Galipoli said. "She wanted me to slap her, so I did; she liked that, man. She wanted more. I told her to wait until we got to her place, and I'd give her what she was asking for."

It was obvious even from Galipoli's facial expression that this was simply his fantasy version of what had happened, but Medveded took it for what it was: a way in.

"Most women just reject me," he said absently, as though changing the subject. "I usually just end up going home to jerk off."

"That's bullshit," Galipoli said, looking almost pityingly at him. "I never let them get away with that kind of crap. A bitch rejects me, she gets what's coming to her."

"How do you mean?"

"You know, just—they get their comeuppance, that's all."

Medveded saw that he'd have to put a line out. "I mean, I think I know what you mean," he said, quickly thinking up a story. "I pulled this rich girl over once for driving drunk, back in my patrol days, and—"

"The fucking rich ones are the worst," Galipoli said, shaking his head.

"Yeah, she was a piece of work. She just seemed so fucking arrogant, you know? I wouldn't have done anything otherwise, but I knew she needed to learn a lesson, so I made her blow me."

Galipoli laughed. "That's good," he said. "Still small-time, but that's the idea."

"Small-time?" Medveded looked offended. "I thought it was pretty goddamn risky at the time."

"Oh, brother, the shit I could tell you," Galipoli muttered, half to himself.

"Come on," Medveded prodded him.

Galipoli scoffed. "It's not something I ought to be talking about," he said.

"How much worse could it be than forcing a girl to blow you?" Medveded laughed. "I didn't mention that she was basically a teen-ager—some fucking club girl."

"Yeah, well, I got some stories about those," Galipoli hinted again, rolling his eyes as he took Medveded's bait.

"Well—?"

Galipoli leaned in eagerly. "There was this one girl, total freak," he said. "I met her in a transgender club downtown. Said she was exploring a part for a role as an actress. She was full of shit—just a freak. I asked her if she wanted a real man, and she had the balls to say, *Tell me when you see one.*"

Medveded chuckled. "Nice. How'd you take that?"

"Oh, fine. I bought her a drink anyway—I'm a good guy. But she refused to drink it. *That* pissed me off. Bitch wanted freaky, so that's what she got." Galipoli hesitated. "I really shouldn't be telling you this, man," he said.

Medveded knew he was close. It was time to pull out the stops. Slipping a hand into his pocket, he rubbed it against his leg, making just enough noise for Galipoli to hear him.

"Come on, just tell me," he said.

"Hey, are you—" Galipoli started, his eyes widening.

"Listen, you gotta tell me, man," Medveded said. "This shit is why I got into the job in the first place. You don't think the pay's what gets me, do you? Come on, I need to know this bitch got what was coming to her."

Galipoli looked shocked. "Are you serious?"

Medveded let out a sigh. "Look, it's not like I'm going to pass *this* on, right?" he said. "It's between us."

"No one else?"

"No one else." Medveded raised his right hand. "One cop to another. I swear it."

He could see Galipoli's excitement rising. Finally, he had someone who truly understood him, admired him even, with whom he could share his exploits. His voice lowered almost to a whisper.

"All right," Galipoli said. "So this bitch comes out of the club, and I'm waiting for her. It's pretty dark, and I walk up behind her; she turns around and doesn't even remember me from the club. Stupid cunt. I punch her square in the face. She goes down like a sack of potatoes."

"Incredible," Medveded said, closing his eyes as though in appreciation of the justice of it. "Bet she didn't see *that* coming."

"Oh, definitely not. And I was going to leave her there, but decided I ought to have a little fun with her first."

"What'd you do? You fuck her?"

"Man, way worse," Galipoli bragged. "I picked that bitch up and threw her in my car."

"How the fuck did you get away with that?"

"I just played the Good Samaritan, the guy who found her lying on the street when she came to. She was real shook up. She told me her address, and eventually told me she lived alone too. The rest was easy."

Medveded pretended to gloss over this crucial detail, hoping to lock in the location first. "Lived alone, huh?" he asked. "Rich bitch, was she?"

"Yeah, totally. She lived in fucking Gramercy."

Bingo, Medveded thought. He couldn't believe Galipoli had copped to it so matter-of-factly. It seemed the guy was really getting carried away. And he was so remorseless about it, too!—Medveded had imagined there'd be at least a little compunction mingled in with these confessions, but so far he hadn't seen any at all. Galipoli had started to rub himself under the table, none too discreetly, and his breathing had become ragged as he'd begun to inwardly relive the thrill of his crime. It looked like the excitement alone could take him all the way, to say nothing of his braggadocio. Medveded decided to try and make things completely explicit between them.

"Wait, so—*this* was the girl from Park Avenue South?" he asked, incredulous.

"Yeah," Galipoli said absently. "And nobody knew. They still don't. And they couldn't prove it if they wanted to," he added, smiling, "so don't get any ideas."

Medveded waved the idea away, as though nothing could be more absurd between men like them. "But what about all that stuff the other guys had used—the rope, the tape, all that shit—are you telling me *you* put all that together?"

"Hardware store on Twenty-Third," Galipoli grinned. "I went by there the next morning to pick it all up."

"Weren't you afraid someone would see you going back to her place?"

"No, I wore a big hoodie when I went back. Besides, quiet building like that? No one even knew I was there."

Medveded whistled again. "Man, I knew you were smart, but I didn't know you were brilliant."

"Man, that was nothing," Galipoli beamed. "The one on Thirtieth Street—now *that* was a work of art."

Medveded feigned utter amazement. "You did the girl on *Thirtieth* too?"

Galipoli laughed coyly. "Well, you know, I'm not saying anything incriminating here. Just—you do some things right, you know? Some things just—they just go exactly the way you want them to."

"How so?"

"Oh, you know—some women, they just want it so bad. They keep begging you to do it harder. I gave that one everything I had."

"I've always suspected they want it that way," Medveded said.

"They do," Galipoli said. "They really do. Makes you think some-times, you know. I'm sure she knew it," he trailed off absently, as though recalling a fond memory.

"Knew it?"

"Yeah." Galipoli shook his head contentedly. "Not all of them did, but she knew was going to die."

Medveded smiled. It was as close to a flat-out admission as he was going to get. This game was over; the rest was icing.

"You said 'not all of them'—so tell me, Lou," he said, "in all these good times of yours, were those the only two women you killed?"

Galipoli's smile came crashing down. His eyes went dark as he glared at Medveded.

"You piece of shit," he said quietly.

"Hey, no need to get nasty," Medveded said coolly. "Just a friendly conversation we're having."

"And *have* been having, for hours," Galipoli said. "You trying to get something out of me, you slick motherfucker?"

"Trying?" Medveded said, his smile fixed.

"I'll *kill* you!" Galipoli shrieked suddenly, leaping up, his hands shooting out toward the detective as he spun around the table.

Medveded was quicker. In a blur, his hand emerged from his pocket as he swung his arm up. The blackjack landed home perfectly, connecting solidly with Galipoli's temple. There was a deep thud as Galipoli went down hard to the ground, followed by the answering crash of the kitchen door swinging open.

Kasak and Marchioni were the first through the door. Galipoli, sluggish but conscious, swung out at them with fists and feet as he struggled to get to his feet. They were the wrong guys to get physical with. The two detectives rained down blow after blow to his body, pummelling his ribs and abdomen until he was forced into submission. Cuffing him once more they dragged him out, kicking and screaming, to the squad room cell.

Medveded straightened up and shook the tension out of his hands. His calm restored, he walked into Morrison's office and closed the door behind him. Morrison stood and, without a word, opened up his cabinet.

"I know it isn't your usual," Morrison said, pouring him a tall shot of Jameson. "But I'm sure it'll do."

"None for you?" Medveded asked.

"Nah, I might be giving that up," Morrison smiled. "I've got something better going, these days."

"Understood. I, on the other hand"—Medveded raised his glass. *"Na zdarovje,* Captain." He tilted the glass back and swallowed. "Cap, that guy's one sick fuck," he said.

"And the ego on him!" Morrison said. "I don't know how you do it, Alex; it got so the rest of us couldn't listen for more than a few minutes at a time."

"Hmm." Medveded cocked his head at him. "So you might not have heard the big part, the stuff outside the homicides. Did you happen to catch what he said about the chain of command—about his promotion, and all that?"

Morrison raised his eyebrows. "Must've been in my office for that part," he said. "What'd he say?"

Medveded smiled. He gestured toward the bottle of Jameson. "Better pour me another of those, Captain," he said. "And with all due respect to this 'something better' you've got going these days, you might want one yourself, when I've told you."

41

It had been a grueling day already, and the subsequent mountain of paperwork carried everyone from Morrison's taskforce long into the night. Exhausted as they were, though, when the door to the squad room opened in the early hours of the morning, they all snapped to attention when they saw who it was.

Police Commissioner Robert Harrington walked casually through the squad room, stopping at each desk to shake the hand of every detective and sergeant in the room. Walking by the cell, he peered in at Galipoli, who'd been sound asleep on his bench practically since they'd locked the door on him.

"What a disgrace," Harrington said under his breath. He turned from the cell to see Morrison standing in his office doorway, a bigger smile on his face than Harrington had seen him wear in years. "Bill," Harrington said, walking toward him with an answering smile.

"Commissioner, thank you for coming in—especially at this early hour," Morrison said as they shook hands.

"Are you kidding?" Harrington laughed. "I couldn't get dressed fast enough. Hell, I almost walked out without my shoes on, I was in such a hurry." Laughter rippled through the squad room.

"Well, come on in, Commissioner," Morrison said, ushering

Harrington into his office. He closed the door.

"Commissioner, I have some big news for you," he said.

"Quite a day you're having, Captain," Harrington smiled. "Is it as big as what you've already told me?"

"In a way it is, yes."

"Good news, then, I hope."

Morrison chuckled. "Well, I guess *I'd* say it is, but you probably won't," he said. "During Galipoli's talk with Detective Medveded, he admitted to having been on the take."

"What?" Harrington said. "From whom?"

"Councilman Cook."

"Dave Cook, out in Brooklyn? District 43?"

"That's the one."

"You're kidding me."

"No, sir. Galipoli claims he was paying him for campaign appearances, on the strength of his war record. And there's more: according to him, Chief Arndt, who introduced them, was getting fatter envelopes from Cook—and it sounds like he may have sold Galipoli his shield, too."

"Jesus," Harrington said, obviously blown away. "Why would he do that? That's your soul, your dignity on the line—to say nothing of your professional reputation! For what—a few bucks?"

"Agreed. Though it was probably a few more than a few."

"How much?"

"On which end?"

"Either!"

"Galipoli claimed he was getting a grand per appearance. He said Arndt was getting ten times that."

"Ten times—! What about the shield?"

"He didn't say how much that cost him, but he copped to paying Arndt something for it."

"This is beyond belief. Do you have reason to believe he's telling the truth?"

Morrison laughed again, looking hard at Harrington. "Aside from my personal knowledge of Arndt's character?"

Harrington nodded. "Fair enough," he said. "We'll have to look into it. If money changed hands over it, as you say, that should be something we can pin down. It's not something I'm happy to hear, but I'm glad to have the lead; we can't have that sort of thing in this department." He took out his cell phone and dialed a number. "If you'll excuse me a moment, I'm going to call back to the office and have someone escort Arndt out of the building for the day—if what you say is true, we can't have him getting the jump on us."

"By all means, Commissioner," Morrison said.

As Harrington was making his call, there was a knock at the door, and Rivera poked his head in.

"Chief Arndt's on the phone for you, Captain," he said.

"Send it in," Morrison said. "If you don't mind, I'll put it on speaker, Commissioner," he said.

Harrington nodded. Morrison picked up.

"Captain Morrison—how can I help you?" Morrison said.

"You know exactly how you can help me, you son of a bitch," Arndt's voice came through. "You can get the fuck out of my detective bureau. Who the hell do you think you are, arresting a war hero, and a decorated member of this department, without my authority? This is the last time you make me look like a fool! Everyone on that goddamn task force is going to be transferred before this phone call is—"

"Understood, Chief, understood," Morrison said, smiling at Harrington. "Listen, Chief, I don't want to interrupt you, but the PC just walked in, and he wants to talk to you."

"Good," Arndt said, after a slight pause. "I'm looking forward to telling him what you've done."

Harrington spoke up. "Chief Arndt, Commissioner Harrington here," he said, his voice cold.

"Commissioner, good to speak to you," Arndt said. "As I'm sure you're already aware, we have a problem that needs dealing with."

"Yes, so I understand," Harrington said. "I'd like to deal with it as swiftly as possible."

"I'm glad we see eye to eye, sir," Arndt said. "What would you like me to do first?"

"Nice to hear you're on board," Harrington said. "The first thing I'd like you to do is to head home for the day."

There was a long silence. "I'm sorry, Commissioner—what did you say?" Arndt finally managed.

"I think you heard me, Arndt," Harrington said. "Or perhaps you had Councilman Cook speaking in your other ear?"

"I—I don't know what you mean, sir," Arndt stammered, his voice close to breaking. *Good old weepy,* thought Morrison. *Never disappoints.*

"You might as well know that I'll be on the phone with Internal Affairs and the District Attorney's Office as soon as I hang up with you," Harrington continued, "and there should be an officer there with you now, ready to escort you out of the building. You may leave your department car keys with my secretary on your way out. That will be all, Arndt."

Harrington nodded to Morrison, who hung up the phone with a rare thrill of vindication.

"Commissioner, I'd like to thank you," he said, "not only on my behalf, but on that of everyone that man has ever fucked over."

"Never a doubt, Bill," Harrington said, straightening his jacket as he stood. "Now get back to work, and keep me posted. I've got a few phone calls to make in a hurry, if you don't mind my using your office."

"Not at all, sir—anything you need."

He stepped out of the office, leaving the Commissioner to do the Lord's work. As he did, a thought occurred to him.

"Frankie," he called to Rivera, "get the Medical Examiner on the phone, will you? I need to know what's going on with that DNA from the gym bag."

"You got it, Cap," Rivera said. In another moment he was handing Morrison the phone.

"James, how are you—Bill Morrison here," Morrison said. "Do you have any news for me on those new DNA samples?"

"Whoa, Bill, you're in quite a hurry, huh?" James Fernandez answered with a light laugh. "Not even waiting for my pleasing voice to give you a hello back—! Must be really important, huh?"

"Sorry, Jim," Morrison said, catching himself, "but yeah, it is. As we speak I have a detective locked up in my squad room under suspicion of two homicides and an attempted rape. I really need to find out if you have anything on those new samples we sent the other day."

He heard Fernandez whistle. "Understood—my apologies, Bill," he said. "It sounds like you're up to your ass in alligators over there. Hold on, let me check for you."

While Morrison listened to the hold music, he tried to calm his nerves. A case was like a chain: if one link was weak, no matter how strong the rest was, the whole thing could fall apart in a second. He'd seen too many cases lost on the weakness of one piece of evidence, to think otherwise; the burden of proof "beyond a reasonable doubt" meant a shrewd attorney could turn a case at any moment, and although their case against Galipoli was very solid so far, these DNA results would be critical. He was positive the DNA from the panties would match one of their two victims, and he was also pretty sure the DNA from the shorts in the gym bag would come back as Galipoli's; but if either of those turned out otherwise, it could mean big trouble for them.

Finally the music stopped. Morrison thought of musical chairs, and hoped he'd found a seat.

"Bill, sorry for keeping you so long," Fernandez said, "but I do have some good news for you. We have a positive match from the cigarette butts, to the homicides on Twenty-First and Thirtieth Streets. We also have a positive match on the shorts in the gym bag —they're all from the same person."

Morrison breathed a sigh of relief. "That's great news, Jim," he said. "And there's no doubt on that, right?"

"Absolutely not—they're off the charts, as far as the numbers are concerned."

Morrison pumped his fist in the air. Once again, however, his moment of ecstasy was short-lived.

"We do have one problem, though," Fernandez added. "The panties did test positive for DNA, but they don't match either of the homicides you have.

"What? But that means—"

"Yeah. Looks like you might have another victim out there somewhere. We'll run them in our database, as well as through CODIS, to see if they match any other reported crimes, but we're going to have to get back to you."

"Okay, Jim, I understand. Thanks very much for you help on this."

Morrison hung up the phone and called Medveded into his office.

"What's up, Captain?"

"Did Galipoli say anything about other victims?"

"He'd mentioned something to that effect, but that's when everything fell apart in there."

"Exactly what did he say?"

"He said *not all of them* had known they were going to die. When I asked him about others is when he flipped out. Why do you ask?"

"The panties in that gym bag don't match our two homicide victims' DNA."

"Shit," Medveded said. "I hope he wasn't just talking things up."

"Yeah, exactly," Morrison agreed. "That means he probably had other victims in the car with him, too. Hopefully that warrant will—"

Just then, there was another knock at the door and McNamara leaned in.

"Cap, O'Dell's got the search warrants for Galipoli's house and car in hand," he said. "He's heading back from court now. Who do you want to execute the warrants?"

Morrison stood and grabbed his coat. "You guys and I will do the house," he said. "I'll have Simmons and Garriga get on the car. Let's get going."

Not quite forty-five minutes later, McNamara, O'Dell and Morrison arrived at Galipoli's home in Bay Ridge. It was in a fifteen-story residential building facing the Verrazano bridge. An Emergency Services unit was standing by at the scene; Morrison had Galipoli's keys, but wanted the help available if they had to make a forced entry. Not even the guys from Galipoli's former command knew much about him, so Morrison didn't know what to expect.

They walked into the building and found the super in the lobby, emptying out a trash can.

"Excuse me," Morrison said, showing his badge. "We're detectives with the NYPD, here to conduct a search on one of your residents' apartments. Do you know Lou Galipoli?"

"Yeah, I know the fucking jerk," the super said gruffly. "And about time somebody came for him. His mom was just getting on the elevator with some shopping bags; you'll find her in the place."

"He lives with his mother?" Morrison asked, surprised.

"Yeah, nice lady too," the super said, shaking his head. "How she made such a son—I never understood it."

"Thanks," Morrison said. "We're going to have to do this delicately," he added to the others.

"Hey, at least it isn't another Galipoli we're going to be dealing with," McNamara said.

Leaving their Emergency Service cops in the lobby, the three of them headed up to the seventh floor. When Morrison knocked on the door to 701, an older woman with a pleasant face answered.

"Can I help you?" she asked doubtfully.

"Hello, ma'am. I'm Captain Morrison with the NYPD," Morrison said. "These gentlemen with me are Sergeant McNamara and Detective O'Dell. Can we come in, please?"

"Of course—of course. Come on in."

She led them into a tidy, carpeted living room. Morrison asked her to sit before explaining their warrant and what they were doing there. It was a good thing. As soon as he'd told her that her son was under suspicion for murder, she fell back into her chair and wept loudly, claiming she couldn't believe her boy would do anything to hurt anyone. It pained Morrison to hear, as it always did but it was a pretty common story in these cases. The same obsession with manipulation that led many people to kill, helped them keep it a secret from those closest to them.

"Well, it isn't certain, ma'am," he eventually interjected, "but we need to carry out our investigation here. Do you mind showing us to his room?"

"Of course," she said, rising. "It's just this way."

She led them down a hallway to a room at the other end of the apartment. The door was padlocked.

"He always likes his privacy," she explained. "I'm not allowed in here—he calls it his man cave. But it isn't that I distrust him," she was quick to add. "I've always tried to respect his privacy here."

"That's very considerate of you, Mrs. Galipoli," O'Dell said, turning her away from the others. Not knowing what they were going to find, it was important that she not be there when they entered. "While they carry out their search, do you mind if I ask you a few questions out here in the living room?"

When he'd led her away, Morrison and McNamara pulled on rubber gloves, and Morrison got out Galipoli's keys. He tried a few of them on the padlock before he found the fitting one. It stuck a little, but eventually the lock popped. Cautiously, he swung the door open and stepped into the room.

The room was dark—almost impossibly dark. The windows were all covered with thick, dark curtains against the sunlight. Morrison flipped on the light and he and McNamara winced. There were at least thirty pictures of women in various state of undress taped on the wall. Most of them had been taken in the street, candid-style—some of women in cars pulling their tops down, others spreading their legs for the camera—but the two detectives soon spotted a few familiar photos among them: shots of the last two homicides, apparently taken immediately after they'd been murdered.

"This guy is one sick fuck," Morrison said.

"Yeah," McNamara agreed.

The two conducted a cursory search over the rest of the room. Once they were satisfied there weren't any additional victims locked inside, they called for the Crime Scene Unit to come and process the scene in depth, and went back out to join O'Dell and Galipoli's mother in the living room.

"Well," McNamara said on their way out, "I'll say this: if Garriga and Simmons are finding anything like this in the car, this one's going to be pretty open-and-shut."

"Let's hope," Morrison agreed.

When they rejoined the others in the living room, it seemed O'Dell had been able to calm Mrs. Galipoli down. Clearly proud of her son, she was speaking of his accomplishments in an almost reverent tone as she showed the detective a small stack of photos.

"This is Louis at a bodybuilding competition," she was saying, holding up a faded Polaroid. "Can you believe those muscles? He was just fifteen." She looked up as Morrison and McNamara sat, and eyed them with silent apprehension.

"Mrs. Galipoli, we're going to have to have Crime Scene in to look at things a little more closely," Morrison said. "Do you mind if we sit and speak with you while they work?"

"No, that's fine," she said hastily. "You didn't find what you were looking for?" she added hopefully.

"We'll have to have them look," Morrison said evasively. "It's just normal procedure."

It was then that Morrison noticed the urgency in O'Dell's eyes.

"Captain, Mrs. Galipoli was telling me about Lou's father," he said.

"Yes—where is he?" Morrison asked.

"God rest his soul, he passed years ago," Mrs. Galipoli said, standing. She retrieved a photo album from a low shelf and brought it back to them, flipping the pages. She showed them a photo of a young Galipoli, his face inscrutable, standing with a stern-looking man.

"This is the only picture I have of the two of them," she said, her voice trembling with emotion. "Silvio died not long after it was taken."

"I see," Morrison said. "Was Louis close to his father?"

Mrs. Galipoli's brows knitted for an instant as she looked down. "No," she said quietly. "Not really. Silvio was—he was very demanding. He could be hard on Louis. He was hard on everyone," she added, and her fingers twisted the tissue she was holding.

"Was Louis's father ever violent toward him?"

Mrs. Galipoli nodded, her eyes still averted. "He loved us, but he had a temper," she said.

"How did he pass?" Morrison asked.

The bluntness of Mrs. Galipoli's answer was almost shocking. "He was murdered," she said simply, and burst into tears. Morrison looked at O'Dell and McNamara as they tried to console her.

"I know it's difficult, Mrs. Galipoli," he said when she'd quieted again, "but it could be important to our investigation. Could you please tell me a bit about your husband's death?"

She nodded, wiping her eyes. "It's all right," she said. "It was so long ago—I'm used to talking about it. I'm more upset that Louis is in trouble."

"I understand completely, Mrs. Galipoli. Go ahead. Where did it happen?"

"It was a few blocks from here, at the park. We were living in a little place on Ninety-Fifth back then, right across the street from there."

"What happened?"

"Well, Louis was late for dinner, and his father went looking for him," she said. "I begged him not to go, but he was in one of his moods. He went out with—with his belt in his hand."

"Go on."

"Louis came home a little later, maybe an hour later. He was scared he was in trouble. I told him I'd always protect him, and I wouldn't let Silvio hurt him. I was afraid of Silvio, but I was angry too. We were both angry, under the fear; Louis was always very angry at his father.

"In the middle of the night, I heard a knock at the door. I thought it was Silvio, but when I answered it, it was a policeman. They'd found Silvio in the park. He was beaten to death. Whoever did it took his money, but left his wallet."

"Whoever did it? They didn't find his killer?"

"They never did, no." She wiped her eyes again. "Just imagine that, as a boy—being so angry at your father, fighting with him all the time, then *that* happens. How could he be expected to deal with that?" She looked at them imploringly, as though to plead with them for under-standing. "All these years—how does *anyone* deal with that?" She broke off, the tears flowing freely again. Morrison held his tongue.

He knew, too well, the way some people dealt with that.

A few hours later, they were still talking when one of the Crime Scene detectives pulled Morrison aside.

"Cap, we're wrapping up here, if you want to take another look in the room," he said.

"Thanks," Morrison said. He headed down the hallway and walked in, seeing a good-sized group of bags marked by Crime Scene piled up by the door. The walls were bare.

"I see you found the photos," he joked. "Anything else of interest?"

"Yeah, a bit," the detective told him. "Some hardcore porn, a paper bag with some panties in it—pretty standard-issue stuff, though, all things considered."

"We'll have to see what the lab makes of that."

"Yeah." The detective pulled up short. "We did find another photo you should see, though," he said. He handed Morrison a plastic bag. "This one wasn't on the wall—it was in a box on the top shelf in the closet."

Inside the bag was a Polaroid photograph, so worn and dilapidated that at first Morrison didn't see what it was of.

Then he took a closer look, and almost dropped it.

It was of a man lying contorted on the ground, a belt wrapped tightly around his neck. The grass around him, trampled in places from the struggle, still shone vividly with fresh blood. His pale face wore the ubiquitous slack expression of the dead. Beyond this, it was almost unrecognizably battered; but Morrison knew in an instant who it was, and what it meant—though he also knew he'd almost certainly never be able to prove it.

It was a photo of Lou Galipoli's father, taken within minutes of his death.

42

There truly was no rest for the weary.

Everyone but Koreski was back in the squad room, taking congratulations and going over case notes. It had been decided that Medveded was going to take the arrest for the task force, but everyone had done their part in securing a rock-solid case against Galipoli—who'd been moved downtown to await trial—and the rest of the precinct had been coming in and out of the squad room congratulating them on a job well done.

Still, it was hard praise for the team to enjoy. None of them had slept more than a few hours over the last two days. Among other loose ends, they still didn't know where or who Galipoli's additional victims may have been. Had his comment to Medveded been truthful, or only another empty boast? Even the last speculation about his father, as shocking as it had been, was inconclusive; it only proved Galipoli had been there shortly after his father's death, and didn't tie him to any of the current crimes. Garriga and Simmons, along with a team of Tyvek-suited Crime Scene detectives, had gone over every square inch of Galipoli's car, and found some intriguing additional evidence there—particularly the bottles Galipoli had given to Koreski to drink out of, and a Pennsylvania license plate hidden in the trunk—but nothing they were able to draw any ready conclusions from.

In the midst of the hubbub, a call came through for Garriga. He raised his hand for quiet, scribbling on a pad. The rest of the room went silent as they waited for him to hang up.

When he was off the phone, he looked around the room.

"I think we've found the other victims," he said.

"Oh, no," Sergeant Rivera said, speaking for them all. "How many more bodies do we have?"

"Actually, it's not quite like that," Garriga said. "Apparently he's been busy on the Hutchinson River Parkway, pulling over women and sexually abusing them. They have about twenty cases reported, and probably a lot of others that didn't report it. He apparently tried to pull it with an off-duty female sergeant from White Plains."

The room laughed in spite of themselves.

"So what's the connection?" McNamara asked. "How do we know it was him?"

"Well, that's what I'm getting to," said Garriga. "Apparently he had pulled this off-duty cop over, but took off when a Westchester County PD came up behind them. The sergeant got his license plate number— and guess where the plate was from?"

The room reverberated as practically everyone present shouted their answer at once.

"PENNSYLVANIA!"

"You got it," Garriga said. "Looks like our boy's looking at up to twenty additional counts of sexual abuse."

"Thank God," McNamara said. "We got him. Twenty additional counts!"

"Lord knows the bastard deserves them," Simmons said.

"And an off-duty cop, too!" Rivera pointed out. "Guy really likes to fuck around with the wrong women, huh?"

As if on cue, a high voice came from the back of the squad room.

"Hey, I know you're all busy, but can a girl get a seat around here?"

The room erupted in shouts and and applause as Tina Koreski came in, fit as a fiddle—aside from a light bruise across her cheekbone where Galipoli had slapped her—and smiling from ear to ear. One by one, each of the team stood to hug her and shake her hand. She blushed as Leo Kasak self-effacingly offered her his chair.

"Ah, you're making a lot of it," she said. "I couldn't have done it without you guys."

"And you think *we* could've flirted with that asshole all night?" Kasak laughed. "Think again."

"Hell of a job, Detective," Marchioni agreed. "Hell of a job."

"How're you feeling?" O'Dell asked. "You get enough time in that hospital bed?"

"Enough to last me a good long while," Koreski said, smiling. "I'm doing fine—great, really. A hundred percent."

"Hundred percent, huh?" Rivera laughed, looking around the room. "That good enough for Kelley's? I know nobody here's slept in a day or two, but *I* for one couldn't rest without raising a glass to you, if you're up for it."

"I'm in," she said, beaming as her team cheered her again.

Later that evening, after everyone else had headed out, Bill Morrison sat alone in his office.

He'd just hung up from a long conversation that had needed to happen for a while, but which he hadn't thought himself capable of initiating—a call with his wife Kathleen. He'd always dreaded bringing up their distance, as it had never led to anything but hostility between them before; but lately, with Claudia in the picture, the need had become pressing. There was not much guilt to it for him—they'd been living on separate planets too long for that to be the case—but he felt it as a weight, an attachment to a previous life that, until he finally and decisively freed himself from it, would hold him back from the life that could be.

So today, in the first real breathing space he'd had since their case had escalated, he'd made the call. To his surprise—but then, why would it surprise him?—Kathleen had anticipated what he had to say, almost to the word. She had arrived at the same conclusion differently, and though it was difficult, she knew as well as he did that a final separation was the right thing for both of them.

They spent the better part of an hour talking, about their lives, their kids, and most conspicuously, Bill Junior. His death had been the breaking point for them, and their inability to speak to each other about it had provided each of them with an ongoing proof of that crucial divide.

Now they talked about it, to such an extent as they still could with one another; and the conversation was pleasant, unpressured, the undisguised communication of two people who had nothing to hide from one another anymore. There was a definite tinge of melancholy to it—they both seemed to have known that this sort of conversation was the only context within which they would ever truly open up to each other again—but it was more than they'd talked at once for five years, and when it drew to an end, it ended well.

Now, the strange warmth of their conversation still with him, Morrison picked up the framed photo of his son he'd been looking at as they'd talked.

"Billy, I—uh—I think I'm going to be okay," he said at last, touching the photo. "It really feels like some things could be turning around for me. I know you're in a better place—I have to believe that—but if I can help it, I'm not going to be seeing you anytime soon."

He kissed the photo and returned it to its place on his desk, then picked up the phone again. The others were all out at Kelley's, celebrating Tina, but he had one more call to make before he joined them. This one, at least, he was more excited about. He hadn't spoken to Claudia since their pursuit of Galipoli had kicked into high gear. Now he had good news for her on all fronts.

"Bill!" her light voice greeted him. "I've missed you so much, darling. Are things settling down a bit for you?"

"Oh, relatively speaking," he laughed. "God, Claudia, do I have a lot to talk to you about!"

"Good news, I hope?"

"Definitely—a few different pieces of good news."

"Ooh! I'm intrigued. Are you done for the night? You can come up now, if you'd like."

He smiled at her eagerness; it was so unusual a happiness for him. "I'm going to get a couple of celebratory drinks with the team, and get some much-needed sleep—but I can drive up in the morning, if you have time then."

"Of course. I'll be looking forward to it until then! Have a good time tonight."

"Thanks, babe." He caught his reflection in the window, smiling like a jackass. *And so what if I am?* he thought. *That's what happy men do.* "I love you, Claudia—I'll talk to you in the morning, all right?"

"I love you too, Bill. Have a good night!"

He hung up and stood, grabbing his coat. It was odd; he didn't particularly feel like drinking. This was better than any buzz, this new feeling he'd found; it was like he had a new chance at life.

But he wouldn't miss Kelley's for the world tonight. It had been a long day, and his family was waiting for him.